A **LIAM HARPER** THRILLER

FINAL CLAIM

NEW YORK TIMES #1 BESTSELLER **TONY LEE** WRITING AS

JACK GATLAND

Hooded Man MEDIA
INSPIRATION • PRODUCTION • PUBLICATION

Published by Hooded Man Media.

Cover design by L1graphics

First Edition: March 2025

PRAISE FOR JACK GATLAND

'Fast-paced and action packed, Jack Gatland's thrillers always deliver a punch.'

'This is one of those books that will keep you up past your bedtime, as each chapter lures you into reading just one more.'

'This book was excellent! A great plot which kept you guessing until the end.'

'Couldn't put it down, fast paced with twists and turns.'

'The story was captivating, good plot, twists you never saw and really likeable characters. Can't wait for the next one!'

'Totally addictive. Thoroughly recommend.'

'Moves at a fast pace and carries you along with it.'

'Just couldn't put this book down, from the first page to the last one it kept you wondering what would happen next.'

LIQUIDATE THE PROFITS

FOLDED HANDS

Declan Walsh. Ellie Reckless. Tom Marlowe. Liam Harper. Ryder Waites. Damian Lucas.

Also by Jack Gatland

DI DECLAN WALSH BOOKS

LETTER FROM THE DEAD

MURDER OF ANGELS

HUNTER HUNTED

WHISPER FOR THE REAPER

TO HUNT A MAGPIE

A RITUAL FOR THE DYING

KILLING THE MUSIC

A DINNER TO DIE FOR

BEHIND THE WIRE

HEAVY IS THE CROWN

STALKING THE RIPPER

A QUIVER OF SORROWS

MURDER BY MISTLETOE

BENEATH THE BODIES

KILL YOUR DARLINGS

KISSING A KILLER

PRETEND TO BE DEAD

HARVEST FOR THE REAPER

CROOKED WAS HIS CANE

A POCKET FULL OF POSIES

CHEATING MY DESTINY

STAND AND DELIVER

WE PLAY WITH DEATH

TOM MARLOWE BOOKS

SLEEPING SOLDIERS

TARGET LOCKED

COVERT ACTION

COUNTER ATTACK

STEALTH STRIKE

BROAD SWORD

ROGUE SIGNAL

SNIPER ALLEY

SHADOW THREAT

ELLIE RECKLESS BOOKS

PAINT THE DEAD

STEAL THE GOLD

HUNT THE PREY

FIND THE LADY

BURN THE DEBT

LIAM HARPER BOOKS

FINAL STRIKE

BLOOD RIDGE

DAMIAN LUCAS BOOKS

THE LIONHEART CURSE

STANDALONE BOOKS

THE BOARDROOM

As Tony Lee

STANDALONE

TWELVE TASKS

THE PLAYING CARD WAR

KNAVE OF SPADES

QUEEN OF BLADES

For Mum, who inspired me to write.

For Tracy, who inspires me to write.

CONTENTS

1

WELCOME TO PROSPERITY

The Goldrush Diner in Prosperity, deep within the arid Nevada highlands was a third-generation business, passed down from grandfather to mother, and then to daughter. The current owner, Maisie Brown, was a strong-willed, stocky woman in her fifties who could, with a wink and a smile, charm her way to a large tip, but also grab you in a vice-like grip and toss you out onto the street if you got too unruly. Which, unfortunately for Maisie, seemed to be more common than not these days.

She'd spent her entire life at the diner. As a child, she'd sit on the high seats at the diner's bar, listening to stories from truckers and bikers while her mom manned the counter, raising an eyebrow every time they used inappropriate language in front of her daughter. Maisie hadn't minded the swearing; it made her feel grown-up if she was being honest. She'd even started working at the diner as a waitress when she was fifteen, earning money during weekends and evenings, and eventually took over when her mom had a stroke, twenty years back. It had been tough, working as both waitress, owner, and carer, but she hadn't complained.

Maisie Brown never complained.

Even when the rents went up and the mayor added new tariffs, she stayed silent. When the biker gang turned up fifteen years ago, she hadn't complained either, but she'd raised a glass in celebration when they were finally run out of town about five years later by Sheriff Cortez. Although, through one of their dealers, they gained revenge by shooting him as he left the department one night in a goddamned sneak attack.

Maisie didn't get involved; it wasn't her place. Maisie was someone who understood her place in life. She hadn't even complained when her mom passed away five years earlier, either. In a way, it'd been a blessing, although Maisie would never say that aloud.

Maisie Brown had no ambitions and no regrets. Throughout her journey she'd met many people along the way, and was proud to still call quite a few of them friends, and some even lovers – though she often wondered why the hell she'd stayed with Keith as long as she did.

Or Kyle, for that matter.

Still, every day Maisie would rise at five in the morning, open the diner for breakfast, allowing Caleb, the cook, to come in with stock from the market, before the two of them would start prepping for the day. It was a simple diner for locals, though tourists did come by around lunchtime. After all, Prosperity was a heritage town, and had its fair share of visitors. But, most of the time, it was the usual crowd and the occasional passing regular, trucking down to Virginia City, or catching the red-eye route for travel.

Today, though, the man at the diner counter was different.

He had ridden in that morning, around ten-thirty, maybe eleven, just as the breakfast rush turned into the early lunchtime crowd. She'd heard him before she saw him; the diner was on the main road out of town, and the engine of his motorcycle echoed up the street before he appeared, bringing back memories of the biker gangs of old.

It wasn't a Harley. That had a different kind of purr. This engine, though familiar, was one she didn't recognise, which was odd since she spent most of her time listening to the sounds of bikes and cars passing by, tuning out the same fifties playlist the diner played every day. The motorcycle pulled up outside and, as she glanced out of the diner windows, she watched as the rider climbed off, pulling off his helmet – a full-face one with a visor, more akin to those worn by racers – and taking a moment to look around, looking up at the sun, smiling as he felt it on his face, before he locked his helmet to the bike's seat and walked into the diner.

'You don't want to leave your helmet out there,' Maisie said as he approached the counter. 'Some kid'll pinch it.'

The man shrugged.

'Then I'll buy another,' he replied, 'and the thief will have a story to tell, and an item to sell. Do you have a menu?'

With that, he sat down at the counter. He was young – well, young to Maisie's eyes; he was mid to late thirties, perhaps younger. His hair was kept short and flattened, most likely from hours of wearing the helmet while riding. But, despite the disarray, she could tell he normally kept his hair neat with a side parting; it was dark-brown, leaning towards auburn, shorter on the sides and his sideburns just about matched the stubble on his face. He was a good-looking man, and built more like a gymnast than a bodybuilder, maybe six-one at best, and probably no more than two hundred and twenty pounds – although from the way he moved, she wondered how much of that was muscle.

He wore army boots, jeans and a brown leather biker jacket, battered from years of use. His only notable feature was a one inch scar above his right eyebrow, cutting into it and dividing the eyebrow in two.

As he sat, he cricked his neck and stretched his back, the pops audible across the counter.

'Been riding long today?' Maisie asked.

'Feels like for years, ma'am,' the man replied, his accent strange – British, but not quite. There was an American twang to it, possibly East Coast. 'Started late yesterday and carried on through. Clear night made the stars beautiful.'

'I'm guessing from your accent you're not from around here,' Maisie smiled.

The man shook his head, but offered nothing else.

'Coffee?' Realising he wasn't likely to give anything until he had a drink in his hand, Maisie waved at one of the coffee pots behind the diner counter.

'Please.'

'How d'you take it?'

'Black, no sugar.'

Maisie grabbed the pot and poured a mug, sliding it across to him.

'I gotta ask,' she said, nodding at the window, 'what's that bike? Don't sound like nothing I know around here.'

The man followed her gaze but didn't speak immediately. Maisie realised he was probably just checking that his helmet hadn't been stolen yet.

'It's a Triumph Bonneville,' he eventually replied.

'A Triumph?' Maisie smiled. 'Thought I recognised a bit of your accent. You're English.'

'Kind of,' the man replied. 'My dad was American.'

'You live over here?'

'Visited more than lived. My mum and dad split when I was a kid.'

'You reconnecting?'

'It'll be difficult. He passed away six months ago.'

'Sorry,' Maisie mentally grimaced.

Way to go, girl. Now your tip's just halved.

The man held up a hand, however, still giving a smile.

'You weren't to know,' he replied as he glanced at her name tag. 'Pleasure to meet you, Maisie.'

'You got a name?' Maisie couldn't help it; she'd already turned on the charm, and not just for the tip. He was way younger than her, but he was cute. 'Or do I just give you one?'

'Harper,' the man replied. 'First name's Liam, but most people call me by my surname.'

He glanced down at the menu.

'I'll grab the eggs on toasted rye bread, sunny side up and still dippable, crispy bacon on the side,' he said. 'Largest orange juice you do, and this coffee. I can sit anywhere, right?'

'Honey, you can sit wherever you want.'

'I'll just be over there, then,' Harper rose as he spoke, pointing at a booth as far from the door as possible, over to the right of where they stood.

As Maisie put the food order through to Caleb, the newcomer walked over, sat down, then rose and approached another booth where an old man, Hank Longstead, the local veterinary surgeon, had placed a discarded newspaper on the table.

'Excuse me,' he said, overly polite for a diner. 'Can I borrow your paper?'

'It's not a national one,' Hank muttered.

'No, that's fine. I was looking for a local.'

'Sure.' Hank didn't even glance at the man asking as he handed over the paper. Harper took it and returned to his booth, almost hiding behind it as he read the sports news on the back. After a while, Maisie almost forgot he was there, placing his brunch order down on the table when it was done and refilling his black coffee when she noticed it had nearly emptied, turning her attention back to the regulars.

It was another twenty minutes before the next customer walked in. Well, more accurately, customers *plural* if she was being accurate. Two of them; goddamn *Aegis* goons, the idiots who worked for Mason Carrick up at the mine. They'd been in before and rarely caused any trouble, but today, they had a different air about them – an edge Maisie couldn't quite explain. She thought the devil himself might be within them; they'd been scuffling outside for half an hour, smoking roll-ups and shouting at people passing in their vehicles, and eventually came in laughing, bringing with them the pungent, unmistakable smell of weed.

'I hope you're not smoking that inside here,' Maisie said. 'You know we don't allow it.'

'Don't know what you're talking about,' the first man, a squat blond with a cheap bottle tan, said. He was in his late twenties, maybe early thirties, and his face was pockmarked, though Maisie had never bothered to ask from what. He wore a denim jacket with the sleeves ripped off, over a grey T-shirt, khaki combat trousers and army boots. The man next to him was Hispanic, about ten years older, with shoulder-length hair and a tiny goatee that looked more like wisps of bum fluff than an actual beard.

Maisie held back a smile at that thought.

He was wearing a hoodie with a letterman jacket over the top, which really aged him – men in their forties shouldn't try to dress like college students. Maisie didn't recognise the university logo, nor was she sure it even belonged to one. His jeans were black, and he wore white leather sneakers, again ageing him more than he probably wanted.

The two of them walked over to the counter and plonked themselves down in the spot the stranger had vacated earlier.

'Looking pretty today,' the pockmarked blond said with a leer.

'Thank you,' Maisie replied coldly. 'What can I get you?'

'Question is, what can I get you?' the pockmarked blond retorted.

Maisie sighed.

'I'm double your age, old enough to be your mom. Let's stop with this stupidity right now.'

'Maybe I liked my mom,' the pockmarked blond said, winking. 'Maybe I like 'em older. Maybe I like *you*.'

Maisie sighed again. This wasn't the first time she'd heard this kind of talk. But today she noticed that the stranger with the British motorcycle had lowered his newspaper, and was now watching the scene closely.

Were these two here for him? Was that why they'd come in?

'Honey, give me your order or go,' Maisie said firmly. 'We're busy.'

The pockmarked blond looked around, his mouth curling into a half-smile.

'You call this busy?' he sneered. 'Looks like one step away from bankruptcy.'

As he spoke, he glanced down to the far end of the diner, and Maisie thought for a second he was looking at Tucker, a hippy in what looked to be his forties, with long hair and a beard, maybe thinking of scoring some more weed – but instead his gaze carried on to where an elderly man was seated by the back window, poring over some academic papers, thin as a rail with wispy white hair, and wearing a tweed jacket with those elbow patches teachers used to wear decades ago. Eddie Hawkins was in his seventies, one of those fellas that people in town knew by first name, and had been coming to the diner for years.

Unfortunately, it seemed today he was the goons' target.

'Hey!' the pockmarked blond called out.

Eddie looked up, his eyes widening at the grin spreading across the blond man's face.

The pockmarked blond left the counter, his older Hispanic friend trailing behind, and swaggered over to Eddie's table. Once standing over the elderly academic, he casually picked up one of the sheets of paper he'd been studying.

'What're you looking at?' he asked.

'I'm checking numbers,' Eddie replied.

'Yeah? Numbers we should be worried about?'

'No, not at all.'

'You sure about that?' The pockmarked blond leaned in closer. 'Because last I heard, you weren't supposed to be looking at numbers. You were supposed to be hunting maps.'

'These have nothing to do with you,' Eddie said, his voice shaking slightly. 'I promise.'

The pockmarked blond turned to his friend with a mock-serious look.

'Did you hear that? He *promises*.'

'Well, that's alright then, isn't it?' the Hispanic with the goatee said with a smirk.

With a sudden slam of his fist onto the table, the pockmarked blond startled Eddie.

'You lying to me?'

'No! Of course not!' Eddie replied, fear now evident in his voice.

''Cause if you're lying to me, I'm gonna have to kick your ass.'

'I swear, I'm not.'

The pockmarked blond leaned in even closer, speaking in a low, casual tone.

'You know, old man ... I swear I heard my boss tell you to leave town if you weren't fulfilling your side of the deal.'

'I've lived here all my life,' Eddie replied desperately. 'My daughter lives here.'

'Well, your daughter ought to move with you too,' the Hispanic with the goatee suggested in a disturbingly amiable tone. 'You two could be all happy together somewhere else.'

Maisie was about to yell out and tell the guys to leave Eddie the hell alone, but she paused when a loud smashing noise from the other end of the diner – the familiar sound of a coffee cup hitting the tiles – caught her attention.

'I'm so sorry,' Harper said loudly, enough for everyone to hear, gaining their attention. 'Didn't mean to knock my mug off the table. I'm not usually that clumsy.'

The noise and his voice also drew the ire of the two goons, who now turned to look at him.

'It's just ... well, I was so fascinated by the street theatre over there, I didn't even realise I'd knocked something over,' Harper added as he placed the newspaper to the side. 'Sorry to interrupt you guys. Keep going – loving it. No notes.'

'No *what?*' the pockmarked blond asked, frowning.

Harper rose from his table, casually walking past the other diners towards them.

'I said I had no notes. Your performance is spot on. Cadence is great. Accents are a bit ropey, but hey, you can't have everything.'

'Who the hell is this guy?' the pockmarked blond muttered, not really directing the question at anyone. Maisie, sensing something brewing however, was worried. She'd also noticed something important, though; since the man with the motorcycle had stood up, the two men had completely forgotten about Eddie.

'I'm sorry, I'm just passing through,' Harper replied, his tone level and calm. 'I'm guessing this has to be street theatre or some kind of prank because, in my experience, two men in their, what, twenties? Thirties? Maybe forties in your case, goatee man, who are clearly together – I'm not judging – wouldn't usually gang up on a seventy-year-old man unless it was theatre, or a prank.'

'It's nothing to do with you,' the Hispanic with the goatee muttered, possibly sore he'd been correctly aged.

'No, I get that. It isn't. I don't want it to be,' Harper nodded amiably. 'So, here's the deal; leave the guy alone, let him read his papers and enjoy his brunch or whatever he's doing, get whatever you came in for from the nice lady at the counter, and then go, yeah? Carry on with your day, so that he can carry on with his and I can carry on with mine.'

'Who the hell are *you* to tell us what to do?' The pockmarked blond spat.

'Oh, no, don't get me wrong, brother, I'm not telling you anything,' Harper replied, his voice low, shaking his head slightly. 'I'm just suggesting.'

'I ain't your brother, mister,' the pockmarked blond sneered. 'You a faggot?'

'Why would you think that?'

''Cause you've got a faggot's bike outside.'

'The Bonneville? You think that's a faggot's bike?' Harper raised an eyebrow. 'Man, you've got no idea about bikes.'

'I know a faggot when I see one riding a faggot's bike,' the pockmarked blond shot back, obviously spoiling for a fight.

'Okay, whatever, sure, it's a faggot's bike,' Harper sighed. '*Now,* will you leave the guy alone?'

'What if we don't?' The pockmarked blond cracked his knuckles, his eyes narrowing as he sized Harper up, weighing the fact the stranger had buckled so quickly on the bike comment as a point to his advantage. Though shorter, the pockmarked blond was stockier, all muscle and bulk, and there *were* two of them.

Maisie, watching from behind the counter, wasn't sure what to expect. The stranger didn't seem to have much to him – he was lean, almost too lean for a fight. But there was something, a casualness that made her wonder whether he was more than people saw. He didn't seem concerned at all.

Maybe if he knew who they worked for, he would be.

'If you want to take this outside, we can go outside,' Harper suggested, his tone calm and measured. 'But I'll only fight one of you.'

'Oh, what? You scared to take us both on?' the pock-marked blond mocked.

'No,' Harper replied, his voice still steady. 'It's just that when I break one of your arms, the other's going to have to drive you to the hospital. I don't think anyone in here's going to do it – I'm not actually sure how far it is, but I'm guessing it'll involve a drive – and believe me, you *will* need to go to the hospital.'

'Bullshit,' the pockmarked blond growled, pulling off his jacket. 'Come on then! Me and you!'

Harper nodded sadly, and with an expression of resignation began pulling off his own leather jacket, walking back and placing it carefully on the back of the booth he'd risen from, in the process revealing a T-shirt. As his bare arm came into view, however, the Hispanic man with the goatee noticed the tattoo on his upper arm and froze.

'Leave it,' he said to his stockier, pockmarked friend. 'Let's just go. We can come back to this later.'

'What? No way, I'm not—'

'You're going to do *nothing*,' the Hispanic with the goatee insisted, gripping the pockmarked blond's arm. 'Trust me. Let's just leave it.'

He turned to Harper now.

'We didn't mean anything, mister. We were just messing around.'

'I know,' Harper said, his face still emotionless. 'And I'll be happy to keep on "messing around" outside.'

'There's no need for that,' the Hispanic replied, glancing at the tattoo again before subconsciously flinching back. 'I served in Helmand Province. I know you.'

The pockmarked blond, now visibly frustrated, muttered angrily under his breath as his friend forcibly dragged him out of the building. A few seconds later, the sound of clattering metal filled the diner, as he furiously kicked over the parked Bonneville.

Harper sighed, cricked his neck from side to side to release tension and walked outside. Pulling it back upright, he straightened the bike and, after a moment, came back inside, sitting down again at the booth and grabbing the paper once more, as if nothing had happened.

'Sorry,' he said, noting the still smashed mug. 'Can I get a cleanup and a refill? I'll obviously pay for the breakage.'

Maisie walked over to him.

'Your tattoo,' she said as she cleaned up the spillage. 'The one on your arm. It seemed to spook them.'

She glanced at it again; it was a stylised sword, positioned upright behind a Corinthian-style helmet, with what looked to be a scroll across the bottom.

'Did it? I wondered why the other one backed off,' Harper shrugged. 'I assumed he just got bored with playing.'

'You serve?' Maisie pressed. 'He mentioned Helmand Province. I watch CNN. I heard of that.'

'He might have been there, but I never was,' Harper replied pleasantly, as if trying to divert from the subject. 'I heard it was a nightmare.'

'Look, mister, what's the tattoo?' Maisie was tiring of the games now.

Harper placed his hands on the table, folding the local paper before looking up at Maisie, nodding his head at the bare arm and the tattoo.

'It's the symbol of the Special Reconnaissance Regiment, or SRR.'

'That some kind of British unit?'

'Yes, ma'am.'

'You served?'

'Every day of my tour.'

'You see action?'

'As I said, ma'am, every day of my tour. Although not at Helmand.'

Maisie now understood why the Hispanic with the goatee man had pulled the pockmarked blond away.

He'd recognised the tattoo.

'If you're just passing through,' Maisie said, 'you might want to do it a little quicker. Those two might've been dumb as stumps, but they've got friends.'

'Great,' Harper replied with a shrug. 'I'm looking for new friends.'

He paused for a moment, his brow furrowing slightly.

'Actually, you might be able to help me. I'm looking for a place to stay. Is there a guest house around here you'd recommend?'

Before Maisie could answer though, Eddie Hawkins approached, holding out his hand.

'Thank you for what you did,' he said, still nervously looking outside the diner, in case more goons were planning on entering. Harper also noted this, rising to face the older man.

'I did nothing,' he replied, shaking Eddie's hand. 'You know a good guest house?'

'My daughter Maggie.' Eddie smiled. 'Tell her I sent you, and you'll get the special deal.'

'I'm always happy for a special deal,' Harper gave a nod to this. 'But can I ask what you were reading that pissed those men off so much?'

'Geological samples,' Eddie replied. 'Just stuff from the hills. You know the story about this place, right?'

'Prosperity?'

'Yeah. Gold mining town. Made millions back in the day—'

'And then it died overnight when the gold was stolen,' Maisie added helpfully.

'Stolen?'

Eddie straightened, and Maisie groaned.

'Never ask a historian to explain something, Harper,' she muttered as Eddie began.

'1875, at the height of Prosperity's gold boom, a massive shipment of gold, valued at two million dollars at the time, equivalent to about fifty million today – and that's without the historical value – was being prepared for transport to San Francisco,' he explained. 'This shipment represented months of excavation from the town's mine. However, on the night before its scheduled departure, the entire shipment vanished without a trace. The town awoke to find the specially fortified vault empty, with no signs of forced entry. The gold, along with all documentation about its exact quantity and form, had simply disappeared.'

'Suspects?'

'Initial investigations pointed to everyone, from disgruntled miners to sophisticated thieves from San Francisco. Some said it was William Bickford, a local landowner who was even suspected to be the mine owner himself—'

'You didn't know who owned the mine?' Harper seemed surprised by this.

'It's a weird one, as, with a hundred and fifty years of hindsight, we can see it was Bickford, but at the time, publicly it was a Bickford stooge, Jonathan Caldwell that was the "mine owner" and people at the time believed he was guilty of orchestrating the theft to avoid paying his investors.' Eddie had become full on tour guide now. 'However, no concrete evidence was ever found, and no one was ever charged with the crime. Roadblocks – well, as much as you'd call them "roads" in 1875 – were set up, and the plains were combed. Anyone who took that much gold would have been seen, but nobody reckoned they saw a thing.'

'So, it what, simply vanished?'

'Well, as it wasn't seen being taken away, well, people believed it got buried, kept hidden until a later date, you know? Maybe somewhere deep in the mines, so whoever stole it could come back and dig it up when the heat settled. But nobody ever did.'

'That we know of.'

'Well, of course. It's become a bit of a tourist trap because of that.'

'Yeah, it's done us well, and since the papers announced it, we've had people coming every year for over a century now, all looking for the damn thing,' Maisie added. 'But recently, there's been a lot of renewed interest in the gold, and the anniversary celebrations at the start of the year gave it a massive social media presence. More importantly, people are trying to figure out how to get to it, or even if it *is* hidden in the mine, still.'

She sighed, realising she'd forgotten the other diners.

'Anyway, that's just all stories and hearsay. Why are you looking to stay? I thought you were just passing through.'

'I am,' Harper replied, leaning back in his chair. 'But I'm doing it slowly. You see, I'm hunting for something.'

'Yeah? What?'

'Missing gold.' Harper grinned.

2

FAMILY HISTORY

Helping the old man had been a mistake – Harper was aware of that, but there was something about the old guy Eddie that reminded Harper of old Pete.

Of course, old Pete wasn't his name; his name was Peter Harper, he was Harper's grandfather and had pretty much raised him from the age of fourteen after Harper's mother, Pete's daughter, had died in a car accident. Harper had been in America at the time with his father, and when he returned, his life had changed completely.

Growing up, Harper had a strange, alternate life, in a way. His father had been a US soldier working in the engineering corps. He'd been stationed in the UK on diplomatic duties and had met Harper's mother, Maureen, through mutual friends. They'd hit it off and started a relationship that then became a marriage after Maureen found she was pregnant with Liam. It wasn't a "shotgun" wedding, though; they truly loved each other, and Harper's early years, although foggy by time, showed him a father who loved him, a mother who adored him, and a family dynamic that, although he spent some of it bouncing around the world, staying on military bases and constantly meeting new friends, was generally quite calm and planned out.

However, this all changed when Harper was ten; his father had become more distant, spending more time in America. He had left the services around this point, was working for an American-based security company, and looking to create his own, smaller equivalent. Harper didn't know what he'd been doing back then, but now, with hindsight, Harper was aware he'd been working for, and then effectively creating for himself, a mercenary unit to be utilised by large corporations, going into places where it was deemed un-optional for sovereign militaries to go into. On paper, his father was a "troubleshooter", a term given to someone who could come into a situation and find a way to fix it.

But as far as Harper was concerned, as a boy turning into a teenager, his father was very much a man who saw trouble and *shot* it.

Harper had found himself spending a lot of time on different continents at this point. His mother had returned to her family in England, living in a two-bedroom house in Essex near her parents, returning to her maiden name with her son, Liam, following suit. Meanwhile, Harper's father had moved to Washington, probably because the work was more lucrative there, working with people who wouldn't give their names whenever the now teenage Harper met them; men in suits who spoke calmly, and definitely had connections to organisations that were spoken of in letters rather than names: CIA, NSA, and such like.

Harper would spend his summers in America with his father, his winters and Christmas at home with his mother and family, and then two or three times a year he would travel back and forth for birthdays and events.

If he was being honest with himself, it was this that made him a loner.

Sure, there were friends he had gained in both places, but it was hard to make friends at school when your plans for summer involved not being around, and it was harder still to make friends in America, when you were only there for the holidays and once school started you were gone once more. He was a constant cuckoo, flying into people's nests, hanging around and then leaving.

In a way, it was probably also where Harper gained his commitment issues.

And then, when his mother was sideswiped by a car in the middle of Cambridge on a wet November evening, Liam Harper expected his life to change again but, instead of taking him to his bosom and bringing him to the United States, Harper's father effectively gave up all interest in his fourteen-year-old son overnight.

There had been discussions on where Harper should live, but he'd eventually stayed with his widowed grandfather – Old Pete, an ex-RAF corporal who had worked in the Queen's Silver Service Department – and his father became nothing more than a voice on a phone, a card sent on birthdays with money inside, and the occasional Christmas invite. But only then for a week or two at some random location, where Harper would be told to "sit and be quiet" while his father spent his time talking to strangers, constantly working, the men in suits still keeping to the shadows, still watching from the side.

When Harper was sixteen, he joined the RAF.

There was probably some kind of connection between his

grandfather's role in the RAF and some need to be like his father; to travel the world and find his own family, but instead Harper had found that, actually, he had a talent for things. In fact, after a couple of years and at a rather youthful eighteen years of age, his commanding officers had already realised that Liam Harper was destined for bigger things than the RAF.

But even then, staring at the gawky teenager, still trying to convince them he could be an adequate pilot down the line, they had no idea how right they were.

Harper sat on his Triumph Bonneville considering this, staring down the Main Street of Prosperity. The two men were arguing beside their car, some kind of black SUV. He couldn't make out the make and number from this distance, but he could see that the pockmarked blond had decided he was driving, even though he was probably too baked to sit behind a steering wheel, and stood there arguing angrily with his Hispanic friend, probably still not understanding why he'd been pulled out of a fight he'd wanted.

Harper stretched his back muscles, feeling the knots loosening. Even though he'd sat in the diner for an hour, the confrontation had tensed him back up, preparing for a fight, and now he needed to relax once more. He was about to give up on the pair of them and start the motorcycle when he noticed a white Ford Expedition Special Services Vehicle, or SSV, driving towards him. It was a Prosperity Police Sheriff's wagon, a green stripe along the sides, and it looked to be driven by a woman in her twenties.

It pulled up next to Harper, and the woman climbed out

carefully, looking him up and down as he sat on his motorcycle, his helmet still in his hands.

He'd been correct. She was in her late twenties, and slim – more toned than skinny. She wore the beige shirt of a deputy, with the badge on the left-hand side, her gun at her hip, and she carried herself with a cautious gait. Her long black hair was pulled back into a ponytail, and she wore minimal makeup, which was understandable considering her job. There was also the slightest of bruises on her left orbital bone, Harper noted. Either she was incredibly accidental, in a poor relationship, or being a deputy in Prosperity was a little more physical than he would have expected.

'Deputy,' he said calmly, the helmet in his lap.

The black-haired deputy stood in front of Harper, looking down at the motorcycle.

'Nice,' she said simply, before looking back at him.

'Can I help you?' he asked. 'It's not for sale, if you were about to ask.'

'Can *you* help *me?* Well, that depends,' the deputy replied. 'Name's Cortez. I've been told there was an incident at the diner, and that a British man was involved? One who came into town on a bike?'

Harper smiled.

'It wasn't really an incident,' he said, shrugging, nodding down the street. 'Two guys were hassling an older man. Eddie, I think his name was. I felt I had to step in. Asked them politely to leave, and eventually, they did.'

Cortez watched Harper, and he wondered if she believed what he was telling her.

'They just left,' she commented, the words spoken with utter disbelief at the story. 'Without any fuss.'

'Feel free to ask the waitress,' Harper nodded back at the diner. 'I think her name's Maisie? She saw everything.'

'Don't you worry, I will be,' Cortez looked back at the diner momentarily before returning her attention to the stranger in front of her. 'Can I ask why you're in Prosperity?'

'Sure,' Harper pointed back at one of the panniers of his Triumph. 'I was going to do some sketching. Some good mountain ranges around here. My sketchbook's in there if you want to look.'

Cortez looked as if she was considering the question, but then shook her head.

'I think we're fine for the moment,' she replied. 'So, you're just here to sketch some mountains and shit, purely passing through?'

Harper tried to give a winning smile, but knew this wasn't one of his strong points.

'My father came here once, talked about the place,' he added, in case it helped.

'Is your father with you now?'

'He died six months back,' Harper shook his head.

Cortez softened as he said this, her confrontational stance slightly lessening, and Harper knew what was now going through her mind. It was why he led her to the question, after all. This was no longer a man riding through the town; this was a man doing some kind of last journey, promised to his father on his deathbed maybe, travelling to places his father had loved. Harper could see the revised storyline running through her head, and he wasn't going to change it.

'Will you be here long?' she continued, her tone definitely warmer now she realised he wasn't the potential threat she'd first envisioned.

'A few days, nothing more,' Harper shook his head. 'I've

got some business to take care of, family stuff, and then I'll be on my way.'

'You have a place to stay?'

'I've been suggested to go to Maggie's Guesthouse, but there's a hotel just down the road I saw as I came in.'

Cortez nodded.

'Don't go to the Goldstrike, that's just a glorified bar that wants to play at being a casino, and they'll fleece you out of everything you have – maybe even this pretty bike,' she replied. 'Go see Maggie. She'll give you a good price. Tell her Cortez sent you; you might even get a discount.'

'I've already had a suggestion about that from Eddie, the historian guy,' Harper laughed. 'Apparently, she's his daughter or something.'

'Oh, yeah, you'll get a better discount if you use his name,' Cortez chuckled, looking back at the two men, still arguing down the Main Street. 'Do you want to raise a complaint about those guys?'

'Oh God, no,' Harper shook his head vigorously. 'They were young – well, at least one of them was. The other was ... unfortunately styled, shall we say. They were just throwing their weight around.'

He leaned closer.

'Got the impression they weren't locals, though.'

'No,' Cortez replied. 'You'd be right about that. They're here on work.'

'Work?' Harper asked, looking around the street. 'I didn't realise you had that much outsider help around town.'

'We don't need any outsider help,' Cortez said, and for the first time, Harper heard the slightest hint of anger in her voice. 'So, whatever you've been told ...'

Harper held his hand up to stop her.

'Deputy, I've not heard a thing,' he replied calmly. 'I was just going on what I saw in the diner, and what I heard after they left. Maisie and Eddie? I got the distinct impression they weren't happy these guys were there. I also got the impression though, they were some kind of personal security somewhere local. This wannabe casino, perhaps?'

Harper waited, wondering if Cortez would give something away. He already knew the answer that he wanted. That the pockmarked blond and the Hispanic with the goatee were both employees of an independent security company called *Aegis*, a company that had taken a strong interest in Prosperity over the recent months.

But Cortez wasn't biting. She simply kicked the tyre of his Triumph gently to test it, looked back at Harper, and smiled.

'You have a good day,' she said. 'And your name again?'

'Harper, ma'am. Liam Harper.'

'Well, as I said, you have a good day, Mister Harper. Maybe I'll see you around.'

'Hopefully not in an official capacity.' Harper gave another smile and realised it probably made him seem creepy. 'I mean, I didn't ...'

Cortez simply smiled, nodded, and turned back to the SSV.

'Hey,' Harper called out. 'There is one thing you could do for me.'

Cortez paused and slowly turned to face the newcomer, probably wondering what was about to be asked.

'This guest house,' Harper shrugged. 'You couldn't tell me where it is, could you? I forgot to get the address.'

'You know what?' Cortez nodded amiably. 'It's a slow day. Follow me, I'll take you there myself.'

Harper wasn't dumb; he knew she was taking him purely

to confirm his story checked out. But that was fine by him, as he knew she would likely have followed him anyway. Also, with her beside him the two idiots by the SUV were less likely to do anything stupid, and at the end of the day he genuinely was looking for the guesthouse, and he had nothing to hide from her, or any other law enforcement officer here.

Yet, anyway.

3

HOUSE GUEST

MAGGIE'S GUESTHOUSE, ON THE OUTSKIRTS OF PROSPERITY, WAS exactly what Harper had wanted; small, homely and owned by somebody who didn't care too much about asking questions. That Harper had helped her father had already put him in her good books, so Maggie Hawkins, the owner, was happy to invite him in. Harper noted, as he hefted his rucksack in one hand and his bike helmet in the other, that she hadn't seemed as happy to allow Deputy Cortez in; however, Cortez had followed and hung around, claiming she "just wanted to make sure that Harper got the best discount". Once she'd confirmed he'd paid his deposit and booked his hotel room, she tipped an imaginary hat and left, her Ford driving back towards Prosperity.

Maggie watched her ... while Harper watched Maggie.

'No love lost?' he asked.

Maggie looked back at him. She was in her early fifties with short black hair, cut in an almost military style. She was more muscled than Harper had expected on first meeting, and had the wiry grace of somebody who was a crossfitter, or perhaps somebody who played an endurance sport. She wore a baggy jumper that hid this, possibly even deliberately, the sleeves pushed halfway up her forearms, and as she turned to face him, he noted the slightest edge of a familiar tattoo.

'Cortez is fine,' she said, shrugging as she returned her attention to the keys behind the counter, flicking through them with her index finger to find the key to Harper's room. 'She's just a little green.'

'Didn't seem that way to me,' Harper said. 'She took in the situation, made sure I was taken somewhere safe.'

'Oh, she's good at escort duties, don't get me wrong,' Maggie said. 'But in Prosperity you need to have a little more *gumption*, if you know what I mean.'

Harper frowned.

'I might've only arrived today, but I don't see this place being a hive of criminal activity.'

Maggie returned her attention to Harper.

'It's not a case of who the homegrown criminal element is,' she said. 'It's more the visitors.'

Harper got the impression she wasn't talking about him.

'How long have you been here?' he asked.

'All my life,' Maggie shrugged. 'My dad came here when I was one year, maybe eighteen months old. And I've been a child of Prosperity ever since.'

'Apart from your tours, I'm guessing,' Harper replied, nodding at her tattoo. 'I couldn't help but notice that's three stripes over crossed rifles, right? U.S. Marine Sergeant?'

'Hoo-rah,' she said, raising an eyebrow. 'Master Sergeant, SRT. Nobody really knows what it is around here.'

'Special Reaction Team?' Harper nodded, impressed. 'You guys do good work.'

'Impressed you've heard of us. You serve?'

Harper pulled off his jacket, revealing his own tattoo, the stylised sword positioned upright behind a Corinthian-style helmet over the scroll.

Maggie whistled, recognising the symbol.

'Special Reconnaissance Regiment? I met some of you guys once,' she nodded in response. 'Gave me a killer hang-over. What brings you to a sleepy town like this?'

'Well, I quit the services recently,' Harper shrugged as Maggie, now finding the key, motioned for him to follow her. 'Wasn't the best of endings.'

'Dishonourable?' she asked, but there was no judgement to her voice.

'No, nothing like that,' Harper shook his head. 'My choice, not theirs. It was just ...'

He paused and stared at Maggie, his eyes intense. He knew it would have been the kind of look she would have seen before; the look of a soldier who had seen too much, which was exactly what it was supposed to be, because Harper had.

'There was an op,' he said. 'It went south. People died.'

'That happens all the time,' Maggie said. 'And people die all the time, too.'

'This one was different.' Harper stopped and said nothing else, and Maggie, with whatever knowledge the US Marine Corps would have given her about the SRR other than their partying habits, knew not to push anymore.

'Well, you get used to being out,' she said. 'I became a civilian again about eleven years back.'

'Planned?'

'IED,' Maggie tapped at her thigh. 'Got half a ton of steel in here. You wouldn't know to see, but Christmas can be a bitch when the weather's cold.'

As if realising she'd talked too much, she sniffed, and looked back at the key.

'Your room's upstairs, second floor,' she said. 'It's small, but it'll do you what you need. How many days do you think you'll be here?'

'Unsure,' Harper replied. 'I've got some business nearby, and I wanted to sketch the landscapes.'

Maggie laughed at the comment.

'Painters,' she said. 'Painters, poets and goddamned sculptors. That was half of my unit. I get it, I really do.'

'You find things to do when you're on base,' Harper shrugged. 'Some, it was carving things out of wood, maybe making small sculptures out of spent ammunition. Me? I'd spend hours learning about weapon history, and when I tired of that, I'd find myself on point staring out across landscapes. Gained myself a love of it.'

'Yeah?' Maggie was already walking up the stairs but paused, looking back at him. 'Not in Prosperity, you won't. You know the story?'

'I do,' Harper said as they carried on up. 'Maisie in the diner mentioned it as well. Your dad's some kind of historian, I believe?'

'He's not *some* kind of anything,' Maggie replied tartly. 'He's *the* historian, the eminent expert in the area. Him and Moses literally wrote the book. It's in the library. Worth a read, too.'

Pausing at a door, she took a long metal key, inserting it into the lock and turning it. The door opened with a click, and Maggie stepped aside to allow Harper through.

'He's been investigating the Bickfords, Old Man Caldwell, and that damned mine since he was a teenager,' she said. 'If there's anyone in this godforsaken town who knows where the gold is, he'll be the one. You been told the story of the gold, yet?'

'I got the crib notes in the diner, but I'll admit I knew about the story,' Harper said. 'It's one of the reasons I came. My dad passed through here once. It was on a list of places he'd always wanted to return to.'

'Well, he should have stayed with the memories,' she said. 'As should you. There's nothing here now. The tourists still come along, but they're being pushed away.'

'They are? How come?'

'The mayor, for a start,' Maggie shrugged, pointing towards a side door. 'Your bathroom's in there, there's towels. You can be served breakfast and dinner if you want it. Most don't.'

'I'd appreciate breakfast at least,' Harper smiled. 'Is it extra?'

'Everything's extra in Prosperity,' Maggie said, and Harper caught the slightest hint of anger or frustration with the comment.

'And everything's cheap,' she added.

Harper raised an eyebrow at this, waiting for Maggie to continue. Eventually, like all good gossips, she couldn't help herself.

'Look, I don't usually gossip, but you'll need the lay of the land if you want to stay out of trouble,' she explained, as if justifying the gossip she was about to give. 'See that big old white house on the hill when you rode in? Belongs to the Bickfords. They've been running this town since before I was born. Tom's the mayor now, but don't let that fool you. They're richer than they act, and twice as greedy.'

'The mayor's lining his pockets?'

'Let's just say he finds ways to grab "consulting fees" and

"agent percentages",' Maggie grumbled. 'Guy's a showboater. The family own most of the buildings around here, have for over a century, but he has to rub it in our faces.'

'How?'

Maggie pursed her lips.

'The Bickfords bought up land after the mine closed, but they treat the gold theft like some kind of golden goose. Even had a celebration this year, for the hundred and fiftieth anniversary. Bickford brought his special rifle out and put it on display for a week in the library, like it was the goddamned Turin Shroud or something.'

'Special rifle?'

'Doc Holliday's Winchester. Apparently he gave it to William Bickford, the great grandaddy of them all, when he joined the hunt for the gold.'

'Doc Holliday hunted the Prosperity Gold?'

'Oh yeah. He was heading from Virginia City down to Colorado, and offered to help, but it was nothing more than an excuse to whore and gamble a few days. Anyway, the Bickfords treat it as if they were touched by God, and it's been the totem of the town ever since.'

She chuckled.

'Damn fool couldn't work it, though. Sheriff Coble had to take it off him to fire it in the celebrations. Christ, Bickford was furious. A week later, a firm turns up. Their name's—'

'Aegis.'

Harper raised a hand, pausing Maggie from replying as she stared at him, confused.

'The two guys hassling your father,' he explained. 'Cortez said they worked for Aegis. Security firm?'

Maggie nodded.

'The mine's where the gold was believed to have been

lost, well, it's been held as a site of historical importance for over seventy years, no drilling, but Mayor Bickford, well, he likes his kickbacks. Aegis turned up about six months ago, right after the celebrations, claiming they were security for a team of corporate researchers who wanted to check for more deposits. Got the rights to do some sample tests, do some test holes, even got a gold mining permit, to see if they can find gold – whether the hidden bars or new seams – once again. You know, prove to the masses whether it was nothing more than a drunken man's myth, or a story for prospectors. And with Bickford owning the land, he's arguing it's his right to do that, no matter the "historical importance", or what the academics and environmentalists say.'

'Not many security companies have "gold prospecting" on their books,' Harper placed his motorcycle helmet on the bed.

'Oh, they're just the security, but from what I can work out, they're doing the bulk of the work,' Maggie replied icily, standing by the door now, her face cold and emotionless. 'We thought they'd be here a couple of weeks, have a look around, and then, like everybody else, piss off back to wherever they came from.'

'But let me guess, these guys don't know when to give up?'

Maggie smiled.

'They're tenacious, I'll give them that,' she said, but her smile quickly faded. 'But there's more to it. They're violent. They're not like us.'

Harper motioned between her and himself.

'Us? You mean—'

'No, not soldiers,' Maggie said. 'They're not like the townsfolk. You know, we've grown up with this story. It's important to us, but these guys? I think they'd take down the entire goddamn mountain if it meant they'd find one bar of gold.'

She shook her head again, her lips pressed into a tight line.

'There's more,' she muttered. 'We've had more drunken fights, thefts, you name it, in the last few months – the town's gone downhill since they turned up.'

'Well, hopefully, they'll leave soon,' Harper suggested.

'It'd be nice,' Maggie smiled faintly. 'If only for my father.'

'Why do they hate him so?'

She laughed.

'Oh, they don't hate him at all,' she said. 'If anything, they need him. You see, he's the guy who told them where the gold probably was, and promised them a survey map that could help. Problem is, the map's a bedtime story, and he's no good at those. Trust me.'

Harper nodded, understanding now. If Eddie *had* been the man who told them where to dig, and the gold still hadn't been found months later, he could understand why they'd have a problem with him – especially if he'd not given them a map he'd promised.

'Tucker at the diner? Don't ask him about Aegis Security either, unless you want an earful about the "Men in Black" and government cover-ups,' Maggie was on a roll now. 'Man's been off his rocker since they arrived. People reckon he went for a job back at the start, but they shit-canned him when he started asking too many questions. Though, the only question he usually asks is where the liquor cabinet is, so I reckon he was fired for another reason.'

Realising she'd spoken too much, Maggie shrugged and cricked her neck.

'I'll let you settle in, soldier,' she said. 'As I mentioned, you're more than welcome to share in my dinner. I've got another couple, the Parsons, who are staying until the end of the week. They're two doors down. Apart from that, you've pretty much got the building to yourself.'

'Quiet season?'

'All seasons have been quiet for the last year or so,' Maggie shrugged. 'The tourists either turn up, take snaps and leave, or they show up with metal detectors like it's some kind of adventure park. "Where's the treasure?" they ask. I tell them if I knew that, I wouldn't be renting out rooms, would I?'

She chuckled to herself.

'Usually I'll aim them at Old Charlie Rivers – he's still out there with his metal detector. Guy's gotta be, what, eighty? Woke up one night swearing he'd seen the ghost of a miner showing him where to dig. Or I'll point them at the Fool's Gold Mine.'

'The Fool's Gold Mine?'

'It ain't exactly on the tourist brochures, and even when it was, it didn't bring in the kind of crowd you'd want,' Maggie explained. 'The name says it all, really. They called it the Fool's Gold Mine because that's all it ever spat out – pyrite. Looks just like gold, shines just as pretty, but it ain't worth more than the dirt it's stuck in. By the time they figured it out back in the day, the Bickfords had already pocketed their cash, left them broke and humiliated. These days, it's mostly sealed up. Used to be a tourist spot – "Pan for gold like the old-timers!" – but that dried up quick once people realised they were paying to play in dirt with no chance of payout, and we had some deaths.'

'Deaths?'

'Bad air,' Maggie shrugged. 'The whole reason miners

used to take canaries into mines. Took a few lives over the decades, and thinned out the herd, the cautious, intelligent tourists deciding they'd rather pick up their "gold" from the gift shop rather than clamber down a hole.'

She straightened, her expression souring at the memory.

'I still see them now and then – old-timers with pickaxes, travellers with metal detectors. People always think they'll be the one to find what everyone else missed. The funny part is, there's a tunnel system in the back to the west, past where they let the tourists go, up from the Goldstrike and Aegis haven't even realised – or they don't give a damn about it. Real narrow, real steep. Folks say that's where the real gold is. Some reckon Moses Mathers was working that tunnel right before he vanished. Left everything behind, tools and all. Miners don't do that without a reason. Makes you wonder, don't it?'

'Moses Mathers?'

'Another crazy old fool used to work with my father until he disappeared a couple of months back,' Maggie replied, but didn't seem to want to explain past that. 'Anyway, you used to be able to leave your doors unlocked. Not now. Since the mine opened back up, we've had break-ins, stolen cars, even a couple of fights at the diner. Never used to be like that. I don't like drunks, late nights or girls in my rooms. If you feel the urge to pay for something, go to another town.'

'Yes, ma'am,' Harper smiled. 'I don't think you'll be having that problem.'

'Get yourself settled.' Maggie paused by the door. 'Is there anything else I can help you with before you go?'

'Before I go?' Harper asked, tilting his head. 'Actually, yes. How do I find the mine?'

'You want to go there?'

'Why not?' Harper shrugged. 'As I said, I'm here to sketch interesting things and, well, that sounds very interesting to me. And you said tourists still visit.'

'Yeah, they visit, but not for long,' Maggie shook her head. 'You get within a hundred feet of the entrance and you'll have a welcome party come out and stop you. Bickford gave the Aegis bodyguards carte blanche to do whatever the hell they want up there.'

'Well then, I'll sketch them, too,' Harper smiled.

'You know what?' Maggie walked off now, chuckling. 'I daresay you would. Semper Fi, Mister Harper.'

4

PUBLIC AFFRAY

ONCE HE'D UNPACKED, HARPER PULLED TOGETHER A SMALL everyday carry pack, shoving it into a satchel and throwing it around his shoulder before locking his bedroom door and making his way out into Prosperity. He knew if he'd laid down on the bed, as comfortable as it looked, he probably wouldn't have got up for a good day or so; he was still bone-tired from the journey, and was missing a night's sleep.

In his satchel, he had his sketch pad and some pens and pencils, a small metal water bottle, and a few other bits and pieces he always carried with him. He wasn't hiking or going out into the mountains, but he'd always been of a nature to be prepared. As he pulled out a familiar grey stone from his pocket, stroking it absently with his thumb, the worn smooth edge proof this was a common occurrence, he considered using the motorcycle – but that would have involved returning to the room and grabbing the helmet, so, placing his lucky stone away, Harper decided to carry on by foot.

It was early afternoon now, and the November weather

was quite clement, if chilly. The Nevada sun provided enough glare to need shades, but a peaked cap could suffice.

Harper had one; an old grey *New York Mets* cap he'd had for years. It was battered and frayed, but he loved it dearly, one of the last happy times he'd spent with his father.

And so, with the battered grey cap on, satchel over leather jacket, jeans, and army boots finishing the ensemble, Liam Harper went for a stroll. His plan had been to go to the library, look up some local maps, and check into the area; he hadn't lied when he said he was here to sketch, but he also hadn't lied when he said he was looking into the gold.

He had a more *personal* reason than most of the tourists, however.

PROSPERITY'S HIGH STREET WAS LAID OUT LIKE MOST OF small-town America, but as Harper looked at the storefronts, he felt it was a town with almost an embarrassment of its past.

A fresh coat of asphalt stretched between tired concrete sidewalks, each stamped with a fake wood pattern that fooled nobody. The *Goldstrike Inn & Suites* dominated one end, its vinyl siding and illuminated sign a far cry from the frontier hotel it had once been. As he passed it, Harper was glad he'd listened to Deputy Cortez and Eddie Hawkins, and chosen the smaller, more independent guest house; this looked more like a sports bar with rooms available, than an actual tourist hotel.

Chain stores lined both sides – *Subway, Dollar General, Starbucks* – their modern facades interrupted only by a gift shop with its awkward mix of tourist tat and local necessities. Harper checked the window, and chuckled as he saw the Fool's Gold deposits, held in fancy glass cases. The tacky reproduction lamp posts the council had likely installed during their last attempt at historical charm bore fading celebration banners, swaying in the November breeze.

The street was quiet this time of year, just a few locals' pickup trucks parallel parked. The entire scene felt like small-town America desperately trying to forget its Wild West origins, while simultaneously unable to let them go completely.

As he turned down one of the side roads heading towards Prosperity's library, he slowed down as he saw a confrontation beginning outside it.

Once more, it looked like Eddie Hawkins, the historian he'd already saved once that day, was being hassled. A black SUV – the same one that had been driven by the pockmarked blond and the Hispanic guy with the crappy goatee – had pulled up and, as he paused to watch, three men emerged. One of them was the pockmarked blond, but Harper didn't recognise the other two. It was obvious even from this distance, though, that Eddie didn't want to go with them, and was trying to argue, almost as if they were accusing him of something and he was trying to claim innocence.

Harper sighed, picked up his pace, and headed towards them.

'This ain't your fight, faggot,' the pockmarked blond said, seeing him approach. 'We told you before, back off.'

'Can't do that, I'm afraid,' Harper replied calmly. 'I'm staying at his daughter's guesthouse. Kind of feel I owe it to her to keep an eye on her old man.'

'You ain't his keeper. You ain't part of this. Leave before we kick the crap out of you, too,' the second man said, glaring at Harper. He was taller, broader in frame, and with jet-black hair and a beard that looked like you could shave it at nine in the morning and find a full beard back by the end of the day. The third man, slimmer, standing to the back and wearing round "John Lennon" glasses, had decided not to get involved, however, and was already on the phone, tapping out a message – probably to ask for backup.

Or for orders. Aegis were soldiers, after all. Just not for a country.

Eddie glanced back at Harper, and his face broke into a smile of relief – and that was all Harper needed to see.

Whatever was going on, it was bad.

Harper continued walking towards them, closing the distance, hand casually in his pocket as he did so.

'Guys, I don't know what this man's done to you, but if there's a problem here, maybe we should take it to the police,' he suggested.

'You ain't got a clue what's going on here,' the pockmarked blond replied. 'Why don't you just keep walking?'

'I already told you, I can't.' Harper stopped, as the three men, now tiring of Eddie, turned to face him. 'Just tell me what's going on, and I'll be on my way ... if, of course, I believe you're in the right here.'

'If *we're* in the right? Listen to the balls on this guy!' Blackbeard scoffed. 'What's going on here, is we're beating the shit outta *this* guy ... and then we'll start on you.'

Harper now faced Blackbeard, as the taller man squared up.

'We ain't met,' he said. 'I've met the blond guy and his

goatee-wearing friend earlier today. You two? You're new to me. I'm guessing you're Aegis as well?'

At the name, Blackbeard raised an eyebrow. He glanced at the man in Lennon glasses, as if to ask for help, before returning his attention to Harper, which made him wonder if the guy in the glasses was the one in charge, while Blackbeard was simply the loudest.

'So what if we are?'

'It just seems strange that a usually government-funded private security organisation has such a fixation on an old guy,' Harper replied.

'This old guy stiffed us,' Blackbeard said. 'He promised us things he hasn't delivered.'

'And you're asking for them nicely?'

'We're taking him to our boss, so *he* can ask him nicely.'

'Awesome,' Harper looked at the SUV. 'That holds, what, five people? With me added, that'll fit us all fine then.'

'You think you're coming with us?'

Harper stepped closer, now near enough to touch Blackbeard if he wanted.

'I'm saying that unless you take me with you, there's *no way in hell* I'm letting you take this man with you, wherever you think you're going,' he said, his voice cold and purposeful.

There was a moment of confusion at this; Harper could see the three men weren't sure what to do. On one hand, Harper had offered them a way to take Eddie – but it meant taking him along, too. He was an unknown quantity, fresh into town, and with a history that the pockmarked blond had seen scare his buddy in the diner. More importantly though, regardless of whatever this newcomer brought, their hesitance also meant that whatever they planned to do, it likely couldn't happen with a witness.

Harper clicked his neck from side to side. He knew what was coming – he always did. Since childhood, combat situations had played out like slow-motion chess in his mind; two, three, sometimes four moves ahead.

His father had called it a gift.

His SRR instructors had called it intuition.

Harper just called it *staying alive.* He couldn't play chess, however. It only seemed to work in violence.

Blackbeard telegraphed his first move like an amateur; a vicious right cross that Harper read before the man's weight even shifted. Harper moved with practised efficiency, his feet planted as his upper body swayed back just enough to let the punch whistle past. In one fluid motion, he caught Blackbeard's extended arm, using the larger man's own momentum to guide him face-first forwards into the fake-wood-stamped concrete.

The pockmarked blond moved next, more cautious after seeing his friend dropped. He circled left, trying to flank while Lennon glasses backed away, still fumbling with his phone. Harper kept his stance relaxed, hands loose at his sides – a posture that suggested vulnerability while actually allowing for quicker response.

'Last chance,' Harper said quietly, tracking both men's movements without turning his head. 'Walk away, leave Eddie alone.'

The pockmarked blond's response was a quick combination – jab, cross, hook – professional moves that told Harper that although he was young, a hothead and most likely had a weed issue, this one had actual training. Harper slipped the jab, blocked the cross with his forearm, and stepped inside the hook's arc. In close, he drove a short elbow into the pockmarked blond's solar plexus, followed by a knee to the thigh that buckled the man's leg.

But Blackbeard was up again, and this time he had a collapsible baton in his hand. The metal rod snapped out with a distinctive click that brought a flood of memories to Harper – Baghdad, Kabul, a dozen other places, where the sound of extending weapons meant things were about to get serious.

'Really?' Harper sighed. 'You're going to escalate this with a weapon? In broad daylight?'

He shifted his stance, keeping both men in view while positioning himself between them and Eddie. His satchel now felt like a liability, but it could also be an asset. As Blackbeard charged in, swinging the baton in a wild arc, Harper used the bag's leather strap as a makeshift bracer, letting the baton slide down his arm before swinging the strap up to tangle the damned thing. A quick twist disarmed Blackbeard, sending the weapon clattering across the pavement.

The brief clash, however, gave the pockmarked blond time to recover. Both men now circled Harper, looking for an opening. They came at him together this time, but Harper had been expecting it, and side-stepped Blackbeard's charge, letting the bigger man's momentum carry him past. In the same fluid motion, Harper drove his elbow up and back, catching the pockmarked blond square in the jaw as he tried to close in from behind.

The crack of impact echoed off the storefronts.

The pockmarked blond staggered, but before he could recover, Harper had already pivoted. His knee shot upwards, driving hard into Blackbeard's side as the man tried to turn back into the fight. With this, the bigger man folded with a grunt, dropping to one knee.

Harper finished the combination with a short, brutal right hook that caught the still-dazed pockmarked blond across the temple. The man's eyes rolled back as his legs gave way, and he crumpled to the pavement beside his partner.

The entire sequence had taken a matter of seconds. Both men lay groaning on the ground, Blackbeard clutching his ribs while the pockmarked blond, beginning to recover his senses, tried unsuccessfully to push himself up.

Harper hadn't even lost his cap in the exchange.

He glanced over at the man in Lennon glasses, who had wisely refrained from joining the fight, still staring at his phone screen. Harper wondered if reinforcements were already on their way and, as if in answer to his thought, sirens echoed down Main Street. Harper looked over to see two police SSVs speeding around the corner, lights flashing.

They screeched to a halt on either side of the SUV, boxing it in.

Deputy Cortez emerged slowly from the second SSV, but it was the driver of the lead vehicle who commanded Harper's attention; an overweight, red-headed man with narrow eyes who drew his pistol with surprising speed, levelling it at Harper's chest.

Harper stayed perfectly still, his hands visible at his sides.

'Hands in the air!' the man shouted. 'Drop your weapon!'

'I don't have a weapon,' Harper called back calmly, raising his hands. 'I was defending myself. These guys attacked me.'

'What's your business with these men?' the man demanded.

'They were attacking this old man. I stepped in.'

'What's your connection with Eddie Hawkins?'

'What's that to do with you?' Harper frowned. 'That's not the point here—'

'I ask the damn questions! What's your goddamned connection?'

Harper tried to keep his voice level; the gun still aimed at his chest felt a little more oppressive now.

'He's the dad of the woman who runs the guesthouse I'm staying in,' he replied, glancing over at Cortez, noticing she hadn't pulled out her weapon.

'That's true, Dan,' Cortez interjected. 'I saw him there earlier.'

The Deputy – evidently called Dan – glanced dismissively at Cortez before turning back to Harper.

'What did you do to these guys?' he asked.

'They attacked me. I defended myself, Dan—'

'You can call me Deputy Carson,' the red-headed man said curtly. 'We had a call saying you were hassling these guys, threatening them.'

Harper looked at Lennon glasses, tipping his head almost respectfully.

'I thought you were calling backup,' Harper said. 'Didn't realise you were aiming for a different kind of backup.'

'Just making sure my men are looked after,' Lennon glasses replied smoothly. 'I'm sure you'd do the same.'

Eddie stepped forward, waving wildly at Harper, the men on the floor, and then the SUV.

'He's telling the truth,' he said, addressing Cortez rather than Carson – this intrigued Harper, and gave him even more of an impression of the guy still holding the gun at him. 'These men wanted to take me to see Carrick. I said I didn't want to go. They were quite insistent. If this man hadn't turned up, I'd have been kidnapped.'

'Is that what you were doing?' Carson asked sharply at Lennon glasses. 'Dragging Mister Hawkins here to see Mason Carrick?'

Lennon glasses shook his head, giving the most hurt, innocent expression he could provide as he answered.

'Mister Hawkins owes us a survey map of one of the mines,' he said. 'We've been waiting for it for quite a while. Yes, the conversation got heated, but then this man appeared out of nowhere and escalated it into a fight.'

'That's bullshit, and you know it,' Harper retorted, but Lennon glasses stepped back with a slight, wry smile. Carson, meanwhile, had already decided the next stage of this.

'Hands on the car,' he ordered.

'You're kidding me.'

'Hands on the car.'

Sighing, Harper placed his hands on the vehicle. Carson stepped forward, kicked Harper's legs apart, and frisked him, pulling out an old, battered pocket knife, known as a "Swiss Army Knife" from Harper's pocket.

'Offensive weapon.'

'It's a tiny knife,' Harper protested. 'That guy there had a goddamned extendable baton.'

'What do you use it for?'

'Sharpening my sketching pencils, or pretending I'm *MacGyver*,' Harper already disliked Carson. 'Look, check the two of them. At no point did I use the knife.'

'I'll be the decider of that,' Carson snapped.

'*Evidence* will be the decider,' Harper muttered, wincing as his hands were wrenched behind his back and handcuffs clicked into place. 'Wait, you're arresting me?'

Cortez seemed just as surprised.

'Dan, we can't just—'

'We can do what we damn well want, *Deputy Cortez,*' Carson cut in angrily, now rummaging through Harper's other pocket, pulling out the worn stone. 'What the hell's this?'

'Lucky charm,' Harper said calmly. 'Stone Age fidget spinner.'

'It's a piece of crap you probably stole off a gravel track,' Carson raised his hand to throw it. 'Here, let me get rid of it for you—'

He wasn't sure what had happened, but even with Harper handcuffed, in one swift motion Carson was slammed back against the car, with Harper, angry, leaning in.

'That's my personal property,' he hissed. 'And I swear to you, if you throw it, I'll make you *go find it*.'

'Threatening an officer?' Carson looked to Cortez for support. 'You heard that, right?'

'Stop being a prick and give him his goddamned stone back,' Cortez shook her head angrily. 'And if you're going ahead with this bullshit detainment, then we should take the others. These guys attacked—'

'These guys were attacked without warning,' Carson interrupted, reluctantly placing the stone back in Harper's pocket. 'You heard the witness.'

'And the other witness—'

'You know ...' Harper interrupted calmly, as he glanced over at Carson. 'I'd love to know how you do it.'

'Do what?'

'Your psychic powers.'

'What do you mean by that, funny man?' Carson spun him angrily around, slamming him backwards against the car door, reversing their positions.

'I mean you can tell without any doubt I attacked them,

when you weren't even here, and the only real witness says I was defending him.'

'I was told,' Carson growled,' by text.'

He nodded at Lennon glasses.

'Mister Ashfield here is a stand-up member of the community. Of course I'll listen to him over ...'

Carson paused, looking Harper up and down.

'Over some kind of vagrant, who has a rock for a best friend—'

'It's a river stone, not a rock.'

'Who's already admitted he has a connection to the only other man here – a man who's obviously in debt and looking to squirm out of a legally binding deal.'

Harper said nothing. There was no point. He could see Carson had already decided.

'I get a call, right?' he asked.

'Eventually,' Carson replied.

'Can I at least ask one thing?' Harper turned to Cortez. 'You're not arresting these guys. I get that. But can you at least take Mister Hawkins somewhere safe, so they can't keep attacking him?'

'Eddie, do you want a lift somewhere?' Cortez asked, ignoring Carson's angry gaze.

'I'd appreciate it,' Eddie replied, his voice trembling.

'Come on, I'll take you to Maggie's,' Cortez said gently.

Carson, grabbing Harper from behind, pushed him towards the Ford SSV, opened the back door, and bundled him inside. As the door shut, Harper sighed. The pocket knife had been returned to his pocket, his satchel still slung over his shoulder, and as he sat there, he realised this was little more than a show of force.

Placing his head back against the seat, Harper smiled. In

a way, he'd gained more than they'd realised when they spoke.

For a start, he had information he desperately wanted, and it was intel that confirmed a lot of things.

For a start, Mason Carrick still ran Aegis.

And that meant Harper was still on point and aiming straight at the target.

5

MAYORAL VISIT

METAL GROANED SOMEWHERE IN THE DEPTHS OF THE container ship.

Harper advanced down the corridor, MP7 raised, the beam of his weapon light cutting through steam from burst pipes overhead. There were four men behind him, all SRR operators he'd helped train, back in Hereford.

All of them were good. None of them made a sound.

The ship's manifest had shown twelve crew. They'd found three bodies on the bridge, executed ...

Captain shot in the back of the head.

Radio operator too.

Navigator had fought back – died for it.

That meant there were nine more, possibly dead, possibly captured.

And a security that didn't give a shit.

The corridor ahead split three ways. Standard procedure said to hold position, send for backup. But backup meant helicopters, and helicopters meant the insurgents would start executing hostages, if they'd bothered to keep any.

Harper signalled the team to split. Cardy and Dillon peeled right. Laverick and Ashbee took left.

Harper went straight, alone.

Twenty yards in, he saw there was movement ahead, and Harper killed his light.

Two figures in black tactical gear.

The mask design was familiar; he'd seen it in briefings about a new militant group operating out of Myanmar.

They were getting bolder.

His brain then went into overdrive, the next three moves mapped out before he even began. The first one died without seeing Harper, who quietly dropped his MP7 on its combat sling, drew a razor sharp Fairbairn-Sykes fighting knife, clapped a hand over his target's mouth and slit his throat, the body caught before it hit the deck. The second fighter had better training, and got his own knife out, slashing at Harper's throat; Harper blocked and parried with his Fairbairn-Sykes, then crushed his opponent's windpipe with the knife's steel tipped pommel.

There was the hurried sound of boots on metal, and a third insurgent appeared at the corridor's end, weapon already shouldered. Harper went to fire, but stopped – this wasn't an insurgent, it was the tanker's security.

But the intel they had said the security had stepped back from—

'Get down!' the masked security operative shouted, raising his weapon. The AK's muzzle flash strobed the passage; 7.62x39mm rounds whipcracked past Harper's head, and punched holes in another fighter who had materialised *behind* Harper—

One he hadn't seen.

Hit by two AK rounds, the wounded insurgent still

returned fire, two controlled pairs, before he folded to the deck – as did Harper's saviour.

Harper moved forward, weapon trained on the fallen insurgent; he was dead, his glassy eyes staring up at the sky.

No love lost there. But damn, that was close.

Returning to the operative, Harper was leaning closer, checking for a heartbeat. It was there, but it was fading. Blood pooled on the deck from a neck wound – it looked like one round had hit the vest, but the other had struck him in the throat, and nicked the jugular. Standard procedure was to confirm the kill, call it in, move on, but this man had saved him at the cost of his own life, and Harper's hand was already reaching for the mask, to give some final words of thanks and comfort. Also, something about the way the man had moved was familiar.

He grabbed the mask. Pulled—

HARPER HAD BEEN IN THE HOLDING CELL FOR THREE HOURS before the mayor arrived.

It wasn't the first time Harper had been arrested, or even placed in a holding cell for crimes he hadn't committed. Nor was it the first time he'd been in one for crimes he *had* committed. He'd been arrested all over the world, locked up in cells from Cairo to Caracas. Most of the time, it was thanks to the antics of his drunken friends. But he'd come to understand the process – a kind of ritual, a tradition, a formal dance of the justice system.

He'd been brought in, processed, fingerprinted while cuffed – at Carson's insistence – his ID checked, and seen the faces frown when they saw how much was redacted from his records. His items were taken from him and bagged up before finally the cuffs had been removed. Rubbing his wrists, he'd taken stock of his surroundings: a standard barred cell at the back of the main sheriff's office. It held little more than the essentials: a metallic bench bolted to the wall with a thin camping mat on top, with no blanket, no pillow. There was a toilet too, although he wasn't planning to use it unless absolutely necessary. It wasn't the kind of place where people stayed long; it was more of a limbo – a pit stop before being released, or transferred somewhere larger and less forgiving.

Harper sat down on the metal bench and gave the mattress a test.

Thin, firm, and unforgiving.

Taking off his jacket and folding it behind his head as a makeshift pillow, he laid down and closed his eyes. One of Harper's few consistent talents, honed since his teenage years, was the ability to fall asleep anywhere and at any time. His time in the UK Special Forces had only reinforced this skill; you learned quickly to take sleep where and when you could because you never knew when your next chance would come.

He was asleep within seconds.

However, even in the holding cell, Harper's internal clock ticked on. He didn't need to check the time to know exactly how long he'd been lying there. Three hours, give or take, had passed before a familiar, recent nightmare woke him from sleep, snapping him awake, eyes wide and staring at the stark, jail-cell ceiling, his hand outstretched to pull a memory of a mask off a dead man's face.

The usual background noise had been easy to tune out; the hum of fluorescent lights, the occasional clink of a mug against a desk, muted conversations. But now there were mutterings, arguments, raised voices. He was wide awake immediately and, pushing back the tension and fear he'd gained from the nightmare, Harper turned his head lazily to see a man in a suit having an animated argument with Cortez.

The man was short – no more than five foot five – but stocky. Not fat, but built like someone had taken his photo and stretched it sideways by about ten percent. He looked like he was mid-fifties, but as if he hadn't slept for half of those years.

Harper sat up, watching the man as he argued with the deputies. Eventually, however, the man realised Harper was watching and turned with a wide, shit-eating grin on his face.

'Well, hello there,' he greeted, as if addressing some kind of parishioner. 'Have a good nap, did you? Excellent. Sleep off the alcohol.'

Harper frowned, then realised what the man was insinuating.

'If you're suggesting I was drunk,' he replied calmly, 'I'm more than happy to do a breathalyser test. It wouldn't have left my system in three hours, and I can guarantee you there's not an ounce of alcohol in my body.'

'Sure,' the man grinned. 'We'll keep that a little secret.'

He gave a knowing wink, as if Harper was obviously lying. Harper sighed and leant back.

'Please tell me you're not my court-appointed lawyer,' he said.

'Why do you need a lawyer?' the man replied. 'You don't think you've been arrested, do you?'

'I'm being detained. That's good enough,' Harper said, straightening as he stood, stretching his back muscles and linking his hands behind him to pull down, clicking any stiffness out of place. 'You seem to know who I am. Who are you?'

'Mayor Tom Bickford,' the man replied. 'I run this town for my sins.'

Harper nodded.

'Heard about you,' he said.

'Really? Nothing bad, I hope.'

Harper didn't reply, simply staring at the man, letting the long, awkward silence stretch out.

'So, is this common in Prosperity?'

'What's that?'

'That the mayor visits anyone who's arrested?'

'Mister Harper, you were detained for your own good. Seems you had a mental breakdown, maybe due to ... well, you know ...' Bickford mimed a drinking motion, 'and attacked men on the street.'

'Is that what Deputy Carson's saying now?' Harper smiled.

'You disagree?'

'Absolutely.' Harper shrugged. 'The men – the ones Deputy Carson didn't bother arresting – were attacking an elderly man I'd met earlier today. One of them was the same guy who'd confronted him in a diner. All I did was act as a good citizen.'

'Good citizen? Well, if only that were the case ... you see, I'm afraid that's not what we've been told.' Bickford flashed another wide shit-eating grin. 'Unfortunately, we're in a world of "he said, she said" here, and, well, the guys you attacked, they're fine, upstanding members of the town, who'd *never* do the things you claimed.'

'Really?' Harper shook his head, frowning. 'I was under

the impression they were hired mercenaries brought in by a security company. They're as much outsiders as I am.'

'They've spent money in the town, Mister Harper,' Bickford replied. 'A shit-ton of it. They've shown themselves worthy of the trust a town gives to newcomers. You, however, are an unknown quantity.'

'I can see that,' Harper muttered, as he sat back down on the bench, as if without a care in the world. 'When do I get my phone call?'

'What exactly are you doing in Prosperity, Mister Harper?'

'As I said to your deputy there—' Harper nodded towards Cortez '—I'm travelling through on a road trip. My father was here a while back. He'd mentioned it. I thought I'd pop in, you know, retrace his steps.'

'And what was your father's name?'

'Dad.'

'Now, come on, Mister Harper—'

'I'm sorry,' Harper shook his head and rose. 'I don't see why I should be telling you anything right now. After all, you said I wasn't arrested, right?'

'Do you have a place of residence in the US?'

'You're asking if I'm a vagrant?'

'I'm asking if you have a place of residence in the US.'

'Fine then. I do.'

'Then perhaps you should return to your place of residence,' Bickford said. 'It seems you're finding yourself in a lot of trouble on your "holiday" right now.'

'I do, don't I?' Harper shook his head in disbelief. 'You know what though, you're correct, mayor. Thank you for pointing that out. When do I get my phone call?'

If Bickford was angry, he wasn't showing it. But Harper

could see, as he smiled back, that the mayor's grin was slowly fading, his eyes narrowing, growing unfriendly.

'Mister Harper, you attacked people in the street. We need to sort this out before deciding what to do. Whether we arrest you properly and put you in court tomorrow, or ... perhaps, considering your military service ... I understand you served; maybe this is some kind of PTSD that caused you to confront people in both the diner this morning, and then later in the street? I understand you talk to a rock? We could bring in a therapist about that.'

'Do you have my phone?' Harper asked. The sudden change of topic seemed to throw everyone.

Cortez, however, nodded.

'It's in the evidence box,' she said.

'Could you open it?'

'Now's not the time to check your messages, Mister Harper.'

'Oh, no, I'm not checking those,' Harper replied. 'I'm more than happy for you to do it for me. But since you've not provided me with my legally appointed counsel, and you seem keen to believe the word of a man who blatantly lied, I thought I'd give my side of things. Could you open it?'

'Is there a passcode?' Cortez asked.

'Do I need one? I'm amongst friends, aren't I?'

Cortez forced back a smile as she brought the phone to life.

'There's a passcode.'

'One, two, three, four,' Harper said with a shrug.

'You really ought to get a better passcode,' Cortez muttered.

'I find it easy to remember.'

Cortez entered the code, the phone unlocked, and she looked back at him.

'What am I looking for?' she asked.

'Voice app. Last note.'

Cortez scrolled through the phone, found the recording, and frowned.

'It's dated today.'

'Exactly,' Harper confirmed. 'It's time stamped for the exact moment I met your fine, upstanding citizens. You see, after meeting the blond man and his friend in the diner earlier, I thought it prudent to record the conversation as I approached. I have a double-tap shortcut set up on my phone, in case I need to leave a voice note, and I used it earlier. Feel free to play it.'

Cortez hesitated, catching a subtle shake of the head from Carson, but then ignored him and pressed play. The phone's speaker filled the room with the unmistakable voices of the confrontation.

'Guys, I don't know what this man's done to you, but if there's a problem here, maybe we should take it to the police.'

'You ain't got a clue what's going on here. Why don't you just keep walking?'

'I already told you, I can't. Just tell me what's going on, and I'll be on my way ... if, of course, I believe you're in the right here.'

'If we're in the right? Listen to the balls on this guy! What's going on here, is we're beating the shit outta this guy ... and then we'll start on you.'

Cortez paused the recording and looked up, her expression grave.

'This is pretty damning, Dan,' she muttered, turning to Carson, who currently looked like he wanted to throttle someone, his jaw tight as his gaze flicked to Bickford.

The mayor's expression was also one of controlled irritation.

'Well, there seems to be a bit of confusion,' Carson said weakly.

'There's no confusion at all,' Harper replied firmly. 'I was assaulted, and I'd like to press charges.'

Bickford slowly turned to face Harper, his eyes narrowing, almost calculating, as he tried to weigh up the man in front of him.

'Who exactly are you, boy?' he asked, cautious now.

'Just a traveller,' Harper replied. 'One that found himself up against people that you seem to be looking after.'

'Oh, I ain't looking after anybody,' Bickford muttered. 'If the law says they've done wrong, then I'll have them punished.'

He glanced over at Carson, and for a moment Harper wondered if he was about to throw the deputy under the bus. He was correct.

'My deputies made a terrible error here,' he said, looking from Carson to Cortez and back. 'I'll make sure they're reprimanded for their actions.'

'Make sure *she's* not,' Harper replied, nodding over at Cortez. 'From the very beginning, she was actually understanding the situation for what it was. Your red-headed friend there was the one who went in all gung-ho.'

'Now you listen here, you piece of trash—' Carson stopped as Bickford's hand rose.

'Boy, are you too stupid to understand when you're in trouble?' he asked. 'This man here has been illegally detained. There's a goddamned *recording*. You took the wrong person's statement. You've caused us a lot of hassle.'

'But I—' Carson started, but then stopped once more at a second glare from Bickford.

'Now, how about we let you out,' Bickford said, returning his attention to Harper, 'and we call it a day? Some youthful indiscretion on their part?'

'No,' Harper replied calmly. 'Those men attacked me. I had to defend myself. I want to press charges, as I've already said.'

'And as *I'm* saying, Mister Harper, the last thing you want to be doing right now is—'

'The last thing I want to be doing right now is sitting in a cell in a town that I'm travelling through,' Harper snapped quickly, looking over at Cortez. 'Am I still being detained?'

'No, sir.'

'Good. Give me my phone.'

Cortez glanced at Bickford rather than Carson and at a slight nod, passed the phone across. Harper dialled a number, holding it up to his ear.

'Hey,' he said as it connected. 'Can I speak to Senator Casey?'

He looked directly at Bickford as he continued.

'Tell him it's his *godson*.'

'Now, we don't need to go down this route,' Bickford mumbled, with the tone of a man realising things were rapidly progressing past his pay grade. Harper, meanwhile, ignored Bickford.

'No, I'm happy to wait. I know he's a busy man. I've got a bit of a problem I need fixed.'

With the phone to his ear, he looked back at Bickford.

'Those two men,' he said. 'You don't want me pressing charges? Fine, I won't. But I want their names, and I want them to stand in front of me and apologise.'

'Well, I'll see what I can do—'

'You won't *see* anything, Mayor Bickford,' Harper snapped. 'You'll contact Mason Carrick and you'll tell him to get his men to apologise to me. But I don't want them here; I'll come and see them tomorrow, first thing in the morning at the mine that Aegis apparently now owns. Also, so I know when I give the name in a moment, are you a *Tom* or a *Thomas* on the mayoral register?'

Bickford wasn't an idiot. He picked up immediately at the familiar way that Harper had stated Mason Carrick's name. There was definitely something more going on here, and the last thing he wanted was to be involved in it or in whatever phone call Harper was making. Reluctantly, and with a quick nodding of his head, he agreed to the request.

'I don't know their names,' he said. 'Carson might.'

'Blaine and Lucas,' Carson said sheepishly. 'I'll speak to Mister Carrick. We'll arrange something for you.'

'Good.' Harper held a finger up as his call obviously clicked off hold, listening for a moment before replying. 'No, that's fine, just tell him I called to say hi and I'll catch him later on.'

He placed the phone back in his pocket, and this done, he grabbed his jacket pillow and pulled it back on as he walked over to the bars of the cell and tapped on them, as if knocking on the door.

Understanding the request, Carson almost leapt forward to open it.

'Just so you know,' Harper said as he looked at the man, 'I have no problem with law enforcement, and I have no problem with any suspicions you may have had with a stranger in your town. What I have a problem with, at this point ...'

He turned and faced Bickford as he continued.

'... is cronyism.'

Taking a deep breath, he smiled at everyone in the room.

'Now we're done,' he finished, 'can I get a lift back to the library before it closes?'

THE JOURNEY WAS QUICK, THE COMPANY CHILLY, AS CORTEZ drove Harper back to the Prosperity Town Library.

'I don't know what your game is, Mister Harper,' she said.

'Just Harper,' Marlowe replied. 'Only pricks I don't like have to call me *Mister* Harper.'

Cortez flushed a little as she gave a slight smile.

'Still, *Harper*,' she continued, 'you're playing a dangerous game. Bickford's not a man to play chicken with.'

'And what makes you think I was playing chicken?'

'You were bluffing him,' Cortez quickly snapped a glance across. 'I saw your phone. You didn't make a call. And if I asked to see your phone records, I'd see there was no outgoing call made, wouldn't I?'

'Sometimes you have to use the same tools that are being used against you,' Harper grinned. 'Why do you work there, Cortez? You're clever, you understand the ground you walk on. Rather than Carson, you don't seem to be working for "the man", so to speak, and Bickford has no love for you.'

'My dad was the sheriff here,' Cortez replied. 'Until about ten years ago.'

'What happened ten years ago?'

'Shot in the line of duty. I was about to go to university; I had a scholarship for Harvard. Threw it in the same day. Joined up in his name.'

'Some might say you threw away your future.'

'Some might say that,' Cortez smiled. 'Some might say I took a different path. I was always intending to be in the police. I just thought I'd go a more, you know, university-orientated route – maybe join the FBI, do something that mattered.'

'You don't think policing Prosperity matters?'

Cortez pulled in by the pavement. They weren't at the library yet, and Harper turned to face her as she shifted in her seat to confront him.

'I don't know why you're here, *Mister* Harper,' she said, deliberately using the title. 'But you don't get to decide on the people who *do* live here, who *do* have to deal with what's been going on.'

'I apologise,' Harper replied. 'I didn't mean to.'

He glanced across at the bar opposite them.

'Is that a good place to drink?'

If she was thrown by the sudden change of conversation, Cortez didn't show it, leaning forward, glancing past Harper to see where he was pointing.

'O'Malley's,' she said. 'Better than most, it's large, has bands on most nights. You should come along. We'll teach you line dancing.'

'I don't dance,' Harper replied simply.

'That's what everyone says, but once they get a good do-si-do going ...' Cortez grinned. 'It's a better place than most. There's an online newsletter, *The Prospector*—'

'That's the name of the local paper, right?'

'Yeah, but that's a weekly, while the site's up to the minute and free,' Cortez smiled. 'Anyway, they have a list of what bands play each night. You might find you like one.'

'Aegis drink there?'

'What is your fixation with those guys?'

'They seem to have a fixation with Eddie Hawkins,' Harper replied. 'Kind of feel like I should make it my business to know a bit more.'

'The impression I got, Harper, was that you already knew more than you're letting on,' Cortez started driving again, turning right towards the library. 'I don't know what your game is, but there's a lot of good people in Prosperity. And anyone coming in and starting a war with those guys? It's going to hurt us, not you.'

'Don't worry,' Harper replied as they pulled up outside the library. 'I didn't come here to start a war.'

'Then what did you come here for?' Cortez replied. 'Because I checked through your pack, and sure, you can sketch, but that ain't why you're here. You're *off-kilter*, Harper. Sure, you're friendly and all that, but it's too artificial, too sweet. There's something sour here, like a bad taste in the back of the mouth.'

'Give me time,' Harper grinned. 'I'm an acquired taste.'

6

FIZZY GUINNESS

PROSPERITY LIBRARY, SURPRISINGLY, WAS CLOSED FOR THE DAY, a taped A4 sheet of printer paper informed that because of some power outage, the library would reopen the following morning. There was a part of Harper that wondered whether Mayor Bickford had actively done this to stop him entering, but it was quickly blown away.

Nobody was that omniscient.

And even though he'd asked for a lift to the library ten minutes earlier, Bickford couldn't have closed it that quick.

There was a man sitting on the pavement outside; he looked like he was in his forties, but Harper couldn't be sure. He had long hair and a beard that was whitening out, his skin was tanned and almost leathery, and it gave him an agelessness that was definitely older than he truly was, but could have been anything.

'When did the library close?' he asked the man.

The man looked up, his piercing blue eyes staring at Harper.

'About three hours back,' he replied. 'Like, there's no power issues. It's because *they're* in there.'

'They're in there?' Harper frowned. 'Librarians?'

'Aegis. They've taken over the survey map room. It's what they do whenever they want to look at stuff we're not allowed to see in there.'

'Really?' Harper looked back at the door, then walked to the side of it, trying to peer through one of the glass windows. There was no movement that he could see, but there was every chance they could have been in a room further into the building. 'And why are you here?'

'When they're finished, I'll be able to go back in.'

'It says on the paper that they're closed until tomorrow,' Harper looked at his watch. 'And it's coming up to five now. Surely the library wouldn't bother opening back up that late.'

'Then I'll wait until tomorrow.' The man looked up at Harper, squinting, his hand coming up to shade against the slowly setting sun behind Harper's head.

'You're the guy from the diner this morning,' he said. 'I saw you.'

Harper seemed to recall seeing the man in the diner, but he hadn't really been on full alert, having just ridden into town after riding through the night.

'Name's Tucker,' the man said, and Harper almost let out a laugh.

'I've been told not to talk to you,' he said. 'Maggie Hawkins at the guesthouse said you're a bit of a conspiracy nut.'

At this, Tucker started to chuckle, darkly.

'Yeah, Tucker's the conspiracy loon here,' he said bitterly. 'Nobody believes what Tucker says. Tucker's the crazy one. But Tucker knows what happened, Tucker sees the deaths for what they are, Tucker knows how Moses died.'

'Tucker shouldn't talk about himself in third person, perhaps,' Harper replied. 'Maybe less people would think you're crazy.'

Tucker rose now, brushing down his jeans as he stared across the porch of the library at Harper.

'You one of *them*? The swanky security bots?'

'No sir,' Harper replied, 'and you should've picked that up when I confronted them in the diner.'

'Could've been an act,' Tucker shrugged. 'You could've been playing a part, just turned up, didn't know who was on whose side.'

'So there are sides?'

'Oh hell man, you are *definitely* new to Prosperity,' Tucker laughed. 'Sure there are. You've got Bickford on one side, you've got Chen on the other.'

'Chen?'

'Rachel Chen, town's doctor. She's been against the mines being reopened and dug into since it started. Her family used to be involved in them.'

'Chen doesn't exactly sound like a long-standing local name,' Harper frowned.

'Married.' Tucker smiled. 'Damn shame, that was. She's Prosperity born and bred.'

'Yeah, well where can I find her?'

'She's around here and there.' Tucker looked down the street. 'She's always on the ball when it comes to new people in town, so chances are she'll find you before you find her.'

Harper stretched as he stood there, shifting his satchel.

'Hey, you said something about Moses,' he asked. 'Do you mean Moses Mathers? Maggie mentioned he'd gone missing, vanished ... but your comment ...'

'Moses is dead, I know it,' Tucker replied coldly.

'How?' Harper continued.

'How does Tucker know how Moses died? It's more a calculated guess,' Tucker admitted, checking the street for anyone overhearing, and Harper was convinced the man added the third person into the statement purely to annoy him. 'He died of curiosity.'

'Curiosity?'

'Yeah. He asked the wrong questions to the wrong person.'

'And who would that be?'

Tucker didn't reply for a moment, and then his face softened.

'So, what are you going to do now?' he asked, looking back at the library as if he hadn't been talking about death a moment earlier. 'Library's closed and there's no more Aegis people to punch out.'

'You heard about that?'

'Everybody heard about that,' Tucker said. 'I think they even have a poll about you on *The Prospector*'s website.'

Harper looked around the street. It was quiet for the time of afternoon; too late for the afternoon crowd, and just too early for the evening revellers.

'I think I might get some early dinner, and then I might go do some sketching,' he said.

'Sketching? Sure,' Tucker replied, and once more the paranoid conspiracy theorist seemed to come out. 'You do that, Mister Man.'

And with this cryptic statement made, Tucker turned and wandered off.

Harper watched him for a moment, shrugged, and then walked back down the street. He was feeling hungry now; the diner had been five, maybe six hours ago, and he hadn't eaten while he was riding here.

His stomach was already growling as he continued towards O'Malley's.

O'Malley's was a traditional Irish pub; and by that, Harper knew it was exactly the same as every other traditional Irish pub. In fact, Harper, before he entered, could have shut his eyes and described it in incredible detail, based on the other Irish pubs he'd been to over the years, all around the world: deep mahogany wooden benches, equally deep mahogany wooden beams, limestone walls and Irish music being played. There would be a fiddle and a bodhran on the walls, probably a few steel-printed Guinness posters. If he was lucky, there'd be half a dozen four-leaf clovers scattered around the pub.

It did not disappoint.

Entering, Harper walked up to the bar, examining the various pumps.

'What can I get you?' the woman behind the bar asked. She was young, early-to-mid-twenties, with long red hair. It wasn't the ginger hair that Carson had; this was more bottle-red. Harper hoped she hadn't had to dye her hair to look like an "Irish lass".

He nodded at one pump.

'How good's your Guinness?' he asked.

'It ain't fizzy,' the woman replied, and at a frown from Harper she shrugged. 'Some folks down the street at the Goldstrike were complaining the Guinness there was being put through the wrong pump, which started to carbonate it. Fizzy Guinness ain't great.'

She tapped at the pump.

'Though, I'll be honest, from the twang in your accent the chances are you've had better. Let's just say it's not Dublin level.'

'Nothing's Dublin level.' Harper smiled. 'I'll grab a bottle of beer.'

'Any in particular, or dealer's choice?'

'I'll go with whatever you think.'

'Probably a better option than the Guinness,' the woman said. 'I'm Cassie, by the way.'

'Harper.'

'Now that's an Irish name if ever I've heard one,' Cassie turned, looking back at him.

'Irish ancestry,' Harper grinned. 'Unfortunately, I wasn't born in the motherland.'

'None of us are,' Cassie said, passing him a bottle of light beer. Harper wondered what it said about him that he was happy with this. 'Open a tab?'

'If you don't mind. Have you got a menu?'

'Find a place to sit, I'll pass one over.'

Harper looked around. It wasn't quite evening yet, and the bar was only half-filled.

'Busy for the day,' he commented. 'I'd have expected it to be dead before seven.'

'We've got a mixture of tourists, drivers, townsfolk ...' Cassie replied.

'Aegis?'

'Why? You looking for them?'

'Actually, I was hoping this is a place they don't drink.'

'They prefer the Goldstrike,' Cassie smiled. 'However, their boss, he don't like them drinking during the day, so you won't find anybody around town until evening.'

'Good.' Harper grinned, looking around and seeing a booth to the side. 'I'm going to grab that one.'

But Cassie wasn't listening, as she'd looked at a man who'd just walked up to the bar.

'Jack Daniels, straight.'

'Please, Cass.'

The order was given as a statement rather than a question, and as Cassie went off to fulfil the drink order, the man looked back at Harper, gave him a friendly nod and continued checking his phone. Deciding Cassie would work out where he went, Harper took his beer, walked over to the booth he'd indicated and went to sit down, but then paused as he saw *The Prospector,* the local paper on the booth table next to him. There was nobody at the booth, so he reached across, picking up the paper and started to read it as he sat down, continuing from where he'd left off in the diner.

A couple of minutes later, though, he felt rather than saw somebody move up to the side. He spun quick, instinctive—

Cassie jerked back.

'I brought your menu,' she said, holding a sheet of A3 laminated card. 'I didn't mean to startle you.'

'Sorry,' Harper said. 'It's been a day.'

'I bet,' Cassie grinned. 'You're the guy, aren't you?'

'The guy?'

'The one that took out the mercs? Saved old man Hawkins?'

'Is there something about this town that anybody over the age of sixty has to start with the term "old man?"'

'It just seems to happen,' Cassie shrugged. Harper went to reply to say how patronising it probably was and then realised that his grandfather had been known for his entire life as “Old Pete” when the chances were he wasn't even in his fifties when Harper had moved to live with him.

'I'm guessing you saw it on *The Prospector*'s webpage?'

'Hell no. I work in a bar. The news comes from here *to* the paper,' Cassie laughed, but before Harper could say anything else, there was more movement to the side of her as the man with the Lennon glasses appeared.

'Mind if I sit down?' he asked, as Cassie made space for him to approach. Harper frowned, wondering what the plan was here, but then shrugged.

'Sure,' he said, 'it's a free country. It's Mister Ashfield, right?'

'My friends call me Ash,' the man with the Lennon glasses, now named Ashfield said, sitting down and looking up at Cassie.

'What can I get you?' she asked, her voice definitely cooler.

Ashfield glanced back at the bar, squinting as he looked at the bottles. Eventually, he clicked his tongue against the top of his mouth, looked back at Harper, and just pointed at the bottle in front of him.

'I'll have what he's having,' he said, 'and another, on me, for him.'

Cassie nodded and walked off, leaving the laminated menu on the table. Harper picked it up and gave it a quick perusal, but he'd already decided what he wanted. Taking his bottle, he took a mouthful, staring at the man sitting in front of him.

'So, Mister Ashfield ...' he said.

'Please, call me Ash,' Ashfield replied.

'How about I meet you midway and lose the “mister”?'

Harper replied. 'Somehow don't think I'm at the stage of calling you by a friendly name, after what you did to me.'

Ashfield gave an almost embarrassed smile.

'Sorry about that,' he said. 'It's my job to look after my men, yeah?'

'Your men.' Harper leant back on the booth's seat, observing the man in front of him. Ashfield looked bookish, like middle management, but that didn't mean he wasn't dangerous. Private security firms would often have soldiers, ex-marines and suchlike as their core market. Personal security, after all, had to be trained to a high level. But when you looked at the people who would control those security officers – or rather mercenaries – you needed somebody higher up the food chain. Often, this was somebody from the officer class, or even from other areas of the military. There was every possibility that the bookish man in the Lennon glasses sitting opposite him was somebody who had done his time with the CIA, or worse. Knowing Aegis, that was possibly true.

'I feel we got off on the wrong foot,' Ashfield continued. 'My men—'

'Blaine and Lucas,' Harper replied. 'I've already been told their names.'

'I think Blaine and Lucas were a little gung-ho, shall we say,' Ashfield continued without skipping a beat. 'That's the problem with private security. You're reliant on a dwindling pool of resources.'

'Are you saying your soldiers aren't good enough for the job you need?'

Ashfield took a moment to compose his comment. Harper appreciated it. *This was a man who wasn't going to give away much in a conversation.*

'Aegis has many arms,' he replied carefully. 'Peacekeeping is one of them, law enforcement, security obviously. Some of our better operatives are used in personal protection or corporate work. But then sometimes ... well, you just need a button to be pushed.'

Harper understood what Ashfield was saying. The Aegis men in Prosperity were likely to be button pushers, grunts, point-and-click people who were there purely for bodywork.

Meat suits. Cannon fodder.

The list of names they'd go by was long, and none of them were complimentary.

'I understand you've moved into the treasure-hunting department,' Harper took another draught of the beer.

'Who told you that?'

'The mayor.'

'Tom Bickford is desperately hoping that we'll find money,' Ashfield chuckled as he shook his head. 'It's doubtful, though. That gold's been gone for over a hundred and fifty years now. Somebody would have found it before now.'

'Then why are you bothering?'

'To look for the gold?' Ashfield shook his head. 'We're not. We've been employed to keep an eye on the people who *are* looking for the money, to make sure that if they find anything of worth, they won't be mugged or robbed by it.'

'I see,' Harper smiled, nodding at Cassie as she walked back over, placing down the two new bottles of beer before walking off. 'So what you're saying to me is you're actually protecting the mine.'

'Protect and serve,' Ashfield replied.

Harper nodded.

'And this here is what, you warning me away from the mine?'

'Not at all,' Ashfield replied. 'After seeing you in action, I'd almost want to offer you a job.'

Harper raised an eyebrow at this.

'You think I'm Aegis material?'

'Possibly.'

'Lucas ... his accent was East European,' Harper replied. 'So, I'm guessing you're not primarily American in your target pool.'

'We don't discriminate,' Ashfield smiled. 'Especially when it's somebody from the UK Special Forces.'

'You've read my jacket.'

'We didn't need to,' Ashfield settled back now, beer in his hand, sipping from it for a moment before looking back at Harper. 'Gomez. He was the—'

'Guy with the crappy moustache and chin fuzz.'

'That's the one. He recognised your tattoo. Said you're SRR; Special Reconnaissance Regiment. You give the SAS a run for their money.'

'We've got the same mother,' Harper replied. 'Grew up together. You know how it is with family.'

'Either way, you scared him enough to make him shit himself. He didn't want nothing to do with you. And Gomez ... well, I pay attention to what Gomez says. He's a clever man, even if he chooses friends poorly.'

'And Blaine?'

'Well, he's slower. But then what you did with him outside the library ... impressive.'

Ashfield shifted on the chair, leaning closer.

'There's an opportunity here, Mister Harper. Do you mind if I call you Liam?'

'I'd rather you didn't,' Harper replied. 'Nothing personal, it's just sitting in an Irish bar being called Liam? Someone's gonna want me to sing "Oh, Bring Me Home Kathleen" or something.'

He also leant forward now, matching Ashfield, elbows on the table.

'The problem you've got is I already have a job.'

'Really?' Ashfield's eyes sparkled with interest. 'Because from what we've been told, you were fired six months ago.'

'You should get your intelligence people to check better,' Harper said coldly. 'I left.'

'My mistake,' Ashfield held up a hand, apologetically. 'The story we'd been told was there'd been a bungled op. Shortly afterwards, you left. I assumed ...'

'To assume makes an ass out of you and me,' Harper replied, taking a moment to sip at his beer to bring his anger back down. 'Don't for one second think that you know me, or that we're brothers in arms.'

He raised his bottle, tapping the second on the table with the base.

'I appreciate the drink, but right now I'm not really looking for a new career change.'

'Then what are you looking for, Harper?' Ashfield pulled out his phone, looking down at it. 'Wikipedia claims your regiment performs clandestine intelligence, surveillance, target acquisition, and reconnaissance missions, with a focus on counter-terrorism and counterinsurgency. Are you looking at us as counterinsurgents?'

'Should I be?'

'We're just security guards, nothing more.'

'Who beat on old men.'

'That was unfortunate. I didn't realise your earlier confrontation with Blaine had forced him to want to prove himself. It was—'

'Wait,' Harper furrowed his brow at this. 'Are you saying that the reason they wanted to beat up an old man was because *I stepped them down earlier?* Come on, Ashfield. I'm not some rube.'

'No, *Captain* Harper, I can see that.'

Harper once more toasted with a raise of the bottle, noting Ashfield's use of the rank he'd been when he left.

That wasn't something to be found easily.

He then smiled, sipping the beer, letting the moment drag out.

'Look, I'm just fulfilling my dead dad's wishes,' he said. 'And when I'm done, I'll find somewhere nice to spend the rest of my days. Are we done?'

Ashfield took off his Lennon glasses, pulling out a cloth and cleaning them. Harper couldn't work out if he was delaying the moment or if he genuinely wanted to see Harper clearly as he continued.

'I'm here to invite you to the mine,' he said, placing his glasses back on. 'Tomorrow at ten hundred hours. You can have a tour, see what we do, and both Blaine and Lucas will be there to apologise for what they did.'

'Thank you,' Harper replied. 'That's very gracious of you. I'll be there.'

'I'm sure you will. We'll even provide you a car to pick you up,' Ashfield finished his beer and went to rise, pulling out his wallet to pay the bill for the two bottles. As he did so, Harper leant back, watching him.

'How did you know I was here?' he asked.

'Purely by chance,' Ashfield replied. 'I was coming in for some food, saw you were here, thought I'd speak to you, but I don't want to bother you any further, so I'll take my leave.'

'Drink here a lot, do you?'

'It's one of the nicer watering holes.'

Harper shook his head at the comment, and saw Ashfield pale, as if realising he'd said too much ... or even not enough.

'You see, that's where I get twitchy,' he explained. 'You know, when people lie to me. I already know that Mason won't let people come here during the day. He doesn't like his men drinking until the night. Which means that either A, you're someone very special to him, or B, you're lying. You also claim you came here for something to eat, but you've not once looked at the menu on the table.'

'Maybe I know what I want?'

'No,' Harper shook his head. 'Because when Cassie asked what you wanted to drink, you didn't know. You looked at the bar as if you were trying to work out what to have, and someone who comes here a lot would probably have a usual drink they'd order. And more importantly, Cassie, who – from what I can work out has a knowledge of who the locals are – when she knows someone, she'll state that drink immediately. No question, a pure statement of intent. If she doesn't, she asks, "What would you like?" Like she did to me, and more recently, to you.'

Harper's voice lowered now, cold and threatening.

'You can tell me whatever you want as an explanation, Mister Ashfield, but that woman did *not* know who you were; only that you worked for Aegis. So the next time you want to follow me into a bar to try to hire me, tell me the goddamn truth.'

Ashfield paused for a moment, gave a wide smile, then, tossing down a twenty-dollar bill, walked off.

Harper watched him leave before relaxing back, staring at the menu, though his appetite had gone now. He scanned the bar, his gaze eventually settling on Cassie, who had been watching him, concerned from the bar. He made a sign for the check, and, rising pulled a ten-dollar bill out of his own pocket, adding it to the twenty.

With his satchel over his shoulder, Harper left O'Malley's.

7

HOUSE HUNT

ALTHOUGH HARPER MIGHT HAVE LOST HIS APPETITE IN THE BAR, it didn't mean he wasn't needing to eat anytime soon. An army marched on its stomach, and all he'd had that day were eggs, bread and bacon for brunch.

He decided he'd return to the guesthouse, and perhaps take up Maggie Hawkins on her offer of dinner, but it was still light as he left O'Malley's. Estimating there was still an hour or so of visibility left, Harper wondered if he still had time to have a further look around.

The main street of Prosperity led out towards the mountains – and apparently the mines themselves – but as Maggie had pointed out to him when he checked in, before the mountains the streets widened into a more suburban area, with larger houses dominating the landscape. It was here where the Bickford house Maggie had mentioned was situated, and Harper found himself walking up the trail towards it, noting the high fence and metal gate, the barred entrance. When he was almost outside, he paused on the road as he looked through the gate at the building on the other side.

The mansion stood in the middle of the Nevada grasslands, white brick and old, with wide columns running along the front porch. It was the kind of house built to impress, even if it had little to back it up anymore. As it had looked the last time he was there, the roof still loped gently, and the shutters were still warped, the paint peeling, but they still hung in place.

Stubborn.

Harper stood at the gate, a heavy iron thing locked with a new video-call doorbell to the side that didn't match the rust eating into the bars. The driveway stretched from the gate up to the house, and might have been grand a hundred years ago, maybe owned by a cattle baron or a silver tycoon.

Now, it was just tired.

The windows were tall and arched, their glass catching the setting sunlight in a way that made it hard to see inside.

Harper almost wanted to pull out his sketchbook and start sketching, but even he wasn't that stupid. He did notice, however, as he paused to stare through the gate, that a black SUV had started from the house towards him. Harper didn't want to cause any more problems so he carried on walking; it was only a half-mile walk back to the town, and it was probably safer to stay there for the moment, although the term "safe" and Harper never really went too well together.

As he continued away from the house, however, he heard the sound of the electronic gate opening and closing, and after a further moment the SUV exiting through the gate pulled up beside him. The back window dropped slowly, and Harper turned to see Mayor Bickford smiling at him.

'You look lost, Mister Harper,' he said. 'Would you care for a lift back into town?'

Harper went to refuse – an automatic response – but then, looking back up the road, he gave Bickford a smile.

'Don't mind if I do,' he muttered.

'Then book a goddamn taxi,' Bickford snapped, waving for his driver to continue and, as the SUV drove off, Harper could hear their laughter.

He couldn't help it. He started to chuckle to himself.

Bickford might have been a grade-A prick, but at least he wasn't hiding it.

He continued towards the town, enjoying the evening air. The sun was almost gone, the evening now arrived, leaving shadows across the mountain's red brick, looking like blood splashed upon the face of the mountains – which, in a way, Harper assumed, it had been. He considered cutting through them, maybe taking a diversion to see what came out of the stroll, but his stomach had rumbled again. He knew he'd be back there the following day, so he now considered the imaginary dinner Maggie Hawkins was cooking up for her other guests, hoping she had enough for an extra portion.

He had barely walked another two hundred yards before another vehicle drove up. It was a familiar-looking Ford SSV, and Harper groaned internally, wondering if once again he was about to be arrested, or rather "detained" as Prosperity didn't seem to arrest people here. The Ford pulled up next to him, and Deputy Cortez leant out of the window, elbow resting on the sill, smiling at him.

'I understand you were looking for a lift,' she said.

Harper paused, looking back up the long road ahead, before shaking his head.

'Did Bickford send you?' he asked.

'We got a call,' she replied. 'Apparently you'd asked for a lift, and he felt uncomfortable having you in the car.'

The hand, resting on the edge of the window, raised to pause Harper from replying. It was a lazy movement, relaxed for that time of day.

Or perhaps Cortez was finally warming to him.

'Don't worry,' she said. 'I can tell that was "Bickford speak" for he was a prick to you, left you standing and then probably felt bad about it.'

Harper shrugged.

'He is what he is,' he replied. 'I can't really complain. I was having a look at his house.'

'You've been up to the mansion?' Cortez smiled. 'It's a hell of a place, isn't it?'

'I've always been more of a country cottage kind of man,' Harper replied. 'Never really saw the need to have such ostentatious buildings.'

'Well, I know *I'd* like something a bit bigger,' Cortez said, nodding to the other side of the jeep. 'Come on, Cortez cabs is here.'

'You know, when I heard you were good at escort duties, I didn't think this was literally what you did,' Harper replied as he climbed into the SSV. It was an offhand comment, but Cortez's eyes turned steel as she spoke.

'Maggie Hawkins say that?' she asked.

'Problem?'

Cortez brought her demeanour back under control, but Harper hadn't missed the eyes flashing.

'Her and my dad, they had a thing going,' she said. 'Didn't help that she went off to join the army, came back a goddamn war hero. My dad stayed here.'

She looked aside, starting the car and driving off.

'And all he got was a bullet in the back.'

'So, what, did Maggie and your dad see each other?'

'Childhood sweethearts,' Cortez shrugged. 'Fell apart when they were in high school, though.'

She gave a mock shiver.

'Imagine how bad it would have been if they'd have stayed together. Maggie Hawkins would have been my goddamn mother.'

'She seems a good woman,' Harper replied carefully. 'Unless you know something else.'

'No, she's good,' Cortez replied cagily. 'She'll look after you. She's also a volunteer fire chief, so she'll put out your pretty bike when someone throws a Molotov at it, and the Marines made her a trained combat medic, which will probably help when you start having the utter crap kicked out of you for a second time.'

'I don't recall having the crap kicked out of me the first time,' Harper raised an eyebrow. 'Are you warning me off, deputy?'

'You've been in town less than, what, eight hours?' Cortez replied as the Ford turned onto Main Street. 'In that time, you've seen what Aegis has to offer. You've met our mayor. And you've spent almost half that time in a police cell. What do you think?'

'I think it's nothing I've not seen before,' Harper replied, looking out of the window at the shop fronts as they went past. 'I'd also say it doesn't matter what I think. Until I've done what I need to do, I'll be staying around, jail cells or not.'

'And what is it exactly that you're here to do?' Cortez asked. 'You mentioned your father came through here, but you've not exactly done anything to explain why you need to be here. All you've done is cause disruption.'

'Is that what you think?' Harper gave a smile. 'There I was thinking what I'd done is save an old guy from a beating.'

'That's what the police are for, Mister Harper,' Cortez replied, and Harper felt there was a hint of professional insult in the words.

'Don't take it the wrong way,' he explained, looking back at her. 'I'd have you back me in a fight at any time; you seem to know what you're doing. But your red-headed buddy? I get the impression he's a little less cautious about the law, and more about who he wants to piss off or not.'

'You think he's in Bickford's pocket?'

Harper cocked his head.

'You tell me,' he said. 'There's definitely something going on between them. Bickford walking into the sheriff's office like he's the chief, and Carson, bending down to his whim. Do you guys even have a sheriff?'

'Sheriff Coble, but he's out of town,' Cortez said, and as she did so, she indicated right, pulling into one of the bays outside the Goldstrike Inn & Suites; not because she thought he was staying there, but more because it was one of the few spaces on the street to do so. 'Look, Mister Harper—'

'Please, just Harper.'

'Look, Harper.' Cortez warmed a little. 'I don't know what your game is, and I still don't trust that you're not gonna come out of this without burning our town to the ground. But Bickford's not a man to screw around with, and neither are his men, although I get the impression that you're already aware of that.'

Harper paused, not saying anything. He assumed she meant Aegis when she said "his men", and it made him wonder whether it was Bickford, or Carrick who controlled the mercenaries.

Cortez slapped him on the arm.

'Come on, man,' she urged. 'I don't know what your

problem is here, but it's pretty obvious that you know who Aegis are.'

Harper leant back in the passenger seat, staring at the roof of the car. After a moment, he nodded.

'I know them,' he replied. 'Not in the biblical sense. More, I've found myself facing them here and there. Border skirmishes. Pirate vessels.'

Cortez watched Harper as he spoke.

'What kind of soldier were you?' she asked.

'The kind that got sent in when nobody else could do things,' Harper muttered. 'People who had a skill set that was required to get the job done, no matter what.'

'I thought that was Liam Neeson, or the SAS,' Cortez grinned.

'SAS? SBS, SRR, they're all part of the UK Special Forces,' Harper replied. 'Each one has their own area of expertise. Mine, well, we were the guys who went in and came out quickly, without anyone the wiser. When you wanted a door smashed in, you went for one of the others.'

'So, how well did you know Aegis?'

Harper didn't reply, still staring up at the roof, lost in thought.

'There's a lot of them around, you know,' he said eventually. 'Private security firms, or mercenary units, whatever you want to call them. When you work in the military, it becomes a way of life, you know. One day you're a soldier, a pilot, a sailor, whatever it is, and then the next day you're doing something mundane, ordinary—'

'Like running a guesthouse,' Cortez chuckled.

'If that was Maggie's choice, then that's what she wanted,' Harper nodded. 'I mean, don't get me wrong. While you're sitting there waiting to deploy or when you're in a plane, flying across to God knows where, armed to the teeth and with more kilograms of unnecessary kit on you than you care to mention, you dream of having a normal life. You dream of opening guesthouses and bakeries and things like that. Having a marriage where your partner doesn't need to worry if you're coming home that night. Although I'm guessing as a cop, you can relate to that one.'

Cortez gave a shrug.

'But once you actually get out and you find yourself out of the action, there's a withdrawal phase,' Harper continued. 'To many of us, it's easy enough to get through. If your job has been during peacetime, then it's an easier transition than for someone who has been constantly at war.'

'And were you constantly at war, Harper?'

Harper said nothing, turning back and fixing Cortez with a steely gaze.

'There's always a war somewhere,' he said. 'But I'm not talking about me here. I'm talking about others. People who, when they leave the military, whether by their own decision or not, still want to carry on, or who have unfinished business. And they're annoyed, angry even, that they're not getting a chance to do it anymore. These are the people who you need to worry about.'

He was staring out of the window again, and Cortez realised that he was looking into the Goldstrike Inn & Suites, staring intently, almost as if trying to see through the walls and guess who was inside.

'There are a lot of good people who work in private security,' he continued, 'and I've worked with a tonne of mercenaries who are the top of what they do. But if you've got a bad recruiter, then you've got a bad unit, and Aegis ...'

'On a scale of one to ten?'

'On a scale of one to ten, they're middle ground. And that's only because they've got some units that are good at what they do, and some that are terrible. They average out. You get what I'm saying?'

'Yeah, you don't rate the guys that are guarding the mine.'

'Why exactly *are* they guarding the mine, Cortez? Impression I got was the mine was a no go area for mining, but that changed somehow after the celebrations?'

'Look,' Cortez shuffled around. 'Speak to Eddie Hawkins. He knows the history. Then speak to Rachel Chen, and she'll tell you the science.'

'The science?' Harper frowned. 'What kind of science would I need to be knowing about?'

'Those mines, they're dangerous,' Cortez explained, 'and not just because of the guys guarding the doors. There's pockets of gas, have been for decades. When you dig too deep, you pop them out. It can be fatal and it's why they were closed in the first place.'

'What kind of gas?'

Cortez shrugged.

'I never bothered asking,' she replied. 'I've never cared for the mines and I never will. But people have died up there.'

'Moses Mathers?'

'Possibly,' Cortez nodded. 'He disappeared after likely going in, so there's every chance he struck the wrong rock, found himself overpowered somewhere deep inside that mine ... he could be laying there, long gone.'

Harper stared at Cortez.

'Do you really believe that?' he asked.

'Why wouldn't I?'

'Because from what I heard, Moses Mathers' equipment was found outside,' Harper continued. 'Which begs the question, how the hell did he manage to dig a hole or break open a rock if he *didn't have a shovel or a pickaxe?*'

He took one last glance at the Goldstrike Inn & Suites, opened the passenger door and climbed out.

'I'll make my way from here,' he said. 'I wouldn't want to force you to be my chauffeur any further.'

'Pleasure's all mine,' Cortez replied, and her tone was just as sarcastic as it had meant to be.

Harper tipped his cap, closed the door, and carried on up Main Street, away from the Goldstrike, from Cortez, and from the black SUV that he had noticed following them since they'd left the mansion.

Whether Cortez had noticed it or not, he didn't know, but one thing was for sure. Aegis was keeping close tabs on Liam Harper.

8

MACGYVERING

It took another fifteen minutes to walk to Maggie Hawkin's guest house. As he walked, he found himself following a young couple – a man and a woman – whom he assumed were the guests staying two doors down, who Maggie had named as "The Parsons". They were chatting to each other, scrolling through photos on a phone as they carried on down the street, Harper keeping a sensible distance behind them. If they were his neighbours, the last thing he wanted to do was spook them, although they'd jumped when they first saw him behind them.

As they continued, Harper overheard a couple of snippets of their conversation. They'd been hiking through the mountains, looking for old gold panning streams, but rather than panning themselves, it seemed mainly for Instagram pictures. Harper assumed they'd been far enough from the mines to not be hassled by Aegis – *they* would have provided some far more interesting social media posts.

Arriving at the guest house, the two carried on upstairs to

their room, while Harper headed through the back into the kitchen.

Maggie Hawkins looked up.

'Guessing you want dinner after all,' she said.

'It would be appreciated if you had a little extra.'

'Put some on the stove just for you,' Maggie grinned. 'I heard O'Malley's wasn't to your taste.'

'Christ,' Harper started to chuckle. 'Is *everyone* glued to the bloody *Prospector* web page?'

'Nah, I just have my sources,' Maggie shrugged. 'It's always good to know when new people are in town and need a guest house, for example. I just keep those people on retainer for anything else. You know, like strangers causing fights. And being arrested – right after I pointed out it was something I didn't appreciate.'

Harper didn't wince or even look apologetic, simply standing there, waiting for her to finish.

'I started no fight,' he muttered, once she had. 'I finished one fight, sure. And I got stuck in a cell for three hours for doing it.'

'Don't worry,' Maggie laughed. 'I'm aware. Cortez brought my father home shortly afterwards. I think you're his new favourite person.'

'As long as he's safe, that's all that matters,' Harper replied.

'See anything else exciting today? You know, after they let you out?'

'Met the mayor, he's a prick.'

At the comment, Maggie snorted loudly.

'Maybe keep your impressions a little more personal, soldier,' she said. 'I might agree with you. But there's others who ... well, they voted for him, after all.'

Harper grinned back in response.

'I've got a meeting with Aegis tomorrow,' he said, 'up in the mines. Apparently, the two men who attacked your father are going to personally apologise to me for what they did.'

'Either that or they'll dump you somewhere deep inside and no one will see you again,' Maggie waggled her wooden spoon at him. Harper shrugged, picking up a carrot from the table and munching on it absently.

'Well, class this as me telling you that if I don't turn up again tomorrow, you know who's got me,' he said, looking back at the food. 'Chilli?'

'US Marines recipe.'

'There's a lot there.'

'Big table,' Maggie looked back at him. 'Me, you, the Parsons – that's the couple who are staying – my father and Rachel Chen.'

At the name *Rachel Chen*, Harper's ears pricked up. Maggie noticed his change in expression.

'You've heard of her already? Don't worry, she ain't here to see you,' Maggie chuckled as she carried on stirring. 'Her and my dad have been working together on the mines for years. it's a hobby of hers.'

She looked back at Harper, noticing that he hadn't moved, his carrot caught mid-journey to his mouth.

'Are you having a stroke or something?' she asked.

'Cortez said if I wanted to learn the history of the mines, I should speak to your father, but if I wanted the science, I should speak to Chen,' he replied.

'*Doctor* Chen,' Maggie corrected. 'She's been the town locum for the last few years. But yeah, she'll tell you all you want to know about the science of the mines, although expect most of it to be, "don't go in there, you'll die".'

'I heard. Something about gas?'

'Sure, why not?' Maggie was obviously tiring of the conversation, and Harper realised it was probably one she had had many times in the past, and was distracted by the bubbling-over pot. Taking it as a cue to leave, Harper tipped the remains of the carrot to his hat and turned to go.

'Dinner's in an hour,' Maggie said. 'Make yourself presentable.'

Harper looked down at his jeans, sweater, and jacket.

'Am I not presentable now?'

'You stink of a jail cell, Harper,' Maggie replied calmly. 'Go take a shower. You have about half an hour before the hot water stops.'

THE MOMENT HARPER ARRIVED AT HIS BEDROOM'S DOOR, HE knew something was wrong.

Someone had been inside.

If you looked at the door to the room, you'd have noticed nothing different. The door was still shut and locked, the key in Harper's pocket. There was likely a master key downstairs, but he didn't see Maggie Hawkins as the kind of person who would rummage through someone's underwear.

But the door had been opened.

An inch from the bottom of the doorframe – where the door opened inwards – before leaving, Harper had placed a tiny Steri-Strip from his first aid kit; a thin adhesive bandage used often by medics as a backup to dissolvable stitches, or to keep a wound secure after regular stitches had been removed. Quicker and easier than stitches, Steri-Strips were a mainstay in the SRR kit. Only an inch and a half in length and an eighth of an inch in width, this small piece of tape had been placed against the door frame and door itself, bridging the two, the tape matching the white paint and effectively becoming invisible. The only way that it wouldn't be attached to either part would be if the door had been opened, the inwards motion pulling off the tape from one side.

Looking down at the door now, Harper could see the tape was indeed removed on the right-hand side. In fact, it looked as if when somebody had entered, opening the door, the tape had pulled off the door frame – and when the door was closed and relocked, it'd been pressed against the edge of the door in an L shape, something that couldn't have happened if the door had stayed closed.

Harper slowly pulled out the key to the room, and with his other hand removed the Swiss army knife from his back pocket, unlocking the larger of the two blades. It wasn't big, and it wasn't vicious looking, but if someone was waiting in his room—

No, he shook his head. *No one would be in there. They'd come to look, not attack.*

Slowly, Harper unlocked the door and pushed it inwards. To his complete lack of surprise, there was nobody inside his room, and it looked exactly like it had before he'd left. Carefully, he walked into the room, scanning the walls as he did so. He'd emptied his panniers when he checked in, and the contents of his rucksack had been dumped onto the bed. The small amount of clothing and necessities he had, he'd placed into the drawers – ones he now proceeded to pull out, checking them, looking to see if anything had been moved.

There was a small safe in the cupboard, one of those basic hotel ones you'd type a four-digit code into and it would open or shut, depending on what you wanted. But even looking at it now, he could see that there was every chance someone could have opened that without a problem. It was cheap and cheerful and therefore a reason to give the impression of security rather than actual security itself – the very reason Harper had only placed in some money and his passport.

On searching the room, however, Harper knew someone had done the same movements he was doing now. Some of his shirts had been slightly moved, no longer crisp against each other in a straight line, something that Harper had started doing while in the military. His bag had been opened as well and checked through, and his helmet was at a slightly different angle on the side table than it had been when he had arrived in the room. They were small inconsequential things, but they were details that Harper *knew*. When you lived as part of a military unit where every small detail could cost a life, you learned to focus on the small things.

Someone had been in, had checked through his items and left, but they were good.

Too good.

He stopped in the middle of the room, hands on his hips, scanning for what they'd left behind. *Something felt wrong. Too clean. Too deliberate.*

And then it hit him.

Moving quickly to his bag, he pulled out a few items: a pocket analogue multimeter, mainly carried to check his Triumph Bonneville's battery, the coil of wire for his phone charger, and a flashlight powered by a 9V battery. He stripped the ends of the charging cable wire with his pocket knife, and twisted one end into a crude coil. Then he attached the other stripped end of the wire to the multimeter's positive terminal, with the coiled one going to the negative. Finally, he connected the 9V battery from the flashlight to the multimeter's power terminals, completing the circuit.

The device wasn't pretty, but it didn't need to be. It'd pick up any stray electromagnetic fields – exactly what a transmitter would emit.

Harper adjusted the multimeter's dial to measure small voltage changes, and held it steady. The needle twitched as he passed it through the room, staying steady near the bed and dresser. But as he swept it near the lamp by the mirror, the needle jumped sharply into the red.

He stopped, watching the needle slam forward again as he repeated the motion. Each pass confirmed it – the spike wasn't random. Harper set the makeshift scanner down and approached the lamp slowly, careful not to disturb anything.

No need to alert whoever might still be listening.

Beneath the shade, partially hidden along the frame, was a small microphone.

Harper leaned in, studying the device. It was about the size of a coin, and a thin transmitter wire ran down the length of the lamp, blending seamlessly into its base.

His jaw tightened as he studied the bug. Whoever planted it wasn't just good –they were thorough. But now, they'd made one mistake; they hadn't expected Harper to find it.

With the bug discovered, Harper stood back. The rest of the room was clean, which meant there weren't any cameras that he could find. All they had was audio.

It was probably all they expected to need.

But, if they wanted to know what he was up to, well, then he'd give them a show.

Stepping close enough so that his voice could be heard clearly, he began to speak.

'It's me,' he said, as if talking on a phone. 'I can't talk for long. I'm having a shower and then dinner.'

He paused, as if listening for orders, or to a conversation on the other end.

'I've made contact,' he continued. 'You were right. It's definitely the mayor.'

He waited a couple more seconds, smiling as he did so.

'I'm seeing Mason Carrick tomorrow,' he continued. 'We'll see then if he understands why I'm here. Although I understand he's been informing on his men to us for years.'

Harper stifled a snort as he gave a moment's pause.

'No, they haven't found the gold yet,' he replied to his imaginary voice in his head. 'But they're getting close. From what I hear, they might find it within the next week or two.'

Another pause, then, 'Exactly, sir. I couldn't have said it better myself. I'll keep you updated.'

He couldn't help himself.

'Hail Unity,' he barked as he ended his imaginary phone call.

He didn't know if there was even an organisation called Unity; it just seemed a fun thing to say, something that would get them searching for the rest of the night, most likely – right after arguing whether the guy who ran everything was a snitch.

This done, he walked away and prepared for a shower. If someone *was* listening, then it was probably Aegis. Few people in Prosperity likely had the infrastructure to use listening bugs. And if Aegis had bugged him, and if Aegis *were* listening, well then tomorrow morning's meeting would be very interesting. He'd let them sweat, and then point out that he'd found the bug, but by then it wouldn't matter.

By then, Mason Carrick would probably know who Liam

Harper was, and everything would be out in the open, anyway.

As he waited for the shower to heat up, he smiled, shaking his head as he did so. He'd been in Prosperity less than twelve hours and already he'd caused a shit ton of disruption.

What would things be like by this time tomorrow?

9

DINNER PARTY

MAGGIE'S US MARINE CHILLI WAS SURPRISINGLY GOOD, AND the company around the table provided an interesting dinner party of sorts. Maggie sat at the head of the table with her father, Eddie, to her left, and following the table clockwise were Alan and Diane Parsons, the two hikers who were staying at the hotel as well, while opposite them was Harper, and then to Maggie's right, Doctor Rachel Chen.

Doctor Chen was a slim, pale, blonde woman, with long hair pulled back into a ponytail, she had an angular, almost skeletal face. In fact, she seemed overly thin for her height, which was almost six feet. This had been explained away quickly early in the dinner, however, when a passing comment had revealed that she was an ultra-runner in her spare time, and would run daily through the mountains around Prosperity. The fact she seemed to enjoy the chilli made Harper also wonder whether she was working with a strict calorie intake, because if so, she'd shot past it today.

For the first half an hour, while the food was being served, there had been barely any conversation, just small talk here and there. The Parsons discussed their hike, Doctor Chen suggested some new routes for them based on her own running trails, Maggie explained she'd never even *attempt* to run after the injury to her leg, and throughout this Harper smiled and nodded, allowing the conversation to pass him. He hadn't mentioned the listening device in his room and had spent most of the meal working out who could have done this.

The obvious suspect was Maggie, even though he'd already dismissed her from the list of suspects. She was, after all, the one who had his room key. But Harper knew also that the key itself was large and clunky, the house old and Victorian, and it wouldn't take much to both unpick and re-lock a door if you had the skill, which anybody with the military training to take apart a room without looking like they'd been there, and to attach a listening device without detection, would have had.

Eddie had also talked about the day, gushing praise onto Harper. And if Harper hadn't been there himself, he would have thought that the conflicts he'd had, both in the diner and outside the library, had been fierce, action-packed moments where he'd ridden in like a white-hatted hero cowboy in a fifties western, the ones Old Pete used to watch and enjoy. He politely nodded, corrected Eddie when the elderly man expanded a little too much, but enjoying the home-made food, he generally kept himself to himself.

Alan and Diane Parsons had that West Coast look of people who seemed younger than they really were. Alan's hair was short, dyed black and spiked out in a trendy style. Diane's was also neat and tidy, a bob of auburn hair contrasting against Alan's darker cut. The hiking had obviously been good for them, though, and they both looked fit, tanned and healthy, even.

Alan, at one point during the meal, nodded out past the bay windows of the guest house, out onto the unseen driveway.

'Saw your bike,' he said. 'Triumph? Nice ride.'

'Are you a biker?' Harper asked. At the question, however, Alan laughed.

'Christ, no,' he said. 'Diane would kill me if I got on a bike. Too dangerous.'

'And hiking around the mountains isn't?' Doctor Chen asked before holding out a hand to stop herself. 'Sorry. Force of habit. You know, being a doctor and all that.'

Harper laughed.

'It's a safe bike,' he said. 'If you ever want to try it, feel free to.'

Alan glanced at Diane, and the two of them laughed.

'Maybe next time,' he said, before turning to his chilli, taking a large mouthful. 'This is amazing, Maggie, you have to give us the recipe. It tastes so familiar.'

'I learned it in the Marines,' Maggie said with a smile. 'There were times on base you had to feed a lot of people with a little amount of food, and chilli was always a popular serving.'

Alan nodded, but his face paled slightly as he ate, almost as if he had said something he shouldn't. Harper also noticed the glance Diane had given him the moment he had spoken.

It was one of *annoyance.*

'So, what's the deal with Cortez?' he asked, deciding to change the subject.

'What do you mean?' Maggie frowned.

'She seems like she's a solid officer,' Harper started. 'But I get the feeling she's in the wrong police department. I look at Carson and he feels right for what Prosperity wants. Cortez is a little ...'

'Too clean?' Maggie suggested.

'I didn't want to insinuate that Carson was dirty—'

'It's okay,' Eddie smiled. 'We'll do it for you. Do you know her story?'

'That her dad was sheriff, and he was killed?' Harper nodded. 'She turned down University to take on the task of being the last Cortez on the force or something.'

'She joined so she could solve his murder,' Doctor Chen replied. 'She had high beliefs. She had spent her life in the department as a kid. Sitting on desks as cases were worked through gave her the belief that she was cleverer than she was. Genuinely thought she was sheriff level the day she walked into the room.'

'Not that she wasn't, I'm sure she'd do a good job,' Maggie added, and Harper remembered the comment about Maggie and Cortez's father once dating. 'She was just too green.'

'Did she catch the man who killed her dad?'

'No.' It was Maggie who spoke now. 'They'd found the guy, a meth dealer named Clinton Hackett. He'd been a suspect in a case that Robbie – I mean her father – had been working on, connected to a biker gang he'd just run out of town. They'd had confrontations, and he fitted the bill. Shortly after Sheriff Cortez died, Clinton was ... well ... I think he realised his time was up.'

'How would you mean?'

Eddie shifted uneasily on his chair, and Harper gained the impression that this was gossip they didn't want to talk about.

'Let's just say Clinton was on a ticking clock,' he

explained. 'He'd pissed off a dozen different people all the way over to the Dixie Mafia in Mississippi, which is impressive. He'd had a few problems, his major supplier had been run out of town, add to that a massive drug addiction ... he knew his ticket was going to get punched. Either by a judge, or in a more permanent fashion.'

'He decided to take things into his own hands, and we found him dead from an overdose,' Doctor Chen added. 'It seems he decided that no one else could have his supply, and took it all in one big go. There's almost an element of injustice in the fact that he went out with such a high. The man should have suffered for what he did.'

'And he was who people believed killed Sheriff Cortez?'

'He was, after he died,' Maggie replied. 'They found paperwork in the house when they searched it. He'd been tracking Sheriff Cortez, working out his movements. It was believed he'd found a time when he was on his own and taken him out.'

'The police also found a gun,' Doctor Chen added. 'A Smith & Wesson Model 29, famous as the "Dirty Harry" gun. Cortez was killed by a .44 magnum bullet, and this gun ...'

'Fires them,' Harper understood now.

'By the time Cortez joined up to solve her father's murder, it was solved,' Maggie shrugged. 'So, she took out her anger on other people instead. Still, at least the chip on her shoulder meant she wasn't easily bought.'

'Like Carson,' Eddie added. 'So I understand you're getting an apology tomorrow. Impressive.'

'We'll see,' Harper shrugged, thrown slightly by the change of subject. 'They reckon they're going to apologise, but I think to be perfectly honest, it's more a case of them wanting to check me out.'

'And they probably want to dump him down in the mines,' Maggie suggested to her father with a wink. It was a joke, but Harper caught Chen's stricken expression.

'You don't want to get caught deep in those mines,' she said.

'Oh, I'm sure I'd find my way out if something bad happened,' Harper shrugged it off, not wanting to make a fuss here. He'd noticed that as they started talking about the mine, both Alan and Diane had leant slightly forward to catch it all.

'That's not what I meant,' Doctor Chen replied. 'If you go too deep, you get poisoned.'

Harper nodded, placing his fork down.

'Cortez pretty much said the same. Said there's gases down there, but didn't say what they were.'

'Hydrogen sulphide. H_2S,' Chen confirmed. 'What else did she tell you about the mines?'

'Not much,' Harper admitted. 'But between her and Maggie here, I've picked up a bit. Gold mining was big until eighteen seventy-five when the shipment disappeared. I got the impression people didn't find much more, and the mining faded away.'

'More that the whole mountain range is filled with crap,' Eddie muttered. 'For most of the tourists, when they turn up here, there's a couple of local "experience" companies that'll take you up into the hills by ATV—all terrain vehicle, that is, take you to a few creeks and let you spend an hour or two panning for gold.'

'Doesn't sound so bad,' Harper remarked.

'It is when you realise that all you're getting is fool's gold,' Maggie smiled.

'Fool's gold is common around here. Wherever there's gold, there's always fool's gold,' Eddie replied, 'and that's the problem. Where you find large pockets of it, well then you also find HS2. The deeper you go, the more dangerous the pockets become.'

'What exactly does HS2 do?' It was Alan who asked, curious.

Now Doctor Chen took over.

'In gold mining, it's particularly dangerous, because it forms when iron pyrite – fool's gold – gets exposed to water and air. The chemical reaction of this releases this gas.'

'But fool's gold is usually found outside, though?'

'Sure, it can be, and that stuff's fine, because the hydrogen sulphide disperses quickly. But our mountains are full of pyrite deposits, interleaved with the gold seams.'

'So, if you're deep in the mines, it's more common?' Harper asked, munching on some tortillas.

'Hydrogen sulphide's heavier than air, so it sinks and collects in low spots, old tunnels, anywhere that dips,' Doctor Chen confirmed. 'At low concentrations, you get that "rotten egg" smell. But at higher concentrations – and this is the truly terrifying part – it paralyses your sense of smell. You can walk right into a lethal pocket and never know it.'

She paused for a moment, allowing the statement to sink in.

'At high concentrations, just one or two breaths ... you get an immediate loss of consciousness. Your respiratory system just stops. The particularly cruel thing is that if someone goes down, the rescuer trying to help them often dies too. We call them "double fatalities" in mining documentation.'

She placed her fork down, now on a roll.

'The victims ... their faces often show extreme terror,' she continued. 'Not because they're scared, but because the gas causes muscle contractions. And since it's heavier than air, trying to crawl to safety can actually make things worse, as you're crawling right into the highest concentration.'

'Surely this is all guesswork?' Alan looked concerned now. 'I mean, it can't be that common?'

'This isn't theoretical,' Eddie interjected now. 'The Comstock Lode mines in Virginia City had several H_2S incidents. Sure, back in the 1860s they called it "bad air" or "foul air", but they were hunting sulphide ores, including silver sulphide. When they hit water pockets in pyrite-rich areas, they sometimes had to evacuate entire sections. Up in the mines, they called it "the devil's breath" as miners would just ... drop. No warning, no chance to escape. When William Bickford – or Hawkins, if you believe the "official" records – opened up the mine for anyone willing to pay to play, we had our own "bad air" deaths, matching Comstock in all but name.'

'The really dangerous part?' Doctor Chen took over, happily eating while she spoke. 'Once you expose a pyrite seam to air and water, it can keep producing hydrogen sulphide for years. That's why some of these old tunnels, even after a century, are still death traps – because of the damned condensation down there.'

'Wow,' Alan shook his head, paling a little. 'Glad we're staying on the surface.'

'This is great conversation while eating, guys,' Maggie muttered, staring at her food, but nobody seemed to listen.

'It's one reason why the mine was closed down in the end,' Eddie explained, once more the historian. 'There'd been a few deaths, but no one understood why back then. During the nineteenth century, miners had limited knowledge of toxic gases like HS_2, and ventilation systems were rudimentary. Miners relied on canaries or personal experience as warning systems.'

He wiped his mouth with a napkin and sat back to continue.

'When the gold was stolen, the mines were closed while federal authorities started looking for it down there. A couple of their guys died while hunting too deep, and it was decided to close the mines permanently for public safety.'

'So, the legend about the mines being closed because of the missing gold is a lie?' Diane asked. 'It was this gas?'

'There were a few who carried on mining, staying closer to the surface, believing they were clever enough not to get killed,' Eddie shrugged. 'But by eighteen eighty, without the mine and with the authorities banning deeper excavation, Prosperity became a ghost town.'

'So, what happened?' Harper asked. 'I mean, it really doesn't look like a ghost town right now.'

'The Bickfords,' Maggie said, and her voice dripped with disdain. 'When the townsfolk started to move out, panic selling, getting away from the "cursed mountains that could kill you", William Bickford bought up the land at a bargain price. But the problem with buying land in a cursed town is that if it becomes a ghost town, that land's worthless. So he, and his children after him, had to find a way to keep the people coming.'

'And that's when the legend of the gold started,' Eddie continued. 'Around the turn of the century, local newspapers started talking about ghostly visions. A couple of elderly locals talked about stories they had heard when they were younger, all of which conveniently hinted that "there was gold in dem'dar hills", millions of dollars' worth. The story began that the gold hadn't been taken away, had never been discovered; it was still there, hidden. And of course, people started to come to look.'

'But surely they would have been affected in the same way that the miners were?' Harper frowned.

'Not as much,' Doctor Chen replied. 'You see, the tourists didn't go deep. Some may have, but a death here and there could be attributed to other things; heart attacks, a fall – normal, natural causes – and over the years it became more of an urban mystery than an actual treasure hunt.'

'Yup, this is a fun dinner,' Maggie sighed, still trying to stop the current train of conversation.

Harper smiled at the comment, but then turned his attention back to Eddie.

'So, is that why Aegis were annoyed at you?' he asked. 'You wouldn't give them maps that led too deep?'

Eddie gave a "who knows" kind of shrug, his mouth filled with chilli. After chewing and swallowing, he replied.

'They're already too deep, god knows why,' he said. 'I was mainly protecting my own work. They never paid me for my last set of research, and I wasn't going to give them what I found this time.'

'Why not?' Alan asked. 'Maybe they would have paid you for both?'

'Spoken like someone who's never worked off invoices,' Eddie laughed. 'The honest truth is, though, and I told them this, that the data I have isn't connected to the gold. It's long gone, I reckon.'

Eddie looked uncomfortable talking about this, and Alan went to speak again, but Harper noticed Diane nudge him to pause his question. He reddened and relaxed back.

'So, why are you in town, Harper?' Diane now turned her attention across the table.

'Just visiting, tourist stuff, same as you.'

'Maggie mentioned your father came here once?'

Harper glanced quickly at Maggie, seeing her stricken face – the gossip had likely been passed on a "don't ask, don't tell" basis – and looked back at Diane.

'Yeah, he passed through.'

'What did he do here?' Alan pushed.

'I don't know,' Harper replied calmly. 'I wasn't there at the time. Probably the same as you though – hiked, did the usual tourist thing ...'

'What did your father do for a job?' Alan asked, but then at a nudge from Diane amended it. 'I mean what *does* he do?'

There was a moment of silence as Harper stared at Alan; the man opposite looked as if he knew he'd screwed up, and Harper knew why he'd think that. Maggie might have mentioned he was following his father's route, but he hadn't told her his father was dead when he'd checked in. The momentary use of the past tense meant someone else – likely from the sheriff's office or the mayor's residence – had been speaking to Alan and Diane Parsons.

'He's dead,' he replied, and watched as both husband and wife pantomimed a shocked expression, followed by the expected "I'm so sorry for your loss" responses.

After they settled back, Harper decided to test a hypothesis.

'So, what do *you* do for a living?' he asked them both.

'I work in tech,' Alan replied, as Diane shrugged.

'I'm between roles,' she admitted.

'What was your last one?'

'I ...' Diane smiled nervously as she seemed to claw for an answer. 'I worked in tech, too.'

'Tech,' Harper nodded, as if that one word explained everything. 'Sounds exciting.'

'Can be, I suppose,' Alan replied.

'Cool,' Harper now smiled, but it didn't reach his eyes. 'Tell me about it.'

Alan gave a similar, emotionless smile back.

'It's boring. I'd bore you.'

'You just said it could be exciting,' Harper insisted. 'Tell me about the exciting parts.'

'It's getting late,' Alan replied. 'We have an early hike planned for tomorrow.'

'Oh yeah? What time?'

'Oh-eight thirty—' Alan started, but then stopped himself. And, with a sigh, he rose from the table.

'Thanks for the dinner, Miss Hawkins,' he said. 'It was great.'

'Just like the US Marines make,' Harper replied casually, spooning more chilli.

The silence was immediate. Diane's hand tightened on her spoon, while Alan's face stayed neutral ... but his eyes changed. However, it was only for a second before releasing the spoon, Diane joined her husband and, with a nod, the two of them left the dining room, heading up the stairs.

After a moment, Maggie glared at Harper.

'And what the hell was that?' she asked.

Instead of answering, however, Harper reached into the satchel he'd brought down with him, pulling out his makeshift bug sweeper, quickly and quietly moving it around the room. With no significant movements of the needle, he nodded to himself and sat back down.

'Did you go in my room today?' he asked Maggie as he placed the device back in the satchel.

'Of course I damn well didn't!' Maggie snapped. “What kind of guesthouse do you think—'

'Someone did,' Harper interrupted, his voice low. 'Someone picked the lock, searched my room and then left, acting as if nothing had been disturbed. Oh, but not before they left a listening device in the side lamp. I'm guessing that's not one of the added extras you provide?'

Maggie stared at Harper in stunned silence.

'And you think ...' Eddie said, trailing off as if scared to speak the thought aloud, but staring off towards the stairs.

'They're Aegis, I'm pretty sure,' Harper replied calmly. 'They used military time when mentioning their start tomorrow, Alan – or whatever his real name is – recognised a military-style chilli, they're in touch with probably either Carson or Bickford, because I didn't tell Maggie my dad was dead, and their “hiking” allows them to visit the mine area without anyone asking. Alan has that military bearing he's trying to hide by slouching, while Diane's attempt at hiker-casual was betrayed by how she automatically positioned herself to watch both exits. While you were serving, they discussed their supposed trek through Nevada's mountain trails, but their knowledge felt researched rather than lived.'

'I felt that,' Doctor Chen admitted. 'I run those trails daily, and it almost felt like they didn't travel the same routes.'

'But why stay here?' Eddie asked, frowning, before pausing, realisation hitting his face. 'They're keeping an eye on me, aren't they? I mentioned last night at dinner I thought I'd made some progress, and today I'm being hassled by their goons ...'

He went to rise, but Harper shook his head.

'Currently, they don't know I know, and therefore don't

know *you* know. They suspect, but they can't leave on a suspicion. I'll find out tomorrow what's truly going on.'

'And why do you care so much, Mister Harper?' Doctor Chen asked, hands folded on the table.

'Because I wasn't lying when I said my father came through here a while back,' Harper replied. 'And after hearing what you said, I think the mines are where I'll find answers as to why he told me to come here after he died.'

'*After* he died?' Eddie frowned.

Harper nodded.

'Yeah, it's a mystery's isn't it?' he replied. 'Maybe those two can answer it. Or, if not, maybe Mason Carrick can, tomorrow.'

He looked back at Eddie.

'On that note, do you have a map I can examine?'

10

APOLOGIES

THE FOLLOWING MORNING, AFTER A BREAKFAST MADE BY Maggie of bacon and eggs – followed by a long conversation where Harper explained that the *last thing* he wanted was for Maggie to go to the Parsons' room and visibly kick them out, requiring her to casually keep an eye on them while allowing them to think that "they'd got away" with whatever lie they'd given the night before – Harper was sitting on the porch steps to the guesthouse when Carson's Ford SSV pulled up.

Harper had wondered who'd be coming to pick him up; the choices were an Aegis SUV, Cortez, or Carson, and it looked now like he was getting the worst option of all three.

The deputy had the window wound down, and his forced smile suggested someone had given him a talking-to that day, most likely to place him back in line.

He looked as happy to be there as Harper was to see him.

'Come to arrest me again?' Harper asked as he rose from his spot on the steps, brushing his jeans down and placing his satchel over his shoulder. Inside, it held his usual sketch pad, pocket knife, and a few other items, including the makeshift bug sweeper. Harper didn't feel he needed that right now, but he didn't know what to expect, so it was always good to be prepared.

'Get in,' Carson replied testily. 'Apparently it seems I'm your transport to the mine today. Probably to make sure you don't get into more trouble on the route. I hear last night you got lost.'

'I didn't get lost,' Harper shrugged, and the Ford's suspension creaked as he climbed in. 'I was exactly where I wanted to be.'

He noticed Carson had cleared the passenger seat of the usual police detritus – forms, clipboards, the general debris of law enforcement – that he had in there the last time Harper had ridden with him, and this effort at politeness felt wrong, slightly, like Carson was playing a part he hadn't rehearsed.

It definitely wasn't Carson's nature to be so clean; Harper had, after all, had a backseat view on the way to the station the previous day.

'You armed?' Carson asked.

'No,' Harper replied calmly, holding out the satchel. 'Just my pocket knife. And my stone. Feel free to check through it, if you want.'

'Nah, I reckon you're clean,' Carson muttered as they pulled away from Maggie's guesthouse. 'You're a "good guy" after all, aren't you?'

Harper chuckled.

'Listen, Carson,' he said, 'if we started off on a bad foot, I apologise, but let's face it, you've not exactly endeared yourself to me. Either way, you really don't need to make small talk on the journey.'

'Just doing my job,' Carson replied.

'And which job would that be?' Harper asked politely. 'Town deputy or Aegis courier?'

Carson's hands tightened on the steering wheel at the question, but he kept his voice level as he replied.

'You know, for someone who's "only just passing through", you seem awful interested in town business.'

Harper laughed now.

'If you hadn't arrested me, or if your Aegis goons hadn't been attacking old people, I might have been gone by now,' he replied, but he knew it was a lie. What he'd come to Prosperity to do hadn't been done yet.

But the last thing he was going to do was allow Carson that knowledge.

THE DRIVE TOOK THEM THROUGH PROSPERITY'S MORNING routine. Late risers were heading to the diner, and Harper was convinced he could see Maisie through the window as they passed, finishing up the breakfast rush. There were a few locals who had likely been at O'Malley's or the Goldstrike the evening before on Main Street, now looking worse for wear, but what caught Harper's attention was how everything—the people, the buildings, even the way folks walked—seemed to exist in relation to the mine. The drive also gave Harper his first proper look at how the mine dominated Prosperity. He hadn't really taken the time to consider that the previous day on his walks around town and up to Bickford's house. The main shaft rose above the town like a sentinel, visible from every street corner, the mountain behind it an ominous guardian, its shadow casting across Prosperity. Even the roads seemed to have been laid out in deference to it, all leading up to the dark mouth in the mountain.

'Before we get in there, you'll need to listen to the safety briefing,' Carson said, his professional mask back in place.

'I thought I was turning up, they were apologising, they'd give me a tour and then I was coming home,' Harper replied, frowning, playing the part. He knew there was no way Aegis would let him walk away so easily. But there was no reason for Carson to think that he knew that.

'All people hear the safety briefing,' Carson said. 'There's gases up there that are nothing to mess with. We've lost men up there over the years.'

'I heard,' Harper replied. 'Eddie Hawkins was telling me last night.'

'Right, Hawkins. He's so trustworthy.'

'You don't think so?'

Carson shrugged while driving, his hand still on the steering wheel.

'Look, Mister Harper, you've been here, what, twenty-four hours now? You've made a real pain in the ass of yourself in that time, so congratulations on that. But you've got no earthly clue what's going on here.'

'Yeah?'

'Every person you've met, who've lived here all their lives? They've been owned by the Bickfords since before they were born,' Carson muttered. 'Nothing happens without Tom Bickford's say. So, before you start blaming everybody and accusing people of whatever you *think* they're doing, just know that we're all just trying to live our lives and get on with things. People like Eddie Hawkins, they just want to see the town burn down.'

'Or they want to be freed,' Harper suggested.

'Freed from what?' Carson glanced over at Harper angrily, and the Ford swerved slightly as he did so, the deputy returning his attention to the road as he continued. 'We're a good town, Harper. You've spent the day walking around, so I know you've seen it. Yeah, sure, the Aegis guys need to blow off some steam here and there, and it's up to people like Sheriff Coble, me and Cortez to calm shit down, but we have good lives here, and the tourists are happy ...'

Realising he'd probably said too much, Carson trailed off.

'Look, let's just get this over with,' he said. 'Get your apology, have a chat with the mine manager, do what you need to do, and then piss off back to wherever you came from.'

'Sounds like a command.'

'Yeah, well, if I had my way, I'd drive you to the edge of the town, drop you off, and send you on your way.'

'I wouldn't do that,' Harper replied casually. 'That's how the Stallone movie *First Blood* started, and we all saw how that progressed.'

'No offence, Harper,' Carson looked across and shook his head sadly. 'You ain't no Stallone.'

Harper couldn't argue with that.

THEY WOUND UP THE ACCESS ROAD, PAST WARNING SIGNS weathered by decades of sun and wind. Harper started counting them, idly at first. A new one appeared every fifty yards, each one threatening death by invisible gas or erosion or even falling rocks. The impression was given repetitively; *this mountain was dangerous.*

The repetition felt deliberate; this was a town that had built its identity around fear of what lay beneath the mountain, while at the same time building its identity around curiosity of what had been *hidden* beneath the same rock.

The mine entrance was already busy; trucks were moving, men in hard hats checking equipment. Most of it looked new, Harper noted. The vehicles had that rental gleam to them, and the workers moved with the careful precision of men still learning their cover stories.

And cover stories they were, Harper was sure of that now. He didn't know why they were pretending to "mine the upper tunnels" or, rather, "guard the people who were mining the upper tunnels", but this felt more like a charade for his benefit than anything else.

To the side, his Lennon glasses on, Ashfield stood waiting with another man, white-haired, cut short, standing with a military bearing. They were both in clean corporate overalls that looked as if they'd never seen real mining work, and the sight was almost comical – two men playing dress-up like children in their father's clothes. But there was nothing childish about the man with the white hair; his eyes cold and calculating as he tracked Harper's arrival.

As they pulled up, Harper noticed how Carson's demeanour suddenly shifted. The deputy might be wearing the badge, but it was very clear who really gave orders in Prosperity.

'Right on time,' Ashfield smiled, pushing his Lennon glasses up his nose. 'Ready for the tour?'

Harper stepped out of the Ford, feeling the mountain's presence in front of him. The morning sun hadn't yet crested the peaks, leaving the mine's entrance in shadow. A cool breath of air leaked from the darkness, carrying an almost metallic taste of old iron and something else, something chemical perhaps ... a smell that definitely didn't belong in a gold mine.

'Wouldn't miss it,' Harper grinned.

Carson shifted in his seat, clearly unsure if he was supposed to stay or go. The deputy's discomfort was telling; he was used to being the authority in Prosperity, but here, at the mine's mouth, well ... different rules seemed to apply. Harper watched as Ashfield gave the slightest of nods, dismissing the lawman like a servant.

'We'll take good care of him, and let you know when it's time for Mister Harper to leave,' Ashfield assured the deputy, but his eyes never left Harper. The implied threat wasn't particularly subtle, but then it wasn't really meant to be. *This was nothing more than theatre,* Harper realised, every moment choreographed to remind him and Carson who held power here. Workers moved around them, their paths creating a careful distance between the corporate men and the labour, and Harper caught fragments of conversation as they did so. Some were local accents, but most of them weren't – Aegis had obviously brought their own people, wearing coveralls that were just a touch too clean and tool-belts that had never seen proper use.

Before they moved, however, Harper turned and faced the white-haired man.

'Don't think we've met,' he said.

'Mike Delaney,' the man replied. 'I'm the manager of the mine. And for my sins right now, I'm the head of Aegis Security.'

'I thought Mason Carrick was head of Aegis Security.'

At Harper's mention of the name, Delaney paused, and Harper could see him already re-evaluating the conversation he was about to have.

'Carrick's had to go back to Los Angeles,' he said. 'While he's there, *I'm* head of Aegis security. When he's here, *he's* head of Aegis security.'

'Right,' Harper nodded slowly. 'So basically what you're saying is you're the mine manager ... with delusions of grandeur.'

Ashfield, to the side, stifled a laugh, and Delaney positioned himself to face the bespectacled man, his eyes glaring, even if his face was emotionless, until Ashfield turned it into a cough.

'Lead the way,' Harper said, waving towards the mine entrance while still observing the two men. Delaney's positioning – always keeping clear sight lines, professional paranoia in every movement – gave away the fact that the man had training, and from what he'd been told about, before he'd even arrived in Prosperity, it matched exactly what Harper expected.

Ashfield, giving a shrug, aimed Harper and Delaney towards the offices. Behind them, Carson's Ford SSV retreated down the mountain, leaving Harper alone with men who would rather see him dead than be asking questions.

He almost missed having Carson beside him.

Almost.

THE SAFETY OFFICE THEY ENTERED SMELLED OF NEW CARPET and fresh paint. There was a screen dominating one wall, a one hundred-inch monitor, ready for what Harper guessed would be some kind of masterclass in corporate theatre. It looked exactly as corporate as Harper had expected: glass walls, enormous screens, and enough expensive equipment to make the MSHA, or *Mine Safety and Health Administration,* happy.

A technician was setting up gas monitors on a side table – likely standard procedure for any mine safety walkthrough. What caught Harper's interest was the calibrator sitting beside them. It was a *BW MicroDock*, the latest model, about the size of his phone but half as thick. The technician was using it to run diagnostic checks on the monitors, and Harper felt a strange familiarity here as he'd seen similar techs using chemical detection gear just like this before, but it wasn't a corporate mining operation back then.

The same protocols, but different packaging.

Mike Delaney, mine manager and apparent current head of Aegis Security, took up a position by the door, while Ashfield gestured Harper over to one of the plastic chairs, arranged classroom style.

It seemed that although Delaney claimed the title, Ashfield was truly the boss here.

'Before we start, you must have heard the rumours about the gas,' Ashfield began.

Harper nodded.

'I've been told,' he replied. 'Cortez mentioned it, so did Carson, and you don't exactly miss the signs as you drive up here.'

'Gas safety is our priority,' Ashfield ignored the response, clicking through his presentation as he continued. Harper noted how he stood; it was a military parade rest, poorly disguised as a corporate stance. He'd thought the previous day that Ashfield could have been CIA or something along those lines, but now he could see that Ashfield definitely had military training of some kind.

Which made him even more dangerous.

"Hydrogen Sulphide is heavier than air, so it collects in low spots, old tunnels, anywhere that dips,' the slideshow that he began showed diagrams, death statistics, the science behind hydrogen sulphide. All of it seemed carefully researched and perfectly presented, but it almost felt too perfect, Harper thought, like someone had spent a lot of time and money making sure that this briefing, to whoever it was given to, would stand up to scrutiny. 'At low concentrations, you get a rotten egg smell, but at higher concentrations—'

'It paralyses your sense of smell, and you can walk into a lethal pocket and not even know it,' Harper finished as he watched Delaney rather than the presentation. The security chief's attention never wavered, eyes constantly assessing, analysing. This wasn't about safety protocols; they were studying Harper's reactions, looking for something specific. 'I already know this, Ashfield, and if you're delaying because you don't have an apology for me, I'd rather you just call Carson and bring him back. I don't want to waste my day being talked to about stuff that I don't really care about.'

'Oh, but you should care about this,' Ashfield clicked to a new slide. 'Now, our monitoring systems are state-of-the-art, sensors every fifty feet, emergency breathing apparatus at regular intervals. Our safety is expensive—'

'But cheaper than lawsuits?' Harper questioned.

Ashfield's smile didn't reach his eyes.

'Exactly.'

Harper sat back and listened to more talk about emergency procedures, evacuation techniques, and other such requirements for anyone entering this mine, wondering if he was one of many that had watched it, or if this was purely for him and created the previous night. The technician had long disappeared by now, but the briefing continued, and everything as far as Harper could tell was by the book, almost *too* by the book. It was like someone had taken MSHA regulations and polished them into some kind of corporate mythology. He wondered how many of these procedures were actually followed once the inspectors who saw this left.

At the end, Ashfield wound the briefing down by handing over a small gas monitor from the table the technician had been working at; sleek and compact, with a digital display and a single red button, it'd been recently calibrated, and Ashfield smiled, holding it out to Harper like he was presenting a gold watch instead of a plastic box.

'This is your personal gas monitor,' he began, with the same rehearsed precision Harper had come to expect. 'You'll wear it clipped to your belt or jacket at all times. It's designed to detect hazardous gases – hydrogen sulphide, methane, carbon monoxide. If it picks up anything, it'll vibrate, beep, and flash this light here.'

He tapped the side of the device, where a small LED sat.

'The display will show the concentration levels. If it hits the threshold, you leave immediately. No exceptions.'

Harper took the device, turning it over in his hands like he was checking a counterfeit bill. It was lightweight but solid, almost too new, like everything else he'd seen so far. He flicked his eyes to the display, noting the calibration.

'Simple enough,' he said, examining the screen. 'What's the range on this?'

'Twenty feet or so,' Ashfield replied smoothly. 'More than enough to keep you safe if you pay attention. Any more questions?'

'Actually, yeah, a couple,' Harper held up the monitor.

'First off, why do these have a higher detection threshold than standard mining equipment?'

There was the smallest pause. Most people wouldn't have caught it, but Harper wasn't most people.

'I'm not sure what you mean.'

'Standard detectors alert at ten parts per million. These are set to fifteen,' Harper tapped the display. 'Gives you a larger margin before evacuation protocols kick in.'

'Our equipment's calibrated to MSHA standards,' Delaney muttered from the doorway, and his tone suggested the conversation was over. 'You said you had a second question.'

'Yes,' Harper now turned to face Delaney. 'Where's my apology?'

There was a long, quiet moment, and then Delaney, with his fist, banged twice on the safety office door. After a second, it opened, and the pockmarked blond, Blaine, and "Blackbeard", Lucas shuffled in, both looking uncomfortable in their clean coveralls. The bruises from the fight were still visible, Lucas's eye particularly purple. Harper noticed with the slightest of smiles how they positioned themselves, trying to look tough while maintaining a safe distance.

'These gentlemen have something to say to you,' Ashfield prompted, like a schoolteacher with unruly children.

'Yeah, I'm sorry about yesterday,' Blaine muttered, not meeting Harper's eyes. 'Got carried away.'

Lucas nodded, looking at Blaine rather than Harper.

'Yeah, it won't happen again.'

The performance was perfunctory and rehearsed. Harper had caught the glance between them; this wasn't about making amends; this was clearing a deck, moving this on before it became a thing, allowing Blaine and Lucas to return to an almost anonymity. But either way, everything that Harper had been promised had been delivered.

'Water under the bridge,' Harper replied easily. 'Though, I am still curious why you were interested in Eddie's research.'

Blaine's face tightened, but Lucas cut in smoothly.

'Just doing our job, making sure site security ain't compromised.'

'Really?' Harper frowned. 'Because he told me last night you thought he'd stiffed you on a deal, saying he owed you for things you'd already paid for, while he claimed you hadn't paid the invoice. Perhaps you expected him to provide you a route into the mine that you wanted, one that he maybe felt wasn't safe?'

The question had started with Harper facing the two men, but ended with him staring at Ashfield.

'That'll be all,' Delaney snapped, dismissing the two men who left quickly, relief evident in their posture. 'We ain't here to talk about loony old men. You came here to get an apology and to see what we're doing.'

Harper watched them go, noting how as he watched through the window, they headed not towards the main entrance, but instead towards one of the newer buildings on site.

'I know what you're doing,' Harper said almost dismissively. 'And I wanted Mason Carrick.'

'Well, Carrick isn't here, so you can say whatever you were gonna say to him, to me.'

'You sure?'

'Absolutely,' Delaney replied. 'Just pretend I'm Carrick, if it helps.'

'Okay, sure,' Harper shrugged. 'Okay, *Mason*, this might come as a shock ... but you're my biological father.'

There was a moment of stunned silence, broken by Harper laughing.

'Christ, you should see your face,' he gasped. 'Come on then, show me your sodding mine. After I take a piss, though. Where are your washrooms?'

WHEN THEY FINALLY STOOD TO LEAVE, HARPER MADE SURE TO be last out, and as he waved for Ashfield to pass, the BW MicroDock calibrator on the table beside him slipped easily and unobtrusively into his jacket pocket; just another piece of safety equipment among many. Following Ashfield out, they stepped out into the morning sun, and Harper felt the work site had taken on a distinct atmosphere since they'd entered the building. There were fewer workers visible now, and those that remained seemed to move with a practised efficiency. Harper noted how they created empty spaces around the main tunnel entrance, like water parting around a stone.

As they walked across, Ashfield pointed out an equipment locker holding a variety of hard hats. Everything was clean and felt new, but it somehow didn't make Harper feel any safer.

To the side were some portable cabins, and Delaney waved Harper towards them.

'Go on, take your damn piss,' he muttered irritably.

Gratefully accepting and making his way into the cabin, and then into one of the washroom cubicles, Harper knew he had only moments to work before their suspicions were aroused. The MicroDock's case opened easily with the help of the pocket knife's screwdriver, taking out the four small screws. Inside, the circuitry looked familiar; he'd seen similar testing stations used for chemical weapon detectors instead of mining equipment, and the principles were the same.

Reaching into his satchel, still amused they'd been so desperate to get this all over with they'd not bothered checking him, he pulled out components from his makeshift multimeter bug detector; the coil that detected Aegis's surveillance would work perfectly to boost the test signal here, while the multimeter's oscillator could override the MicroDock's timing circuit, forcing it to think it was constantly starting a new calibration cycle.

'You good in there?' Ashfield's voice called out.

'Dodgy food last night,' Harper shouted back. 'Give me a moment.'

'Chilli does that,' Ashfield replied without thinking, and Harper smiled.

Without realising, he'd just proven the moles in the guesthouse. Or had he realised, and provided a "mistake" as a way to give the information?

The modification was precise work in the confined space. He bridged the timing circuit with the oscillator, using the stripped wire from his phone charger to make the connections. The coil he wired in parallel with the test signal generator, effectively turning each calibration port into a broadcast point. Now, instead of waiting for detectors to dock, once turned on, the modified MicroDock would continuously transmit test signals. Any detector in range would think it was being calibrated, forcing it into a reboot test mode. Multiple failed calibration attempts would trigger failsafe protocols, all in the space of microseconds, and a hard reset would kick in. They were simple changes for someone used to working with military detection systems, and was something that, deep in the mines, could really screw with the systems.

It was a last chance resort, but Harper wasn't an idiot. Everything here – the talk, the apology – was all to take him deep into the mines, for whatever reason.

He wasn't going unarmed.

He had the device reassembled now, looking perfectly normal but currently capable of disrupting every gas detector in the tunnel. Sliding it into his pocket, he flushed the cistern and left the cabin, where he saw Ashfield raise an eyebrow.

'Do we need to light a candle in there?' he asked with amusement.

'False alarm,' Harper shrugged, taking the offered hard hat from Delaney. 'Shall we?'

'I ASSUME YOU'VE BEEN IN UNDERGROUND MINES BEFORE?' Ashfield asked, adjusting his own hard hat.

'Once or twice,' Harper didn't elaborate on that. He knew they'd seen his military file, and he also knew they'd seen it was heavily redacted; he decided to let them wonder about his experience.

'When's Mason Carrick coming back?' he asked.

'Why are you so desperate to chat to Carrick?' Ashfield asked, turning and facing Harper, almost blocking his entry to the mine. 'And no "biological dad" bullshit, please.'

'You know damn well why I want to speak to him,' Harper said, deciding that subtlety was over and it was time to play a different game. 'You've been listening to me, you probably heard my phone call last night.'

'And how would—'

'You know, on the microphone your guys in the guest house stuck in the lamp,' Harper snapped. 'Let me guess, they're there to monitor Eddie, right? You must have been over the moon when you realised I was staying there, too. They're good ... but I'm better.'

Ashfield said nothing for a long moment and then gave a slightly dismissive shrug.

'Don't know what you're talking about, Harper,' he said, 'and the hikers are just hikers.'

'I didn't say which guests I was talking about.'

'There's only two other guests at the guesthouse,' Ashfield replied, getting irritated, either by the conversation or because he'd been caught out. 'It wasn't that hard to work out. Anyway, we're going to go for a stroll now, so stay with the group, follow instructions, and don't wander.'

Delaney's smile was professional, empty as he took the gas monitor device and clipped it to Harper's jacket lapel.

'You ready for this?' he asked.

The mine entrance gaped before them, dark despite the industrial lighting. It was weird, but Harper almost felt the mountain's weight above him, pressing down with generations of secrets. And it was very likely that somewhere in there, Moses Mathers had found something worth dying for.

Harper just hoped he wasn't about to *join* him.

'Sure,' he said. 'You first.'

11

RE-CALIBRATION

THE TUNNEL PATH, GRAVEL PLACED DECADES EARLIER, WAS dimly lit by harsh pools of light every twenty feet or so, probably more for psychological comfort than true illumination. Harper was walking slightly behind Ashfield, watching how the Aegis man with the Lennon glasses' shadow danced between the pools of light, while Delaney brought up the rear, his footsteps echoing with military precision. The sound echoed off old stone, marking their descent into the mountain like a metronome.

He wasn't sure if it was real or not, but it felt to Harper that the air was changing with every step he took deeper. Surface warmth was definitely giving way to cave coolness, carrying traces of oil and machinery that didn't quite mask something older – the metallic taste of exposed rock that had waited millions of years to meet the air, before some poor bastard with a pickaxe decided to hit it.

Their breath made small clouds visible in the space between lighting pools, as their descent followed what Harper thought of as the "tourist route"; very much reinforced walls, proper drainage, even handrails in places. Everything was too clean, too new up here, almost as if it was *Disneyfied* for the tourists, not a working mine so much as a movie set idea of what one could look like. The walls had been recently shotcreted, the floor levelled with fresh concrete. Someone had spent a lot of money making this section look safe and accessible.

'Watch your step now,' Ashfield pointed at a drainage channel. 'The original workings date back to eighteen fifty-one. It's amazing to think what they achieved with hand tools and black powder.'

His voice, surprisingly, carried the practised enthusiasm of a museum guide, and for a moment Harper wondered if Ashfield truly enjoyed or believed what he was saying.

'Of course, modern safety regulations require significant upgrading of—'

'You're going the wrong way,' Harper interrupted. The sound of their footsteps changed as the tunnel widened, Ashfield's voice now bouncing back too loud in a confined space.

'I'm sorry?'

'The old goldworks, the ones that we all hear about in the legends of Prosperity's mines, they're east of here. This tunnel's turning west, heading downwards.'

Harper watched the shadows on the wall, noting how Delaney's posture behind him had shifted at his words. The security chief's hand had drifted closer to his overall's side pocket. There was also the smallest pause in Ashfield's stride, almost imperceptible.

'We've found it safer over the last six months to approach from this direction,' he explained. 'The gas tends to pool in the eastern sections, you see. Our monitoring systems have mapped the flow patterns extensively.'

'Then why were the western tunnels closed up?' As they continued down the path, Harper now noted how Delaney's footsteps had changed rhythm, becoming more alert, less heavy – the man had shifted to some kind of combat stance, without seeming to move.

'The geological surveys showed this was now safer—'

'Funny thing about that,' Harper interrupted, tasting metal on his tongue that wasn't entirely from the rock. 'The geological surveys show the pyrite deposits mainly in the lower western reaches. If hydrogen sulphide was the real problem, this is exactly where it would pool.'

He pointed forward.

'You know, just down there. Where they closed the mine, decades ago.'

Water dripped somewhere in the darkness ahead. The sound echoed off stone that had never seen tourist lights or safety rails.

'You've been doing your homework.' Ashfield's voice remained pleasant, but something had shifted in the air between them. 'I wasn't aware you'd had access to geological surveys. Perhaps Eddie Hawkins was showing you some of his maps? They're bullshit, by the way. He's a crazy old man who's taken us for a ride, as I've already told you. The geological surveys you've probably seen are old ones, where the gas was in the western tunnels, but, um ...'

'The geological surveys don't exist, I was just seeing how far you'd go to argue it,' Harper smiled in the darkness, watching their shadows merge and separate in the rhythmic lighting. 'But you just confirmed that I'm right.'

The silence that followed felt heavier than the mountain

above him. The footsteps echoed off walls that had probably kept secrets for well over a century now, and Harper was very aware that each step was taking them further from the carefully maintained fiction of tourism and safety, deeper into whatever truth lay hidden in Prosperity's bones.

The silence held until Ashfield sighed, turning slightly, one hand brushing at his spotless coveralls.

'Look, Harper, the sensors tell us we're safe down here, just like I said in the briefing,' he replied, pointing at the green sensor lights visible every ten yards, and tapping his gas monitor. 'If they go red, then we have a problem.'

'Especially if we can't smell it,' Harper added. 'Any deaths down here?'

'A few, sure.'

'Well, let's hope the sensors carry on working,' Harper continued as they moved into a slightly wider section of the tunnel, with side tunnels branching off from it.

'There's water dripping ahead,' he said, noting a genuine leak of some kind.

'So?'

'So you were the one going on about it in the safety briefing? Or did you forget what happens when you expose a pyrite seam to air and water?'

Ashfield muttered, sighing at Delaney.

'Let's check just in case.'

It was perfect timing; Harper needed them distracted just long enough to activate the device. There was a moment where he thought Delaney would argue this, but with a sigh from the latter, Ashfield and Delaney moved forward to inspect the dripping water. The moment they stepped away, however, Harper's hand slid into his pocket and thumbed the MicroDock's power switch. The modified circuitry powered up silently, and if he'd repurposed it correctly, it'd now be sending out continuous calibration signals. Any detector within range would think it was being tested, forcing it into calibration mode, and then hard reset.

'It's just condensation, and the levels are safe,' Ashfield returned to Harper. 'So, don't worry, okay? Let's continue.'

'Fine by me,' Harper shrugged. 'Lead the way.'

AFTER ANOTHER MINUTE OR SO OF SLOW WALKING, ASHFIELD slowed to a stop, cricking his neck as he sighed.

'Well,' he said, 'I believe we should take a break right now, and have a... conversation.'

Harper had been waiting for this, as the scuff of boots behind him confirmed Delaney's movement. The security chief was good; his steps whispered more than echoed, each one bringing him closer, but Harper had learned silence in places darker than this, from men who had made death their profession, and who were very good at it.

'I wouldn't,' Harper said quietly.

'Come now, Mister Harper,' Ashfield's corporate mask had slipped, showing something harder underneath. 'We both know how this plays out. These tunnels are dangerous, and accidents can happen.'

There were more footsteps in the darkness. Not Delaney's – the sound came from a side tunnel, one of the many alcoves to the right, places Harper had noted and catalogued on their way down. Water dripped in the darkness ahead, the sound deeper now. The tunnel was widening, opening into what mining maps would call *Chamber Four*; Harper had memorised the layout from Eddie's documents the previous night just in case, but something about the space ahead felt *wrong*. The air moved differently, for a start, as if others were down here, waiting.

But so was Harper. Now, standing still, his sabotage device had gone to work. He watched the first LED on the wall change from green to amber – *calibration mode*. Then red – *failed test*. The effect rippled down the tunnel as each detector received the signal and failed the forced calibration. Mining safety protocols were unforgiving – a failed calibration meant unreliable readings.

Unreliable readings meant shutdown and reboot.

One by one, all the sensor lights winked out.

'You're right, Mister Ashfield, they do happen,' Harper agreed, tensing, ready for anything. 'Especially when someone forgets to check their monitors.'

Ashfield's hand froze halfway to his collar, where his own personal gas monitor was clipped. It was silent, its power light dark, the forced calibration rebooting it as well. Harper smiled, knowing he only had minutes before they came back online, looking back at the two men, now glaring at him in confusion.

'Looks like failed calibrations,' Harper said, keeping his voice neutral. 'Multiple units, too. Safety protocols require immediate evacuation when testing fails, right? You said it in your briefing.'

'Or we could continue,' Ashfield suggested. 'Since we know the air was safe a moment ago.'

'Without certified detectors?' Harper watched the last lights shift to red, and then turn off. 'That's a lot of trust in these old tunnels.'

Delaney's face darkened.

'Can you smell rotten eggs?' Harper quickly added, sniffing. 'I do hope not. Surely our little safety boxes would be beeping, and buzzing, and flashing ... twenty feet or so, right? I wonder how far we've walked since they became useless down here ...'

Delaney went for his gun, but Ashfield blocked him.

'Don't be a fool,' he said. 'If it sparks off a rock, and there *is* gas ...'

'Boom,' Harper smiled as he made an explosion motion with his hands. 'So, here's what's going to happen next. Either we continue this tour, just the three of us, nice and friendly, and you show me what the hell you're really doing down here, or we find out how many of your men will risk a fire-fight in a tunnel with no working gas monitors, because I reckon that's pretty much against safety protocols – and suicidal. Or, we all make our way out, nice and safe.'

A long moment passed, measured in drips of water and held breath.

Then, as if nothing had happened, Ashfield's smile returned.

'Of course,' he said. 'Although I have to say this isn't very sporting of you.'

'Neither is having men waiting in the shadows,' Harper gestured into the darkness. 'You can stand down now, gentlemen. Let's keep this professional.'

One by one, lights appeared in the tunnel's shadows; six men, each trying to look like they hadn't just been caught setting up an ambush. Harper counted weapons; holster bulges, enough firepower to make their intentions clear. Weapons that, without the sensors, could ignite unknown gases that could kill them all.

'Shall we continue?' he asked pleasantly. 'I believed you were about to show me the western tunnels that we're not allowed to go into, and then I was going to have a chat with Mason Carrick.'

'I told you, he's not—'

'I don't give a shit where you say he is,' Harper replied. 'After what happened yesterday, I can pretty much guess he's already on a private jet back here ... and I can wait.'

The lights caught Ashfield's expression; a flash of something flickering deep beneath the polished veneer.

'The western tunnels are restricted, safety concerns – there's nothing to see that way,' Ashfield said. His corporate manner had hardened into something more genuine now, and definitely more dangerous. 'Collapsed workings, mostly. We're still assessing structural integrity. My apologies, I must have got turned around, thinking we were heading eastwards.'

'Those are some expensive humidity sensors for collapsed tunnels,' Harper nodded towards the sensors along the tunnel wall, the currently powerless devices. A drop of water hit Harper's hard hat, the sound oddly metallic. He looked up, noting how the rock above had been recently worked; fresh tool marks scored the ceiling, trying to look old.

'Sometimes, Mister Harper,' Delaney's voice had dropped to match the tunnel's darkness, 'curiosity can be fatal. Especially in old mines. Especially when a man doesn't know what he's looking for.'

'But I do know,' Harper turned, facing Delaney directly. 'That's what's bothering you, isn't it? The question is, do you know what *you're* looking for?'

Delaney's answer, if he even had one, was lost in a sudden burst of static – systems coming back online as the MicroDock's limited charge, forced into a continuous cycle of calibration, finally died. Harper watched the change sweep through the tunnel; gas sensors blinking awake, security lights intensifying. Another drop of water hit Harper's helmet, and this time he caught the chemical tang beneath the mineral smell. Something was leaking in the western tunnels, something that didn't belong in a gold mine. The air felt different here; heavier, with an edge that made his tongue tingle.

'Your plan seems to have failed,' Delaney smiled.

'Did it?' Harper asked. 'Knowing I've somehow been in your systems, can you truly confirm I'm not giving you false positives now?'

'You'd die too.'

'You've seen my heavily redacted file. Do I seem like a man who's bothered about possibly dying?'

There was a pause as the two men facing Harper considered this.

'I think,' Ashfield said carefully, 'we should conclude our tour. These tunnels can be treacherous, even with proper safety equipment. We wouldn't want to risk any ... accidents.'

'Funny thing about accidents,' Harper took a step closer to Ashfield. 'They leave evidence. Marks on rock. Chemical traces. The kind of things a good forensics' team might find interesting.'

'Are you threatening me, Harper?'

'Not at all, just making conversation. You know, like you were yesterday at O'Malley's,' Harper caught the flicker in Ashfield's eyes. 'Though I notice we're having a very different conversation now. Amazing what a few hundred feet of rock can do to a man's honesty.'

He looked around the tunnel now.

'So, what was the plan, guys?' he asked. 'You were going to

what? Shoot me in the head? Find me somewhere to be left to die?'

'Of course not,' Ashfield shook his head, looking ahead, not turning to face Harper as he spoke. 'The plan was to scare you, perhaps warn you off. Let's face it, Harper. You've proven yourself *not* to be the kind of person who would be warned off easily – we thought that a large group of us, in a scary location, could do what we needed.'

'And how's *that* worked out for you?'

Ashfield finally stopped and turned.

'What do you want here?' he asked.

'Answers,' Harper replied.

'To what?'

'A lot of things.'

Ashfield sighed and gave a little shudder.

'Look,' he muttered, and Harper could see genuine concern on his face. 'We don't go down here that much anymore; we've had gas pockets appear, and I'm not lying to you. Your stunt with your jammer means we could be in the middle of one, and we wouldn't know. Sure, they're on again ...'

'But you don't know if they're genuine,' Harper nodded. 'I get it.'

'Are they?'

'Light a match and see.'

They started back, Harper watching as Ashfield took them on what looked to be a safer route to the surface. Another drop of water hit Harper's helmet, and this time he caught Ashfield's quick glance upward. Was it concern? No, *recognition*. Whatever was leaking from the western tunnels, Ashfield knew exactly what it was.

Quietly and without causing attention, Harper pulled a

handkerchief from his pocket and wiped the hat's surface, folding it up and placing it back in his jacket pocket.

They'd walked for another five minutes, a new route that seemed to move parallel to the old one, Delaney muttering that Ashfield was going the wrong way, and that they weren't gaining height, while Ashfield argued it was safer ... when they suddenly paused.

Harper felt the change before he saw it. A shift in the air currents, a stillness that didn't belong ... like the mountain itself was holding its breath.

'You feel that?' he asked, glancing at Delaney and Ashfield.

Ashfield didn't respond, his attention fixed on the tunnel walls, eyes scanning the jagged seams of rock overhead.

'Probably just a pressure pocket shifting,' Delaney muttered, though his tone didn't sound convinced.

Before anyone could say more, there was a low groan from somewhere deep in the mine. A sound like the mountain itself was alive, stretching and cracking its joints. The groan became a rumble, and Harper barely had time to brace himself before a deafening crack split the air. The tunnel shook violently, loose rocks and dirt raining down as Harper instinctively threw an arm over his face for protection. The ground beneath him shifted, just slightly, but enough to make him take a stabilising step to the side as a section of the wall ahead crumbled, dislodging a spray of debris, and opening a wide, jagged fissure where a narrow corridor had been, ahead of them, moments before.

'Everyone all right?' Delaney barked, his voice sharp and commanding now. Gone was the “mine manager” persona. Now he was all military.

'Fine,' Harper said, straightening and brushing dust from his sleeves. 'What the hell was that?'

'Gas pocket igniting, maybe,' Ashfield offered, but the way he avoided eye contact told Harper he was guessing. The fissure gaped before them, narrow and irregular, the edges sharp where the rock had cracked further apart. Harper stepped closer, his helmet light cutting into the darkness beyond.

'Hold up,' Delaney warned.

Harper ignored him. Something was catching the light inside the fissure, a pale shape half-buried in the rubble. He crouched, angling his helmet light for a better look, and the shape resolved into something unmistakable A work boot, but not military – unlikely to belong to Aegis's operation, but too new in style and material to be an old-timey prospector.

'There's someone—' he began, but Delaney was already moving, trying to block his view.

Too late.

Harper's light found what remained of Moses Mathers.

The body sat propped against the tunnel wall, almost mummified by the mine's constant temperature and dry air. Moses's face was frozen in an expression Harper had seen before, in men who'd died seeing something they couldn't comprehend. His hands were raised, not in defence, but as if trying to ward off something that couldn't be stopped. It brought to mind Doctor Chen's comment the previous night, of how victims' faces often showed extreme terror, because of the gas causing intense muscle contractions.

'Well,' Ashfield's voice was carefully neutral. 'That looks to be Moses Mathers, the prospector who disappeared. This is unfortunate.'

Harper studied the scene, scanning his torch across the

body; Moses' clothes were undisturbed; no signs of violence. The old man's notebook was still in his jacket pocket, his pen fallen beside him. This wasn't a robbery, and definitely not a fight.

Could Aegis be innocent of this?

However, the rock around the body told a different story. Strange crystalline formations surrounded him, too geometric to be natural. And beneath the mineral smell of the mine, there was something else, the same chemical tang he'd smelt from the dripping water. It wasn't rotten eggs though, and a quick check of his gas monitor showed it was fine.

Ashfield, noting this, smiled, and Harper didn't care that he'd given away his ace.

'We need to call this in,' he breathed.

'Of course,' Ashfield's corporate manner was back, but Harper caught the quick hand signals to Delaney. 'We take safety very seriously. If you'd like to return to the surface, I can have someone—'

'I'll wait here,' Harper kept his torch beam steady on Moses' face. 'Wouldn't want to disturb a crime scene.'

'Crime scene?' Ashfield's laugh echoed off the walls. 'Harper, this is clearly a tragic accident. The gas—'

'Doesn't crystallise rock.' Harper knelt, careful not to touch anything. 'Doesn't leave chemical burns. And doesn't make a man look like he's seen something worse than death.'

Ashfield's smile remained fixed.

'Of course. Though I should point out, technically this is private property. We have our own procedures for—'

'A man is dead.' Harper's voice was quiet. 'Your procedures just became evidence.'

'And we're standing beside a body that has died, possibly

due to fatal gas inhalation, while wearing no gas mask,' Delaney replied, finally pulling his gun. 'I really don't want to use this, Harper, but we're going to the surface. You can call the cops the moment we're there, but on your own convenience or at the barrel of a gun, you're leading us out of here before Mister Mathers there isn't the only one who dies of something strange and unnatural.'

Harper went to reply, to state that Delaney had better be ready to *eat* that weapon, but it was Ashfield who broke the stalemate.

'Put the damn gun away before he feeds it to you,' he snapped, before looking back at Harper. 'I think you owe us an answer. You know too much about what's going on. You know too much about us. Are you law enforcement? You're not local. Bickford would have warned us of you.'

Harper shook his head.

'I'm not law enforcement,' he replied. 'I'm here on my father's business.'

'And just what is it about your goddamned father that makes it so important for you to come here? And don't give us none of that bollocks secret society nonsense you played into the microphone last night.'

Harper smiled. *Ashfield had just proven that they were the ones that listened.*

'My father was Dominic Kane,' he said.

There was a long, quiet moment before Delaney whistled.

'You're shitting me,' he said.

'No,' Harper replied. He leant over the body, closing the eyes before rising, making a faint bow to the body, hands clasped before eventually turning around. 'He divorced my mum when I was a kid, moved back to America. We kind of got estranged after she passed away twenty years ago. We met here and there. I knew he was part of Aegis, but I had my own journeys.'

Delaney looked at Ashfield.

'You know Kane?'

Ashfield said nothing, and Harper now wondered whether Ashfield was as deep into Aegis as he believed.

'Probably above your pay grade,' Delaney chuckled. 'But I knew Dominic Kane. Met him once, too. You know how Mason created Aegis?'

He looked back at Harper as he continued.

'Well, he had a partner when he did it,' he explained. 'Kane. Man died recently, leaving everything to his sole heir. Which means, if Mister Harper really is his son ... then he owns half of Aegis, and he's our goddamned *boss*.'

Now he put the gun away.

'So, what *next*, boss?' he asked, almost mockingly.

12

CSI: PROSPERITY

THE RADIO CALL TO PROSPERITY'S POLICE FORCE WAS BRIEF.

Cortez had taken the call, and Harper had kept it simple; there was a body found, a possible mining accident, but he stretched the words "possible accident" just enough to catch her attention. If it'd been Carson, the chances were it would have been ignored completely, but her response was equally measured. From her undertone, Harper could tell she understood.

'No one touches anything,' Harper instructed the people around him. 'This is now a potential crime scene.'

Ashfield's smile remained fixed.

'Of course. Although ...'

'Although there's a chance this guy owns us,' Delaney finished the comment. 'Well, I mean, if he's telling the truth, his dad owned us, so I'm assuming *he* owns us. And if the boss tells you—'

'I'm not your boss,' Harper interrupted. 'My father helped create Aegis, but on his death the shares went back to the board, or something along those lines. It's a discussion that needs to be had, and one of the reasons I wanted to speak to Mason Carrick.'

If Delaney was surprised at this, he didn't show it, simply standing more at ease.

'Well then,' he said. 'It's going to take a while for the police to turn up. Shall we go have a drink in the office?'

Harper gave a smile.

'I'll wait here,' he replied. 'Best to make sure nobody disturbs the scene.'

'Okay then,' Ashfield walked over to the tunnel wall and sat against it. 'Looks like we're here for a while then.'

CORTEZ AND CARSON BOTH ARRIVED WITH PROPER PROCEDURE: lights, crime scene tape, and a small team of crime scene officers, all wearing gas monitors and masks. Having been brought down to where the body had been found, a teenager with long hair under a hard hat, mask and a hoodie was now photographing the scene, his face betraying nothing.

As he worked, Cortez explained he was the town's crime photographer, but Harper suspected he was more of a photography major, or perhaps a local high schooler doing this on the side, and wondered whether they'd all had to sit through the bullshit safety procedurals presentation he had.

The photographer was young and probably green to this, but Harper could see how he lingered over certain details: the crystalline formations, the burns on Moses's clothes, and the expression that death had frozen in place.

Cortez stood beside Harper as they watched him work. She had brought her forensics kit, there being an apparent lack of a localised forensics department in Prosperity, and had been checking the area, under duress, from Aegis.

'Gas?' she asked, her tone professionally neutral.

'That's our assumption,' Ashfield answered quickly. 'Our sensors indicate—'

'I wasn't asking you.' Cortez turned to Harper. 'What do *you* think?'

'I think,' Harper said carefully, 'that in my admittedly limited experience, gas rarely leaves chemical burns or crystalline deposits.'

Echoing down from the entrance, Harper heard the distinctive rumble of vehicles. The cavalry was arriving, although he wasn't sure whose side they were on. Bickford would likely be here soon, too; the mayor would need to maintain his fiction of authority, even if Aegis seemed to pull the strings right now.

How many accidents had the man covered up, and how many stories had he buried in these tunnels?

Emerging outside, he saw the mountain was casting long shadows, the lunchtime sun given way to mid-afternoon, turning the mine buildings into dark silhouettes.

A small crowd had gathered over the last hour, too. The performance of official investigation was playing out as though scripted; the Prosperity coroner's van stood open and, as Harper stepped aside, with the first examination and photos taken, Moses's body was being sealed away into the vehicle by Aegis "miners" under the watchful eye of Doctor Chen, who had apparently driven the van here.

Harper also noted Bickford's arrival, the mayor working the gathered folk with his usual flair. Some townsfolk had come up as well, the presence of police, medics, and fire services having drawn volunteer servicemen and women;

Harper could see Maggie Hawkins moving around in the crowd, wearing the uniform of a volunteer fire chief.

The mayor had arrived ten minutes after Cortez, late enough to maintain his authority while avoiding actual involvement. He moved between clusters of onlookers, his concerned expression unwavering. He was the picture of a concerned citizen, not a conspirator. Grief replaced guilt in all aspects here.

'It's a terrible tragedy,' he was saying to anyone who'd listen. 'The gas, you know. We've been saying how dangerous these old tunnels can be. It's a shame somebody wouldn't listen to us, or follow the signs we'd left on the roads.'

The story was already forming. Harper could see town elders nodding, sharing their own tales of mining deaths and invisible killers lurking in the dark. Bickford was building the narrative to explain away one more body, hiding one more secret; but something felt different this time. Harper caught it in the way Doctor Chen stood apart from the crowd, her doctor's eye catching details others missed.

Eddie Hawkins, who'd arrived with her, was studying the mine entrance, probably connecting dots that didn't quite align. He also didn't seem scared of Aegis at the moment; Harper noticed that Ashfield and Delaney hadn't moved towards him either, aware that to do so would raise even more questions. Meanwhile, Cortez's unease as to what was happening here was clear. She kept her distance from Carson, marking the divide between actual law and bought authority.

'Don't worry, everybody. The autopsy will confirm our initial findings,' Ashfield said smoothly, appearing at Harper's shoulder. 'These accidents, while terribly tragic, are unfortunately common in old mining operations.'

'That they are,' Harper replied pleasantly. 'Though I've never seen one that leaves marks like that on a man's clothes. Have you?'

The corporate mask slipped for a moment. Then Ashfield adjusted his glasses, buying time before responding.

'I'm sure the coroner will explain everything in his report.'

'I'm sure he will,' Harper said, meeting the man's eyes. 'Just like he explained the other deaths, the ones that also probably don't quite match their official stories.'

At this, Doctor Chen's voice cut through the murmuring crowd.

'I would like to examine the body.'

Bickford had been mid-sentence, beginning some long speech about tragic accidents and safety protocols, keeping the same party line going, but Doctor Chen's interruption silenced him. His politician's smile didn't quite reach his eyes as he turned slowly to face her.

'Doctor Chen,' he said, 'I understand your concern, and thank you for driving Doctor Wolfman's van here, but—'

'But Wolfman is forty miles away, already helping the police on a case, and won't be back here until tomorrow,' Doctor Chen stood her ground, her medical bag clutched like a shield. 'I drove the coroner's van down here with Eddie Hawkins beside me. I've got experience with mining deaths, I've studied every H2S fatality in these hills for the past decade, and I'm the most qualified person to make an initial assessment.'

'Now, Rachel,' Bickford's voice carried just enough condescension to ripple through the crowd, 'I get that your pop died the same way, and this'll be personal, but there are procedures.'

'Damn right this is personal, and absolutely there are

procedures. Procedures that allow for preliminary examinations by a licensed medical professional,' Doctor Chen replied sharply, pulling papers from her bag. 'County Code forty-seven point three. I've already signed the forms ... and it's not *Rachel*, Mayor Bickford. It's *Doctor Chen*, because I am a *licensed medical professional.*'

Harper watched the interplay with interest. Doctor Chen's confidence wasn't just professional. There was something personal in how she stood, and how she faced down the mayor's authority. This wasn't just about Moses Mathers' body, or her father's apparent death years earlier, and this wasn't the same woman he had spoken to the previous night at a homemade chilli dinner party.

'The scene's secured and examined, sir,' Cortez added, authority in her voice. 'And Doctor Chen is right. We need her expertise right now.'

Bickford's smile thinned as he glanced at Delaney. Harper guessed that some kind of silent communication was passing between them; a calculation of risks and consequences if they let this carry on.

'The sheriff—'

'Sheriff Coble isn't here,' Cortez replied firmly, cutting Bickford off. 'It's me and Carson, Mayor Bickford.'

'Carson has seniority in time served—'

'Carson might have been an officer for longer than me, but my father was the sheriff before Carson was even in the force, and I grew up in that building, as well you know,' Cortez snapped now. 'The Cortezes have been the law here for generations, and until Sheriff Coble returns, I'll take responsibility.'

'Of course,' Bickford finally said, holding a finger up to pause Carson as he went to object. 'And, of course, if something goes wrong, *you* will be the name that is placed on the report, and take the responsibility for that, too, right, Cortez? Although I'm sure our enthusiastic *licensed medical professional* here will find this is just another tragic case of—'

'I'll find what I find,' Doctor Chen cut him off, already moving towards the coroner's van. 'And it will be in my official report.'

The threat in those last words was clear. There was no cover-up being made here, no convenient stories to be told.

Bickford wouldn't be in charge.

'A moment, Mister Harper,' Eddie's voice was barely a whisper, appearing at Harper's side, using the crowd's attention on Doctor Chen and Mayor Bickford to mask their conversation. The old historian looked shaken, but his eyes were sharp, and Harper wondered whether he had been hassled again by Aegis, although he was sure he'd have noticed if it had happened.

As they moved away from the crowd, Eddie nodded towards the entrance.

'Moses had no reason to be in that part of the mine,' he said quietly, watching the mayor from afar. 'None at all.'

Harper studied the older man's face for a moment.

'You sound certain of that.'

'We mapped the goldmines together for years,' Eddie said, his voice catching, the memory probably triggering something. 'That western tunnel was sealed and condemned after a collapse in fifty-two. Moses knew that. He had the documentation – hell, he wrote half of it.'

The sun still caught the mine entrance as Harper watched Ashfield, who was watching them; the corporate mask couldn't quite hide his interest in their conversation.

'Yet they reopened it,' Harper said softly, 'without permits, I'm guessing.'

'Without anything,' Eddie's hands shook slightly as he pulled out his notebook. 'Moses called me a few months back, said he'd found something on the old survey maps. Something about the western reaches. Said it didn't make sense.'

'What didn't?'

'The mineral deposits, the composition.' Eddie's voice dropped lower, and his face turned slightly away from Harper's, looking towards the wall, as though afraid someone might read his lips. 'He said he didn't think gold was the only thing they were mining. That maybe it never was.'

A shadow fell across them; Delaney was moving closer, trying to look casual about it. Eddie tucked his notebook away.

'He wasn't a rookie, Harper,' he said, now louder, his voice carrying. 'He was always too curious about these tunnels, but he wasn't somebody who'd walk into something unaware. And never that deep without a reason.'

Delaney said nothing, pretending to check his phone. Eddie's eyes met Harper's, and the message was clear.

There was more to say. Much more.

Harper nodded, and, looking back to Delaney, he spoke, his voice also louder.

'I hope Mister Hawkins here isn't going to be hassled while he's around.'

'I've already made the call,' Delaney said. 'It was just over-eagerness on my men's side. They won't touch him until Mason Carrick returns. Besides, whether you own the company or not, your father was still a hell of a man. So, therefore, because of that, we'll give you a little respect, listen to what you have to say for the moment. And, if you're vouching for Eddie Hawkins, then we'll give you that, as well.'

Doctor Chen was closing up the coroner's van. Harper, nodding to Eddie, walked over to her quickly.

'Doctor Chen,' he said, pausing her from entering the van. As she turned to face him, he quickly and quietly passed the folded handkerchief to her.

'There's a liquid in the middle of this which I wiped off my hard hat,' he said. 'It's dripping in the tunnels, and I don't think it should be there. If there's any way you can find time to check it out, I'd greatly appreciate it.'

Doctor Chen stared at him, narrowing her eyes as she tried to work out what he was doing. 'Why do you care?' she asked.

'Just curiosity.' Harper gave the smallest of smiles.

As he moved away and looked around the remaining townsfolk, he caught Maggie Hawkins watching him, but the look she gave him was one of utter hatred. He wasn't sure what had changed her opinion, but he'd work that one out later as he saw Mayor Bickford making a beeline towards him.

'I understand you're more than we thought you were, Mister Harper,' he said, his shit-eating grin back on his face. Harper had watched him talking to Ashfield and Delaney, and guessed the mayor of Prosperity now had a vague idea of who Harper's possible father was. It wasn't ideal, but it was expected at some point. Bickford, meanwhile, hadn't waited for Harper to respond, continuing to talk.

'You know, when I asked you in the jail cell who your daddy was, it would have been a lot easier for you if you'd just answered.'

'When you asked me who my "daddy" was, it was none of

your business,' Harper replied coldly. 'Just as it's none of your business right now.'

'I think you'll find that anything that Aegis, or any of its employees, board or even owners do is my business,' Bickford muttered.

'I can assure you he's definitely past tense right now,' Harper retorted. 'There's no "do" here, only "did".'

Bickford's expression didn't change.

'Nevertheless, Mister Harper,' he said, outstretching his hand. 'I met your father several times over the last couple of years. He was a good man, and it was an honour to have known him.'

'I'm sure it was.' Harper almost refused to shake the hand, but then decided that for the moment it was better having Bickford as a confused ally, than somebody going against him.

'So when you said you were visiting some of your father's locations, was this just a check-up ... or are you now part of the board?' Bickford's eyes narrowed, and Harper knew he was hunting for anything that could give him an idea of what his current situation was.

'No offence, Mayor Bickford, but I have no idea what your connection to Aegis is, even though you claim it's your business, and I don't think I should talk about this until I get confirmation,' Harper confirmed, looking back at the street. 'Even those guys aren't sure why I'm here. So, why the hell should I be telling you?'

'Because I'm the elected official?'

Harper turned back to Bickford.

'I don't think anybody's been "elected" in Prosperity for a very long time,' he said calmly but crudely. 'And I'd appreciate it if you left me to my own devices.'

'Mason Carrick will be here within the hour,' Bickford almost pouted.

'Great. Then you'll find out after I speak with him later.'

With this stated, Harper turned, looking around for Cortez. He realised he'd arrived without a lift back into Prosperity, Carson's escort duties no longer likely to be happening, as the other deputy now glared impotently at Doctor Chen as she drove the coroner's van away, Eddie Hawkins sitting beside her, likely receiving a lift home, or back to Maggie's. Harper still wasn't sure if Maggie's was Eddie's home, or if he just visited a *lot*.

As it was, it was Maggie Hawkins that walked over to him.

'Looks to me like you kept a lot of things from a lot of people,' she muttered, glancing back at the mine. 'All that time I thought you were an ally.'

'It's complicated,' Harper replied.

'Well, you can tell me all about it while you're checking out,' Maggie glanced back at the mine, and at Ashfield. 'Everybody knows that if you work for Aegis, you stay at the Goldstrike.'

'Goddamn it, Maggie,' Harper growled before halting himself. 'Did you drive here or did you come with others?'

'I drove. Why?'

'Good,' Harper replied, looking around for her car. 'Drive me back to the guest house and I'll explain everything.'

'And why should I trust you?'

'Because when I examined Moses, I swiped his notebook,' Harper said, patting the pocket he'd placed it into after closing the dead man's eyes. 'And you'll note I didn't give it to *them*.'

Maggie glowered at Harper.

'One journey,' she said. 'And only because I want you out faster.'

'One journey's all I'll need,' Harper replied.

13

TRUTH SEEKER

'Go on then,' Maggie Hawkins snarled as they drove away from the mines towards Prosperity. At least Harper felt it was a snarl; it was interesting to see Maggie's posture, her expression, her tone, her entire personality had changed the moment she found out that he was connected somehow to Aegis. Gone was the friendly guesthouse owner. Now, she was every inch the US Marine she'd once been.

'Look, honestly, there's more going on than you realise.'

'What I realise, Harper, is you came into my town over twenty-four hours ago ... and in that time you've caused fights with Aegis, bonded with my father, found a spy in my guesthouse, been secretly bugged, and now, arriving at the mine to gain a simple apology, you've managed to find the body of Moses Mathers, a man who's been gone for two months.'

Maggie glanced at him angrily.

'And now I hear your pop, who you claim is dead, is Mason Carrick's late partner, and that he *created* this goddamn company? Was anything you told me legit? Did you get that tattoo in a dime store?'

'I *earned* this bloody tattoo,' Harper snapped, tired of being attacked. 'And you're not the first person to kick off with me today, so please, if you really want to, get it out of your system now because you're not getting a second chance.'

Maggie went to speak, paused, and shook her head, gritting her teeth, her lips thin.

Harper took a deep breath.

'Ashfield and Delaney took me down into the mine to teach me a lesson – whether they were going to attack me and leave me for dead next to the body of Moses Mathers, I don't know,' he explained. 'All I know is I was able to outsmart them and it was only at the end that I had to give up who my father truly was.'

'He *was*?' Maggie asked. 'So that part's true?'

'He's dead,' Harper confirmed. 'But look, I never really knew my dad, okay? When I was a kid, him and my mum divorced, he moved back to America and I saw him every now and then. Around twenty years back he quit the military and started up his own security company with Mason Carrick.'

'Aegis?'

Harper nodded.

'I think it had a different name at the time, but it was Aegis in all but identity,' he muttered. 'Over the next few years, whenever I came to visit my dad, it wasn't really visiting. It was sitting in corners while he spoke to senators and politicians and recruited soldiers to do his bidding. Same as I'd done when I was a kid, really, but this was more cold, more "business", if you get what I mean. More boardrooms, less cookouts. After a while, I simply stopped visiting. By the time I was sixteen, I didn't even know where he was. I'd gain the occasional postcard from him, usually somewhere tropical or with a dictatorship that needed something fixed. You know, the Silk Road, but for mercenaries.'

Maggie reluctantly nodded and Harper realised she probably knew the post-service route for mercenaries better than most people; US Marines were a common candidate for such agencies.

'Anyway, I wasn't lying when I said I was SRR,' Harper continued. 'I joined the RAF at sixteen. By the time I was nineteen, I'd been pegged for better things and I was moved. I joined the SRR when I was twenty-one. Worked my way up the ranks, was sent to officer training, all the usual stuff. By the time I left, I was a captain. My father, meanwhile, made millions off the backs of South African warlords and companies that required strong-arming. You know, small towns that weren't listening to the "authority". Sometimes he'd be the carrot, most of the time he'd be the stick.'

'Towns like Prosperity?'

'You tell me,' Harper shrugged. 'Over the years, I kept an eye on him. After all, when you're working for UK Special Forces, you have an element of leeway when it comes to checking into people. Then about six months ago, we went on an op, my squad and me. There'd been militant pirates attacking trade vessels off the coast of Myanmar. There was talk that the security firm that had been looking after the vessels had been taking backhanders, though. Can you guess the name?'

He looked around as they pulled into the main street of Prosperity, driving through it.

'We gained information that there was going to be an attack on one of the vessels and we went to intercept it; we helo'ed down to the port and then came up beside the vessel itself on speed boats. We arrived during a firefight; the militant insurgents had already tried to take over, and it was at this point we gained new information. Aegis wasn't actually defending them – the warlords that controlled the pirates had paid more money than the shipping company it seemed, and Aegis decided they were going to be Switzerland, and sit back and do nothing. That wasn't our remit, however, so we went in guns blazing.'

He stared out of the window, remembering the scene.

'There was a battle in the container area. I took down two insurgents, but there was a third with a bead on me. An Aegis operative, masked and armoured, came out and warned me, even though they weren't supposed to. I would have been dead – he took them down as they gained a bead on me, but in the process was shot. He was wearing body armour, but the bullet clipped him on the neck, and he was bleeding out. I pulled the mask off ... and I realised it was my father.'

'Shit.'

'I later found out he was personally commanding the operatives on the ship as part of the financial agreement. Taking down that insurgent was his last act, and it saved my life. I pulled off my helmet and knelt beside him, we had maybe three minutes before I watched his life fade from his eyes. He couldn't really speak; he spluttered blood at me, but he kept repeating one phrase over and over. "Make it right. Make it right."'

'What did he mean by that?' Maggie asked, now invested in the story.

'I didn't know,' Harper admitted, 'until months later. You see, with an SRR op, there aren't any public briefings or medals. We come in, do the job and then we leave, explain what happened in a report and move on, all under the table. As far as anyone else was concerned, Aegis had heroically stopped the pirates, led by my father, who died in the process – and I was happy to keep the lie. But then, about two months later, I received a message.'

He turned to face Maggie.

'By this point, we're talking three months ago,' he explained. 'I'd left the service—'

He paused, shaking his head to stop Maggie's inevitable next question.

'My choice. I felt I couldn't carry on right then, and they understood. Finding my father dead in my arms was enough to give anybody PTSD, and knowing I'd caused his death with my own lack of situational awareness was even worse. They didn't want someone with the yips in charge of a squad, and speaking to me, they could see I needed time. So, I was discharged, with the option that if I wanted to, I could always come back.'

'So, like a sabbatical?'

'Yeah, but they never work,' Harper shook his head. 'Think about it. When you were a Marine, if you gained a captain who everyone knew had been discharged due to mental health reasons, would you have blindly followed orders if they came back?'

'Maybe eventually.'

'Yeah. *Eventually*. The SRR? You need *immediate*. And if I'm being honest, I knew I'd done all this to prove myself to my dad. Now ...'

He sighed audibly.

'I'd gone to my father's funeral in Washington, and nobody spoke to me – I hadn't been part of his life, they didn't know me. It was like I was a ghost. After that, I returned to my family home, staying with my grandfather ... and a couple of months later, a disc turned up in the post. It had been sent from America, apparently from my father, and was one of those "if you're watching this, I'm dead" videos. A lot of soldiers make them, I've filmed one myself more than once. I'm guessing you've probably done something similar.'

'I wrote a letter,' Maggie admitted.

'Well, there you go.' Harper gave a smile. 'I don't know who sent the disc. What I do know is whoever did would likely have watched it first, and would have known exactly what my father was telling me to do.'

'Which was?'

Harper went to reply, but then paused, unsure how to explain this properly.

'Take down Aegis,' he muttered. 'Make it what it was supposed to be, not what it's become. Stop Mason Carrick from bastardising my father's creation.'

Maggie whistled at this.

'So what, you're going to use your father's shares to make the company better?'

'I didn't get any shares,' Harper admitted. 'After he died, there was a meeting with a lawyer in New York. They made a point of explaining to me that the board had a process. If either Mason or my father died, their shares would go into a trust, shared out amongst the operatives. I was fine with that – after all, this was a man I'd barely seen for years. What I did get given, however, was my father's other assets. A house in New York, some other properties, his bank balance, a few stocks, shares, crypto, all that kind of thing. Enough to give Liam Harper, recently retired from the UK Special Forces, a comfortable life if he so wanted it.'

'So, you're what, a millionaire?' Maggie smiled for the first time that drive. 'Because no offence, Harper, you could absolutely do better, style wise.'

'I don't want the money,' Harper shrugged. 'And I sure as hell don't deserve the money.'

'That's guilt speaking.'

'Well, whatever it is, I put most of the properties on the market, the profits to be funnelled into veterans' charities, and set up a trust with a solicitor to manage the rest of the fortune; he arranges a modest monthly allowance, and sets aside a portion for other charitable causes.'

'No offence, but this sounds like you're spotlighting here, and using it as atonement.'

'Whatever you want to call it.' Harper was rolling the flat stone over his fingers now, grounding himself with it.

'You could buy a better fidget toy though,' Maggie suggested.

Harper looked down at the small, smooth river stone, as if not having realised he was even using it.

'It's from the banks of the River Wye in Herefordshire, near where I did my training,' he explained. 'I picked it up on my last day, just before my first deployment.'

He held it up now, no larger than a fifty-pence piece, worn smooth by years in the river, and his rolling of it over his knuckles.

'It became my lucky charm, I suppose. I use it now as a grounding tool, especially when my, well, I suppose they're PTSD symptoms, flare up. The feel of the cool, smooth stone in my hand helps centre me, bringing me back to the present when memories threaten to overwhelm me,' he explained. 'And being from the River Wye, it's also a reminder of the skills I learned and the person I was before everything changed; a tangible connection to a time when things seemed simpler. I roll it between my fingers when I'm formulating a plan or making a difficult decision. Despite its small size, it's the one item I'm never without, even when I'm travelling light.'

'I have a lucky charm, too,' Maggie nodded. 'It's a Desert Eagle 1911 single-action, gas-operated, semi-automatic pistol.'

Harper laughed at this, the ice between them broken. By now, they had arrived at the guest house, and he turned to face Maggie.

'Look,' he said, 'I understand you suspect me. But I hope you can understand why I didn't want people to know. I'm not here to either help or hinder Aegis, I came here to see what they were doing, because they sure as hell aren't being some kind of private military service for people wanting to examine the mines. There's something far more going on here.'

Maggie nodded.

'So, what *are* you going to do, Harper?' she asked.

Climbing out of the car, Harper shrugged.

'Cards are on the table now,' he said. 'I reckon Mason Carrick will be back soon, and there'll be a reckoning. They'll either think I've come back to be the prodigal child, demanding what should be mine, or they'll think I've come back to raze Aegis to the ground. Either way, they'll be ready for a fight, and Prosperity is the battlefield.'

His tone grew dark now as he continued.

'We both know that something dodgy is going on, and now Mathers has been found. It's connected to Bickford, and I'll put money on the fact that he's the one who brought them in rather than them turning up themselves. All I need to do is prove what's going on—'

'And then what? Take it to the board?'

'The board don't care,' Harper shook his head. 'I'll be

closing Aegis's operations here down in a more permanent way.'

He grinned.

'And I could always do with an ally or two.'

'What about the notebook?' Maggie asked. As she did so, Harper pulled it out, examining it.

'I got the impression from your father that Moses was a man who liked to keep copious notes,' he said. 'With luck, something in here will help.'

'What, you can read gold prospector now?'

'Hell no,' Harper laughed. 'I'm giving it to your dad to do that. That's why I asked for a lift back.'

14

MAPS

After pulling up at the guesthouse, Maggie explained that she'd have to return later to evict Harper – although it felt a little more tongue-in-cheek and relaxed than the earlier conversation – as she needed to return her volunteer firefighter's gear back to the firehouse.

Entering the guesthouse, Harper saw the "hiking couple", Alan and Diane Parsons, heading up the stairs. They said nothing to him, and he wasn't sure if they even realised he was there. However, he did find Eddie in Maggie's kitchen, the elderly historian sitting at the long wooden table, with a variety of ancient-looking papers spread out in front of him.

He looked up as Harper approached, nodding at the fresh pot of coffee sat on the counter behind him.

'Help yourself,' he mumbled.

'Are you sure you should offer Maggie's items to everybody?' Harper smiled.

Eddie looked past Harper to see if Maggie had arrived with him, but Harper shook his head.

'She's gone to drop off her uniform at the firefighters' place,' he replied.

'Oh, that's good. Figure we've got an hour or so to ourselves,' Eddie started moving more sheets of paper around, as Harper poured a mug and sat opposite Eddie. Through the open window came the sound of the front door slamming, and both men tensed until they heard the Parsons heading down towards Main Street. They had obviously decided, now Harper was in the house, it wasn't worth staying around.

'Living with the enemy,' Eddie muttered to himself. 'Maggie's not happy about that.'

'Me neither,' Harper said as he reached into his jacket and pulled out the small notebook he'd taken from Moses's body. It was slightly water damaged and had stains, some of the ink blurred, but it was still readable.

'I need to show you something,' he said as he placed it on the table. 'Recognise it?'

'Of course. Jesus,' Eddie's breath caught as he stared down in horror. 'Where did you ...?'

'Took it when I found the body,' Harper replied. 'I was being watched, but I figured if I didn't do it, it'd disappear into an evidence bag and never come out. Or worse, it wouldn't even reach an evidence bag. Somebody somewhere would find a notebook in their pocket, and we'd never, ever find out what Moses Mathers had found.'

'Moses was always making notes,' Eddie said softly, still not touching the book. 'Even when we were kids, he said you never knew what might be important later.'

He gave a bitter laugh.

'I guess he was right about that in the end.'

'I think he might have left you a message,' Harper

suggested, opening the notebook to a dog-eared page halfway through. 'I was flicking through this while I was driving back with your daughter. I saw this, look.'

Eddie squinted at the hasty scrawl.

'Found something in William's journal, second survey, hidden in plain sight. Need to check ...' His voice trailed off. 'That's the last thing he wrote in this. Probably went to the mines directly afterwards. Stupid bastard.'

'You don't seem surprised.'

'He didn't write that before he died,' Eddie shrugged. 'We spoke about it a day before he disappeared. I was all for running through the books, he wanted to go straight to the source.'

'He mentions a second survey?' Harper asked.

At the question, Eddie started pointing at the maps and documents on the table.

'The original Geological Survey of Prosperity is the survey he's talking about,' he explained. 'These are the ones that started the gold rush. Thing is, there were rumours of another survey, a private one commissioned by the Bickfords, but no-one ever found it.'

'Bickfords were still big back then?'

'Oh, God, no.' Eddie looked up at Harper. 'Bickfords were one of many people scrabbling around at the time. They weren't anything like the people they are now. But they had the mine rights, such as they were back then. Seth Bickford, the pappy of them all won it in a card game. Imagine that! Winning a goddamned mountain in a card game, and for ten years not being able to do anything with it until someone found gold, by which time your son has the power.'

'So, if people were finding gold, I'm guessing the Bickfords made money?'

Again, Eddie shook his head.

'They leased out areas, but they didn't expect profits, so they didn't *demand* profits,' he said. 'They spent years watching people make thousands off their gold, and the contracts were cast iron. They didn't have a way to make money from them, even with their new fake "owner" pushing to change the terms.'

'Did that work?'

'Hell no. All he could do was hold the gold for the miners in a vault, deep in the mountain. But we know how that ended.'

'So, if they didn't make money from the mountain, then why would they look for another survey? Why not keep with the official one?'

'No idea. And until someone found it, we wouldn't know.'

'And you think Moses might have?'

'Look at the margin.' Eddie pointed to a tiny notation, almost lost in the water damage on the notebook. 'WB, personal ledger. Survey bound cover.'

'William Bickford's accounting records?'

Eddie nodded.

'The son I mentioned. Moses told me he found a reference in William's journal – the Bickfords, they were meticulous record keepers. Still are. Tom Bickford's got filing cabinets full of paperwork going back generations in his mansion. But they don't have this survey,' Eddie's eyes lit up with the enthusiasm of a historian on the trail of something. 'That's what's beautiful about it. You see, William was clever. He knew at the time the gold rush was about to kick off. Gold had been found in the eighteen-seventies. People were coming from all over the state to look. His father's money-pit poker win was finally gaining interest, but they were locked out because of badly written contracts. However, he'd found what he believed to be another motherlode, outside the areas leased.'

'I'm guessing they never found anything, though?'

'We don't know. He hid the real survey inside a ledger. As far as anyone else was concerned, it was just another dusty account book. Who'd bother looking there? And the Bickfords, well, once William died, they never knew, because the stupid bastard didn't trust his kids enough to tell them. Each generation just kept the records, never knowing what was hidden inside one of them.'

Harper took a sip of coffee.

'Is that why they closed the library?'

'Has to be. They're searching for something, but they don't know exactly what they're looking for ...'

'Eddie?' Harper asked. 'You're a historian. They hired you for the history. Did Aegis hire you to find this survey?'

Eddie licked his lips, reached across for his own mug of coffee, and downed the remainder.

'Yeah,' he admitted eventually, his voice quiet, almost contrite. 'Bickford's been looking for decades. He knew Moses and I were hunting it as well; amateur treasure hunters, rather than a family affair. Moses got drunk a few months ago and mentioned he had an idea where it could be. When Bickford brought in Aegis, they spoke to Moses about it. When he disappeared a couple of months back, they came to me and asked *me* to find it. Offered me a lot of money for it. Of course, I protested, said I didn't know, I'd have a look for them, but after several weeks of nothing, with me mainly trying to work out where the hell Moses had slunk off to, they obviously got tired.'

He stared off, distant now.

'I always wondered if they'd questioned Moses before he disappeared. Asked him what he knew. Maybe they assumed that whatever he had in his knowledge was the same as I had, and therefore I was playing them. The thing is, they don't need to keep searching.'

'Why not?'

Eddie smiled.

'Because I found the survey three days ago.'

He walked over to his battered leather satchel, sat by the door. Picking it up, he returned to the table, his movements careful as he eased the satchel onto a chair.

'Three days,' Harper said. 'You've been sitting on this for three days.'

'I had to be sure,' Eddie's hands trembled slightly as he pulled the ledger from his satchel. His fingers traced the cracked leather binding, and it was almost as if he was hesitating before opening it.

'Is this why they came to you yesterday?' Harper asked. 'Did they know you'd found this?'

'There's no way they could have,' Eddie protested, looking up. 'I mean, sure the library knew what I was looking for and I didn't tell anybody apart from ...'

He trailed off.

'Let me guess,' Harper asked. 'You mentioned you might have found a really important document to your daughter over dinner in front of the Parsons – and then the following morning, Aegis appears and starts asking you to come and have a chat with them in the mine.'

Eddie said nothing, just weakly smiling, knowing that Harper had pretty much hit the nail on the head.

'You had this at the house.' Maggie's voice came from the

doorway, as both men jumped. 'You had this here the whole damn time.'

Harper watched as Eddie's hands instinctively moved to protect the book, even as his daughter advanced into the kitchen, the evening light now catching the dust motes stirred up by his movement.

'Where else could I keep it safe?' Eddie wouldn't meet his daughter's eyes. 'The library's been compromised. My office, my house, they're watching me!'

'So, you bring it here?' Maggie was already moving to the windows, checking sight lines. Harper recognised the economy of her movements; Marine training never faded. 'You put us all at risk?'

'I didn't put anyone at risk.' Eddie tried to play down the argument. 'If any of those pricks had turned up here, I knew you could talk them down.'

'And what about the spies upstairs?'

'Well, I didn't know they were spies back then, did I?'

'You bloody idiot old man,' Maggie was furious, glancing back at Harper. 'Did you know about this?'

'Hey, I've only just found out.' Harper held his hands up. 'Don't evict me on this as well.'

'You're evicting Harper?'

'No, I'm not evicting Harper, goddammit.' Maggie shook her head.

'I can take care of myself, you know.' Eddie's voice carried the stubbornness of age.

'Really?' Maggie turned, placing her hands on her hips. 'Just like Moses could?'

The words hung heavy in the air. There was a moment of uncomfortable silence as Harper watched Maggie's face soften immediately, regretting them.

'Dad, I ...'

'As I said to Harper here before you appeared to chastise me, daughter, Moses found a reference to this,' Eddie interrupted haughtily, carefully opening the ledger. 'William Bickford's personal journal mentioned hiding the original survey inside an accounting book. It's taken me two months, literally since the day he went missing, to figure out which one – every day checking the library.'

'I thought you said the Bickfords had all their paperwork at the mansion?'

'They do, but the more public items are on display in the museum,' Eddie smiled.

'Museum?'

'Bickford's got his own family museum in the library,' Maggie added. 'Prick thinks that if he does that, he can make himself look like he's king of the town or something. Anyway, he swaps things in and out now and then, mainly for the tourists to "ooh" and "aah" at, and you're allowed to look at them.'

'Carrie the librarian doesn't really give a damn about them though, and if you want to sit down and have a flick through, as long as no Bickford's in the area, she's quite happy to let you,' Eddie explained. 'A few days ago, I found the right book. Funny enough, he was about to ask for it back, as it'd been on display for almost a year. No one had realised what they had.'

Harper leant forwards to see what the ledger showed. Between pages of mundane nineteenth-century bookkeeping lay the truth; a carefully preserved survey map, its ink still crisp after over a hundred and fifty years.

Harper frowned as he looked at it; the geological formations marked on them bore little resemblance to the public records he had seen, but even then it was almost like reading another language. But he could notice, by comparing this survey with the one that Eddie held next to it, that areas on one, officially marked as worthless, showed extensive mineral deposits in the other – and in the margin, handwritten notes detailed something labelled only as “anomalous formations”.

'Bloody hell,' Harper muttered, noting how the western tunnels, the same ones Aegis now claimed were too dangerous to enter, were extensively mapped with these in the Bickford survey. 'No wonder they've been tearing the library apart.'

'Look at the dates,' Eddie said, tapping the corner of a yellow map. 'William Bickford commissioned this survey in eighteen seventy, five years before the gold vanished.'

Eddie looked up at his daughter, who, against her better judgement, had moved closer towards the table, looking down at the pieces.

'The Bickfords were losing money back then, you see,' he began. 'The mine was making money for everyone else. Jonathan Caldwell was the mine owner, shall we say, but he was nothing more than a figurehead. The Bickfords owned the mine, but still couldn't afford the federal taxes. So Caldwell was brought in to “buy” the land from them for a dollar, which meant the fees they had to pay were far smaller. Caldwell wasn't local and came in as a stooge for them. But we know the Bickfords were in charge still because several of the older institutions still have some of their letters to creditors, begging for more time to pay off the fees and loans.'

He pulled out a folded sheet from between the maps.

'But here, look, after the gold was stolen and the “bad air” deaths started, suddenly they're flush with cash. Buying up half the town while everyone else is running scared and Caldwell, by this point, is on the run from the authorities.'

'They knew what was down there. Was the story about stolen gold just that, a story?' Harper asked.

'More than that, it was *their* story.' Eddie's eyes now gleamed. 'Think about it. Your mine's failing, the gold's pretty much tapped out – but hell, you never made any money from it anyway – and the debt collectors still want their flesh, but you can find something else in the ground, something valuable but dangerous. You can't mine it, not with 1870s technology, but you can wait.'

'So, you create a legend about stolen gold,' Maggie added, catching on. 'Blame the deaths on "bad air", ignoring the fact they're men you sent down to the closed off areas. Throw Caldwell under the bus. Make people think he stole it, while it's in your possession. Then buy up the town cheap, when everyone runs.'

'And then,' Harper finished, 'one hundred and fifty years later, when you've got the right experience, equipment, and the right buyers, you bring in a private security force to help you dig it up. Only now it's not the Bickfords doing the digging; they're just taking their cut ... but they still don't know where to dig safely.'

He looked back at Eddie.

'But Moses figured this out?'

'He was getting there,' Eddie touched his friend's notebook reverently. 'That mad bastard Tucker gave him the clues. He'd gone for a job with Aegis, and they gave him a tour, and he saw there were reopened pathways and routes underground that, as a local – someone who grew up in the town – he knew you didn't go down. He mentioned it to Moses, and, well, Moses knew the stolen gold story never added up. Two million in gold bullion back then doesn't just vanish. He kept saying follow the money, and the money led to the Bickfords.'

Harper went to reply, but a faint rumble of engines in the distance paused him.

Cars were heading towards them.

'I bet you these'll match the chemical traces you found on Moses,' Maggie had moved back to the table, her anger forgotten in the face of revelation. Harper had started to reply but stopped; the car engines were louder now, and through the window, he caught the glint of a setting sun on black paint.

'Looks like your daddy's best friend's turned up and wants to have a chat with the prodigal son,' Maggie spoke darkly, staring at the road. Through Maggie's kitchen window, they watched the motorcade roll to a stop. Three black Suburbans, flanked by Aegis vehicles, chrome gleaming in the setting sun. The entire street had gone quiet, curtains twitching in windows as neighbours watched. Eddie carefully closed the ledger as the sound of car doors opening carried clearly through the window.

'Where are you going to hide it?' Harper asked, already scanning the room for an exit strategy in case one was needed.

'Sometimes,' Eddie replied with a slight smile as he placed the map back into the cover of the ledger, 'the best place to hide something is where they've already looked.'

He moved quickly for his age, sliding the ledger back into his satchel just as footsteps sounded on the porch. The knock, when it came, was precise and corporate. Three sharp raps that expected to be answered. Maggie opened the door to find Mayor Bickford and Ashfield standing there, their expensive suits somehow making them look more dangerous than tactical gear would have.

Behind them, Aegis security had taken positions around the vehicles; professional and obvious about it. Harper couldn't see Delaney though, and wondered if this was deliberate – Ashfield once more trying to establish his dominance.

'Miss Hawkins,' Bickford's politician's smile didn't reach his eyes. 'Is Mister Harper available?'

'That depends,' Harper said, walking through from the kitchen. 'Who's asking?'

'Mason Carrick would like a word,' Ashfield's tone was carefully neutral. 'He's very interested in meeting Dominic Kane's son.'

'I'm sure he is.'

'He's waiting at my residence,' Bickford added. 'We have a car waiting.'

'You have several,' Harper replied dryly. 'I'll need witnesses.'

'You don't trust me?'

'I don't trust him,' Harper pointed at Ashfield. 'He tried to kill me in a mine today.'

'Don't exaggerate, Mister Harper, or we might need to discuss your flagrant disregard of safety protocols,' Ashfield replied quite amicably, as if having a chat with a friend.

'Either way, I feel a little exposed. I want witnesses.'

'Fine. Miss Hawkins and her father—'

'Have already had run-ins with Aegis, and I don't trust people like Blaine and Lucas. How about both of Prosperity's deputies? I'm guessing the sheriff isn't back from his trip?'

'That won't be—' Bickford started, but Ashfield cut him off.

'Of course. We understand the need for ... transparency,'

he replied as he pulled out his phone. 'I'll have them meet us there.'

'No,' Harper held his ground. 'We'll wait until they arrive. Then? *They* drive me. You lead, we follow.'

A flash of something crossed Bickford's face – anger? Fear? – but Ashfield simply nodded.

'I'll make the call.'

Maggie didn't invite anyone into the guesthouse, and it was a tense five minutes on the porch steps until a Ford SSV pulled up; Cortez was driving, Carson riding shotgun.

'I understand I'm a goddamned driver again?' Cortez shouted out, and Harper smiled as he climbed into Cortez's Ford, sitting on the back seat like the first time he had when riding in one of these. Through the windscreen, he could see Eddie and Maggie watching from the porch, concerned looks on their faces.

'Either of you armed?' he asked quietly.

'Standard issue,' Cortez replied from behind the wheel. Carson, passenger seat, simply patted his holster.

'Good,' Harper watched the lead Suburban pull away, Cortez pulling out to follow. 'Let's go meet the family.'

15

DOC HOLLIDAY

The Bickford mansion stood defiantly, white brick and old, its wide columns running along the front porch. Through the windscreen of Cortez's Ford, Harper watched it loom closer; a house built to impress, even if it didn't have much to back it up anymore.

The motorcade swept up the long driveway, past the heavy iron gates, with their video-call system that still looked out of place against the rust eating into the bars. The roof sloped gently, its tiles bleached by years of harsh Nevada sun; the shutters were warped, the paint peeling, but they still hung in place, stubborn, like everything else in Prosperity.

The windows were tall and arched, their glass catching the afternoon sunlight in a way that made it hard to see inside.

The Suburban cavalcade pulled up in a practised formation; a protective circle that just happened to block any easy exit. Cortez noticed it too; Harper caught her slight frown as she parked, positioning the Ford for a fast departure if needed.

Leaving the vehicle, Harper studied the mansion. Those columns had seen a lot of history. *How many secrets had passed through those doors? How many deals had been made in those rooms while Prosperity slowly died around them?*

And now Mason Carrick was waiting inside, yet another powerful man come to do business with the Bickfords.

Some things never changed.

Cortez checked her holster, a practised movement that could have been habit or warning.

'All set?' she asked.

Harper nodded, already moving. The front steps creaked slightly under his feet as he climbed them, Cortez and an incredibly reluctant Carson flanking him.

Ahead of them, Ashfield held the heavy front door open, his corporate manner perfectly in place.

'Welcome to the Bickford residence,' he said smoothly. 'Mason's waiting in the study.'

The house smelled of old wood and furniture polish, with an undertone of damp that no amount of money could quite mask. Inside, the grandeur continued with crystal chandeliers, oil paintings of stern-faced men who were probably Bickfords throughout history, and a curved staircase that swept up to the upper floor. But like outside, although it was painted up and looked fresh, there was still a tiredness to it all. The carpet on the stairs looked slightly worn in the middle, and the very faintest of water stains marked the ceiling's elaborate cornicing.

Ashfield led them down a hallway lined with more paintings. These were newer though, nothing more than photographs really, showing the current Mayor Bickford's achievements. Civic awards, newspaper clippings, grip-and-grin shots with politicians. A history of power, carefully curated. Bickford stood in the doorway, smiling widely.

'Welcome, Mister Harper,' he said, hand outstretched to shake once more. Harper didn't really want to shake his hand again, but saw on one wall a rifle, what looked to be a lever-action Winchester. Bickford's chest puffed out, and he reached up to take it off the poles.

'This here is an absolute one-of-a-kind,' he smiled. 'This isn't just a rifle – it's a piece of American history. A Winchester Model 1873, the "Gun that Won the West." They made these beauties during a time when every inch of land, every dusty road, held a story. This rifle was more than a weapon – it was survival, a tool, a trusted companion.'

He held it up to the light, letting the intricate grain of the walnut stock catch the glow.

'See this stock? Solid American walnut, aged beautifully, hasn't warped an inch in a hundred and fifty years. Winchester knew how to make a rifle that could handle the grit and grind of the frontier. Cowboys, lawmen, even outlaws carried these because they could rely on them, rain or shine.'

'Can I?' Harper held a hand up to examine the rifle and almost reluctantly, like giving across a child, Bickford passed it over.

'And you're right, this one's special,' he continued as Harper stared down the barrel. 'Not just because it's still in working condition, but because of who held it. This rifle belonged to none other than John Henry Holliday – "Doc" Holliday, the gunslinger, gambler, and the fastest draw in the West. It's no dime novel tale, either. William Bickford bought this directly off Doc himself in late 1875, when he passed through Prosperity, helping hunt for the thieves of the stolen gold.'

Harper turned the rifle over in his hands, his fingers tracing the smooth wood of the stock and the cool steel of the barrel. He thumbed the lever, testing its action. It slid partway open, but then caught with a faint metallic click.

Harper paused, raising an eyebrow.

'Lever's sticking,' he said, working it gently back and forth. The action refused to move smoothly, catching just short of fully cycling.

Bickford, however, waved a dismissive hand.

'Oh, that's just her age. She's been through more than a century and a half of use. Old rifles like this, they've got their quirks.'

Harper *hmm*ed, not entirely convinced, remembering Maggie's comments.

'Damn fool couldn't work it, though. Sheriff Coble had to take it off him to fire it.'

He adjusted his grip, pulling the lever slightly outward before cycling it again. This time, the mechanism slid smoothly into place, the rifle's internals clicking with precision.

'Ah, there we are,' Harper muttered under his breath, more to himself than anyone else. His fingers hovered over the lever for a moment, feeling for the exact motion that made it work.

Bickford, oblivious, carried on.

'Still fires true, mind you. Smooth as silk when you know her. That's a Winchester for you – doesn't matter if it's a hundred and fifty years old, it's still a masterpiece.'

'It's a beauty. You fire it at all?'

'God no. It's a work of art, not a weapon. I have a guy keep it cleaned and oiled, though.'

'Then how do you know it still fires true?'

Bickford opened and shut his mouth a couple of times, unable to answer this.

'Why did Doc Holliday sell it?' Harper was checking the lever action, impressed.

'Honestly? He'd come for the bounty on the gold, but as he never found it, there was no bounty. So, he sold it to fund his gambling habit,' Bickford said, and the smile left as he took the gun from Harper, placing it back. 'I keep it here as a reminder that every man, no matter how high, has their price. Shall we?'

He indicated the doors ahead, Ashfield having emerged to meet them, closing the door behind him. As they walked towards them, Harper observed the study doors were oak, stretching almost to the ceiling – very much a case of old money trying to look older.

Ashfield knocked twice, waited for a response, then opened them wide.

Mason Carrick stood at a window, his back to the door.

He was older than Harper had remembered, looking closer to seventy than sixty, but he carried it well, and he could have been younger, just with a tough life behind him. He'd left the military at the same time as Harper's father, both deciding to create what would become Aegis, but that didn't mean they were the same age.

That aside, his suit probably cost more than most people in Prosperity made in a month.

When he turned, Harper caught the measure of him – this wasn't some thug who'd gotten lucky. This was old-school corporate power, the kind that could buy towns like Prosperity without blinking.

'My God,' Mason said softly, genuine warmth in his voice. 'It bloody well *is* you. Little Liam Harper.'

He crossed the room quickly, hand outstretched. Up close, Harper could see the sharp intelligence in his eyes – this was a man who missed nothing.

'Last time I saw you, you were what, fourteen?' Mason's grip was firm but not challenging as they shook hands. 'Right after your mother passed. You were staying with your grandfather.'

'Old Pete,' Harper replied carefully.

'Old Pete,' Mason smiled. 'How is the old warhorse?'

'Still breathing.'

'Now, gentlemen,' Bickford interrupted from his position, taken up beside the desk. 'I think we should—'

Mason waved him quiet without even looking.

'Tom, this is family business. Give us a moment.'

Harper caught the flash of anger that crossed Bickford's face; the mayor wasn't used to being dismissed in his own house.

'Did I ever tell you,' Mason turned to Ashfield, ignoring Bickford completely, 'about the time little Liam here got into the server room at Langley? Must have been, what, twelve?'

He chuckled at the memory.

'Your father was still in the military then, in a meeting with the director, and you slipped away from his secretary. Found you an hour later, sound asleep under a desk, surrounded by about two million dollars' worth of computer equipment.'

Harper remembered the incident; he also remembered the secretary's panic, his father's fury, and remembered Mason being the one to find him, to smooth things over.

'Jet lag,' he muttered.

'And that time in New York,' Mason continued. 'The fundraiser at the Plaza. You convinced the senator's daughter to help you raid the kitchen. Came back covered in chocolate sauce. Your father had to cancel three meetings to take you shopping for a new suit.'

He smiled at the memory.

'Your mother nearly burst a blood vessel when she heard about it back in England. Called your father for an hour apparently, ranting about his lack of supervision.'

The mention of his mother caught Harper off guard, and Mason saw it, pressed the advantage.

'You've got her eyes, you know,' his voice softened. 'That same way of watching everything.'

He tapped at Harper's eyebrow scar.

'Thought that would have healed up,' he said.

'Not enough,' Harper replied, his voice cold. 'Only time he hit me. It left a message, though.'

'He regretted it,' Mason said softly. 'He always said you were too damned close to how he was as a kid. Too stubborn.'

He stepped back, giving Harper another look up and down.

'You went into the regiment,' Mason continued after a moment. 'Your father told me. He was proud of that, you know. Called me himself when you passed selection.'

'Did he?' Harper kept his tone neutral. 'We talked little in those days. Basically all that could be written inside twenty years of Christmas cards.'

'No,' Mason's eyes narrowed slightly. 'No, I suppose you didn't.'

He moved back to the window, looking out at the Aegis personnel patrolling the grounds.

'But here you are. In Prosperity, of all places. Following in his footsteps?'

'Just trying to understand what he built.'

'Interesting place to start. We've got operations in fifteen countries, and you choose this little mining town.'

'Had to start somewhere.'

Mason studied him for a long moment, then smiled.

'Indeed you did. Tom, why don't you tell Liam what Aegis is doing here? Since he's so interested in the family business?'

Bickford straightened, puffing himself up.

'Well, as I'm sure you're aware, Prosperity has—'

'We're looking for gold,' Mason cut him off. 'At least, that's what the permit says. Isn't that right, Tom?'

Harper watched Bickford deflate slightly. The mayor might own this house, this town even, but in this room he was just another employee. Cortez shifted slightly by the door, and Harper wondered how much of this she was getting.

'The issue with your gold mining seems to be,' Harper said carefully, 'that people are dying.'

'Accidents happen in mines.' Mason sighed. 'Even with modern safety protocols.'

'Moses Mathers wasn't an accident.'

'No,' Mason agreed. 'No, he wasn't. Bloody fool was trespassing in areas he knew were dangerous, without the right safety protocols. But then you already knew that, didn't you?'

'Excuse me?' Cortez stepped forward, her notebook already out. 'Are you saying Moses Mathers was murdered?'

Mason's face remained pleasant, but his eyes hardened as he looked at her.

'I don't believe we've been introduced, deputy ...?'

'Cortez. And you just admitted a suspicious death wasn't accidental.'

'I admitted nothing of the sort.' Mason's tone remained cordial. 'I simply agreed that his death wasn't a *mining* accident. The medical examiner will no doubt find that poor Moses succumbed to toxic gas exposure after entering a restricted area. A tragic case of trespassing, nothing more.'

'The medical examiner hasn't made that determination yet,' Cortez replied. 'In fact, Doctor Chen is performing the autopsy right now.'

'Indeed?' Mason raised an eyebrow. 'Well, I'm sure she'll be very thorough. Though I understand she has certain ... preconceptions about our operation here.'

Carson shifted uncomfortably by the door. Harper caught the movement, noted how the deputy was trying to fade into the background now that the conversation had taken this turn.

'Tom,' Mason said pleasantly, 'perhaps you could show deputies Cortez and Carson your collection of historical mining documents? I'm sure they'd find them fascinating.'

'I'd rather stay,' Cortez said.

'That wasn't a suggestion, deputy.'

'The deputies stay,' Harper said quietly.

'This is a family matter, Liam.'

'That's why I brought witnesses.' Harper didn't move, but something in his posture changed. 'The only reason I'm here is because they are.'

Mason studied him for a long moment, then laughed.

'You really don't trust me, do you? After everything your father and I built together.'

'Trust isn't really the issue here.'

'Of course it is,' Mason turned back to the window. 'But have it your way. The deputies can stay, although I'm sure they have better things to do than listen to old men talk about family history.'

'The only family history I care about is what my father

did here,' Harper continued. 'Whether any of the dead are red markings in his own mining ledger.'

'Now then, Liam, mining's a dangerous business, even with modern safety protocols.' Mason's voice carried genuine regret. 'Your father understood that. The cost of doing business in dangerous places.'

'The cost of doing business?' Harper said. 'That why you've got Aegis troops patrolling a mining town? Seems like overkill for health and safety.'

'We have significant investment here.'

'In gold that's been missing for a hundred and fifty years?'

Mason smiled, but it didn't reach his eyes.

'If you don't mind me asking,' Bickford interrupted, clearly trying to reassert himself in the conversation, 'how did your father die? I mean, was it—'

'Tom.' Mason's voice carried a warning, but Bickford pressed on.

'Well, it's just that if we're discussing family business—'

'Dominic died protecting a trade vessel off Myanmar,' Mason cut in smoothly. 'Piracy's still a problem in those waters. Sometimes these things ...'

He paused, studying Harper.

'Sometimes these things aren't as simple as they appear.'

'Is that what we're doing here?' Harper asked. 'Protecting company interests?'

'We're a security company, Liam. That's what we do.'

'This isn't Myanmar.'

The words hung in the air; Mason's expression didn't change, but something shifted in his eyes.

'No,' he breathed. 'No, it's not.'

'Myanmar wasn't an accident,' Harper continued, ignoring the comment.

'Your father made his choice that day. The real question is, what choice are you making now? Because I have to tell you, Liam, Prosperity isn't the best place to start asking questions.'

Cortez made a note in her pad. Mason's eyes flicked to her, then back to Harper.

'Of course,' he continued, 'if you're really interested in the family business, there are better ways to get involved. Your father's now vacant position provides movement within the organisation, and openings are now available.'

Harper stared at Mason, his eyes widening slightly, as if not expecting such a suggestion.

'You're offering me a job?' he asked.

'Why not?' Mason replied, walking over to a drinks cabinet and pulled out a bottle of expensive-looking bourbon.

Without even glancing at Bickford – whose bourbon it was – he poured himself a generous measure. To some, it might have been seen as a power play, but Harper genuinely believed this was something that happened regularly. However, Bickford seemed quite content to allow it.

'I've read your files. I've seen what skills you have,' Mason continued. He took a mouthful of his drink, smiling and smacking his lips with delight. 'Ah, Tom, you keep the best stuff in your cellar.'

'I live to serve,' Tom muttered, almost mockingly, although Mason Carrick didn't seem to take it that way, as he turned his attention back to Harper.

'I mean, let's be honest, Liam, most of it's been blacked out. And while that doesn't give me a full picture of what you've done, blacked-out text means important shit. You've been doing a lot of that – enough to gain a position wherever you wanted.'

As he said this, Harper noticed Ashfield out of the corner of his eye, pushing his Lennon glasses back up his nose as he tried to appear unbothered.

Harper wondered how far he could push this.

'Could I have my father's job?' he asked casually.

At that, Mason laughed, spluttering some of the bourbon he'd just drunk, and waggling a finger at Harper.

'You've got a good résumé, and your parentage speaks volumes, but no matter how much black is in your file, I've got people on my books who are higher ranked and more experienced than you, Liam. I couldn't give you your father's role.'

'Don't worry. I wasn't serious,' Harper replied with a smile. 'The last thing I want is to be a nepo baby for a mercenary company.'

'You say it like it's a bad thing,' Mason countered, his smile disappearing.

'So, wait,' Bickford interjected, looking confused, 'are you *not* part of Aegis?'

'No, Tom,' Mason said, waving his glass theatrically, as if for an audience. 'Little Liam here does not want to be part of his father's organisation. And why would he? When his father passed away, he left him everything. No other heirs, no wife to contest it. What did you expect exactly, Liam? Shares in Aegis?'

'No,' Harper interrupted firmly. 'The shares weren't given to me – not that I wanted them, anyway.'

'Don't lie to me,' Mason snapped. 'Everyone wants their share of the spoils, eventually.'

'Not if they didn't earn them,' Harper replied calmly. 'Whatever shares or percentage my father had in Aegis, apparently it was decided long ago that shares in the company shouldn't just go to members of the public, or civilians.'

He smiled as he looked back at Mason.

'I would have thought, as the one who created this with my father, you would have known, or at least have been told of this. Could it be, that you're not as needed as you believe?'

Harper looked around the room.

'If my mum had been alive, she could've made an argument for the shares, but I see where the logic comes from. Military goes to military. The board offered me a cash settlement to keep me comfortable, to keep me quiet about it, but I said I didn't need it.'

'You didn't need a cash settlement?' Bickford asked, horrified.

'No,' Harper said, turning to face him. 'I didn't come from money, and I don't expect to *be* money.'

'But money is what he is,' Mason interrupted. 'Even though the shares might not be in his pocket, everything else is, isn't it, Liam? If I remember correctly, your father had a house – a brownstone in New York. I'm guessing that's in your name now. There's an apartment in Santa Monica, a smaller one in Washington, and a couple of industrial lockups here and there – all transferred to your name. And let's not even start on the stocks, bullion, and crypto he collected.'

He turned to Bickford.

'With all these assets, Tom, little Liam here is probably the richest person in the room. Well, apart from me. The question is, of course, not only whether he has plans for it, but rather whether he thinks all this money will keep him alive right now.'

16

FAMILY TIES

'YOU THINK HE'S RICHER ... THAN ME?' BICKFORD ASKED, aghast.

'Oh, I can tell you now, Tom, if he has everything I've just listed, he's definitely richer than you. But, let's be honest,' Mason said, looking around the room, 'there's old money, and then there's *old* money, isn't there?'

Harper let the moment stretch before clearing his throat.

'I didn't keep the houses either,' he said, not bothering to look at Bickford, who at this comment emitted a strangled choke of despair. 'That is, I kept the New York one. I have fond memories of that place. But Santa Monica, Washington, and the one in Chicago – they're all up for sale. When the money comes through, I'll donate it to the veteran charities my father supported when I was younger.'

He turned his attention back to Mason.

'You know, before he left the military and changed.'

'I didn't see any change,' Mason replied darkly. 'What I saw was a wife and child who turned their backs on him.'

'Then you should've been looking more carefully,'

Harper said, his tone sharper now. 'Whatever happened between my dad and my mum, I have no idea. But I can tell you this – when she died, he turned his back on me. I wasn't lying when I said I had twenty years of Christmas cards. He might've called you and told you he was proud of me for getting into the SRR, but the Christmas card I got that year? All it said was "I suppose it's almost as good as the SAS."'

Harper's voice hardened, a flicker of something raw showing through.

'Nothing was ever great for my dad. The best – *my* best, that is – was never good enough. The last thing he ever said to me before he died was, "I can't speak now, Liam, I'm busy. Call back later."'

'And did you?' Mason asked, raising an eyebrow.

'That was the third time he'd given me that answer in succession,' Harper replied. 'So, yes, I bloody well did. And every time, I was pushed aside. There were always more important things.'

'Some things are more important,' Mason shrugged.

Harper's jaw tightened, but he let the comment slide. Instead, he looked Mason directly in the eye.

'You still haven't explained why you're here,' Mason prompted.

Harper took a moment before responding, his voice quieter but no less firm.

'My father spoke of Prosperity quite fondly,' he shrugged, his expression deliberately casual. 'I was passing through, and I knew this was something my dad had been involved in. I didn't realise I was going to walk into some kind of conspiracy, but, well, let's be honest, Aegis isn't exactly a company that shies away from such things.'

'Careful now,' Mason said, his tone level, almost monotone. 'You wouldn't want to act as if you're against us.'

'Why?' Harper asked, glancing around. 'Am I in danger? I've got two witnesses – members of the law.'

He glanced pointedly at Carson.

'Well, at least one. This one, I think, started working for you a long time ago.'

'Now you listen here, you little shit—' Carson began, but Bickford snapped.

'Shut the hell up, Carson.'

Turning to Harper, Bickford sighed.

'Look, kid, I'm sorry your daddy died, and I'm glad you've reunited with Mister Carrick here. But it seems like you've got an issue with Aegis, and whatever that problem is, it shouldn't be affecting us here in Prosperity. I know you wanted to do some sketching or whatever, but maybe we can find you a better town to hang out in.'

'Are you kicking me out of Prosperity?' Harper arched an eyebrow.

'Of course not, son,' Bickford said quickly, shaking his head. 'I'm just saying things seem a little emotional for you right now.'

'Don't worry,' Harper replied flatly. 'I'll be leaving soon – just as soon as I've fulfilled my father's wishes.'

'And what are those?' Mason asked, sounding tired of the conversation.

Harper took a step closer, standing just a couple of feet from Mason. Though Harper was shorter, his age and intensity seemed to throw the older man off balance for a moment. From the corner of his eye, Harper saw Ashfield reaching behind his back.

'Leave your weapon where it is, Mister Ashfield,' he said

coldly, without breaking eye contact with Mason. 'I just want to make sure my "uncle" here understands what I'm about to say.'

He tilted his head slightly, his expression darkening.

'Although ... are you still my uncle, Mason?' he asked. 'When I was a kid, my dad always told me to call you Uncle Mason, like you were some long-lost brother. But now that he's dead? You're nothing to me – just some guy he worked with, in an organisation that took him away from me and my mum ... one that left me on the sidelines.'

Harper's tone was biting now, each word cutting deeper.

'Sure, you can talk about the wonderful stories you have about me as a kid. The time I fell asleep while my dad worked, the time I stole cookies because he was too busy to notice. But how about you tell me a story about something I did when he *wasn't* working? When he *wasn't* hustling with you? Or are we just going for the default "non-working" story – the one when he backhanded me while drunk, and cut my eyebrow open?'

He stared at Mason, whose face remained unreadable.

'I'll wait for you to come up with one,' Harper said softly, the silence that followed suffocating the room. When Mason gave no response, Harper nodded grimly.

'My father was ashamed of Aegis at the end. And from what I've seen, he had every right to be. You claim you're here as security, helping Mayor Bickford reopen the gold trenches so future generations can prosper, while hunting for missing gold? Is that right? Everyone I speak to seems to have a different idea why you're here, almost as if you deliberately don't want people to know. Why don't you tell us about the western tunnels? Or the gas down there that shouldn't exist? What are you really looking for?'

Harper's gaze shifted to Bickford.

'Because you can't tell me you're still looking for hidden gold,' Harper continued before Bickford could reply, addressing the room. 'We all know the Bickfords used that to buy Prosperity in the first place.'

'That's a goddamn lie,' Bickford snapped.

'Really? Maybe I should have a chat with the town historian,' Harper shot back.

'That historian's nothing but a nutbag,' Mason interjected sharply. 'A lying, cheating one who didn't get us what we wanted.'

Harper smiled darkly as he turned back to Mason.

'Would that, by chance, be the second survey, the one William Bickford paid for, that showed the "anomalous formations" in the western mines?' he asked. 'The one Moses Mathers believed he'd worked out the location of, before he turned up dead in one of your mines?'

'Well, I think this conversation has come to a grinding halt,' Mason said, slamming his tumbler onto the table beside him. 'It seems the apple does fall far from the tree. You're nothing like your father – you have no idea what he was, what he wanted with Aegis. He was one of us until the day he died.'

'Was he?' Harper asked, stepping back now, moving into the centre of the room. His gaze swept across the faces before him, his military bearing unmistakable. His eyes locked with Cortez, her hand casually near her holstered gun.

'That's interesting,' Harper said. 'Because from what I heard, my father died defending a container ship against insurgents in Myanmar.'

'And?' Mason inquired. 'You don't think that's in line with Aegis's core beliefs?'

'Not when you were paid by a Myanmar warlord to step aside and let it happen,' Harper said coldly. 'My father was the only man in that unit who stepped up that day.'

He tilted his head, as if deciding whether to continue. Then, with a nod, he did.

'You see, I might've lied a minute ago,' he said, and as he spoke, his words were cold, calm and struck with every syllable. 'My father's last words weren't "Call me back later." His last words were "Get down," and a second later, the insurgent behind me *shot him in the throat*.'

The room fell silent, the weight of his words pressing down on everyone.

Harper's glare fixed on Mason.

'So, yeah, I think I do know what he was doing on his last day – begging me, as he lay dying in my arms to "make things right".'

Moving quickly back to the older man, he grabbed Mason's tumbler, picking it up and downing the rest of the bourbon in one swig. It wasn't a power play, it was just that his throat was dry, and the emotion was raw. Setting the glass down, he spoke quietly, but with an edge that cut through the silence.

'I suggest you stay out of my way. There are people on the board just as unhappy with Aegis as my father was. And you really don't want to piss off the board, do you?'

Mason glared angrily at Harper but said nothing. And Harper knew this could have been for a multitude of reasons; he could be furious, shocked, even remorseful – but one thing this conversation was ... was over.

Harper turned to Cortez.

'I'd like a lift back to town, please,' he said, his voice

steady despite the tension in the room. 'I understand you're the principal deputy for escort duties.'

Cortez, emotionless and composed, gave a small nod. Bickford, however, had turned red with fury.

'Now listen here, you jumped-up little shit,' he spat. 'You come into my town—'

'And *you're the mayor of Prosperity!*' Harper interrupted sharply, spinning to face him. His voice rose. 'You've let these people come in and run roughshod over it. You should be ashamed!'

As Bickford stared impotently back in shocked horror, Harper turned back to Mason.

'If you want to contact me,' he said, his tone icy, 'you can do so through my solicitors. You know their address – they used to be my dad's.'

With that, Harper nodded to Cortez, signalling he was ready to leave. The two moved towards the exit, but Carson stepped in front of the doorway, blocking their path.

Harper didn't flinch.

'You don't need to come with me either,' he said, his tone dismissive. 'You've shown your colours too many times.'

'You're making a grave mistake here,' Carson warned, his voice low and ominous. 'You walk out of this room in anger, then anger is going to follow you.'

Harper's gaze turned cold as he looked back at Mason.

'I watched my father die in my arms,' he said. 'A death that needn't have happened if Aegis hadn't been chasing more money. I was always going to leave this room with anger. Just be glad I haven't left it with a body count.'

Carson glanced back at Bickford, who, after checking with Mason gave a reluctant nod, motioning for Carson to step aside.

'I'll lead them out,' Ashfield said suddenly, springing to life after standing silently by the wall for most of the exchange.

Mason nodded his approval, and with Ashfield beside them, Harper and Cortez left Mayor Bickford's residence.

As they emerged into the crisp air outside, Cortez moved towards the Ford SSV, but Ashfield gently grabbed Harper's arm, bringing him to a stop.

'We need to talk,' Ashfield said quietly, his tone cautious. 'When you're not so angry... when this is all over.'

Harper raised an eyebrow.

'And why would I want to do that?'

Ashfield glanced around nervously, ensuring no one was listening.

'Because I talk to the board as well,' he said. 'And I know Dominic Kane wasn't happy with what's been going on. It's one reason I'm here.'

Harper's eyebrow climbed higher.

'You're telling me you were one of my father's spies?'

'More a trusted ally who could monitor things,' Ashfield replied. 'I never brought it up because I didn't know where you stood. But now I think we should have a chat.'

'Make sure it's somewhere open,' Harper said, his tone flat. 'No more mines.'

Ashfield nodded in agreement, and without another word, Harper left him and walked over to Cortez, climbing into the passenger seat of the Ford.

'Hope you don't mind me dragging you out of there,'

Harper said as she slid into the driver's seat. 'But I was hoping we could talk once we're back in town.'

Cortez looked at him, puzzled.

'About what?'

Harper shook his head.

'I think this is a conversation best suited for a drink,' he said finally.

'Why, Mister Harper,' Cortez frowned, 'are you trying to get me drunk? Not while I'm on duty.'

'It's because you're on duty,' Harper replied, his voice quiet but firm, 'that I need to talk to you. But you'll still need a drink in your hand.'

'Why?' Cortez's smile faltered, replaced by a look of concern.

Settled in the Ford, Harper took a deep breath. His voice was steady, but the weight of what he was about to say was clear.

'Because I think I know who killed your father ten years ago,' he said.

17

COLD CASES

IT WAS EARLY EVENING IN O'MALLEY'S, AND THE END-OF-DAY rush was beginning. Although a sign at the doorway pointed out there'd be music at half past seven, Harper assumed that many of the regulars wouldn't be turning up until then. Cortez gained a few confused looks as she walked into the bar with him, several drinkers averting their eyes and trying to look as if they weren't in the bar, but Cortez wasn't paying attention, staring at the back of Harper's neck, even though he wasn't looking back at her, as he led her to a booth.

'Beer?' he asked.

'I'll have a water,' Cortez replied.

'Are you sure?'

'If you're about to tell me who killed my dad—' Cortez snapped, but then calmed herself. 'Maybe a beer.'

Harper looked up and saw Cassie, the same barmaid he'd seen the previous day, walk over.

'Finally here for your food?' she smiled. 'Beer for you both?'

'Two bottles, please,' Harper replied. Looking around, he

could see people watching him and Cortez in their booth, and he returned his attention to Cassie.

'Are they stunned at seeing a police officer in the bar or something?' he asked.

'It's not the deputy they're looking at,' Cassie grinned. 'They're looking at you. You're something of an enigma at the moment, Mister Harper.'

'I don't recall giving you my name last time I was here,' Harper replied.

'You didn't need to,' Cassie chuckled.

'Let me guess, *The Prospector?*'

Cassie nodded.

'All the businesses in Prosperity advertise, so we're always paying attention to what's going on,' she said. 'The body being found, you being revealed to be connected to the company that's been bastardising the mountain—'

'Now wait a moment,' Harper said. 'Just because I'm connected to them doesn't mean I'm part of them.'

'Well, some folk around here might have a different opinion right now of you,' Cassie said. 'I'd get your story straight. Probably a good idea you're walking around with the police escort.'

She looked over at Cortez.

'Ma'am,' she said politely, and Harper gained the impression that this was yet another person who had an issue with the deputy. As Cassie turned and left, Harper returned his attention to Cortez.

'You were telling me who killed my father,' she said coldly.

'I said I might know,' Harper replied. 'I've got a feeling, but I need to know exactly what happened back at the time.'

Cortez sat back in the chair.

'You want me to relive my father's death? Honestly?'

'Yeah,' Harper mumbled apologetically.

'Fine.' Cortez straightened, and Harper felt she was becoming a little more official in the way she continued. 'It was ten years ago. My dad had just ridden out the Los Alamos gang. They were a band of bikers who wanted to turn this place into some kind of meth lab. You know, real *Sons of Anarchy* shit. Took us five years, but we got them to piss off. Anyway, while they'd been around, there'd been a bit of an increase in other things, drug-wise. And we'd found ourselves with a bit of a meth problem. My dad had cleaned that up as well, and he was having problems with a particular dealer.'

'Clinton?' Harper asked.

'Who told you?' Cortez nodded.

'I'd spoken to Maggie and her father.'

'Yeah, well, Maggie's not one to talk either,' Cortez snapped. 'My dad was in a bad place when my mom died. Maggie was his childhood sweetheart, but then she pissed off to join the Marines. However, when she came back, he was a widower, she was single and there was a bit of a love triangle going on at the time.'

'How so?'

'Because Tom Bickford wanted Maggie for himself.'

'Bickford?' Harper sat back in surprise. 'Mayor Bickford wanted Maggie Hawkins?'

'You might not have noticed, Harper, but we're quite insular here,' Cortez replied. 'Maggie, Tom, my father ... they were all at school together. I don't think Tom was in love with Maggie or anything like that. I think it was more a case of my father had something he couldn't have.'

Harper nodded.

'And so then what?'

'There was a problem when she came back from the Marines ten years back,' Cortez continued. 'She was a bit of a mess, although she wouldn't tell you that. We had our fights. I told her to back off. My dad was hurting, saw her as a crutch. She helped him get rid of the bikers, so ... there was that. But it broke the town in two. It's one reason why Aegis has managed to get away with so much.'

'How do you mean?'

'Half the town didn't want to get involved with the biker gang. Said it was dangerous, and it wasn't worth their time. The other half wanted the Prosperity they remembered back. Tourism was going down at that point. The biker gang was ...' she paused. 'Well, they were kind of doing exactly what Aegis is doing now, but without the mayor's authority.'

She cricked her neck, still unhappy at the attention she was getting in the bar.

'Anyway, Bickford was unhappy with the state of affairs. There was a town hall meeting where things got heated, and there were other problems. My dad wasn't exactly the easiest of sheriffs to get on with if you wanted to buy your way through things.'

'He wasn't corrupt.'

'No, he left that to the other people in the department,' Cortez snapped. 'Sheriff Coble, who at the time was Deputy Coble – he was Bickford's lapdog. You haven't met him yet; he's a real piece of work. Spends most of his time at conferences and law enforcement talks. Anything he can do to keep away from doing his job.'

Realising she'd gone off on a side rant, Cortez paused.

'Anyway, shortly after the town hall talk, my father was responding to a callout. It was anonymous, and on attending he was shot in the back, left to die in the street.'

'Witnesses?'

'Nobody,' Cortez spat. 'Or at least nobody who would admit it. Doctor Chen had just arrived in town, and she performed pathologist duties for it. They found it was a .44 Magnum bullet that killed him. Clinton was the obvious suspect and Coble, now acting-sheriff because he had seniority, pulled in a posse to go check out his apartment. Found him overdosed on his own supply.'

'Dead?'

Cortez nodded.

'There was a note written, well, scrawled really, which basically just said "he had it coming", which Coble found while searching, and decided it was a suicide confession, and Clinton had a gun in his name. A Smith & Wesson Model 29.'

'Dirty Harry Special,' Harper nodded. 'Fires .44 Magnum rounds. I heard.'

'Anyway, I came in to avenge the murder, but by the time I turned up ...' Cortez shrugged, leaving the statement deliberately empty. 'But if you're telling me someone else killed my father, then I'd like to know how the hell they got hold of Clinton's gun.'

'That's the thing,' Harper paused as Cassie appeared with two beers, placing them down, waiting for her to leave before continuing. 'I don't think it was the same gun.'

'We looked around,' Cortez replied. 'There weren't that many people with the same calibre, unless it was somebody out of town.'

'I think it might be someone closer than you actually realise.'

'Stop with the Mister Mysterio bullcrap and just *tell me!*'

'Alright,' Harper said, tone clipped, but sure. 'I didn't have long with it, but I saw enough to know something's not right. Listen carefully.'

Cortez watched expectantly as Harper took a sip of the beer before starting.

'I might not know many things, but one thing I do know is guns,' he explained. 'Especially old ones. The Martini-Henry, a single-shot, lever-action, breech-loader used by the British Army, and famous for its role in Rorke's Drift; the Lee-Metford Rifle, the first bolt-action repeating rifle and precursor to the famous Lee-Enfield—'

'Is there a point to this?' Cortez muttered. 'I'm still on duty.'

Harper nodded, checking the bar to make sure they were alone.

'I also know about the Winchester Model 1873,' he continued. 'And Bickford's Winchester is a ringer.'

'It's not Doc Holliday's rifle?'

'Maybe, but it's been adapted since,' Harper continued. 'First thing I noticed when I checked it was the chamber. It's been reamed out – there are fresh tooling marks that stand out against the rest of the metal. That's not original. The Model 1873 was built for .44-40 cartridges, but this one's been bored out to handle a much longer and more powerful round. Then there's the barrel. Original 1873 barrels were hand-cut, and you'd see faint irregularities in the rifling, almost like a fingerprint for the era. This one's far too smooth, far too precise. It's been mechanically re-bored or outright replaced, no question about it.'

'Okay, so it's had some work done,' Cortez frowned, not getting the point.

'Not just any work,' Harper replied. 'The 1873 used a toggle-link system, strong enough for its time, but completely unsuited to the pressures of more modern rounds. That mechanism's been reinforced. Modern steel, too. You can see the difference in how the parts reflect light. It's subtle, but it's there.'

He leant back slightly, resting his hands on the table.

'All of that points to a serious modification job. It's not just been maintained – it's been altered, purpose-built to fire modern ammunition. Whoever did it knew what they were doing, but they couldn't hide the signs if you know where to look.'

Cortez stared at Harper for a long moment.

'What sort of modern ammunition?'

'Well, as you saw when I tried to cycle through the rifle, the gunsmith didn't fully account for the increased pressure of the new cartridge. This put extra strain on the rifle's action, causing the lever to stick slightly when cycling. I had to use a specific motion, pulling the lever slightly outward before fully cycling it. The ammunition would have to still be a .44, but from what's been done there, I'd say—'

'A .44 magnum cartridge? Are you telling me *that rifle killed my father?*' Cortez stared at Harper, almost as if she didn't understand the words coming out of his mouth. Eventually, she started shaking her head, a shaking that continued way past the time when most people would stop.

'No,' she muttered, 'no. I'm sure there's an explanation for that, but it's not what killed my father.'

'How do you know?' Harper questioned. 'Surely you've got to admit that it looks suspicious.'

Cortez shrugged.

'Don't take it the wrong way, Harper, but all I've got is your word on this. I'd have to get a gunsmith to check it out ...'

Harper leant forward.

'Then we find someone to do it.'

'Are you telling me—'

'That your father's murderer could still be walking free? Maybe.'

'For ten years, I've classed this case as closed,' Cortez snapped. 'And now you appear out of nowhere, riding in on your bike like some mad, modern-day cowboy – and you're just gonna tell me that for the last ten years I could have been solving my father's crime while the man who may have killed my father has been standing almost next to me half the time?'

She took a long swig from the bottle.

'Look,' Harper replied, 'I'm just saying this rifle may have been the thing that killed him, and that Clinton may have been an easy patsy.'

Cortez now rose.

'No, I can't accept it. I ...'

She trailed off, frowning.

'It couldn't have been Bickford,' she continued. 'When my father died, he was in Virginia City. I can't remember why, but I remember it was a couple of days before he came back. I had to take the oath of duty in front of him, and they couldn't let me start immediately because of that.'

Harper rested back in the booth. He'd been so convinced that Bickford had been corrupt, and the gun had been so clearly tampered with.

'Besides,' Cortez continued, 'we saw him in the house. He couldn't use the damn thing.'

Harper raised his hands.

'I apologise, deputy,' he said. 'I thought I was helping.'

'That's the problem when people walk into a town with a white hat on their head,' Cortez muttered. 'You think you're the saviour. And actually, Harper, you're kind of being the problem.'

Her phone buzzed, and she looked down at it, frowning.

'Why the hell is Rachel Chen sending me texts for you?' she asked.

Harper straightened.

'Because she doesn't have my number,' he suggested, 'and chances are she was told you were with me. What does it say?'

'She's finishing her preliminary autopsy,' Cortez read the text, 'and suggests you might want to have a chat with her in a few hours.'

She put the phone away, placed her hands on her hips and stretched, staring upwards, letting out a long drawn breath before sitting back down at the table.

'It looks like we're together a little longer,' she said. 'Because there's no way in hell I'm letting you go to Chen without me.'

'It might be nothing—'

'Balls to that,' Cortez growled. 'I'm not talking about Moses. I'm talking about my father. She was the one who did the autopsy, remember? If he was killed by a ringer gun, I want to know exactly why she never worked it out.'

She picked up the menu.

'But you're paying for dinner,' she said. 'It's the least you can do for the driving I've provided.'

18

MYSTERIOUS READINGS

THE EVENING CROWD WAS FILTERING IN, THE PROMISE OF LIVE music drawing them to O'Malley's like moths to a flame. Eating his ordered chicken tenders and fries, Harper noticed Cortez had let her guard down slightly in the hour they'd been there, and since they'd started talking, her professional demeanour had started softening at the edges. Harper noticed things he shouldn't – the way she tucked her hair behind her ear when thinking, how her smile reached her eyes when she wasn't playing deputy.

'Coble rose fast after Dad died,' she said, picking at her fries. 'Within months, he was interim sheriff. By the time I joined up, he was permanent.'

'Fast track to the top?'

'More like a rocket.' Cortez's voice hardened, but her eyes held Harper's gaze a moment longer than necessary. 'And then the conferences started. Law enforcement talks, training seminars ... always somewhere else. Carson basically runs things while he's gone, and he gets his orders from Bickford, or whoever Bickford likes that week.'

'Convenient way to avoid questions and gain plausible deniability,' Harper munched on a mouthful of fried chicken tender. 'Still, must be lonely, being the only honest cop in town.'

'Are you flirting with me, Mister Harper?' Cortez raised an eyebrow, but her smile suggested it wasn't serious.

'Would that be inappropriate?'

'Extremely,' she stole one of his fries, even though she still had some of her own. 'I'm still not sure if you're one of the good guys.'

'Neither am I.'

A burst of laughter from the bar made them both glance over. Cassie was serving drinks to a group of locals, but Harper noticed how her gaze kept drifting their way.

'People are still watching,' he whispered.

'People are always watching in Prosperity,' Cortez's smile was bitter, but there was something playful in it too. 'Difference is, now they're watching you, too. Probably wondering if we're screwing.'

Harper choked on his fries, and Cortez started laughing; a genuine, full on one.

'Ever the gentleman, it seems,' she mocked.

Through the bar's window, Harper saw two Aegis SUVs cruise past, moving slow. Inside, the band was setting up, guitar cases opening like coffins on the small stage.

'Chen was new back then,' Cortez continued, absently swirling her drink. 'Just started as town doctor. Maybe she missed something in the autopsy. Or maybe ...'

'Maybe she was encouraged to miss something?'

Cortez's phone buzzed. She glanced at it, then showed Harper the screen. Chen's message was brief:

Come to the surgery. Bring Harper.

'Looks like we can ask her ourselves,' Harper said, standing. He dropped some bills on the table, catching the faintest hint of a smile from Cortez as she rose to join him.

'You know,' she said, 'most of my dates don't involve investigating murders.'

'Really?' Harper looked surprised. 'Most of mine do.'

Behind them, the band struck their first chord as, chuckling, they headed for the door. The sound followed them out into the darkening street; a wailing country riff that seemed to cry for something lost.

Harper hoped it wasn't Prosperity.

HARPER WASN'T SURE WHAT TO EXPECT WHEN THEY ARRIVED AT Doctor Chen's surgery. He'd grown up in the UK with small-town NHS doctors with tiny general practitioner offices, and Hollywood had given an artificial impression of what the town locum should look like, but this seemed a little more modern. For a start, there was a full-on operation theatre, or what looked to be one anyway, in the back room. The door had been left open, the surgery now out of hours, it being nine in the evening, and Harper had assumed it had been an invitation.

As he entered her office, Doctor Chen looked up from her desk. It looked like she'd turned her small office into an improvised lab, equipment borrowed from the local high school, or maybe a friendly college nearby, as seen by the marker pen names on the equipment, mixed with her own medical tools.

'Harper,' she said. 'Deputy Cortez.'

'Nice place.'

'It is when I'm not sharing it with Hank Longstead,' she muttered. 'I'm allergic to dogs.'

'What do you have?'

'A conundrum,' Doctor Chen replied, rising from the chair and waving for them to follow her into another room. 'Are you squeamish with bodies, Mister Harper?'

Harper shook his head.

'No,' he replied, 'and as I found Mister Mather's body in the first place ...'

'You didn't find him like this,' Doctor Chen responded.

In the back room, Moses Mather's body was on a slab, a sheet over it. He looked at peace, his expression no longer one of fear, muscles almost relaxed.

'I thought I was done surprising myself today,' she said, walking over to a side table where a microscope was set. She leant forwards, adjusting her microscope before continuing. 'But this ... this isn't what I expected.'

'What did you find?'

'Look.' She moved aside, gesturing at the microscope. With a glance at Cortez, Harper walked over.

'What am I looking at?'

'These are tissue samples from Moses' lungs.'

Harper leant in. Looking through the microscope, the crystalline structures looked almost beautiful, with geometric patterns that had no place in human tissue. Under the microscope's polarised light, they displayed distinctive birefringence, splitting the light into two separate beams.

'At first, I thought it was mineral scarring,' Doctor Chen continued. 'You see that sometimes in miners, mainly from years of dust building up. Silicosis presents similarly. But these formations ...'

She adjusted the focus.

'They're too uniform. The crystallisation pattern shows clear dendritic growth – like snowflakes, but metallic.'

Moving over to an iPad on a stand across the room, she pulled up images on the screen.

'See these electron microscope shots? The crystal structure is hexagonal. Natural mineral deposits in lung tissue are typically random, chaotic. These are following precise geometric patterns. And then there's this.'

She held up the handkerchief in an evidence bag; Harper assumed she'd placed it into one to stop contamination, something Harper hadn't even considered doing.

'The liquid you collected? When exposed to air, it's creating identical crystalline structures. I ran it through the mass spec at the local community college.'

She pointed to a printout covered in peaks and valleys beside the iPad.

'The atomic mass is ... well, it's not anything that should be in these mines.'

'You said hydrogen sulphide wouldn't do this?' Cortez frowned.

'H2S kills by blocking cellular respiration. It doesn't create crystalline formations,' Doctor Chen spread out her notes. 'Whatever this is, it's not natural. The uniform crystal size, the precise hexagonal geometry, the reaction with moisture ... if I was a betting woman, I'd say someone's processing something down there, something they're trying very hard to keep secret.'

She pulled up another image on the iPad screen.

'These aren't formations you'd get from raw ore. This is refined material – and by that I mean *industrial process* refined.'

She looked up at Harper.

'Moses didn't just find their operation. Based on crystal size and density, he was exposed to a high concentration of whatever they're processing down there. *That's* what killed him.'

'How do you know it's refined?' Harper asked. 'Could it be natural deposits they hit while digging?'

Doctor Chen shook her head, pulling up another image.

'See these edges? Perfect hexagonal structure. Nature doesn't work like that; crystals in ore deposits show variations, impurities. These are uniform. *Laboratory* uniform.'

Still in lecturing mode, she moved to a small machine that looked out of place among the medical equipment. It had the same black marker pen on it that the microscope had.

'I borrowed this from the community college's chemistry lab,' she explained. 'It works on X-ray diffraction, lets us analyse crystal structures. The patterns I'm seeing ...'

She paused, choosing her words carefully.

'Whatever this is, I can guarantee you it's not gold. Also, it's not copper, iron, or any of the other usual suspects. The atomic structure is all wrong.'

'Could you identify it?'

'With better equipment, maybe. I've sent samples to a colleague at the University of Nevada, but ...' she gave a bitter laugh. 'Funny thing. The courier company just called. Seems my package was damaged in transit. Nothing salvageable. Which is impressive since I only sent it two hours ago.'

Harper caught her meaning.

'Aegis has people watching the mail?'

'They have people watching everything,' Doctor Chen turned back to her microscope. 'But they missed something. These crystals ... they're hygroscopic. They react with moisture in the air, and grow larger. That's why they formed in Moses' lungs. And why they're forming on tunnel walls where water seeps through.'

'You're saying the whole mine could be contaminated?'

'I'm saying Moses found something down there. Something valuable enough to kill for, and definitely dangerous enough to hide,' she met his eyes. 'And they're processing it without containment protocols, or without environmental impact studies. One heavy rainfall? And whatever this is? Well, it could easily reach the water table.'

Chen finished her report, watching the two faces opposite her.

'As you can understand, this throws a slight wrench into things,' she continued. 'We've been thinking that the gas is sulphites and connected to the gold, when actually there's something more happening.'

'Tell me,' Harper asked, 'as the local doctor, how many times has anybody from Aegis come to you with gas inhalation issues?'

'None,' Doctor Chen admitted. 'Well, that doesn't mean they didn't have it. I'm sure the mine has their own medic who could sort out smaller things, keep it off the books, so to speak. We've not had anybody succumb to the bad air or whatever the locals want to call it for decades.'

'Is that because the mine was closed, though?' Harper suggested.

In response, Doctor Chen simply shrugged. Harper looked at the figures on the sheets of paper. The details, numbers, and words meant nothing to him. But then, this wasn't his world.

'I need to tell you both something,' he mumbled. 'But I'm trusting you both.'

Cortez raised an eyebrow.

'You're trusting us?' she replied. 'Harper, no offence, but the one who should be asking for trust is you. After all, your daddy was still—'

'Moses Mathers had a notebook,' Harper interrupted. 'I found it when he was dead.'

'You took evidence?' Cortez questioned incredulously.

'I made sure the evidence was kept,' Harper snapped back. 'You think Aegis would have left it for you to find? That body would have been cleaned by the time Carson and you turned up.'

'Where is it now?'

'I passed the notebook to Eddie Hawkins. In it were notes that Moses made about William Bickford. Did you know he had made a second survey?'

'There was a rumour,' Doctor Chen acknowledged. 'Why?'

'Because it's not a legend,' Harper replied. 'Eddie found it three days ago, hidden in a ledger, exactly where Moses Mathers believed it was. William Bickford hired geologists and surveyors to create a new map, and they found stuff that the first map didn't have – or rather, they found things that the public map had removed. The areas of bad air, the "here be dragons" areas where no one was supposed to go. In there, they had anomalous formations, basically ore and deposits that, at the time, William Bickford didn't understand, but he wasn't a stupid man. He understood that he might not be able to get the items out now, but down the line, they would. He just needed to have the money to do so.'

He shrugged.

'I think William Bickford started planning for the future. He knew his generation wouldn't be the ones that mined this, but maybe the next generation, or even the one after that, his children or his grandchildren. He stole the money, the millions of dollars of gold, to fund his plan.'

'So, wait, that's what they're protecting?' Cortez asked. 'A century-old land grab finally paying off?'

'It's more than that,' Doctor Chen moved to her desk, picking up a folder. 'The samples I've been testing? After the first package disappeared, I've arranged to send a second batch to someone else, an old friend who can help. Someone who won't be influenced by Aegis or the Bickfords.'

'Who?' Harper asked.

'Better you don't know,' Doctor Chen glanced at the clock on the wall. 'I should hear back by morning. Someone I trust is collecting them personally.'

'Like you were trusted with my father's autopsy?' Cortez, finally unable to hold her tongue, snapped.

The words hung in the air. Doctor Chen's shoulders stiffened, but she didn't turn around.

'I was new,' she mumbled. 'Inexperienced.'

'And Coble was insistent about certain conclusions?' There was an edge to Cortez's voice Harper hadn't heard before. 'That what you're going to tell me?'

'Lisa ...' Doctor Chen's use of Cortez's first name carried weight. 'There were things about this town I didn't understand then. Things about your father—'

'Don't,' Cortez cut her off. 'Just ... don't.'

Harper watched the tension build between them. Two

women who'd lived with this for years, each carrying their own guilt.

'Tomorrow,' he said finally. 'We'll know more tomorrow.'

Doctor Chen nodded, grateful for the interruption.

'First thing. I'll call when I hear anything.'

'You'd better,' Cortez headed for the door, pausing only briefly. 'And Rachel? This time, get it right.'

The door closed behind her with a quiet click that somehow sounded like a gunshot in the silent surgery, and the two remaining people said nothing for a moment.

'Her father wasn't what she thought,' Doctor Chen said quietly, still facing her desk. 'None of them were.'

'You mean Maggie and Bickford?'

'And Robert Cortez.' Doctor Chen turned. 'Lisa thinks it's all about Maggie choosing between her father and Tom Bickford, but she doesn't know the entire story. Robert – the sheriff at the time – he'd been looking into something in the mines. He'd been asking Maggie's father questions, talking to old miners. Then he died, and once he took charge, Coble made sure the investigation went the way it was supposed to.'

'What was he investigating?'

'I don't know. But the day before he died, he came to see my father.' Doctor Chen's voice caught. 'Dad was still working maintenance for the mine back then. The next week, he was dead too. Bad air, they said.'

She gave a bitter laugh.

'Seems there's a lot of bad air in Prosperity.'

Harper watched her for a moment, weighing his next words.

'Does Maggie know?'

'About my father? About Robert's investigation?' Doctor Chen shook her head. 'Better she doesn't. Some secrets ...'

She trailed off, leaving the thought unfinished.

'Tomorrow,' Harper said finally, heading for the door. 'We'll talk tomorrow.'

But something in Doctor Chen's eyes made him wonder if tomorrow would be too late.

19

FIRESTARTER

The streets of Prosperity were different at night.

During the day, the whole damned place played at being a tourist town, all gift shops and manufactured charm. But after dark, when the neon from O'Malley's fought the Goldstrike's gaudy logo for the honour of being the brightest light on Main Street, and Aegis vehicles prowled like black sharks through the shadows, you could feel the truth of the place.

This was a town built on secrets.

Harper kept to the walls of the buildings as he walked; he needed the time to clear his head. Doctor Chen's words about Sheriff Cortez were now rolling around his mind, mixing with everything else he'd learned today.

Mason Carrick's implied threat.

The modified Winchester.

A hundred and fifty years of lies that were finally unravelling.

He hadn't intended to cause trouble; he'd come to make sure his father's reputation wasn't tarnished. What he'd told

Maggie about the message he'd been sent was true; someone had sent the last recorded words of his father to him – if it was truly Ashfield, he didn't know. What he hadn't mentioned was that in it, his father had given him a second message, one that led on a dark night to a London-based arms dealer named Deacon Brodie, and an item he'd kept for Kane. It'd been a box, the code Harper's birthday, and in it was a key to a safe deposit box – and another code.

Almost tiring of the "game", Harper had found the box, and on opening it had found a notebook. It wasn't anything special, but had been filled with names and ops.

An analogue, unhackable database that damned Aegis.

But it wasn't to be passed to the authorities. That had been made clear. Of course, Harper could have, if he wanted to, but the point of all the messages was that Aegis was created to do good – and could do so again. If the FBI got involved, it'd be dismantled. Or, worse, taken by the NSA or CIA and used for even darker shit.

And so now the recently unemployed Liam Harper had a *new* mission.

Movement caught his eye – someone in the shadows beside the Goldstrike. For a moment he thought it was Ashfield, but the figure was wrong. Shorter, less composed, and as Harper watched, the man stepped into a pool of light from the hotel's sign, and Tucker's bearded face came into view. The self-proclaimed town conspiracy theorist wasn't stumbling drunk tonight. His eyes were sharp, focused.

'You see them?' Tucker's voice was quiet, measured. Nothing like his usual rambling tone. 'Third truck tonight. Same route, same timing.'

'Keeping tabs?' Harper asked.

Tucker snorted.

'Somebody has to. Everybody else in this town, they've learned not to look. But crazy old Tucker? Hell, I been watching them since they arrived,' he continued, his eyes tracking another SUV as it cruised past. 'Six months of patterns. You think I'm drunk half the time? So does the town. Easier to watch when they think you're just another town fool.'

'What have you seen?'

'Everything,' Tucker pulled a battered small notebook from his jacket. Even in the dim light, Harper could see it was filled with cramped writing: times, dates, licence plates.

'The warehouse on Cedar that's supposed to be empty? Gets deliveries at three in the morning, twice a week. They avoid Third Street on Tuesdays – that's when the school bus uses it. Can't risk anyone seeing what they're moving.'

Harper studied Tucker's face.

'You knew Moses,' he said. It wasn't a question.

'Moses knew what I knew.' Tucker's voice caught slightly. 'Difference was, he went looking. I just watched.'

'And what did you watch?'

Tucker glanced around, then leant closer.

'Two nights before Moses disappeared, Aegis moved something from the mine. Big truck, military grade. The kind with radiation shielding.'

'You sure about that?'

'Twenty years driving hazmat trucks before the company got canned a year back,' Tucker's smile was bitter. 'I know what I saw. Also, I saw one when I started a job at the mine – even commented to the site manager I'd seen it, asked why it'd be there. To anyone else, it was just a truck, but it was my familiarity with that kind of vehicle that warned them about me, and made damn sure they didn't keep me on.'

He sighed.

'Should have kept my mouth shut. First rule – don't stand out. Anyway, same kind of truck came back, but empty, the next morning. That's when I started watching.'

A car door slammed somewhere in the darkness. Tucker melted back into the shadows, his voice barely a whisper now.

'Watch the patterns. They're getting sloppy, rushing something. And whatever it is, it's big enough to make them stupid.'

Then he was gone, leaving Harper alone with the night and the sound of another Aegis vehicle approaching.

Tucker wasn't wrong about the patterns. Even as Harper walked down Main Street, seeing several more black SUVs cruise by, he started to realise a few things. First, the vehicles were driving slower than they had earlier in the day, more methodical. When he'd first seen them, they were nothing more than transport, even if one of them was transporting Blaine and his buddies to the diner, and then to the library. But now, watching from a doorway as another passed, Harper could see the drivers were watching, intent, driving through the town like an occupational force. More importantly, there were more of them than there should have been; more than they'd want if they wanted to stay under the radar.

Mason Carrick – or Tom Bickford – was rattled.

Harper pulled out his lucky stone, running it between his fingers, letting it ground him as he counted vehicles, mirroring Tucker's actions. The old drunk had surprised him. Or rather, the man *pretending* to be a drunk had surprised him, and this got him wondering how many other people in this town were pretending to be something they weren't.

The sound of breaking glass up ahead made him pause.

Looking up the street, he could see it was coming from a shopfront office, the painted sign visible in the streetlight.

THE PROSPECTOR

Why the hell would they want to attack the newspaper?

Moving carefully, Harper edged closer to the building, staying in the shadows. Two men were inside, their flashlight beams bouncing off walls as they moved through the newspaper's offices. Even from outside, Harper could hear them ransacking the place, looking for something.

Or destroying something.

The men wore dark clothing, faces obscured, but their movements were precise, professional. Not local muscle: these were Aegis operatives. As Harper watched, one of them moved to a computer, using an army knife to prise open the casing, pulling out what looked like a hard drive.

'Got it,' Harper heard the man say.

'Torch the rest,' came the reply.

Harper had choices. He could confront them, but he was unarmed, and there was no guarantee these men had the same orders about keeping him alive that Ashfield's people seemed to have. He could call Cortez, but by the time she arrived, the men would be gone.

Or he could follow them.

Following them won the internal debate, but only for a moment. As Harper watched, a vehicle rounded the corner towards him – not the expected Aegis SUV, but rather Cortez's Ford SSV, its headlights flooding Main Street.

The men inside *The Prospector*'s office froze, then quickly moved deeper into the shadows. Harper, caught between revealing himself and staying hidden, made a decision.

'Deputy.'

His voice was loud enough to reach her, and he saw her clock him immediately. She hit her brakes, the Ford gliding silently to a stop.

'Harper?' she called through her open window. 'What are you—'

'Got movement inside *The Prospector*,' he replied calmly. 'Two men. Armed and professional.'

She was out of the car in seconds, weapon drawn.

'How long?'

'Two minutes. They've got what they came for.'

'And you were going to what? Follow them yourself?'

'Thought crossed my mind.'

'Of course it did.' She spoke into her radio, 'This is Cortez, requesting backup at The Prospector. You armed?'

The latter part was aimed at Harper.

'Just my winning personality.'

'Then stay behind me.'

However, as they approached the building, Harper already knew what they'd find. The sound of a door closing around the back confirmed it; the men were gone, along with whatever they'd taken. More importantly, they'd left something else behind.

The smell hit them before they entered.

Gasoline.

'Out,' Harper snapped. 'Now.'

The sound of sirens joined the night, but Harper was already moving, pulling Cortez back—

The blast tore through the building, a bone-shaking

boom that sent what glass remained in the broken windows shattering into the street. A fireball erupted, ripping through the offices, the shockwave throwing them both hard to the ground.

Heat and debris rained down as Harper rolled onto his side, coughing. The flames surged, devouring the building, smoke billowing into the night.

Harper pushed himself up, his jaw tight as he stared at the inferno.

'This isn't random,' he growled, watching the fire take hold.

'What do you mean?'

'Two men, professional, taking hard drives before torching the place?' Something cold settled in Harper's stomach as he realised what was happening. 'They're scrubbing the town.'

As he looked around the street, hearing more sirens in the background, watching people emerge from the bars and restaurants on Main Street, staring in horror at the blaze, Harper thought of Chen's promise about tomorrow, about samples and evidence and answers. He'd been so caught up in uncovering the truth, in playing his little games with Mason and Ashfield, that he hadn't considered the obvious response.

Clean house. Destroy everything. Leave no trace.

He'd been so distracted, he'd made an amateur mistake; the kind of mistake that got people killed.

Cortez's eyes widened.

'Chen.'

They were up and running before the word finished leaving her mouth. The Ford's engine roared to life, tyres squealing as Cortez pulled a sharp U-turn. But they'd only made it to the end of the block when they saw the second column of smoke rising against the night sky.

'That's not the surgery,' Harper said, orienting himself, the cold in his stomach spreading. 'That's the library.'

As they pulled down the side road, Harper saw he was right, but took no consolation for it. The old building where Eddie had found the survey, where Moses had spent his last days researching, where a century and a half of town records lived in dusty back rooms ... was now nothing but fire and heat, the books nothing more than kindle for the fire. Harper's mind raced through everything that might be burning right now, every piece of evidence going up in smoke.

All because he'd pushed too hard, too fast.

Cortez swung the SSV hard right, then hit her brakes. Up ahead, another fire engine was screaming past the intersection, heading in a third direction.

'How many?' she snapped into her radio.

The reply crackled through. A confused, young voice.

'Three confirmed. Maybe four.'

'They're not even trying to hide it anymore,' Harper muttered. His lucky stone felt like lead in his pocket. He'd thought he was being clever, playing both sides, feeding false information through the bug in his room, watching their reactions. But he'd underestimated their response, or he'd overestimated their restraint.

Either way, Prosperity was burning because of choices he'd made.

CORTEZ HAD CONSIDERED STOPPING AT THE LIBRARY, BUT another deputy had arrived, a young man, who looked no older than eighteen, with wild hair to match his wild eyes. Cortez told him to stay on the radio and continued on. The drive to Doctor Chen's surgery took forever and no time at all, each second marked by the pulse of emergency lights painting the Prosperity streets in red and blue. Harper watched the familiar buildings slide past, buildings he'd committed to a soldier's memory, now transformed by smoke and shadow. The town felt different, as if the careful veneer of tourist charm had been burned away, revealing something older and darker underneath.

This was the real Prosperity, he realised. This was what it had always been, beneath the gift shops and manufactured history.

A town of secrets, finally burning under the weight of its own lies.

They found Doctor Chen outside her surgery, watching as Maggie's volunteer crew fought to contain the blaze. Her face was ash-streaked but composed, her eyes cold as she tracked the flames inside, knowing they were eating through her records, her tests, her evidence. Years of medical history, town records, everything that might have helped them understand what was really happening in the mines ... all of it feeding the inferno.

'They're destroying evidence,' she said as they approached, her voice carrying the same clinical detachment she'd used to describe Moses' autopsy. 'All of it.'

Harper looked around at the chaos of emergency vehicles, and the background light pollution in the night sky, multiple fires turning night into day. The air tasted of smoke and something else, fear, maybe, or the death of hope. Somewhere in the darkness, he knew Aegis vehicles were still moving, still watching.

But their patterns had changed.

They weren't patrolling anymore.

They were hunting.

And Harper knew, with a certainty that settled into his bones like old guilt, that this was just the beginning. He'd pushed, and now Prosperity would pay the price.

The question was, how many more fires would burn before this was over?

20

SCORCHED TOWN

SMOKE STILL HUNG OVER PROSPERITY THE FOLLOWING morning.

As Harper looked up, he could see at least three columns of grey drifting into the morning sky, marking the night's destruction like accusing fingers pointing at God. *The Prospector*'s offices were nothing more than a blackened shell, while Prosperity's library's historic frontage showed only scarred charcoal black above shattered windows, with many of the books and papers within burnt beyond trace.

And Doctor Chen's surgery ... well, that had apparently burned the hottest of all.

Tired, covered in soot and sweat, and aching from the night's activities, Harper walked down Main Street, noting faces in shop doorways. These were people who had lived there all their lives, and now they were pale, quiet even, having spent hours in the darkness watching their town change overnight. In a way, the tourist façade had cracked and had shown something far darker underneath. Even O'Malley's was closed, its windows dark, although Harper wasn't sure if there was such a thing as a breakfast rush there. Cassie, the barmaid, however, was sweeping debris from the outside. Even though the flames had been further down the street, ash and burned pieces of books and furniture, scraps of sheets of paper floating on the wind, even, had followed down into the town itself. Over the night, there'd been several smaller fires because of this. Nothing more than a good stamping out could fix, but still concerning, nevertheless.

Harper paused, stretching his back, feeling the kinks clicking as he did so. He hadn't slept.

None of them had.

The fires had drawn out pretty much everyone in town. Maggie's volunteer fire crew had worked through the night, their efforts hampered because the blazes were deliberately spread out, forcing them to split their resources. But then other people had arrived to help; even the Goldstrike Inn & Suites' private fire equipment had been brought out, Mayor Bickford bringing his own from his mansion house, making a show of civic responsibility, while the flames consumed evidence of his family's lies.

Aegis personnel had helped too, bringing down more fire-suppressant equipment from the mines, Delaney coordinating with Maggie's teams. Harper had watched the Parsons taking orders directly from Delaney, not even trying to hide their connection anymore, their hiking gear replaced with more tactical wear for firefighting. Their clean-cut efficiency a stark contrast to their previously casual demeanour, the pretence of being tourists obviously having served its purpose. But now, with Harper outed and Eddie, well, God knows where Eddie was, they'd returned to the "family", helping out while buildings were aflame.

If Harper was being honest, it had been an impressive

performance of community spirit. Aegis vehicles were kept busy ferrying water from the reservoir, their men working alongside locals. Even Mason Carrick appeared briefly to offer support and resources. To anyone watching it would have looked like a town coming together in a crisis, but Harper, working alongside the firefighters, giving what experience he could, had seen the precision of it all.

How the Aegis teams had been first into certain areas, emerging with boxes and what looked to be hard drives before the flames took hold, passing them to Carson for safekeeping.

How other Aegis members, including the Parsons, had focused their efforts on specific sections of the library, making sure that nothing salvageable remained, while ensuring that anything expensive and useless to the cause – but owned by Bickford – was saved.

Most telling was how they'd concentrated on Chen's office and occasional veterinary surgery, as if they knew exactly what might survive intense heat and what needed to be destroyed completely; this, on top of the test results that had mysteriously disappeared before the fires had even started.

The worst part for Harper had been watching the locals accept this, their faces lit by the flames as they worked alongside the men who were systematically erasing their town's history. *Some of them had to know,* Harper was sure of it. They had to understand, but in Prosperity, not looking too closely at certain things seemed to be a survival skill.

As he stood there staring across at the remains of the battered town, two Aegis vehicles cruised past, moving slower than usual. They were different drivers than last night, Harper noted, but they held the same predatory watchfulness. They were waiting for something, but he couldn't work out what it was, as he carried on down Main Street, continuing on past the sheriff's office.

'You look like hell,' Cortez said as she stood in the doorway, shadows under her eyes suggesting she hadn't slept either. Her uniform was crisp though, badge polished.

'Making a point?' Harper asked, pointing at the clean clothing.

Cortez grimaced at the question.

'Sheriff Coble's back,' her jaw tightened. 'Said we had to look our best, make sure the people of Prosperity could see we were there for them.'

Harper said nothing. He didn't need to. Cortez was as unimpressed as he was about that. 'Any word on the cause?' he eventually asked, already knowing the answer.

'Partly. It's an electrical fault, apparently. All three buildings at once.' Her voice was flat. 'Possibly some kind of power surge in all three locations. Anyway, this is according to the initial report.'

'Initial report? It's barely morning.'

'As I said, Sheriff Coble's back. He arrived an hour ago, and he's already making decisions.' She glanced at the Aegis vehicle as it made another pass.

'He's deputised them,' she said, nodding at it. 'Called it a "necessary response to coordinated attacks on our community". Even got Bickford to sign off on temporary emergency powers, although I'm not sure whether he got Bickford to sign off, or whether Bickford convinced him to publicly *get* him to sign off.'

Her lip curled slightly.

'Apparently you, Mister Harper, are responsible for bringing the criminal elements into Prosperity.'

'Me?'

'According to the sheriff, your arrival, and the sudden outbreak of vandalism and arson can't be coincidental,' she shook her head as she lowered her voice. 'He's put Carson in charge of investigating your background. And Mason Carrick's offered Aegis's full resources to – and I quote – "protect the town from outside influences with their own agenda". Do you have an agenda, Mister Harper?'

'You know damn well I do, but it's not against this town,' Harper watched another Aegis SUV cruise past now. That was two in as many minutes. They weren't even pretending to patrol anymore. 'How long before they try to arrest me?'

'They won't,' Cortez's hand moved unconsciously towards her weapon; it wasn't against Harper, as he saw she too was watching the vehicle pass, and wondered whether she wanted to take the fight to them. 'They can't. There's too many people seeing Aegis moving around in the side streets before the fire started. Tucker's been talking, and he's not as drunk as they'd like to think. But—'

'But Sheriff Coble's back.'

Cortez gave a resigned shrug.

'And he's made it clear; he's got the authority, and you're not welcome in Prosperity anymore.'

'Well, at least they're being obvious about it now,' Harper said, unconsciously pulling his lucky stone from his pocket, turning it in his hand, the familiar weight helping him think. 'How's Chen taking it?'

'Haven't seen her for the last couple of hours, probably since dawn. Coble's got her tied up with insurance paperwork, claiming she needs to document everything that was lost,' Cortez's expression darkened. 'Every file, every test result, every patient record.'

'You think he's making sure nothing survived?'

'I think he's making sure nothing can be proven.'

A door creaked open further down Main Street, and Harper watched Mayor Bickford emerge from the Goldstrike Inn & Suites. Even at this distance, his politician's smile looked strained. Harper noted that Aegis personnel flanked him like an honour guard as he made his way towards what remained of the library.

'It seems he's playing his part well,' Harper muttered.

'They all are,' Cortez replied. 'Although I heard he'd spent half the night in the Goldstrike, sleeping like a baby. Still, you should hear the sheriff's speech about outside agitators and protecting our community's values.'

Cortez shifted slightly, positioning herself between Harper and the approaching Aegis vehicle.

'He's called a town meeting for noon, mandatory attendance.'

'Showing who's in charge?'

'I think it's more a case of showing what happens when people ask the wrong questions,' she said as she glanced at her watch. 'You should get off the street, Harper, especially before—'

'Before what, deputy?'

The voice came from behind them, and Harper turned to find Sheriff Coble standing in the doorway of his office, his badge gleaming as bright as his smile. He was tall, slim, and wore a handlebar moustache that aged him slightly. He looked to be in his sixties, although was likely in his early fifties, his peppered brown hair underneath a sheriff's cowboy hat. But his eyes were cold, calculating, and fixed directly on Harper.

'I don't believe we've met,' he said. 'I'm Sheriff Ric Coble. No "K".'

'Short for Richard?'

'Short for Eric. Never liked it as a name,' Sheriff Coble replied amiably. 'I believe we have to have a conversation about your presence in our town, Mister Harper.'

'A conversation or an order to leave?' Harper asked.

'Now, now, let's not be too hasty,' Sheriff Coble's smile widened, and somehow, he showed more teeth without becoming any warmer. 'Although, speaking of orders, Deputy Cortez, if you would, please consider yourself suspended pending investigation.'

'You *what?*' Cortez's hand now dropped to her weapon again, unconsciously. 'On what grounds?'

'Dereliction of duty. Failure to protect town assets. Conspiracy with outside elements,' Sheriff Coble ticked off the points on his fingers. 'Take your pick.'

'This is bullshit, Eric,' Cortez snapped. 'The Cortezes have been here in the station for generations.'

'I don't give a shit about your daddy, your granddaddy, or any others of your immigrant family who wanted to come and play cowboys,' Sheriff Coble snapped, his voice hardening. 'This is nothing more than just procedure, following your dereliction of duty over the last two days. Or would you prefer I add insubordination to the list?'

Harper watched the tableau unfold, noting how Sheriff Coble positioned himself. The man was moving like someone with combat training, not a small-town sheriff. Even the way he approached, coming up behind them, controlling the space, it spoke of some kind of tactical experience. He wondered whether Sheriff Coble had military training, or whether this had been given to him by his friends at Aegis. *Maybe there was something more to these meetings and conferences that Sheriff Coble had visited?* It'd given the impression of a man who didn't want to work, but now Harper was wondering what Sheriff Coble's true job really was.

'You can't do this,' Cortez replied, but her voice had lost some of its edge.

'I already have,' Sheriff Coble nodded towards the door. 'Carson's waiting inside. Don't make this more difficult than it needs to be.'

Two more Aegis vehicles pulled up, bracketing them on either side, and Harper caught sight of Delaney in one, watching the scene with professional interest. They'd been waiting, patrolling the block until they saw Sheriff Coble confront Harper. It'd been a hunt, and Harper had been the target.

'Go,' he said quietly to Cortez. 'This isn't the time.'

'You know what, Lisa? You don't mind if I call you Lisa, now you're no longer an officer of the law? You really should listen to your friend.' Sheriff Coble's smile was pure predator now. 'He seems to understand how things work here. Although I suspect that our Mister Harper won't be around much longer to offer advice, soon to be riding off into the sunset on his crappy British motorbike.'

Cortez hesitated a moment longer, glanced at Harper pleadingly, and then turned towards the office. But, at the door, she paused, staring back at her onetime boss.

'You know what they're doing,' she said. 'You've always goddamned known.'

'Inside, *Lisa*, before we arrest you for obstruction. There's a good girl.'

Harper watched Cortez disappear into the sheriff's office, catching one last glimpse of her face. Her anger was there, but underneath it was something else. Possibly calculation.

Harper wondered whether Lisa Cortez, no longer deputy, was playing a longer game here.

'Now then,' Sheriff Coble turned his attention back to Harper, with all pretence of warmth gone. 'About that conversation.'

'Not interested.'

'It wasn't a request.' Sheriff Coble pointed at the Aegis vehicles. 'Because of what happened last night, the town's now under emergency measures. It's a form of temporary martial law—'

'Which means you can harass locals, suspend deputies and generally throw your weight around,' Harper kept his voice level. 'But I'm not local, am I? And despite your deputising of private security firms, do you really have any legal authority over me?'

'You don't think I do?' Sheriff Coble stepped closer now. 'The way I hear it, you've been interfering with an ongoing investigation. Harassing our town officials. Making threats.'

'Is that what Mason Carrick told you to say?' Harper asked, looking back at the vehicle. 'Is that what your boss told him to say, Delaney?'

Something flickered in Sheriff Coble's eye. Anger, or maybe even fear – *was Sheriff Coble under the thumb as much as everybody else?*

'You think you're clever, don't you?' he said. 'Coming here, stirring up trouble, playing games with things you don't understand.'

'I don't understand?' Harper shook his head, meeting his gaze. 'I understand plenty, sheriff. I understand how a deputy becomes a sheriff overnight, how certain deaths get explained away, and how evidence disappears ... all like magic.'

'Careful, son,' Sheriff Coble's hand rested casually on his weapon. 'That sounds like you're accusing an officer of the law of something.'

'I wouldn't dream of that,' Harper smiled, but kept his eyes cold. 'Although I've been meaning to ask. That Winchester of Bickford's – you know, his special rifle that was supposedly Doc Holliday's? I had time to peek at it yesterday, and I was wondering if you'd let me take another look at it.'

'I don't think that'll happen.'

'You could hold it while I looked. After all, I hear you understand the little quirk it has, jamming when you're trying to fire it. It seemed to me like it had been altered, maybe updated to fire a different calibre of bullet, although I'm sure you wouldn't know about that, would you?'

As he watched, Harper was grateful to see the colour draining a little from Sheriff Coble's face.

Gotcha.

'You've got until noon,' Sheriff Coble said, his voice barely more than a whisper now. 'We have a town meeting then, and I'd prefer you to be riding out of town as it happens. Four hours, I'd say, to pack your things and leave Prosperity. After that, I'll have probable cause.'

'Probable cause? For what?'

'For three buildings burned last night. After all, the town's looking for someone to blame,' Back in control, Sheriff Coble's colour had now returned, along with the artificial smile. 'And you've been awfully interested in our local history, haven't you? Asking questions about old records, fighting people outside the library. The same library, by the way, that's now nothing more than ash.'

'That's thin, Coble, even for you.'

'Oh, please. It doesn't need to be thick,' Sheriff Coble

nodded towards the Aegis vehicles. 'It just needs to stick long enough against the wall for people to see. You have until noon, Mister Harper. Don't make me come looking for you.'

He turned and walked towards the sheriff's office, pausing at the door.

'Oh, and if you're thinking of talking to Doctor Chen before you go, I'd suggest you don't. She's helping us with our investigation, and you wouldn't want to interfere with that, would you?'

The door closed behind him with a soft click, and Harper watched through the window as Sheriff Coble approached Cortez's desk, where Carson could be seen collecting her badge and her gun. Even from outside, Harper could see the satisfaction on Carson's face. On either side of him, the Aegis vehicles pulled back into the street, driving off now the immediate threat was over, Delaney watching him through the window.

Harper placed his hand into his pocket and felt his lucky stone again, feeling its familiar weight once more.

Four hours.

He looked up at the smoke still hanging over Prosperity, and then up Main Street, far towards Maggie's guesthouse where the Parsons were probably now watching and waiting, having been sent there by their boss.

Four hours to figure out how to stay alive in a town that suddenly wanted him dead.

He had a feeling that the Winchester wasn't the only thing Sheriff Coble was trying to bury right now.

21

SUICIDE WATCH

He couldn't help it, but the walk back to Maggie's guesthouse had felt like a surrender. Harper could feel eyes on him; from windows, from passing cars, from the ever-present Aegis vehicles that seemed to be everywhere and nowhere at once, monitoring him as he made his way back to where he'd been told to go, like a good boy.

Four hours, Sheriff Coble had said – four hours before they'd find a reason to arrest him.

No, it wasn't arrest. It'd be four hours before they'd find a reason to shoot him down in the street, and claim that he was the instigator behind all of this.

It was just past eight now, and Main Street was waking up properly, shop owners opening despite the smoke still hanging in the air. There were tourists around, after all, some of whom had been helping throughout the night. But now the shop owners were sweeping ash from their doorsteps, while others just stood and stared at the ruined buildings.

The library's blackened frontage drew the most attention, the broken windows nothing more than dead eyes staring out at the town it had served for probably over a century by now. The destruction felt personal, deliberate even. It was a message that had been written in ash, ember and fire ... and Harper was convinced it was a message that had been made purely for him.

Outside O'Malley's, Cassie was setting out chairs, her movements slow and deliberate. She paused as Harper approached, and he noticed how tired she looked. Not just from the night's events, though; this felt like a deeper exhaustion of some kind.

'So, I guess they finally ran you off, eh?'

'That obvious?'

'Town's got a way of dealing with people who ask questions,' she straightened, studying him. 'Although they don't usually burn down half the town to do it.'

'You think I had something to do with that?'

'I think a lot of things, Harper,' her smile was sad. 'Mostly, I think about how that fire at *The Prospector* took out twenty years of archives. Stories about mining accidents, town council meetings, property sales ... there's a lot of history gone up in smoke. I'd say that's probably killed the paper as well.'

'You think?'

'Nobody reads local papers anymore,' Cassie shook her head. 'Christ, I'm one of the reporters, and I've been working behind the bar for three years to keep myself up above water.'

She turned her back to her chairs, but her movements had slowed.

'You know what's funny?' she continued. 'Last week I was helping put together a piece about the town's history. Old stories, interviews with folks who remembered the mine's heyday. Had this great photo of Sheriff Cortez from when he first took office, standing right where you met Sheriff Coble this morning.'

Harper watched as she arranged the chairs with an almost mechanical precision, anything to take her mind from what she was talking about.

'That story's gone now, along with everything else we had on the Sheriff. Convenient, isn't it? It's almost like someone knew exactly what they were looking for.'

She looked back at Harper.

'You should be careful. Some folks in this town, they've got real experience in making problems disappear.'

The warning hung in the air between them. As Harper looked around, he saw that down the street an Aegis vehicle was making another pass, moving just slow enough for Harper to catch Delaney once more watching from the passenger seat.

'They'll come for you too, you know,' he whispered, 'once they're done with me. People who know too much. That's what this is about.'

'Maybe,' Cassie's smile turned sharp. 'Or maybe some of us have been keeping records of our own, somewhere safer than a newspaper office. You know, working with the digital age, rather than fighting it.'

Harper smiled; the first genuine one he'd had in hours.

'You're the webmaster, aren't you?' he asked. 'Of Prosperity's webpage?'

'Nobody's ever known for sure, as several people take turns,' she replied. 'Gives plausible deniability. But even if I wasn't, I'd know who would have been. And the one thing a fire can't destroy is a cloud server.'

She turned away, disappearing into O'Malley's before Harper could respond. He stood there a moment longer, processing her words, then with a resigned sigh, continued on towards Maggie's guesthouse. As he did so, he crooked his head, looking upwards. The morning sun was climbing, and in a way, it burned away the last of the smoke, but the air still tasted of ash, and now possibly even secrets.

As he approached it, Maggie's guesthouse stood quiet in the morning light. It almost felt *too* quiet. Harper had grown used to the sounds of Maggie's routine over the last couple of days; there was a radio, usually in the kitchen, the coffee maker gurgling, doors opening and closing as she went about her business. Also, Harper could recall Eddie shouting to her, even the Parsons slamming the door as they went for their hikes.

All of these noises were gone. Now there was nothing, just a weight of silence pressing against his ears.

He paused at his Triumph Bonneville, checking it carefully. It hadn't been tampered with, and the brakes were still secured. It was the first thing he'd considered, as he'd walked towards his inevitable leaving of Prosperity; the possibility that someone fixed the bike so that he had a terrible accident outside of town, as then nobody could complain about his death being intentional or deliberate.

"Just a terrible accident," they'd say, and move on.

His lucky stone still felt heavy in his pocket as he climbed the porch steps, weighted down with unfinished business. The front door was unlocked, but then that wasn't unusual; Maggie didn't seem to be one for locking up during the day. But something made him pause, hand on the doorknob.

This was wrong. The silence almost felt deliberate.

Inside, the hallway stretched, dark and empty, as sunlight filtering through the windows cast long shadows across the floor. Everything looked normal, undisturbed even, but Harper had spent too many years in combat zones not to recognise the feeling crawling up his spine.

The house wasn't empty.

'Maggie?' he called out, pulling off the leather jacket, placing it on the back of a chair, knowing there wouldn't be an answer. 'Eddie?'

He hadn't seen Eddie all night. Maybe he'd been hiding somewhere ...

But there was no answer from either of them. There was, however, an answer from a different source.

'She's helping out at the library still.' Alan Parsons emerged from the kitchen, wiping his hands on a dish towel. He looked different to Harper now. Sharper, more focused; the casual slouch of the hiker-tourist now gone. 'No one's seen Eddie since the fire started. Makes you wonder, doesn't it? Diane and I were about to make some coffee. Would you like to join us?'

It was perfectly delivered. Friendly. Open. Concerned, even. If Harper hadn't seen him taking orders from Aegis and Delaney the night before, he might even have believed it. He wondered whether the Parsons, either of them, had noticed him that night.

Maybe they didn't know he was aware.

'Sure,' he said, matching the casual tone. 'Let me just grab something from my room first. I've been told I have to leave, so ...'

'No need,' Diane appeared at the top of the stairs, and Harper noticed how she'd positioned herself between him and his room. 'I'm sorry, Liam. We heard you were leaving. We thought we'd help you pack.'

'Wow, that's very thoughtful of you, Diane.'

'Well, we feel partly responsible, I'm afraid,' Alan's voice carried on, just the right note of sympathy as he continued moving around the kitchen. 'All this trouble since you arrived ... must be overwhelming for you, especially for someone with your ... well, you know, your history.'

Harper caught the emphasis, understood now what was coming.

'My history.'

'PTSD is no joke.' Diane was descending the stairs, each step measured. 'Losing your father like that, then finding the body in the mines, stirring up all these old wounds. Must be really hard to cope.'

'Very hard,' Alan agreed. 'Some people just ... *break*.'

Harper noted the rope at this point – just the end, poking out from behind Alan's back, tucked into the back of his jeans. New rope, the kind you'd buy at a hardware store. Not the kind of rope you'd find in a knackered old guesthouse.

'Is that what Aegis told people about the others?' he asked quietly. 'The ones who asked too many questions ... that they just broke? Is that what you told Moses Mathers as you stuffed him into a fissure, deep in a mountain?'

'You'd be surprised how many people believe something like that.' Alan's friendly mask was slipping now. 'Stranger comes into town, starts causing trouble. Then tragic suicide. It's a tale as old as time.'

'And the suicide letter or confession I supposedly wrote?' Harper glanced towards the bedroom above. 'Let me guess, I'm confessing to all the fires. Apologising for the trouble I caused. Maybe even a few hints about the gold, or other secrets to make it interesting.'

'Already in your room, waiting to be found.' Diane had reached the bottom of the stairs. 'It's very convincing, I promise you. Apparently, you were overcome with guilt. You couldn't live with what you'd done. And as you'd left a sketch and notes diary in your room, I could work out your handwriting from that, so the police will also be able to compare both and see it was you.'

'And any words that don't look right? Well, you're just not in your right frame of mind, are you, buddy?' Alan smiled widely now.

'And the evidence planted?'

'Gas receipts, matches, things a disturbed man might use to burn down buildings,' Alan's smile was now cold. 'The sheriff will find it all very compelling.'

'After they cut me down,' Harper nodded at the rope.

'Eventually.' Diane's hand slipped into her jacket. 'But first you're gonna tell us where Eddie Hawkins is.'

And there it was. The real reason for this little performance. Eddie had gone to ground and nobody knew where he was. And if they were this concerned, this meant that they also didn't know what he had or where he was taking it.

'You're right,' Harper said quietly. 'It's all too much.'

He pulled his stone, the one he'd had for years, kept from the River Wye, and worn down over the years, out from his pocket.

'Do you mind if I hold on to this still? Bit of comfort in my last moments?'

'Of course. We understand about comfort objects, PTSD and all that,' Alan's smirk now was pure condescension.

Harper gave a smile ... and then threw the stone as hard

as he could at the overhead light. As it struck the fluorescent tube, it exploded in a haze of phosphorus and glass—

Harper moved the instant the light shattered. There was no time to think, just muscle memory and survival instinct. He caught Alan low and hard, driving them both into the kitchen. The counter edge cracked against Alan's spine, but he didn't make a sound, just brought his knee up into Harper's ribs with mechanical precision.

Professional, trained and lethal. Figures.

The first shot from the hallway missed by inches, punching through the kitchen cabinet next to Harper's head. Splinters stung his face as he grappled with Alan, both men fighting for dominance in the confined space. There was another shot, closer now. No time for technique, Harper slammed his forehead into Alan's nose, feeling cartilage crack. Blood sprayed, but Alan kept coming, wrapping the rope around Harper's throat with practised efficiency.

'No need to fake it now,' he shouted. 'We have a spare gun. We'll fire it a few times. You came in shooting, decided you weren't going to go down without a fight. We can make this work.'

Harper's vision greyed out as he clawed at the rope. His lungs were burning, and in desperation he drove his elbow back repeatedly, feeling ribs give way to pressure. But Alan still held on through the pain. The room was tilting, darkness creeping in at the edges. His hand found something solid on the counter; one of Maggie's cast-iron pans, and he swung it blind, connecting with Alan's temple.

There was another shot aimed at him, and a spark flew as the cast-iron pan took the bullet. The rope loosened just enough for Harper to suck in a ragged breath, twist and swing again.

This time he felt bone give way.

Alan dropped, but Diane was already in the doorway, her weapon lined up. Harper could see it was a Glock 17, and he threw himself sideways as the round thundered in the confined space. Pain blazed across his shoulder; it felt – or at least he *hoped* – like a graze where the bullet had scraped by, but was still way too close. He kicked the heavy wooden kitchen table over for cover, diving behind as he heard more rounds punch into the wood, one catching the table leg, sending splinters into his face.

The chemical smell of gas now filled the kitchen. In the struggle, they had knocked the knobs on the stove; the hiss of escaping gas was barely audible over his own ragged breathing and the ringing of his ears from the gunshots, as Diane moved like a shadow from the doorway, trying to get an angle. Harper had always considered her to be the more experienced of the two following their meetings, and she wasn't proving him wrong.

There were two shots left in her magazine – he'd counted – but two shots were all she'd need in this space. His shoulder burned where the bullet had caught him, the warm blood soaking through his T-shirt. The table wouldn't stop a determined shot if she wanted to.

There was movement behind him; Alan was slowly stirring, groaning as he did so.

Not dead then. These people were trained to take punishment, to keep on coming.

Harper's throat felt crushed from the rope, each breath a struggle, his vision still blurred, and his head was swimming from the gas and lack of oxygen. One mistake and they'd have their suicide scene, just not the way they planned.

The floor creaked as Diane shifted position. Harper

tensed, ready to move, knowing he had seconds at most. But before either of them could act, another sound cut through the chaos.

'Enough!'

Harper glanced up to see Ashfield standing in the back doorway, his Lennon glasses misted, his normally pristine appearance dishevelled. His own weapon was drawn, pointed at the floor.

'Stand down,' he said to Diane, his voice carrying an authority Harper hadn't heard before. 'This isn't how we handle this.'

'Sir, we have orders—'

'From Delaney,' Ashfield's voice was icy. 'Not from me, and sure as hell not from Carrick, this man's goddamned *Godfather*.'

Harper stayed behind the table, watching the tension play out. On the floor, Alan groaned, trying to push himself up.

'This man is a threat,' Diane said, but her weapon had lowered slightly.

'This man,' Ashfield replied, 'is exactly where he needs to be.'

He looked at Harper then, and something passed between them – not quite understanding, but recognition, perhaps.

Then his corporate mask slipped back into place.

'Clean this up,' he told Diane. 'Get your idiot partner to medical, and next time, wait for proper authorisation.'

'Sir—'

'That's all.' Ashfield turned to leave, then paused. 'Oh, and Mister Harper? Your four hours started fifteen minutes ago.'

He was gone before Harper could respond, leaving only

questions and the lingering smell of gas in the air. He took a moment to rise, staggering over to the stove and turning the knobs off ...

As he turned, he saw that the Parsons were gone.

Now alone, Harper took a moment to search the floor, finding his stone and pocketing it.

Less than four hours to patch himself up, find Eddie, and stop this madness.

He'd done more in less time, that was for sure.

But not like this.

22

SECRETS AND HIGHS

THE BULLET HAD DONE MORE THAN GRAZE HARPER'S SHOULDER.

Standing shirtless in Maggie's bathroom, wincing as he pressed at it, he could see the deep furrow it carved across his deltoid, the edges of the wound ragged and angry. The vanity mirror showed powder burns around the injury because of the close range shot – the heavy wooden kitchen table had thrown off Diane's aim just enough, but the heat of the round must have still seared his flesh.

His sweater was a write-off though, the right sleeve soaked through with blood, which pissed him off royally. It had been a recent purchase, but he'd really liked the colour. He'd had to peel it away carefully, gritting his teeth as dried blood pulled free from the wound, but now, with the bathroom light on, it showed the full extent of the damage. Not life-threatening, but the kind of injury that could slow you down at the wrong moment.

Maggie's first aid kit was, of course, military grade and stowed under the sink in a heavy-duty medical pack, the US Marine style of box he recognised from his Regiment days.

The contents were meticulously organised inside; there was a selection of combat dressings, haemostatic agents, even a suture kit – Maggie had kept up her medical training, it seemed. The iodine stung as he cleaned the wound, but the bleeding had already slowed to a steady ooze. *He'd been lucky.* Half an inch lower and the bullet would have torn through the muscle, maybe hit bone.

The bathroom clock showed just over three and a half hours left of Sheriff Coble's deadline. Each tick felt like a countdown to something inevitable as, working one-handed, Harper applied a pressure dressing, the movements almost feeling automatic from years of practice – luckily, none of which was for him – and the gauze pad went directly over the wound, quickly secured with some incredibly careful wrapping that wouldn't restrict his movement. After wrapping a second dressing for backup, he then taped it all up to hold it in place. The pain was still there, but felt a little distant now, a duller, constant ache Harper pushed aside – training and necessity was always a good enabler.

He dry-swallowed two of Maggie's ibuprofen. Not ideal, but better than nothing, and he still needed to keep a clear head. The mirror showed other souvenirs from the fight with Alan, including rope burns on his neck, and a darkening bruise along his jaw from where he'd caught an elbow. His lucky stone, regained from the floor now sat on the edge of the sink, still spattered with blood from the fight. As a final thought, he washed and dried it, sticking it back into his pocket, where it belonged.

The guesthouse felt different as he moved through it, like the violence had changed something fundamental about the space. Evidence of the fight was everywhere: broken furniture, bullet holes spread across the walls, and fresh blood drying black on the kitchen tiles. The gas smell still lingered as well, despite the open windows, which irritated Harper; he'd wanted to make a fresh mug of tea, but was a little concerned about lighting a hob.

Cold coffee from yesterday's pot it was then.

But, staring at the hob, and re-running the Parsons' rushed attempt at staging his suicide, Harper realised something possibly important.

They'd been sloppy. They didn't expect him to survive.

Which meant they might have left something behind.

When Harper had first arrived, Maggie had mentioned the Parsons were two doors down from him, so he thought as they'd broken into his room to place the listening bug in, he'd return the favour. The door opened with a soft click, not locked – no need to pick the lock now that pretences were gone.

The Parsons, now outed as Aegis, hadn't bothered packing their "things" – mainly as they probably never intended to wear any of the items again. The guest room looked exactly as a tourist couple's should, with clothes hanging neatly in the closet, hiking boots paired by the bed, and a collection of guidebooks and maps scattered across the nightstand.

But Harper had spent years learning to see past surfaces.

He started methodically. Closet first; each garment checked, every pocket searched, wincing as his shoulder wound pulled at a wrong movement. The clothes told their own story, and were very much high-end outdoor gear with the tags removed, worn enough to look authentic but not enough to match their supposed weeks of hiking. There was a half-empty pack of cigarettes in a jacket pocket, American brand. The Parsons had never smoked outside that Harper could remember, but it was a great excuse to go outside to either receive orders, or spy on people.

The bed yielded nothing, even when he stripped it to the mattress. Same with the drawers, with nothing more than tourist ephemera scattered within and carefully curated to support their cover. A journal filled with fake entries about hikes and local colour was found in the travel safe, alongside restaurant receipts and museum tickets, all creating a paper trail of normalcy, contrasting horribly with the Glock 17 that had been placed under them, a spare magazine beside it.

He drew the Glock, dropped the magazine to confirm it was full, slapped it back in and press checked the weapon, confirming a round in the chamber before slipping it into his waistband. The hiking boots beside the bed caught his attention, however. Two pairs, supposedly well-worn, but the scuff marks were too precise, the wear patterns too even. But there was something else ...

They'd been wearing hiking boots when they fought him. Why would they bring a second, equally worn pair?

He picked one up, testing its weight, and realised that the left foot on Diana's boot was heavier than the right. On further examination, the entire sole came away with a gentle twist, revealing a hollow compartment. Inside, Harper found a small field notes book, and what looked like a small burner phone – one of the flip kinds, without the smartphone accessories, nothing more than a basic burner that could make calls and send texts. The notebook contained coordinates and times, all written in a neat hand that somehow didn't match the Parsons' carefully constructed image. Locations around town were marked with time-stamps, many corresponding to the fires, and Harper couldn't help but wonder whether the Parsons had been bugging other places in the town, or whether their long countryside hikes had actually been to find vantage points to stare down with some kind of high-definition binoculars or sniperscope.

It was the phone that interested him the most. These people had maintained their cover for weeks, which meant regular reports to somebody, most likely Delaney or Ashfield. He powered it on, watching the screen light up. Flicking through, he saw a couple of numbers that had been called, and one that had replied back. He almost dialled it now, but decided this could wait as he sat back on the bed, staring at the phone. The chances were that Alan and Diane, or whatever their real names were, were probably only there to monitor Eddie. The coordinates, times and patterns could actually have been them following the old man as he travelled around. The previous day, for example, Harper could see a mention in the notes of Eddie entering the diner around the same time that he had. There was a small note:

Blaine, Gomez. Discussion.

Could this have been when Blaine, the pockmarked blond, and Gomez, his Hispanic friend, had turned up to hassle Eddie? Harper assumed that's what it was.

There was one message from the phone sent to the Parsons earlier today – there may have been more, but they probably deleted them.

Find Eddie Hawkins and terminate the SOB.

Harper hoped the only reason the message was there still was because they hadn't seen it yet, or followed out the orders—

A creak from downstairs made him freeze, but it was probably just the house settling, groaning under the weight of its own secrets.

He checked his watch. There were three hours and twenty minutes left before Coble's deadline ended.

Time to start looking for Eddie before Aegis found him—

A floorboard creaked in the corridor behind him and Harper drew the Glock and spun, his injured shoulder protesting the movement. He squared his sight picture on the hallway in case it was Alan or Diane back for their phone and a second round – but it was only Tucker in the doorway. The supposed drunk, the supposed town conspiracist, looked almost sober, his eyes sharp as he took in the scene, hands up defensively.

'Figured you'd checked their room,' he mumbled quietly. 'Found some interesting reading there?'

'How'd you get in?'

'Back door's been broken since Super Bowl 2014,' Tucker moved into the room now, his movements careful. 'Maggie never fixed it. Gives people like me a way to keep an eye on her guests.'

He nodded at Harper's shoulder.

'Let me guess, that's Diane's work, isn't it? I got the impression Alan doesn't like guns, always a terrible shot. Although that looks like his gun in your hand. You kill him?'

Harper shook his head.

'Found it in the safe,' he replied. 'You've been watching them that closely?'

'As I said last time, everyone thinks Tucker's just a town

drunk,' he pulled a small notebook from his jacket, similar to the one from the hiking boot, but weathered, worn. 'Makes it easier to sit in O'Malley's or the diner, even the library, all day, every day, taking notes. Writing down licence plates, patrol patterns, radio frequencies – you know, if they're stupid enough to reveal them. Anyone see me do it? Well, I'm just a conspiracy theorist who's collecting cars. Maybe I'm checking how many red cars have passed and whether that means the apocalypse is coming.'

He nodded at the gun.

'They go off into the hills and have target contests,' he explained. 'Diane's better and it pisses Alan off. Anyway, that's not why I'm here. Eddie came to see me yesterday, before Moses' body was found.'

'Where is he?'

'Probably somewhere they won't think to look,' Tucker's eyes were clear, focused. Harper nodded at this. Tucker might be here to help, but he still didn't trust Harper with the truth yet. Still, it didn't matter as long as Eddie was safe. 'But that's not why I'm here. I wanted to show you something.'

He punctuated this by waving the battered-looking notebook. It reminded Harper of Moses's one, and he wondered if they bought them at the same time.

'Remember I said I got canned as a trucker?' Tucker's smile was bitter. 'Well, that wasn't all I did. I used to run security logistics for the firm, coordinated transport schedules, mapped travel patterns. The kind of experience that lets you spot when someone's moving something they shouldn't.'

He tapped his battered notebook.

'Three nights ago, they brought something out of the mine. Something that needed special handling,' he said.

'Eddie saw the manifests last night, right before the fire started.'

'How so specific?'

'Because I waited until I spoke to you on the street before looking for him,' Tucker shrugged. 'No offence, man, but you're still an outsider. That's when he disappeared.'

'And you know where he is now?'

'No, but I've got something better,' Tucker's smile turned sharp now. 'I know where he's going to be in about three hours.'

Harper checked his watch. There were three hours and ten minutes left of Sheriff Coble's deadline.

That was too close to be a coincidence.

'Tucker, what's Eddie going to say at the town hall meeting?'

At the question, Tucker grinned.

'I can do better than answering that,' he said. 'I can show you.'

TUCKER LED HARPER UP TO THE ATTIC OF THE GUEST HOUSE. IT wasn't so much a dumping ground for items as many attics were, but instead was a room, likely Eddie's. It was cluttered, but covered the expanse of the house, giving a lot of square footage, with one window at the end that looked out onto the streets of Prosperity, and another on the other side that looked out onto the mountains. In front of the window, looking at the mountains was an old telescope, the type you'd use to look at the stars. Harper peered through the eyepiece and saw it'd been aimed almost as close to the mine entrance as you could get before it went out of sight.

Looking around, he saw files were stacked in precise order, with surveillance photos, taken from closer and half-hidden locations taped to walls in chronological sequence, while a police scanner hummed quietly in the corner.

'How did the Parsons not find this?' he asked.

'Because Eddie has his own room downstairs,' Tucker shrugged. 'The lock's also a lot harder to break through than the average one. Add Maggie commenting on the fact that the attic had been closed off for years, unsafe to walk around ... Eddie was very careful, made sure that guests didn't see him come up here.'

He gave a small smile.

'Or maybe they did know. Maybe they took copies of everything here. Who can tell?'

'What is this?' Harper said as he started checking the walls.

'Eddie's been gathering evidence for months,' Tucker explained, moving over to a locked filing cabinet. 'But last night, while you were out with the deputy, he found something that changed everything. Something in that survey of William Bickford's.'

Harper looked back at him, seeing Tucker smile.

'Don't worry, man. I guessed you didn't tell me because you don't trust me as much as I don't trust you,' he said. 'But I've known about that map's existence for a while. Eddie, Moses, me? We're the last resort, the Three Musketeers of Prosperity.'

Harper's shoulder throbbed as he watched Tucker unlock the bottom drawer with a key taken from his own pocket. The painkillers hadn't yet kicked in, and he was pushing the discomfort aside.

'You've seen the map?'

'No, but Eddie told me what was on it.'

'So, I'm guessing you know about the anomalous formations that are written on it?'

'More than that.' Tucker pulled out a thick folder as he turned to face Harper once more. 'Eddie made copies of everything. Been doing it for years. Keeping one set at the library, one with me, and one here. Figured if anything happened, there'd be a backup.'

He opened up a small folding card table resting against the wall and spread the documents across the green baize. Harper recognised some of these from the research Eddie had showed him the previous day, obviously returned to the room after he'd finished. But others were new. There were geological surveys, old mining claims, modern shipping manifests, all connected by a variety of cramped handwriting in the margins: Eddie's, Moses Mathers', and Tucker's.

'See these tunnel sections?' Tucker pointed to a faded map. It was hand scrawled as if drawn by a miner rather than a surveyor. 'William Bickford had them sealed off in eighteen seventy-five, claiming it was bad air. Recognise the date?'

'Same time as the gold was stolen.'

Tucker pulled out a modern manifest now.

'He might not have been able to mine down in these tunnels with *his* technology back then, but Aegis can. They've got equipment that's come in; military-grade processing facilities. You know, the kind of set-up you don't use for gold.'

He checked his watch.

'Eddie's going to present all this at the town meeting. I was told to come pick it up for him. Three hours from now, he's going to stand up in front of everyone and expose what the Bickfords have been sitting on for a century and a half.'

'Sheriff Coble won't let him finish.'

'Sheriff Coble won't have a choice,' Tucker's grin was fierce now.

'Of course he has a bloody choice! He has Aegis waiting for his order!' Harper snapped. 'They'll kill Eddie before he gets there. The fires, the Parsons trying to stage my suicide ... they're cleaning house, Tucker. Eddie won't make it to the meeting. Christ, there was even a text message telling the Parsons to kill him! I think the only reason they didn't is they weren't sure who'd arrive at the guesthouse first – him or me!'

Tucker's grin faded.

'Shit.'

'Where is he now?'

'I genuinely don't know.' Tucker went pale as the realisation of his plan falling apart was more likely than he'd realised. As he went to continue, the back door opened downstairs, and both men tensed, but then Tucker relaxed at the sound of boots on wooden stairs.

'Maggie,' he said, leaning back towards the door. 'We're up here!'

After a moment, Maggie Hawkins appeared in the doorway, still in her fire chief gear, face streaked with ash. She took in the scene: Harper and Tucker standing by, piles of notes, a torn apart hiker's boot with what looked to be a burner phone inside its sole, Harper's bandaged shoulder and Glock 17, Tucker's clear-eyed sobriety.

'Guess we're done pretending,' she said, as if this was the most normal thing in the world.

'You heard anything while at the fires?' Harper asked.

'Coble's ordered Shen removed,' Maggie pulled off her heavy gloves. 'They're taking her to the mine. Officially, she's been taken elsewhere to give her statement, but I saw our favourite hiker guests turn up, and boy were they pissed.'

She looked around.

'I'm guessing it was because of you?'

'They were a kind of welcoming committee for me,' Harper shrugged. 'Sorry about the kitchen, by the way.'

'What the hell have you done to my kitchen?' Maggie half turned to go back downstairs, but then paused, deciding it was a problem for later. 'Anyway, they were angry. Started shouting at Delaney. Then Ashfield turned up, and it was a barnstormer of a fight until Delaney got sick of their shit and told him to help with the "extractions".'

'Extractions, plural?'

Maggie shrugged.

'Don't know, but he said something about putting Doctor Chen with the others until this is contained. Don't know who the others are, but they're moving her within the hour.' Maggie's eyes met Harper's. 'You should also know, Coble's convinced Mason, or rather, Mason's convinced Coble to "tell him publicly," to shut down the mine completely. No one in or out after noon.'

Harper checked his watch. Just over two and a half hours until Coble's deadline to leave town.

Just under three hours to save God knows how many lives.

'So, Maggie,' he said calmly, 'now we're all done pretending. How's your Marine training? You been keeping it up? Your zone two and your VO2 Max all good?'

'I do my cardio,' Maggie shrugged. 'Which is a pain with my goddamned leg.'

'You good for an assist?'

'Hoo-rah,' Maggie said coldly. 'Let's go get Chen.'

She glanced around the room, as if suddenly realising.

'Where's my dad?'

'We were hoping you could tell us,' Harper replied. 'He's gone to ground.'

'No, he wouldn't have gone to ground while the fires were burning ...'

Maggie was already heading down the stairs, Harper following.

'What do you know?' he asked as Maggie burst into her own bedroom, opening up the wardrobe and swearing.

'Son of a bitch!'

'Maggie, what's going on?'

Maggie turned to face Harper.

'My dad would never have hidden while the fires were burning,' she said. 'He would have found a way to help out, and if he knew Aegis were looking for him, he would have found a disguise.'

She waved a hand at the empty wardrobe.

'My spare firefighter's uniform is missing,' she explained bitterly, 'including the gas mask and the helmet. My father's probably been putting fires out all night and no one's realised.'

She ran her hand through her sweat and dirt-covered hair.

'But there are no more fires to put out—'

'And he'll be visible,' Harper finished the comment.

'We need to contact Cortez,' Maggie was pacing now. 'She'll be in the sheriff's office.'

'No, she was suspended,' Harper replied. 'Coble did it in front of me. Made Carson take her gun and her badge. She looked pissed as well.'

'Really?' Maggie paused from fretting for a moment, and grinned. 'Wow. Looks like everybody's tired of pretending.

Let's go find her, find my dad, grab Chen, and find out what the hell's going on.'

23

AMBUSH

THE ROAD TO THE MINE CURVED BETWEEN RED ROCK formations, and Harper noted as he pulled up in Maggie's truck that it offered perfect ambush points every hundred yards.

They'd arrived here at Maggie's suggestion, and she'd chosen this one carefully; a natural bottleneck where the road narrowed with simple lines of sight in both directions. The late morning sun cast long shadows along the asphalt, and the temperature was already climbing into rather uncomfortable territory. Harper hoped that the fires in Prosperity were out, because without rain, they could smoulder for hours.

He watched the road through borrowed binoculars, his shoulder throbbing despite the fresh dressing given by Maggie while complaining about his own ability, even ignoring his comments about having to do it one-handed. The wound still pulled every time he moved, a constant reminder of how quickly things could go wrong; but it felt more secure, tighter than it had been when he'd done it.

Amusingly, Tucker had watched while she rebandaged this, giving advice. Maggie had eventually sent him out of the room, complaining how Tucker was one of the best practitioners of "Doctor Google", and the worst patient you could ever have, which made Harper wonder whether this wasn't the first time she'd had to clean a wound up in Prosperity.

Staring down at the road, he checked his watch once more; two Aegis vehicles had passed in the last hour, both heading up to the mine. Neither, however, had been carrying Doctor Chen. From his position, he could see the mine entrance in the distance, and peering through the binoculars, he could see Aegis personnel moving with increased urgency.

Something had them spooked. The fires had been meant to destroy evidence, but instead, they'd only drawn attention. Now they were rushing, making mistakes.

He didn't feel that this was Mason Carrick's work. He knew the man; he was a planner, an organiser, and as good at the job as Harper's father was. No, this felt more like Delaney's knee-jerk reactions, maybe Bickford pushing his weight with Sheriff Coble now beside him.

After all, the enemy of my enemy is still an enemy ... unless you've got something on them.

'Are you sure about this route?' he asked.

'It's the only way up that doesn't have checkpoints.' Tucker was a different man now, all business as he monitored the police scanner from Eddie's attic hideaway, propped up on a flat rock as he narrowed his eyes, trying to listen. 'Blaine's careful, but he's predictable. He'll be the one they send in the SUV, and he always takes the path of least resistance.'

'Like a coward,' Maggie muttered. She had positioned herself behind an outcrop, and Harper was amused that her

Marine training was evident in how she'd established fields of fire. The only weapon she had was a shotgun she'd brought from the guest house, but it was a Mossberg 940 Pro Tactical SPX – an 8 round semi-auto, and a hell of a lot better than the average home defence gun. She had also brought a combat vest that she now wore, including shell bandoliers for the Mossberg, tactical webbing, and equipment that suggested she'd been preparing for something like this.

He, in return, was armed with Alan Parsons' Glock 17, left in the safe when he'd searched the room. He had a full 17 round magazine and a spare, and that was enough for him if he needed it. Tucker had no weapon, apart from a small taser in a holster, one he claimed he'd used many times when staying in his cab overnight, stopping car – or rather truck – jackers. Harper wasn't expecting Tucker to be involved in a fight, so he felt the taser was fine. He was their "eye in the sky", their tech help, even if all he had were binoculars and a scanner.

The radio crackled with interference – communications seemed to be jammed around the mine, but Tucker had modified the scanner, stripping it down to bypass the basic blocking signals. Aegis might be professionals, but they were rushed and using off-the-shelf equipment instead of military-grade jammers. Harper couldn't help but remember one comment he'd said to Maggie earlier that week, on how Aegis were professionals, but this was more likely where the runts of the litter were sent for grunt jobs. This could work to their advantage; it meant that the mercenaries that would be sent to face them weren't to the level that most of Aegis would be.

It didn't mean it would be an easy fight, however.

A voice cut through the static. Carson, trying to sound official.

'Package secure, route two clear.'

'That's them,' Tucker switched frequencies, his fingers moving with an actual practised skill across the dial. 'If it's Carson talking, that's the office on Main Street. They're five minutes out.'

Harper studied the road through his binoculars again. He knew they'd have seconds to act once the vehicle appeared, but the plan was a very simple one. Disable the SUV, extract Doctor Chen, and then disappear in Maggie's truck into the maze of old mining roads that riddled the area, heading to Tucker's off-grid hunting cabin, which sounded very much like Tucker's off-grid conspiracy murder cabin. Tucker and Maggie knew all the paths around here, and Tucker had also spent years mapping out alternative routes, for his own paranoid security. Plus, Harper knew that even without Tucker, Doctor Chen's ultra running paths' knowledge of the area would probably help.

A vehicle appeared around the bend, but it wasn't an Aegis SUV. Harper tensed until he recognised Cortez behind the wheel of what must have been her personal car, an ageing Honda Civic that had seen better days.

She pulled up, climbed out, stared around, and somehow saw Harper on the bluff. He couldn't explain it, but she nodded, clambered in and carried on up one of the side roads, eventually pulling up behind their position, killing the engine.

'I thought I'd find you here,' she said, climbing out, nodding at Maggie. As Harper turned, he saw Maggie had a small hand mirror in her grip, and assumed that she must have reflected it down at Cortez to alert her of their location. Cortez's badge and gun were gone, but she was moving with the same authority; even wearing a flannel shirt and jeans, her civilian clothes couldn't hide the cop in her bearing. 'I tried calling, but the signals were being jammed.'

'They're moving Chen to the mine,' Harper said, noting how Cortez automatically moved to the back of her Honda Civic and opened the trunk at the news. Training didn't go away, just because they took your badge after all.

Harper, Maggie, and Cortez were examples of that.

'She's going to be stuck with the others then?' Cortez's face was grim. 'I know, I heard about it. Coble had the entire department looking for Eddie when I was suspended. Whatever he found in that survey, or whatever Chen's discovered in her tests, they're done playing nice.'

'You know about the survey?' Harper asked.

'Everyone knows about the survey, Harper,' Cortez replied testily. 'It's all they're bloody talking about.'

Harper glanced at Maggie and saw the wry smile.

'Everyone's stopped pretending. I told you,' she repeated.

Harper went to reply, but a low rumble echoed off the rocks coming their way. Harper recognised it; diesel engine, vehicle moving fast. The kind of driving that suggested urgency rather than caution.

'Showtime,' Maggie said, clambering around the rocks as Tucker killed the scanner, moving it into a battered backpack. His hands weren't shaking as he did this, and Harper realised this wasn't his first ambush, wondering just how much of Tucker's past was real, and how much was some kind of cover.

The rumble grew louder.

Cortez, meanwhile, had pulled on a Kevlar vest, likely her police issue one, her own shotgun in her hand as she climbed back into the Honda Civic.

'I'll head them off,' she said, starting the car.

'Remember,' Harper said, as Cortez went to drive off, 'we don't know how many are in the vehicle, but Chen's safety is a priority.'

'And if Blaine decides to make it difficult?' Maggie asked.

'Then we'll show him what happens when you piss off an ex-US Marine, an ex-SRR operator and an ex-police officer.'

'Ouch. Too soon with the "ex", Harper,' Cortez gave a smile and drove off. As she did so, the SUV appeared around the bend, moving fast, just as Harper predicted. He could see through the binoculars that Blaine, the pockmarked blond, was behind the wheel, and what looked to be Lucas, his black beard visible, in the passenger seat. Doctor Chen was visible in the back, but she wasn't alone.

Eddie Hawkins was sitting next to her.

'Ah, Jesus!' Maggie's whisper carried equal parts shock and fury as she stared at the scene through her own binoculars. 'That stupid old fool!'

Harper checked again and saw that Eddie was indeed wearing borrowed firefighter gear.

'He's as stubborn as his daughter,' he smiled. 'They must have spotted him.'

This complicated things. Two hostages meant twice the risk, especially with Eddie's age. One wrong move and ...

The rest of Harper's calculation disappeared as Maggie's shotgun blast took out the front tyre. The SUV lurched hard to the left as Blaine fought the wheel, but physics won, sending them into a controlled slide. The vehicle should have rolled, but these people were professional; Blaine handled the skid with a practised skill, bringing them to a stop just short of the rock wall.

Cortez's Honda Civic was already moving, cutting off their retreat, while Tucker had disappeared into the rocks on the other side, taser in hand, covering the only escape route on foot. Harper started sprinting towards them, gaining distance quickly.

'Out of the vehicle!' His voice carried the authority that expected to be obeyed. 'Hands where we can see them!'

Blaine's response, as expected, was to open fire through his now open window, rounds cracking past Harper's position. The passenger – now confirmed as Lucas – was already out of his door, using the SUVs front pillar for cover as he laid down suppressing fire.

Obviously, this wasn't their first ambush either.

'Chen!' Harper shouted. 'Eddie, stay down!'

Three more rounds of 00 buck from Maggie's Mossberg kept the Aegis men pinned. Harper caught movement in the back seat, Eddie pulling Doctor Chen down, shielding her.

Well, they were alive, at least.

Harper's shoulder screamed as he shifted position, getting a better angle, pulling up the Glock 17. His first shot caught the passenger's door just inches from Lucas's head; a warning. His second would have been cleaner, but then Blaine chose that moment to try something stupid, and the SUV's engine roared as he threw it into reverse, trying to ram Cortez's Honda from behind, sending Lucas – who'd been using the passenger door for cover – flying as the door slammed into him.

However, it was all for nothing, as Cortez had expected this. Her car was already moving, giving them space, and the SUV's back tyre exploded as a 00 round fired from her moving Honda Civic found its mark.

With two tyres blown, they weren't going anywhere.

'Last chance, Blaine,' Harper called out. 'You're trapped,

outnumbered, and running out of time. Whatever they're paying you, it's not worth dying for.'

Blaine knew he was on his own as well. His idiot reversing trick had also left Lucas sprawled on the ground, groaning and out in the open. Understanding that he was now a sitting duck, Lucas dropped his pistol and raised his hands in the air.

Seeing this, something changed in Blaine's expression. It was the look of a man doing rapid calculations, and his return fire became sporadic, designed more to keep them back rather than hit anything, as he tried to drive forward to return to the pissed-off Lucas, to give him some kind of cover.

'You know what's in that mine,' he shouted. 'You know what this is worth.'

'What I know is that Carrick's trying to clean house,' Harper replied. 'How long before you're next?'

That hit something. Blaine's shots were more focused now.

'Mason's got federal backing!' Blaine called back, but his voice had lost the edge. 'You really want to take on—'

The rest of his sentence was lost as Eddie suddenly kicked open the back door, glass exploding outward. Before Blaine could even turn around, Eddie had pulled Doctor Chen through the door with surprising strength for his age, both of them rolling clear of the vehicle into one of the ditches to the side.

Blaine turned to fire at them – a mistake, as Harper fired a round from the Glock, catching him in the arm, spinning him back into the driver's seat. As he screamed, gripping his right arm, Maggie's shotgun kept Blaine pinned, while Cortez darted forward, covering Eddie and Doctor Chen's retreat to the rocks.

'It's over!' Harper shouted.

Blaine's answer was to throw his door open, and with his bleeding arm raised his gun again. However, Tucker, who'd been sneaking closer, had been waiting for exactly that. The taser he'd been holding hit Blaine square in the chest, dropping him before he could squeeze the trigger.

'Told you he was predictable,' Tucker said, emerging from his position.

Harper approached the SUV carefully, keeping his Glock trained on Lucas, still lay on the ground, hands behind his head. His eyes were glazed with fear, or maybe resignation.

'You don't understand, Harper,' he said. 'What they're processing up there, what they're planning to do with it ... it's worth more than our lives.'

'We understand plenty,' Doctor Chen's voice was sharp as she emerged from cover, bruised but intact. 'And I've got proof.'

Eddie appeared beside her, looking similarly battered but alert.

'Guys, you need to see what we found,' he said.

Maggie was already zip-tying Blaine, screaming out in agony from his wound, and who had recovered enough now to start swearing. Tucker, having reloaded his taser, kept him covered while she worked.

'We need to move,' Cortez said, looking down the mountain road. 'They'll have heard the shots.'

'What about them?' Maggie nodded at the captives.

'Leave them,' Harper decided. 'By the time they get free, it'll be too late.'

Tucker's scanner crackled with increased chatter, and they heard voices speaking on it. Multiple vehicles had been dispatched, coordinates being shared.

The hunt was on.

'You two okay?' Harper asked.

'She's got her sample replies back,' Eddie said. 'From the western tunnels. The ones they didn't want anyone to see, from the substances on Moses.'

Eddie and Doctor Chen piled into Cortez's Honda, Doctor Chen in the front while Eddie squeezed in behind.

'Get to Tucker's cabin,' Harper said softly, making sure the Aegis operatives couldn't hear. 'We'll follow you in Maggie's Jeep.'

They pulled away, and as Harper, Maggie and Tucker hurried on back up the mountainside, Harper caught the last glimpse of Blaine through the trees.

The man's expression wasn't angry anymore, it was afraid.

'Your time's almost up,' Tucker reminded Harper.

'Don't matter now,' Harper checked his watch, anyway. Just under an hour until the town meeting. 'It's time to end this.'

The rumble of engines in the distance added urgency to their movements, and somewhere up at the mine, alarms sounded.

Noon was approaching fast.

24

SCARY MURDER CABIN

HARPER WASN'T SURE WHAT TO EXPECT FROM TUCKER'S CABIN. Part of him wondered whether it would be some kind of idyllic lakeside getaway, but then the other part of him wondered whether it would be some kind of serial killer, *Friday the Thirteenth*-style off-grid cabin that looked like no one had lived there for years.

As it was, it felt like a combination of the two, crouched against the mountainside like something hibernating, a half mile up a dirt track that was barely visible from the main road, beside a fallen sign advertising NO TRESPASSING lying rusting in the scrub. Harper couldn't help himself, but actually wondered whether this was a cabin actually *owned* by Tucker, or whether the rusting sign had been smashed down to the ground by Tucker as a protest against who actually owned it.

Tucker gave a smile, a proud homeowner, waving his hands out, welcoming them to his building.

'Welcome to chez Tucker,' he announced, waving around.

'It's not much. It's not even home, but, you know, it does what it needs to do.'

'And what exactly does it need to do?' Harper asked as Tucker walked up to the main door to the cabin and unlocked it with what seemed to be a variety of different sized keys, in a variety of different sized locks.

'Oh, you know, hide out when the satellites are too close, or when there's a chance I could be found.'

'Is this where you keep your tin foil hat?' Maggie grinned.

'You mock, but when the "one percenter" Illuminati comes for us, I know I'll be safe,' Tucker chuckled as he entered the cabin. 'I've got my own water supply, my own electricity supply. Not that I need it. I'm completely off grid here. You've seen the film *Red Dawn*?'

'The one where the teenagers fight the Russians?' Harper frowned.

'Yeah, they went up into the mountains. They could look after themselves all through the winter with a shit load less than I have.'

'You are aware that's a film, right?' Harper wasn't sure how much of this was Tucker playing a part, or whether, regardless of his foresightedness and abilities, he was still a little bit of a conspiracy nut.

The interior belied the ramshackle experience, however. If anything, it seemed quite cosy. In one corner there was radio equipment that looked almost military grade, next to topological maps covering the entire wall.

Tucker smiled, wandering off, and a moment later, the lights turned on. He returned, looking up at them proudly.

'Solar powered,' he said. 'I've got a Tesla Powerwall hooked up to solar batteries.'

'You know Tesla's owned by one of the "one percenters"?'

'I know, but it's renewable and you have to make some concessions in war,' Tucker shrugged. 'Anyway, welcome to my *other* office. Aegis patrols won't come up here; they tried once.'

His expression suggested it hadn't ended well.

'They don't know where the cabin is. It's not on any records. My granddaddy built it.'

'Was your granddaddy allowed to build it?' Harper asked, almost smiling. 'Because I'll be honest, Tucker, it doesn't look like you own this land.'

'Bickfords own this land,' Tucker shrugged, 'but they don't care about the scrublands and the woods. All they care about is the mine.'

Maggie whistled softly, examining a rack of rifles that wouldn't have looked out of place in a military armoury.

'It's a hunting lodge,' Tucker smiled darkly. 'I go hunting.'

Harper wasn't sure, looking at the weapons, what exactly it was Tucker hunted.

Doctor Chen knelt by a metal stove, feeding wood into it to start a fire. Eddie hovered nearby, moving aside items on the table, pulling out folded maps from inside his firefighter's clothes and spreading them out. The firefighter's jacket he'd gained from Maggie's wardrobe was stained with blood and dirt, but he moved with the energy of a man half his age.

'You guys need to see this,' he said, and Harper saw that William Bickford's original survey was now on the table.

'No,' Doctor Chen shook her head. 'Before any of that, they need to understand what's really going on in those mines.'

'And what is going on in those mines?' Harper asked.

'So, my test results were sent to Berkeley to be checked,' Doctor Chen explained, the stove now used as a fire, looking back at the others. 'But as we know, before they even got out of the state, Aegis stopped them. But I had other options, and in a way, I expected them to do this.'

'So, you gave them an obvious one?'

'The lesser obvious one was a message I passed through Cassie at O'Malley's. She's also a journalist, she understands how things are. She had a contact in Virginia City, and she got one of her regulars, someone she trusted, to drive out there, taking my samples with them. There was no connection to me, and as far as anybody asking was concerned, they were just picking up some more whiskey for the bar.'

She stared at the flames in the stove.

'But they worked it out, torched *The Prospector* to remove the samples, thinking they were being stored there. We're lucky they didn't burn the bar down, too. Anyway, before I could check any further, the fires started.'

'Aegis cleaning house.'

'Yeah. And this morning, when I was filling out the bullshit insurance details that Coble wanted, I got a message back.'

'Go on,' Harper encouraged.

'What they found in Moses' lungs was unlike anything I'd seen before. Crystalline structures, growing in geometric patterns, cutting through tissue at a cellular level. These aren't natural formations. They're byproducts of mineral processing – specifically, rare earth refinement.'

'What does that mean exactly?' Maggie asked.

'It means that these mines might be played out of gold, but for a hundred and fifty years the Bickfords have known there's something different, something more lucrative in there,' Doctor Chen replied. 'Did you ever hear about the Brook mine in Wyoming?'

'I'm not local,' Harper shook his head.

'Wyoming's not local, Harper,' Doctor Chen chuckled. 'About fifteen years ago, some CEO bought an old coal mine in Wyoming and spent two million dollars to look into it. Place was tapped out, nobody understood why he was doing it ... and then he found that waiting to be discovered all those years was an absolute shit ton of rare magnetic earth elements. They reckon that fifteen years later, that mine's worth about forty billion dollars.'

'Jesus,' Cortez exclaimed. 'And you think that's the same as Prosperity's mine?'

'I don't think that at all,' Doctor Chen replied. 'I know it. Traces showed significant concentrations of Terbium, Neodymium, Europium ... but primarily Dysprosium. It's what we call a unique geological signature. These elements naturally occur together, but never in these concentrations. What makes this deposit extraordinary is the purity. These aren't trace elements, they're concentrated veins of strategic metals that usually require processing thousands of tons of ore to obtain in usable quantities.'

'And here's the fun part,' Eddie looked around. 'Gold goes for what, eighty thousand dollars a kilo? You're lucky if you're making five hundred for a kilo of Dysprosium ... but that's only when you're talking raw Dysprosium. The stuff on Moses was far more refined.'

He tapped the survey map.

'In those tunnels, Bickford found something he couldn't identify, something that wouldn't even be officially discovered for another eleven years; a metal so rare, and so strategically crucial, that today, refined and prepared, it's worth more than its gold equivalent a hundred times over.'

He turned back to face the others.

'These mines are played out – there's no more gold inside them. Each year gave less and less back in the day. But when Dysprosium is refined to ninety-nine percent purity – which some call weapons grade, although that's a term usually held for Uranium and Plutonium – that price jumps. Personally, I'd use Military Spec, or "MilSpec". Normal deposits are measured in parts per million. But this, it's literally pure. It shouldn't exist in nature.'

'So, there's every opportunity to make billions out of this as well,' Maggie said.

'Exactly. In Wyoming they've spent billions to extract trace amounts from old coal seams, California too. But what Bickford found is different, and hundreds of times higher than Wyoming's estimates. And they've had decades to plan how to extract it.'

'But surely if you can mine it out of Wyoming, you can mine it out of Nevada, then—'

'It's rare,' Doctor Chen replied, shutting Cortez off. 'This is a unicorn, Lisa. You don't find them often, especially at this concentration. China controls ninety-eight percent of global production. And they're already using the monopoly as leverage in trade negotiations.'

'A domestic source,' Harper shook his head. 'That's worth killing for. How valuable are we talking?'

'Honestly, I don't think it can be calculated,' Eddie replied, looking up. 'Dysprosium is just one element. You've got Terbium, which is used in optics and satellites. Neodymium is crucial for the strongest permanent magnets in the world; every wind turbine needs massive amounts of it. Every electric vehicle motor, too. Then there's Europium. That's what gives you the red in every LED screen, every optical sensor. Military night vision, missile guidance systems, satellite communications ... they all depend on it. Now imagine this, refined to MilSpec level. A single vein could be worth billions alone. And trust me, in the western tunnels, they've had a dozen veins to pick from.'

There was a moment of silence at this.

'Anyway, Bickford couldn't have known what it was back then, but he knew it was different, possibly because it had a silver sheen,' Eddie quickly continued. 'The geological conditions created something unique. Deposits hundreds of times more concentrated than anything documented.'

'But he also knew it was deadly,' Doctor Chen added. 'That "bad air"? The deaths weren't from gas, they were exposure to unrefined compounds. Those crystalline structures we saw? These form during refinement. When they enter lung tissue, they can trigger cascade failures in cellular respiration. One exposure, without proper protection ...'

She trailed off, and Harper wondered whether she was considering her father, who had also died in the mines.

'That's what killed Moses,' Tucker added quietly, 'and what's been killing people in these mines for over a century.'

'The Pentagon estimates in five years, we'll need ten times the current global Dysprosium production just to meet military demands,' Doctor Chen continued. 'It's essential for everything. And they're not just mining it, they're processing it on-site.'

'But why not just dig it out, load into lorries and then refine it elsewhere?'

'Probably because Bickford didn't trust Mason Carrick,' Doctor Chen shrugged. 'It's more complicated to do it this way, but "on site", so to speak meant nothing could be skimmed off the top. They'd process it here and then send it on.'

'Which would explain the hazmat trucks that Tucker saw,' Harper said, understanding the big picture now. 'And the military-grade security, too. This isn't just about protecting a mine. This is about controlling a strategic national resource. No wonder Bickford went to a security company of Aegis's size to help him here. This wasn't a case of bringing in some "good ol' boys", he needed somebody who not only had the contacts in the American military to provide the money he'd want, but to provide the equipment to create it.'

'If the Chinese get pissy with us,' Tucker added, 'everything from smartphones to stealth fighters stops working. If we have a domestic source, the military applications alone could be worth trillions.'

'Enough to buy a town and keep people quiet for generations,' Harper added.

'Enough to do whatever it takes,' Eddie spoke, his voice carrying weight. 'My father, Maggie's grandpa, he worked these mines, died of bad air. Chen's father worked these mines. He, too, died from bad air. And now Mason Carrick has arrived with federal backing, military contracts, maybe even black budget operations.'

'Which explains the cleaning operation,' Maggie said. 'The fires destroying records—'

'And why they can't let Eddie present his evidence at the town meeting,' Cortez added.

Harper studied the diagrams, remembering Blaine's fear. This was bigger than Aegis, bigger than Mason Carrick. *If this was national security level ...*

'These weren't for mining gold,' he said, tapping some markings on the map. 'The ventilation shaft, the drainage systems, they were designing this for processing something volatile even back then. Generation after generation, all adding to the plan. The "bad air" deaths weren't accidents, they were test runs. Idiots trying to refine something that wasn't ready for the technology; seeing how the mineral behaved, how it could be handled, using townsfolk as canaries in a mine.'

He pulled his lucky stone from his pocket, running it between his fingers as the pieces fell into place. His father had known about this; he *must* have known. It wasn't just chance that had brought Harper to Prosperity.

'Make it right,' he muttered to himself.

'What?' Cortez frowned.

'What my dad said before he died,' Harper replied. 'Not a random plea, but a specific mission.'

Harper understood now. While everyone else saw gold, Dominic Kane had seen what the Bickfords were really building. If this worked, Tom Bickford would be richer than God. He'd no longer control Prosperity; he'd control Nevada.

America.

The world.

All with Aegis by his side.

'We need to think this through,' he said, studying the map. 'What's Aegis's play here?'

'The town meeting's mandatory,' Cortez replied. 'Coble's made sure everyone will be there.'

'Everyone except the troublemakers,' Doctor Chen added. 'The ones they've got up at the mine, probably others who've been asking questions.'

'What?'

Doctor Chen was surprised by the response, but then nodded.

'Of course, you've been up here,' she replied. 'While you've been away, they've been rounding up the dissidents and whisking them off, just like they were doing with us. Probably the main route, which is why you missed them.'

''They're consolidating control,' Harper nodded. 'Get the whole town in one place, have Coble and Bickford sell their story about outside agitators, criminal elements. Meanwhile, anyone who might contradict them is conveniently absent.'

'Mason Carrick will be there,' Maggie said. 'Probably your buddy Ashfield, too.'

'But not Delaney,' Harper tapped the mine on the map. 'He'll be running the facility. They can't shut down processing just for a town meeting.'

'You're right, these refinement processes are continuous,' Doctor Chen nodded. 'Once you process rare earth elements at this scale, you can't just stop. Usually you'd use chemical reactions to leech out the elements, but the chemical reactions, the containment protocols ... shutting down would take days. And if they're preparing for a backup plan, maybe try to hack the seam out, they'll be looking to up the levels to dangerous heights.'

'How so?' Maggie asked.

'Imagine the mine exploding,' Doctor Chen continued. 'The moment it did, well, it'd spew toxic chemical shit everywhere. Hundreds could be hurt. The town would die.'

'Could that happen?' Cortez's eyes were saucers.

'The fissures are already cracking,' Harper said. 'That's how we found Moses.'

He thought back to that moment. *Had Ashfield known that was likely? Had he organised the "split" to happen somehow? Did he lead Harper there to see Moses ... or die beside him?*

'It won't take much more to set off a chain event,' Eddie looked haunted. 'They're too desperate to even consider the risks.'

'But right now, they're split,' Harper said. 'Security divided between the meeting and the mine.'

He looked at Cortez.

'How many deputies does Coble have?'

'Without me? Four deputies, including Carson. Plus, whatever Aegis personnel he deputised.'

'And the mine?'

'Eight to ten regulars,' Tucker said. 'More since the fires. They're running three shifts now, so maybe twenty at best?'

Harper considered their options. A frontal assault on either target would be suicide. But if they split their forces, used the element of surprise ...

'They'll expect us at the meeting,' he said slowly. 'That's where they think we'll make our move – trying to speak, present evidence. They'll be ready for that.'

'But not for both,' Maggie said, catching his thinking.

'Exactly,' Harper turned to Cortez. 'You're law enforcement. More importantly, you're a Cortez. When you stand up in that meeting, challenge Sheriff Coble about your father's murder, about that Winchester ... people will listen.'

'They'll try to stop her speaking,' Doctor Chen said.

'That's why you and Eddie go with her. Eddie, you've got the historical proof, how the Bickfords have been planning this for generations. Chen, you've got the science; what's really in those mines, what's been killing people. Between the three of you, that's too much truth, and too many years in the community between you, for them to bury.'

'And while they're focused on us?' Cortez asked.

'We hit the mine.' Harper looked at Maggie. 'You've got combat experience, Tucker knows every back route in, and I've got enough demolition training to make sure whatever we find in there never operates again—or until we can find a way to stop someone else coming in.'

'And how do we do that?' Maggie sighed. 'Someone could roll in tomorrow, with enough diggers to level a mountain.'

'Not if they don't own the mountain,' Eddie smiled. 'I think we have enough old paperwork from William Bickford's notes to make a claim that they gained the mining rights fraudulently, and they need to be passed back to the original owners.'

'And who exactly is that?'

'I dunno,' Eddie grinned. 'But the legal hoo-ha should give us enough breathing space to work out how the town can gain the rights back.'

'That's great,' Harper interrupted, 'but right now we're focusing on how to get in.'

'Through the old tunnels,' Eddie suggested. 'The ones they don't know about from the survey they've been hunting for.'

He tapped the corner of the survey.

'You get in, free anyone they're holding, then make sure that facility can never operate again – or at least until correct, and un-involved authorities make it safe.'

'They'll have fail-safes,' Tucker warned. 'Deadman switches on the containment systems. One wrong move and that shit could flood the entire facility.'

'Then we do it right,' Harper checked his watch. 'We've got an hour until the meeting. Questions?'

'Just one,' Maggie said, already checking her shotgun. 'What if we're wrong about any of this?'

'Look around,' Harper replied. 'At what they've done to this town, what they're willing to do to keep this secret. We're not wrong. They wouldn't have burned half the town if we were.'

There was a silent agreement between all five people.

'Looks like I picked a bad time to quit drinking,' Tucker smiled.

Harper paused, pulling the Parsons' burner phone out of his pocket.

'Hey,' he said to Cortez, opening it up and showing the message. 'Recognise this number? It was sent to the Parsons, the fake hiking couple in the guesthouse.'

Cortez checked the message, nodding as she read the number.

'Oh yeah,' she said. 'Can I keep this? Because if it's who I think it is, I know just how to use it.'

'Go wild,' Harper smiled.

25

TOWN MEETING

It was almost noon, and Main Street was empty – except for people heading towards the town hall and the big town meeting.

Cortez watched them quietly from the alley beside O'Malley's, noting the armed Aegis personnel at every intersection. They were checking faces and IDs, stopping anyone who looked suspicious. They weren't just providing security, though, these "deputised" men and women; they were screening attendees. Sheriff Coble's decision for martial law to be enforced was turning Prosperity into a military state.

'This isn't going to work,' Doctor Chen whispered nervously. 'They'll recognise us.'

'Not necessarily,' Cortez was studying the flow of people. 'They might have high tech shit to look for us, but they won't want to show it while they're playing the family friendly role. They're also spread thin, so they're distracted.'

Around them, families were arriving together, groups of workers from the same businesses walking along – silent, strangely silent for such a day. This wasn't a social event, even though it was a "social" event. The town had been rocked in the last twenty-four hours with fires, dead bodies discovered and more deaths explained, forcing a complete shift in their belief system.

But they needed to get *loud* again.

The Aegis operatives were focused on individuals, anyone moving alone. Which made sense, they were probably keeping an eye out for Harper.

'We split up, blending with different groups. Eddie, you go with the mechanics from the east side, you've known them for years. They won't think twice about having you in their group.'

Eddie nodded as they watched another group walk past the Aegis soldiers without a second glance.

'And if they catch me?' he started.

'If they catch you, they'll take you to the mine,' Cortez replied. 'And to be honest, by the time you get there, Harper will probably have blown the bloody place up.'

Eddie grinned, already moving to intercept a group of weather-beaten men approaching from that direction. They absorbed him naturally, decades of friendship making the deception effortless.

'You next,' Cortez told Doctor Chen.

'There's no other townsfolk roles that can fit me,' Doctor Chen snapped.

'No, but right now they're not looking for you,' Cortez replied. 'If you notice, they're stopping males, so we need to get you in before they change that order. There's a group over there; looks like the teachers from the school. You know a couple of them, don't you?'

Doctor Chen smiled.

'They owe me enough for the various hangover cures I've given them over the years,' she replied. 'They'll look after me.'

'Join them on the next block.'

Doctor Chen hesitated.

'What about you?'

'I've got my own way in,' Cortez said. 'Don't worry about me; remember I'm not a threat, I'm just a suspended officer.'

THE TOWN HALL OF PROSPERITY DATED FROM 1876 AND WAS one of William Bickford's first civic projects. Its weathered stone façade had witnessed a century and a half of Prosperity's history. Cortez had practically grown up here; she knew every entrance and every service door. Her father's time as sheriff had meant that more than one town hall meeting or event had her father working, monitoring the audience, young Lisa Cortez beside him.

More importantly, she knew which entrances the staff used.

She circled the building while Doctor Chen ran across and merged with the group of teachers and support staff from the local school. The kitchen entrance was locked, but it yielded to a lockpick set Cortez had gained many years earlier, experience with it gained from times when she had to open doors, or even the sheriff's office itself on an occasion when Carson had forgotten to turn up, leaving her without a key.

Coble had been *pissed* about that one.

Inside, she found exactly what she expected – a small amount of catering staff preparing coffee and refreshments.

Town halls were always a thirsty affair, and the speakers would need water.

Sarah Phillips, who had been running these events since Cortez was a kid, barely blinked at her appearance. In her late forties, she'd been in school a couple of years behind Lisa's father, and had always had a bit of a crush on him. When he had died, she was one of the first people to reach out.

'Back storage room,' Sarah muttered, not looking up from her coffee urns. 'There's a clean uniform on the hook. And Lisa?'

Now she did look up.

'I've heard that they might have been the ones that caused the fires. Is that true?'

'I can't comment,' Cortez replied. 'I'm not official anymore.'

'Well, if they are, make those bastards pay, yeah?'

Cortez emerged into the main hall two minutes later, wearing catering blacks and carrying a tray of ceramic mugs filled with water, a pitcher of water among them, for the stage. As she threaded through the room, she kept an eye to the sides; armed Aegis personnel stood at intervals, watching the crowd, but obviously weren't paying any attention to the staff. Their focus was on the main entrance, where they were still screening arrivals, looking most likely for a British man with a slight beard, cute expression, and a bleeding shoulder.

The hall was nearly full now. Cortez moved between the rows, noting faces she'd known all her life. Maisie Brown from the diner sat near the front, her usual easy manner replaced with barely contained anger, and others around her showed similar tension. These weren't people who'd come willingly, and Cortez wondered whether Mayor Bickford had lied to the Nevada authorities, claiming that they didn't need any extra help from the National Guard or inter-state authorities. Using Aegis as their deputised peace force covered a lot of problems, and Nevada had its own budget problems at the best of times.

She saw to the side that Doctor Chen had successfully infiltrated, while Eddie sat with a group of similarly aged men, keeping his head down. But there were conspicuous absences. She couldn't see Cassie from O'Malley's or in fact anyone from *The Prospector*. There was every chance they were still rummaging through the office ruins, trying to find anything that existed, but it made sense for the newspaper, in whatever state it was in, to be here, where news was being made.

In fact, as she looked around, none of the people who'd been asking questions lately were there.

'Where's my daughter?' The question came from an elderly woman Cortez recognised as Jenny Martinez. 'Katie didn't come home last night.'

Cortez stepped back into the crowd as she saw Carson move forward to shut her down, but others were already joining in, more questions about missing faces rippling through the crowd. The deputies – such as they were –moved through the rows practising intimidation with professional efficiency, while the real Prosperity deputies stood to the side, their faces emotionless. Cortez, however, had worked with them day in and day out, and could see they were powerless, rather than uncaring.

Bickford and Sheriff Coble walked onto the raised platform, where Mason Carrick and a row of suited men Cortez didn't recognise were already standing. Possibly government types, maybe, or military. The kind of people who decided about other people's towns, most likely.

Far to the side, but closer to where Cortez was, Ashfield stood, his Lennon glasses hiding his expression as he scanned the crowd.

'About time too,' a woman that Cortez didn't recognise said, motioning for Cortez to walk towards the stage. 'They need the water in front of every chair.'

Shit. Cortez hadn't realised that she was about to walk right up to the people who knew exactly who she was. However, as she walked up to the stage, she felt Ashfield's gaze fix upon her. She kept her movements casual, but her heart rate spiked – one wrong move now and pretty much everything would fall apart.

'Miss?' Ashfield's voice carried down from the stage. 'Can I have a word?'

Cortez turned slowly, keeping her head down, adjusting her grip on the tray full of mugs of water. Years of working with police officers and assets had taught her that movement was key. Staying natural and staying in character saved the day. But as she'd never been any kind of undercover officer, she wasn't sure if she was doing it correctly.

'Miss?' Ashfield's expression remained unreadable behind his glasses as he crouched to the side of the stage, holding his hands out for the tray. 'We'll need more water during the presentations. Can you get somebody to bring us some?'

Cortez felt the weight of his stare, wondering if he was playing with her, letting her know he had recognised her. But as she looked up at him, he gave her a smile.

'I'll take this,' he said. 'You don't need to come on the stage. And someone else can bring the next load.'

Cortez, surprised, stepped back and was about to reply to

Ashfield, maybe to thank him, but his attention had already shifted back to the crowd. As he started placing mugs down beside chairs, Mayor Bickford approached the podium, his politician's smile firmly in place. Cortez noticed for the first time that in front of the podium was a familiar Winchester rifle.

Bickford was pushing all the buttons today, pushing Prosperity's history as much as he could.

Behind him, Mason Carrick, the man she had met in Bickford's mansion, sat with practised stillness, only his eyes moving as he studied the assembled townspeople. And as she turned and walked back into the audience, she saw that the armed Aegis "deputies" had taken up positions at each exit.

'Friends, neighbours, valued members of Prosperity,' Bickford began, the voice echoing around the hall as the crowd quietened. 'We are here today to address the recent troubles in our fine community.'

'Where's Cassie?' Maisie's voice cut through his opening. 'O'Malley's is still closed.'

Tom gave a slight half bow to her, acknowledging her statement.

'Maisie, if you'll let me finish—'

'Let you finish what? Destroying our town?'

There was a rumble of noise as people talked, and Sheriff Coble rose from his chair, stepping forward.

'Several citizens are being questioned about their connection to recent criminal activities,' he answered smoothly. 'They're helping us with our investigation.'

'Investigation?' Another voice; Bernard Phillips from the hardware store. 'Into what? The fires that you apparently started?'

Murmurs of agreement rippled through the crowd.

Carson moved to silence Phillips, but the damage was already done. More voices joined in, questions overlapping.

'What about the library?'

'Where's Doctor Chen's records?'

'Where's Doctor Chen?'

'Why did you suspend Deputy Cortez?'

Sheriff Coble raised his hands for silence, but the crowd's anger was building. Cortez watched Mason Carrick lean forward, whispering something to Bickford. The mayor nodded and then raised his voice over the growing chaos.

'Please. We understand your concerns,' he said, 'but there are elements in this town, outside agitators, who would destroy everything we have built. The fires, the violence, all of it can be traced to these criminals.'

'What criminals?' Maisie spoke again, her voice sharp with disgust. 'The only violence I've seen came from *them*.'

She jabbed a finger at the nearest Aegis "deputy", who, coincidentally, seemed to be the pockmarked blond, Blaine.

'I'm afraid, Miss Brown, you have been seen conversing with the criminals,' Sheriff Coble said. 'One of them was in your diner two days ago. A British man sent here by enemies of America, to infiltrate our town, and to cause dissent.'

'Are you telling me that man, the one that helped Eddie Hawkins – twice – is the same one who set up three different fires in three different areas before spending the night trying to put them out? That's bullshit and you know it, Eric.'

'Miss Brown,' Sheriff Coble's tone carried another warning. 'Perhaps you'd like to join the others and help us with our inquiries? We'd also like to discuss your involvement, if there was any, in the attack on this deputy, earlier today on the mountain road.'

The threat landed. Silence fell as people processed its

implications, and Cortez used the moment to move towards the kitchen. As she did so, she caught Doctor Chen's eye and saw Eddie shifting in his seat.

It was almost time.

'Now then,' Bickford continued, 'I'd like to introduce you all to Mister Mason Carrick, whose company, Aegis, has been instrumental in—'

'In what?' A fresh voice now spoke, carrying authority and training. Cortez glanced around to see her father's old partner, Jim Reynolds, in his late sixties and still standing, despite Carson's attempt to keep him seated. 'In turning our town into an armed camp? In "disappearing" anyone who asks questions? Last I saw, we were still part of America, not part of communist Russia.'

'Officer Reynolds,' Sheriff Coble's voice hardened. 'You're out of order, and actually a little behind the times and racist with that comment.'

'I ain't no officer anymore,' Reynolds stayed standing. 'I retired when I realised how bad this town was going to be, when that idiot boy-child became mayor and his goddamned lickspittle servant became sheriff. Yeah, I watched you all your life, Tommy. You were never gonna result in anything worth my spit. I served this town for thirty years, served alongside Robbie Cortez when he was sheriff and back then people were proud of Prosperity.'

'I get your concerns,' Bickford said, reddening at the insult, but trying to rise above it. 'Even if you don't feel I was ever going to rate to anything, I understand that. But we're here to address the recent troubles in our community.'

He gestured to the rifle mounted in front of the podium. Doc Holliday's Winchester, positioned like some kind of talisman.

'This rifle represents our heritage, our history of standing strong against—'

'Standing strong against what?' Hank Longstead, the town's veterinary surgeon snapped, standing up now Carson had moved his attention to Reynolds. 'That rifle's something your great-granddaddy bought from a drunkard. You keep saying this is like how the West was won.'

He glared around the hall.

'The West wasn't won, the West was bought by their goddamned family ... after stealing the gold.'

It was about then that the shouting started.

Cortez glanced at Eddie and shrugged. Things were going bad for Bickford right now ...

And *they* hadn't even started.

26

TUNNEL RATS

THE ENTRANCE TO WILLIAM BICKFORD'S PROCESSING TUNNELS hadn't appeared on any official mine document since 1870, and even then Harper was convinced they'd only been in his own, secret surveys. Which made sense, considering that as Bickford paid for the survey, he was already making plans for his family's future.

Tucker led them via a series of back trails through the mountainside; these didn't feel like hiking or running trails, these felt like long forgotten smuggler routes, moving through scrub that hadn't seen footprints in decades. The noon sun cast harsh shadows across the rocky ground, making the terrain treacherous. Every few minutes, the distant sound of vehicles on the main mine road reminded them of how close they were to Aegis patrols.

Harper's shoulder burned with each step, the wound from the Parsons' attack still pulling whenever he shifted his pack, regardless of how well Maggie had patched him up.

It was going to leave a scar, no matter what he did.

Who needs a postcard from places you visit, anyway.

The packs of construction-grade C4 inside the pack, provided by Tucker with a suggestion to "not ask" wasn't heavy, but its weight felt significant – there was likely enough explosive to make sure whatever they found up here couldn't be rebuilt, if positioned correctly. Maggie moved behind him, her Marine training never more clear in how she placed each foot, carrying a matching pack, along with the tactical shotgun that had already proved so effective. Tucker led the way, and it was very obvious that this was a route he'd used before.

They'd left the truck hidden almost two miles back, choosing a route that avoided Aegis's security cameras and motion sensors. Tucker had spent weeks mapping their blind spots, watching patrol patterns while everyone dismissed him as just another burnout; now that knowledge was keeping them alive. There wasn't a need to keep the truck nearby, anyway – the plan was to use a second exit from the mine, a long discarded supply tunnel, only visible on the Bickford map, which led out to the hills to the side of Prosperity, a half mile uphill from the Goldstrike Inn & Suites. Harper remembered hearing about this, and couldn't help wondering if this was the reason the Goldstrike had been positioned there. Although, if the map had been lost for centuries, the chances were the tunnel had been, too.

'Here,' Tucker stopped at what looked like a natural rock formation, its surface weathered by over a century of Nevada summers. He pushed aside decades of creeper growth to reveal metal, set into stone; a door, that over the years had become disguised as part of the mountain itself. The lock was old, but Tucker had it open in seconds, his fingers moving with the kind of skill that suggested this wasn't his first infiltration.

'Maintenance entrance,' he explained, testing the hinges, wincing as they creaked a little on touch. 'They used these for ventilation checks back when the mine was supposedly just mining gold. But look.'

He indicated markings on the metal.

'Industrial grade seals. Air-tight when closed. Pressure regulation systems. This wasn't built for gold mining. They're the same as the ones we'll be coming out of, but those won't need to be unlocked as we'll be coming out, not in.'

The tunnel beyond the door was narrow, barely wide enough for single file, and Harper's torch revealed metal-lined walls, and strange-looking, complex ventilation systems that looked far too advanced for 1870. Modern gas sensors had been added, similar to the ones he'd seen in the tour-turned-ambush, their power cables running alongside Victorian-era engineering. The combination was jarring; like finding a Delorean in a medieval castle.

No. That's time travel.

'They've been upgrading these tunnels for generations,' Maggie whispered, her light catching more modern additions. 'Adding technology as it became available. These air scrubbers are military grade. Same ones we used in chemical warfare exercises.'

'Probably testing their processes on whoever got too close,' Harper added, checking one sensor as Tucker, now to the side, consulted a hand-drawn map of the tunnel system.

'Eddie marked which sections have likely been modernised, based on the information he gained from Aegis when they trusted him,' he said. 'Also, a few additions from me, before I asked questions and was shown the door. They've got fail-safes everywhere, pressure doors, emergency seals. Whatever they're processing, they're terrified of it getting loose.'

They moved deeper, Harper marking their route with small markings from a UV pen. They each had a torch that could see these if needed, and if they were in a hurry to get out of Dodge as quick as possible, it made sense not to get locked down there. The air grew cooler, carrying chemical traces that made his nose itch. Somewhere ahead, machinery hummed – the sound transmitted through rock and metal. The walls here showed signs of recent work, fresh welds on old iron.

'Contact,' Maggie hissed suddenly, dropping into a combat crouch.

Two Aegis guards appeared around a bend, their attention on clipboards rather than security. They wore clean hazmat suits with the helmets off, more concerned with readings than watching their sector. Everything about them suggested complacency; these were men used to guarding a facility that wasn't targeted, not expecting anyone to know about these tunnels, let alone breach them.

They went down fast and silent. Maggie's shotgun pressed against ribs was persuasion enough, while Harper's hand over mouths prevented any alarm. The guards' eyes widened as they recognised Harper from his visit the previous day – not only was he the man they'd been warned about, but he recognised one of them from their misguided attack down in the lower levels.

'Tell us what we want to know, and we don't leave you like Moses Mathers,' he hissed. 'Processing control room – and where you're keeping the townsfolk.'

'You'll need a map—'

'Let us worry about a map,' Harper continued, leaning in

close now. 'You worry about staying alive in this gas-filled death trap.'

'Processing control room's through there,' one guard gasped when Harper let him speak, pointing down a side tunnel. His voice shook with genuine fear. 'Please ... those crystals ... you don't understand what happens if the containment fails. The fail-safes, the pressure doors, they're not just for show.'

'How many people have you got locked up?' Harper asked, while beside him Maggie was already stripping the guards of weapons and communications gear. Their radios showed encrypted channels, military-grade equipment that shouldn't be in a civilian mining operation, but they were well past surprise at this now.

'Six, maybe seven. Storage section B.' The guard couldn't stop staring at Harper's eyes, staring coldly down at him. 'In the vault.'

'The vault?' Maggie leant closer. 'That damned thing was supposed to be airtight! They'll suffocate!'

'I don't think they care,' Harper muttered.

'No, they welded bars in the opening,' the guard explained. 'They can breathe. But you need to listen ... if those processing systems go down wrong, if the containment fails—'

'This is already known, and boring,' Tucker's taser dropped him before he could finish. The other guard started to respond but was knocked unconscious with a butt stroke to the back of the head from Maggie's shotgun.

'You should be careful about that,' Harper couldn't help but chide. 'That could cause concussion.'

'I'll apologise later,' Maggie shrugged as they zip-tied both men, gagging them with their own hazmat suit sleeves.

'They're not lying about the containment,' Tucker said, examining the guards' clipboards, turning it to Harper to reveal complex chemical readings, pressure measurements, crystallisation rates – none of it looked like normal mining data.

'They're not just processing rare earth elements, they're trying to find some way to weaponise them,' Harper understood the reticence here as he examined the tunnel junction ahead; three paths lay in front of him. One led towards the processing centre, one deeper into the mountain, and one marked with a faded 'B' that had to be the storage section.

'Get your people out first. Then we'll worry about what they're cooking up down here.'

'We've got another problem,' Tucker was examining the clipboard. 'These notes Huey and Duey were writing? They show they're in the middle of a processing cycle. We can't just shut it down; the containment systems are tied to the main power. Kill that, and everything vents.'

'Then we do it smart,' Harper pulled the first of Tucker's incredibly suspicious C4 charges from his pack. 'Set the charges, get our people clear, then bring it down in sequence. The processing first, then the support tunnels, then the main shaft. Bury it all so deep they'll never dig it out.'

Maggie studied the unconscious guards.

'Will they be okay?'

'They're far enough out to be safe,' Harper nodded. 'They won't be able to get back in though, so I hope they didn't leave anything important in their lockers.

'They'll have check-ins,' Maggie warned, reassured now. 'We need to move.'

THE 'B' TUNNEL NARROWED AS THEY MOVED DEEPER INTO THE mountain, its Victorian-era stonework giving way to modern concrete and steel. Pipes ran along the walls, carrying God knew what deeper into the mountain. The air felt wrong here, becoming constantly heavy with something that made Harper's throat itch. Their flashlight beams caught crystalline formations growing in corners, glinting with unnatural colours, similar to the ones found on Moses Mathers. Concerned, Harper looked at Tucker, who shook his head, checking a gas sensor he'd picked up from one of the secured guards.

'Gas levels are fine,' he replied carefully. 'I mean, don't lick the damn things, but they seem to be old, stable growths.'

Tucker consulted his hand-drawn map again, correlating it with markings on the walls.

'The storage sections were part of the original mine. Used for equipment, explosives, the vault they kept the gold in. But if they've brought people here, they've probably turned them into holding cells.'

Harper's shoulder wound throbbed as they moved, each step carrying them deeper into the mountain. The guards' reactions played through his mind – not just fear of being caught, but genuine terror about containment failures. Whatever Aegis was processing down here, even their own people were afraid of it.

His father had been afraid of it, too.

The tunnel opened into a wider section, with a heavy vault door set into the wall, open to reveal a second, welded-shut entrance with a heavy door with an opening slit, turning the inside of the vault into a kind of holding cell, built into century-old mine workings, with narrow air slits down the side. A guard station stood empty, coffee still steaming in a mug. Maggie moved to check the security monitors while Tucker examined the door controls.

'They're running on a separate power system,' Tucker said. 'Independent from the primary facility. Smart; means they can maintain security even if the processing systems fail.'

'Or if someone tries to shut them down,' Harper added. He studied the monitors over Maggie's shoulder. One large holding cell, currently occupied. He recognised Cassie from O'Malley's, but didn't recognise any of the others, likely townsfolk who'd been asking questions lately. All looking alert, aware ... they hadn't been drugged, at least.

'Can you open it?' Maggie asked Tucker, but he shook his head sadly.

'I'm a conspiracy theorist trucker,' he admitted. 'Not bloody MacGyver.'

'Luckily, we don't need you to be,' Harper held up a keycard taken from the guard he'd spoken to, but a door slammed somewhere in the tunnel behind them. Footsteps approached; multiple sets, moving with purpose.

'Shift change,' Maggie whispered, already moving to cover. 'Shit.'

Harper found position behind the guard station, while Tucker, proving an innate skill of staying alive, melted into the shadows. As he did so, three more Aegis personnel appeared around the bend – two guards and someone in a white lab coat. They were deep in conversation, not expecting trouble this far inside their facility.

'... crystallisation rates are increasing,' the lab coat was saying. 'If we don't adjust the containment protocols—'

They reached the guard station before noticing something was wrong. The first guard's hand moved towards his weapon—

Harper was already moving. A solid elbow strike to the first guards temple that put him down, and his cohort took a vicious throat strike, dropping him before he could draw. The scientist backed away, hands raised, clipboard clutched like a shield.

'Please,' he stuttered, 'you don't understand. The processing systems, the containment down here – one wrong move and ...'

'And what?' Harper kept his voice low, controlled. 'More crystals in people's lungs? More "accidents" to cover up?'

The scientist kept glancing at his clipboard, hands shaking. Harper took the clipboard, passing it to Tucker.

'How long have you worked here?' he asked the scientist.

'Eight months. Aegis recruited me from Los Alamos. Said it was private sector research, better money,' the scientist swallowed hard. 'Didn't know about the deaths until I started seeing the medical data. By then it was too late to walk away.'

'It's never too late,' Maggie said, but her tone suggested she didn't entirely believe it.

Tucker was already at the cell controls, the guard's stolen keycard enabling access. The door opened with a pneumatic hiss, and Cassie emerged cautiously, taking in the scene: unconscious guards, armed intruders, terrified scientist.

'About time,' she said. 'They've got Katie Martinez in here. Girl's having breathing problems.'

Behind her, the other prisoners emerged quickly, understanding their window was limited. Katie Martinez, a young girl, perhaps not even in her teens, looked pale, her breathing laboured even in the short walk to the guard station.

The scientist watched her with obvious guilt.

'Why the hell did they take Katie?' Maggie asked, rummaging around in her pocket. 'She has asthma, you prick. Leaving her down here without her inhaler ...'

'Mom was asking questions,' Katie croaked. 'I tried to help find answers, followed a car, saw them set fire to *The Prospector*. They picked me up before I could—'

She stopped talking, turning her response into a wracking cough.

'The crystalline structures,' the scientist said quietly, glancing from Katie to the cavern walls around them 'They're forming faster than our models predicted. The containment systems weren't designed for this level of production.'

'That's why you've got fail-safes, though, right?' Harper asked. 'Pressure doors, emergency seals?'

'They won't be enough, not with what we're processing now.' The scientist's voice shook. 'We thought the concentration readings were wrong at first. Nothing shows these kinds of purity levels in nature. But the military contracts required higher yields, faster processing ...'

'How many others?' Maggie asked the freed prisoners. 'Anyone else they're holding?'

'Just us,' Cassie replied. 'They grabbed anyone who'd seen the fires started, or asked too many questions. Would've been more, probably, but the fires kept people distracted.'

Harper checked his watch. The town meeting would be going on now – Coble and Bickford gathering everyone to sell their lies while Aegis cleaned house.

'Looks like you missed your deadline to leave town,' Maggie whispered.

'Well, technically, I'm not *in* town,' Harper tried to make his reply more jovial than he felt, but something the scientist said nagged at him.

'What happens if your containment fails?'

The scientist's face went pale.

'The crystalline formations don't just get in your lungs. They, well, grow. Spread. The deeper we dig, the purer the deposits ...'

A radio crackled from one of the unconscious guards.

'Vault guard, status check.'

They all froze. After three clicks, the radio crackled again: 'Vault guard, respond.'

'They'll send someone to check,' Harper said. 'We need to move.'

'The main entrance is watched,' Cassie said. 'They've got cameras, guards—'

'We're not using the main entrance.' Harper turned to Tucker. 'How far to those tunnels that come out on the hills behind the Goldstrike?'

Tucker consulted his map, correlating it with the facility diagrams on the guard station wall.

'Three junctions over,' Tucker said finally. 'But we'll have to pass the main processing centre. No way around it – these maintenance tunnels all feed into the primary facility. They designed it that way, probably for speed and ease.'

'No choice, then,' Harper sighed. He turned to the freed prisoners, properly assessing them for the first time. Katie Martinez's breathing worried him most; that rasping sound wasn't just fear or exertion. Even though she'd only been in the cell a couple of hours, the crystalline formations the scientist kept talking about could be moving into her lungs.

'Anyone need medical attention?' he asked. 'Anyone need to be carried?'

Katie shook her head despite her laboured breathing. The others looked shaken but mobile; locals who'd been asking too many questions, plus old Jim Rivers who, as he explained as they stood around, had been caught taking soil samples near the western tunnels. Cassie from O'Malley's moved among them, checking on each one – even after being locked up herself, she was still taking care of people.

'What about him?' Maggie nodded towards the scientist. His lab coat was spotless, a man who worked with theory rather than practice. But the fear in his eyes when he looked at them was real enough.

'He comes with us,' Harper's tone brooked no argument. 'We'll need him to explain exactly what they've been processing up here. Everything they've been hiding.'

They moved out in pairs, Tucker leading with Harper's borrowed keycard and his small, yellow taser, Maggie bringing up the rear with her shotgun. The tunnels felt different now; not just old mining works retrofitted with modern tech, but something more sinister, although Harper assumed this was just in his head. The chemical taste in the air was stronger near the pipes, still making Harper's throat burn. Every few yards they passed more evidence of recent upgrades; fresh power cables, new sensor arrays, modern ventilation systems grafted onto Victorian engineering.

The first junction showed signs of rushed work, with welds still dark on pressure doors, and a selection of ventilation systems that looked half-finished. Everything about it suggested a facility expanding too fast, and perhaps pushing too hard.

The second junction was worse, as Harper could see small crystalline formations growing unchecked in corners, their geometric patterns catching their flashlight beams.

The scientist kept looking at them nervously, making notes on his regained clipboard, even now.

'They're spreading faster than predicted,' he whispered, more to himself than them. 'The processing creates micro-fractures in the rock. Once they start growing ... the models didn't account for this level of propagation. They exceeded all safety parameters.'

Harper went to respond, but a distant alarm cut off any answer. The sound echoed through the tunnels, mixing with the constant hum of machinery.

Someone had found the unconscious guards.

'How far?' he asked Tucker.

'Two more turns.'

They rounded the corner and stopped. Through pressure-sealed windows, they could see into the processing facility proper. The space was enormous – a cathedral carved into the mountain's heart. Banks of machinery filled the chamber, converting raw ore into something else, likely Milspec and dangerous, while pressure vessels bigger than trucks dominated the middle ground, connected by a maze of pipes and catwalks. The scale of it was staggering, not just a hidden operation, but a full industrial facility, built in secret over generations.

'Jesus Christ,' Cassie breathed, pressing against the window. 'This is what they've been hiding? What they burned the library to protect?'

'This is just the visible part,' the scientist said. His clipboard shook as he gestured towards deeper tunnels. 'The real processing happens further in. They kept pushing for higher yields, faster processing—'

'And people kept dying,' Tucker said quietly.

'That wasn't us!' the scientist protested. 'That was generations of miners, pushing too far! We've only been working on this for the last six or seven months, as we ...'

'Pushed too far?' Harper suggested, and the scientist fell quiet.

Another alarm joined the first, its tone more urgent. Through the windows they could see technicians rushing to control panels, engineers checking readings. The entire facility was waking up to the intruder threat.

'We need to move,' Maggie said, the ex-US Marine in her already checking angles, counting threats. 'Before they lock down the—'

The pressure doors began to close.

The sound carried clearly through the observation windows; massive hydraulic systems engaging, thick metal barriers descending with inexorable purpose.

Through the narrowing gaps, they could see more Aegis personnel appearing, weapons drawn, searching methodically.

Seeing this, Harper cursed. They were about to be trapped in a facility that was never meant to let anyone out.

But this time, he had no backup plan.

27

MISSED CALL

SHERIFF COBLE LOOKED AS IF HE WAS ABOUT TO PULL HIS GUN out and fire it at the ceiling, but the arguments and accusations calmed, and Bickford, waving his arms in a flapping gesture, calmed everyone back to a semblance of silence.

'My family stole nothing,' Bickford's voice was cold and dark, and Cortez noticed the Aegis "deputies" straightening as they stood around the room. 'And I'll have you take that back, Reynolds.'

'You prove to me your family didn't take it, I'll take it back in a second,' Reynolds' voice carried across the now-silent hall. 'But it's mighty suspicious that your family did so well when it disappeared, but hell, at least you bought that oh-so-special little popgun to wave around. We're saved.'

Reynolds looked around the hall to his left.

'And I ain't the only one to think you took the gold,' he continued. 'And I ain't the first to think you didn't shoot Robbie because you wanted Maggie all to yourself.'

There was an intake of breath at this, and Cortez could see in the crowd Doctor Chen preparing to stand, Eddie most likely reaching for the survey map in his jacket – but Reynolds had the floor now, with thirty years of respected service giving weight to every single word.

Unfortunately, it was at this point Reynolds looked around to his right, and as he did so, his eyes caught Cortez's.

'Shit, Lisa, I'm sorry, I didn't mean to disrespect your poppa,' he muttered, not realising that by saying her name, he'd effectively outed her.

She felt and heard, rather than saw, every Aegis "deputy" flick off safeties and bring their assault rifles to low ready at the mention of her name.

Sighing, Cortez reluctantly stepped into the centre aisle, removing her borrowed catering jacket.

'Cortez,' Sheriff Coble's voice carried false calm. 'You're under suspension, and you're not welcome here.'

'You said this was a town hall meeting for the folk of Prosperity,' Cortez replied, forcing herself to sound calm. 'Last time I looked around, I'm one of the oldest families here, so don't you dare tell me I'm not welcome at a townsfolk meeting.'

She pointed at Reynolds, deciding she might as well go all the way.

'And I too would like to know more about that rifle, Eric—'

'Sheriff Coble!'

'—and how you seem to be so good with it,' Cortez finished. 'I understand the lever sticks unless you pull it slightly to the side first. Harper noticed that yesterday. Strange that a rifle that's been on display for years would still have that quirk, that no one would have tried to fix it. But then I suppose nobody's fired it, have they?'

The hall went silent.

"We did try to have it fixed,' Bickford muttered. 'But to do so would involve removing so many parts of the original rifle, the legacy of Doc Holliday—'

'Bullshit,' Cortez snapped. 'I've seen reports of events happening here over the last hundred years, ones that showed off that damned rifle, and not once did any of your ancestors have that sticking issue.'

She smiled, now, on a roll.

'Interesting thing, though, when you let Harper look at that rifle yesterday, he noticed it'd been altered, that a gunsmith had worked on it.'

'As I said—'

'Yeah, we heard, you wanted to keep it as it was.' Cortez held an accusing finger up. 'Your gunsmith was keeping it pure. But, instead, that rifle no longer fires the rounds it was created for, the ones that I'm sure Doc Holliday fired with great abandon if he even owned that rifle.'

'Are you saying my great-great-granddaddy was a liar?'

'I'm saying *you* are,' Cortez retorted, to another hushed intake of breath from the crowd. 'Let a fresh gunsmith examine that rifle. I'm sure we've got one in here. Prove to me that gun *doesn't* fire .44 Magnum bullets like the round that killed my father. Show me that this rifle, that's been on display for years, *isn't* the weapon that killed Sheriff Robbie Cortez.'

Cortez allowed the momentum to keep moving forward, watching for the Aegis operatives to come to stop her, letting her training, her anger, carry her words to every corner.

'You can't even work it properly, can you?' she continued. 'But Sheriff Coble can. He understands how it sticks, and how you have to move it to the outside. Just like he could the night my father died.'

Sheriff Coble's face hardened as he moved towards the podium, but Cortez saw the slight tremor in his hands. Behind him, Mason Carrick was watching the scene with professional interest, while Ashfield was shifting position, adjusting his view of the crowd.

'What was it?' Cortez continued. 'You were pissed that Maggie Hawkins didn't love you? That she didn't want you? You were angry that she fancied my father, her childhood sweetheart, instead? Or was it simply that this was something you couldn't buy, like *every other damn thing in your life?*'

'She was too good for him! He needed to be taught a lesson!' Bickford screamed back, before paling, grabbing the rifle, holding it awkwardly. 'I mean it was a terrible tragedy, but this weapon here is a piece of history, a symbol of—'

'A symbol of what?' Maisie was standing now. 'Of how this town really works? Or how we buy our history, like you bought the town? Or what happens to people who ask questions?'

She pointed at the Aegis men at the doors.

'Again, like what happened to Cassie?'

More people were rising. Cortez saw Doctor Chen standing, and Eddie pulled documents from his jacket. The tension in the hall was building towards explosion, but she kept her focus on Sheriff Coble and on the slight sheen of sweat on his forehead.

'You know what I think?' she was close enough now to see his trigger finger twitching, moving slowly towards the gun at his holster. 'I think that rifle's been fired more recently than people know. I think it's got history beyond Doc Holliday, and I think if we tested it, *really* tested it, we'd find it matches the bullet that killed Robert Cortez. My father.'

'That case is closed,' Sheriff Coble snapped. 'Clinton Hackett confessed.'

'After he was dead,' Reynolds' voice carried the weight of decades on the force. 'Convenient how that worked out.'

'Don't you goddamn start,' Sheriff Coble turned, snapping back at Reynolds. 'You quit the day after he died.'

'Because you were brought up to his position by the mayor standing beside you,' Reynolds cried out. 'I should have been next. I had seniority. But I wasn't somebody Bickford knew he could control. Robbie Cortez was the one who stopped the motorcycle gang from taking over this town, and in return you had him killed.'

The crowd's murmuring grew louder, uncertain what was happening right now. Aegis personnel were moving to stop them leaving, covering the exits, and Carson's own hand was drifting towards his weapon.

Cortez, however, knew she needed to keep pushing.

'Did you do it, Eric?' she asked softly. 'Go on, show everyone how to work that lever. Show them the trick that only someone who's handled it regularly would know. Then tell us what Bickford offered you to use it on my dad, before framing Clinton Hackett.'

Sheriff Coble couldn't stop himself – his anger was building, and he snatched the rifle from Bickford, working the lever without a problem as he aimed it at Cortez.

'You want to die like your daddy?' he cried out. 'I can make sure you get a reunion with him right now—'

'For god's sake, Eric!' Bickford shouted, kicking the rifle's barrel towards the roof. 'That's what she wants!'

The Winchester went off, plasterwork from the ceiling raining on terrified residents, and Cortez laughed.

'Thank you,' she said. 'Now, when we check that fired bullet, we'll see if it matches.'

'You're nothing but an agitator,' Bickford snarled. 'One that needs to be—'

'You want to talk about agitators?' Cortez interrupted, gesturing at Mason Carrick and his suited companions. 'Let's talk about the deaths.'

'That's what we're doing!' Bickford protested weakly.

'I don't mean those deaths, I mean the ones Aegis was doing for you,' Cortez pulled out the Parsons' burner phone. 'The ones where Aegis operatives received messages like this.'

She opened it up, reading the message out.

'*Find Eddie Hawkins and terminate the SOB.* I'm guessing that's son of a bitch? And that terminate means kill? This was sent only hours ago.'

She saw Mason Carrick glare at Ashfield, who shrugged.

'I didn't send that message!' Bickford almost wailed. 'That wasn't me!'

Cortez nodded.

'I know, Tom,' she said, almost sadly. 'You would have been cleverer than to use your personal number to send this. But the person who did ... wasn't.'

She pressed a button and waited. And, at Sheriff Coble's hip, his phone rang.

'Why don't you tell us what's really going on in those mines then,' Cortez smiled as the audience murmured darkly. 'What's been killing people for over a century while the Bickfords got rich?'

'Oh, are we a scientist now?' Bickford snapped, annoyed, glaring at the now reddening Coble.

'No, Tom, but *she* is.'

Cortez stepped to the side as Doctor Chen walked forward.

The hall went quiet again.

'When I performed my autopsy on Moses Mathers, I found crystalline formations in his lungs,' she said, her loud voice carrying across the hall. 'I had these checked – Aegis tried to stop me, but they got through before the fires, and I received the results today. They're not from gold mining, they're from rare-earth metal processing. The kind of processing that's worth billions to the right people.'

'That's enough, goddammit!' Sheriff Coble moved to stop her, but Eddie was already up, waving the mining survey high, like a flag.

'William Bickford knew what he had,' the old historian's voice rang out. 'After the gold started running out, and this new ore was discovered, he redesigned those mines for processing, not mining. Every death, every accident, they were all part of the plan, testing these metals and minerals, waiting for technology to catch up, and now—'

'Now we're helping this town prosper,' Mason interrupted smoothly. 'Providing jobs and security.'

'Security?' Cortez spun to glare at him. 'Is that what you call disappearing people, burning down buildings, and leaving Moses Mathers jammed into a rock fissure?'

The revolution started with Maisie Brown. She'd quietly worked her way towards Carson, and now she knocked his hand away from his holster, pulling the weapon, and aiming it at him.

'Sit down, you corrupt piece of shit,' she hissed.

Others moved to block the remaining deputies, while more confronted the Aegis men at the doors, the mercenaries uncertain on whether they should open fire at unarmed Americans.

'This is your last warning,' Coble's voice shook with barely contained rage. 'Stand down.'

Mason Carrick was already moving across the stage as this happened, speaking rapidly into a radio as he walked calmly towards the steps at the side. Ashfield was heading for the exit also, pausing only to give swift orders to his own men. The suited observers were being hustled out of a side door.

'Listen to me,' Bickford's voice held panic now, as he realised he was being left to the wolves. 'Everyone needs to stay calm.'

An explosion, muffled and distant, came through now, its concussion rattling the town hall's windows. Mason paused, surprised, looking back at Ashfield for confirmation as to what this was, while others in the auditorium instinctively ducked, then immediately began shouting questions.

'That was the processing facility,' Doctor Chen shouted, her voice carrying in the chaos.

'You have no idea what you've done,' Mason's corporate mask had now slipped, showing something darker underneath as he glared at Cortez. 'Those containment systems were the only thing preventing ...'

'Preventing what?' Cortez moved closer to the stage. 'Preventing people from learning what's really in those tunnels? What's been killing them for generations?'

'Enough!' Sheriff Coble had once more loaded the Winchester, and was aiming it frantically around the hall. 'You don't understand what's at stake! These processing facilities are vital to national security!'

'Bullshit!'

Cortez felt the weight of every eye in the hall. These weren't just townspeople anymore, these were her people.

People her father had protected.

People who deserved the truth.

'Let me tell you what's really at stake,' she said, her voice carrying to every corner. 'This ain't about national security or military contracts. This is about Prosperity. About what makes a town more than just a name on a map.'

The room had quietened. Aegis, townsfolk, deputies, all watching her. Not as a suspended deputy, but as a daughter of Prosperity.

'You know, my father used to tell me stories about this place,' she started. 'About miners and shopkeepers and farmers who looked out for each other, who helped when times were hard, who were proud of their town and would tell tourists what happened up in the mines, the prospectors who came here with a dream and often left with nothing, even the few who managed to make a success, who stood together against anyone who tried to take advantage.'

She pointed at Bickford, currently staring at her, dumbfounded.

'Doc Holliday's rifle was a symbol, before *he* bastardised it, but we can take that back,' she turned slowly, meeting eyes, connecting with faces she'd known all her life. 'That's what the Bickfords never understood; what Aegis and their government contracts can't comprehend. Prosperity, we're not about gold or rare earth whatever-it-is, or processing facilities! It's about people – people who have been dying in those mines for generations, while a few got rich. People who have been lied to, threatened, disappeared even, who've lost their livelihoods in the last twenty-four hours alone, but who never stopped helping their neighbours.'

She pointed across at Eddie.

'Eddie Hawkins was being hunted by these men last night. He had to hide, or else they were going to take him away and probably do the same to him as what they did to Moses Mathers. So, what did he do when the fires started? He grabbed his daughter's fire uniform, went out, and he helped put out the fires while these assholes drove around in their swanky SUVs looking for anybody who might want to stop them.'

'That's a lie,' Mason said. 'We helped with the fires.'

'Damn right you helped with the fires,' Cortez snapped.

'That's not what I meant.'

It didn't matter. Maisie was nodding. Reynolds stood straighter. Even Carson looked uncertain now.

'Today we learnt the truth about what's in that mountain,' she continued. 'About what killed Moses Mathers, and what's been killing our friends and family for a hundred and fifty years. But we also learned something else.'

She faced Mason and Bickford now.

'We learned that Prosperity doesn't, and will never, belong to *you*. It belongs to the people who built it, who kept it alive through every bust and boom, who buried their goddamn dead and *still showed up for work the very next day*, a smile on their face, ready to help. It belongs to us.'

'You've killed this town,' Maisie added. 'Year by year, death by death. All those families who lost people in those mines. All those accidents that weren't accidents.'

Bickford's expression shifted as he realised what was happening; his audience wasn't listening anymore.

'Now see here,' he blustered, 'I'm still the mayor of—'

'A town you sold out,' Cortez said.

She turned to Carson, who stood uncertainly by the door. She knew this was a moment, a Rubicon to cross – Carson had very much been on the side of Coble, and had actively helped Mayor Bickford ... but he was still a child of Prosperity, and she'd seen his conflicted expressions during the meeting, even when he was quieting townspeople.

'Deputy Carson? I believe we have enough evidence to arrest Thomas Bickford for conspiracy, corruption, and accessory to murder,' she stated. 'Or perhaps one of the other deputies could do this, and you could turn in your badge and weapon?'

Carson looked between Cortez and Sheriff Coble, decades of taking orders warring with what he knew was right.

Then, slowly, he stepped forward, nodding at Cortez.

'You can't be serious,' Bickford's voice rose. 'Carson, remember who signs your checks.'

'That's the problem, isn't it?' Carson's voice was quiet. 'I've been remembering that for too long.'

He pulled out his cuffs.

'Mister Bickford, you're under arrest.'

'But I didn't do it!' Bickford whined, looking desperately at Cortez. 'I didn't kill your daddy, either! He was looking into the mine, talking to Eddie—'

'He was asking for my blessing to propose to Maggie, you son of a bitch!' Eddie shouted angrily now. 'He wasn't looking into any damned thing!'

Bickford looked horrified at this, but it seemed his mouth hadn't gained the memo as he continued talking.

'Coble was supposed to shoot low, paralyse Cortez and force him to retire from the force, but he screwed up—'

'Shut the hell up, you goddamned coward!' Sheriff Coble moved then, the Winchester coming up as he jumped from the stage, aiming at Cortez again.

'You ain't taking my job—'

The response was fast and brutal. Cortez grabbed the Winchester with her left hand, pulling it to the side, and before Sheriff Coble could respond she swung a meaty right hand that caught him on the chin, lifting him up before landing him on the wooden floor, momentarily stunned. Slowly, he tried to rise, holding his bleeding mouth, but Reynolds and the other deputies – the original ones, not the Aegis mercenaries – were faster. No violence, no drama, just experienced hands taking down someone who'd forgotten what the badge really meant.

'You're under arrest,' Cortez smiled. 'And you're suspended until an investigation can check the text you sent, making you an accessory to attempted murder, and the round you fired into the ceiling, comparing it to the rifle. If it matches, well, with what Mayor Bickford here just said ...'

The accusation was clear.

'This is absurd,' Bickford spluttered as Carson cuffed him. 'I'll have all your jobs. Mason—'

But Mason Carrick was finally gone, having slipped out a side door while everyone watched Bickford's downfall. Only Ashfield remained, his expression unreadable behind his Lennon glasses, as Carson led Bickford out, while Reynolds secured ex-Sheriff Coble.

'Lisa,' Reynolds used her first name, like he had when she was a rookie. 'Your father would be proud of you right now.'

Cortez looked around the town hall, at faces she'd known all her life, at people finally free to speak the truth about what had happened to their town.

There would be federal investigations, corruption charges, hard questions about what had really been happening in those mines, sure.

But for now, Prosperity had taken its identity back.

28

COUNTDOWN

HYDRAULICS WHINED AS THE PRESSURE DOORS DESCENDED ALL around them, each thud of the locking mechanisms echoing through the tunnels. As he stared through the glass, Harper counted six Aegis personnel visible through the narrowing gaps – all armed, all moving with professional precision. He knew, however, that more would come; a facility this size would have more than one dedicated security team, and all would be ex-military.

Fast in, fast out. Do what needs to be done before they react and get the hell away.

Tucker studied his map, comparing it to what they could see through the observation windows. The processing floor stretched out below them, a maze of machinery and catwalks.

'Maintenance is still open,' he muttered. 'We can cross the main floor.'

'We'll be exposed,' Maggie interrupted. She had positioned herself to cover their rear, shotgun ready. 'They'll have clear lines of sight from those catwalks. If we weren't locked in here, that is.'

The scientist looked up from his clipboard.

'They're initiating full lockdown,' he whispered. 'But this is just the testing phase. They'll open again in a minute before they close fully. Once those seals engage for the second time—'

'How long?' Harper asked.

'Six minutes, maybe less.' The scientist's hands shook as he pointed through the small window. 'But you don't understand these processing systems. They're not meant to be interrupted. The crystallisation rates – if they lock down wrong, if the processing cycle isn't contained properly ...'

The scientist swallowed hard.

'We'll have a containment breach.'

Another alarm joined the cacophony, and Harper saw technicians rushing to control panels beside the primary processing vessels dominating the centre of the facility; massive steel containers connected by a web of pipes.

'The whole mountain's infected,' the scientist whispered. 'We thought we could contain it, but the goddamn military requirements exceeded all safety protocols.'

More Aegis personnel appeared on the catwalks, all moving to cover angles – it looked like they were unsure where Harper and his people would come from, so they were aiming everywhere. Harper cursed silently – they had maybe five minutes before the lockdown trapped them in this section.

'Tucker,' Harper said, pulling the C4 from his pack. 'In your opinion, how load-bearing are those main support pillars?'

'I'm a driver, not an architect.'

'You're also a paranoid trucker, so I'm guessing you read and reread everything,' Harper continued. 'Humour me.'

Sighing, Tucker studied the facility's architecture on the copied survey map.

'Well, they're on Bickford's survey, so I'd say they're original mine supports from 1870. Maybe even earlier, from when they first started down here. They've added modern structures around them, but those old wood and iron columns? They're likely still holding most of the weight.'

'So, hypothetically, if we bring them down?'

'We die,' Maggie suggested with more than a little gallows humour.

'Maybe not immediately, but the whole processing centre would collapse around us,' Tucker nodded towards the massive pipes running along the ceiling. 'But we'd take out those primary feeds too, and the containment systems fail.'

'I thought failing systems are bad?'

'Well, if it actually worked, then everything they're processing would get buried under a ton of rock and would seal itself in,' the scientist added, understanding dawning. 'The weight would create a natural containment.'

'Good,' Harper checked his watch. *About five minutes dead until time ran out.* He turned to the group, borrowing the map from Tucker, checking it a last time. 'We move fast. Maggie, get these people across. Use the machinery on the outskirts for cover. Tucker, you know where the maintenance tunnels come out in the hills behind the Goldstrike?'

'It's a ten-minute walk if we go by this map, so five minutes if we push hard,' Tucker nodded, glancing back at Katie Martinez. 'You good for a little jog?'

Katie nodded silently, her eyes wide like saucers.

'Good. Get them clear. Don't wait for us,' Harper handed Tucker the map before he turned to the scientist.

'You want to stay here and work with Aegis, or do you want to live?' he asked.

The scientist shrugged.

'Do I get a choice?'

'Everybody gets a choice,' Harper replied. 'You don't seem too happy about being down here, so why don't you go with them? Make sure everybody understands what's in these tunnels, what's been happening here.'

'Because I might get killed if I do that?'

'You'll definitely die down here,' Maggie growled before looking through the small window. 'What do you want me to do once they're across?'

Harper felt that from her tone she already knew.

'Someone needs to set these charges,' Harper said, checking his weapon. 'And someone needs to make sure if I fail, that the captives get out.'

'No man left behind,' Maggie argued.

'Unless they volunteer for the greater good.' Harper placed a hand, the one not holding C4, on her shoulder. 'Relax, I intend to be right behind you. The survey map shows a ventilation shaft leading straight out. Not great for a group, but a lone man—'

'With a bum arm ...'

'I'll be fine,' Harper smiled. 'They have to catch me first.'

As if on cue, a fresh voice cut through the facility's PA system.

'Harper!' Delaney's tone was conversational, almost friendly. 'Let's talk about this, yeah?'

Through the observation windows, Harper could see Delaney emerge onto a central catwalk. He moved with his usual military precision but carried no visible weapon, only a commander's confidence.

'You don't understand what we're doing here,' Delaney continued, his voice echoing through the speakers. 'The strategic importance, the contracts we've secured – this isn't about money anymore.'

'No,' Harper murmured to himself – there was no way Delaney would hear his answer while they were in the room. 'It's about the people you've killed to keep it secret.'

The hydraulics controlling the pressure doors hummed, the testing phase now over. Any second now, they'd open the doors, and eventually the Aegis guards would work out where they were.

'You know what to do.' Ignoring Delaney, Harper nodded to Maggie and turned to the others. 'Stay close to her. Don't stop moving. Get yourself through the tunnels.'

'Harper, I—' Maggie started, but paused as the doors began to rise.

'Get them out. That's an order, Sergeant.'

Harper moved before they finished opening, drawing the Aegis guards' fire towards himself. Firing back, he made sure anybody watching that door was now following the lone man with the weapon and the C4 in his hands, while Maggie quietly led the others along the facility's edge.

Harper's shoulder wound grated as he rolled behind a processing unit, rounds sparking off the surrounding metal. He moved low and fast between the machinery, keeping solid cover between himself and the Aegis positions on the catwalks. Even though Maggie had patched up the wound earlier, it was screaming again with every movement, each impact felt like a knife driving into the muscle – but he forced himself to push it aside.

Pain could wait. The mission couldn't.

He knew the wound had opened again; torn from effort,

blood soaking into his shirt. None of it mattered, though. The first C4 charge needed to go on the central support column, one of the old Victorian ironworks they'd identified. Everything else until then was just a distraction.

He glanced across the facility and saw Maggie's group moving along the far wall. They were making good progress, using the facility's layout for cover. Tucker had them surprisingly well-organised, moving in quick rushes while Maggie provided overwatch. If anyone could get out, it'd be them. It didn't matter if Harper made it or not – although he classed escape as the preferred option here. He had a job to do first, and years of training had taught him that the job was always the priority.

More rounds slammed into the machinery Harper was weaving through. These guys were proper military – calm, disciplined, picking their shots and conserving ammunition. Possibly, they were even concerned about the rising gas levels. Harper remembered a warning from when he was taken deep into the old mines, as Ashfield and Delaney screamed at their men to *not* fire weapons down there, as the sparks could ignite the gas.

It seemed these guys hadn't received the same memo.

A couple of quick peeks revealed their positions - three on the upper catwalk, two on the main floor, and Delaney somewhere near the glass-fronted environmental control centre. He'd seen more personnel earlier; some of them must have gone searching after Maggie's group.

With luck, they were heading the wrong way.

Reaching the first column, he slapped the C4 charge against the century-old iron. The detonator armed with a quiet beep.

One down, three to go.

'You know what's funny?' Delaney's voice carried across the facility's speakers. 'Your father helped design some of these security systems. That man was a genius when it came to shit like this.'

Harper didn't answer; he was already moving to the second column, varying his sprints between cover and bursts of enemy fire. An Aegis guard appeared around a corner – too close for guns, Harper drove his elbow up under the man's chin, followed by a knee strike that folded him. The move cost him, though; his wounded shoulder flared with pain again, and he leaned against the column for a moment, taking deep breaths to steady himself before placing the second charge.

Something clattered across the floor nearby. *A flashbang—*

Harper dove behind a pressure vessel just before it detonated. Even with his face turned away and eyes tightly closed, the light was disorienting, but he'd learnt long ago to trust his other senses. He heard rather than saw movement to his right – combat boots on metal grating. Spinning low, he swept the approaching guard's legs out from under him and followed up with a *fak sao* strike to the jugular, and it was lights out for his opponent.

'You're good,' Delaney called out, his tone almost mocking. 'But you're also hurt – bleeding badly again, I'd guess. How long before that shoulder gives out completely?'

Harper wanted to shout something back, but he knew that was exactly what Delaney wanted. The moment Harper spoke, his location would be confirmed.

Bang, bang, bang.

He stayed silent, checking his six and noting shell casings scattering on the floor. The Aegis teams were moving to surround him, but they'd have to bunch up to do it.

Tight spaces. Multiple targets.

This wasn't optimal, but emergencies never were - it was still exactly what he'd trained for in the regiment.

Popping up from cover, Harper fired some well-placed shots – while he'd take a direct hit if he got lucky with one, his focus was on keeping their heads down. He bobbed and weaved to the third column on the far side of the cavernous space, rounds slapping into the floor and machinery, several far too close for comfort. He could hear Aegis guards shouting at each other, eventually reminding each other to avoid hitting the metal, and to reduce sparks, which didn't help his comfort level at all. Apparently, someone had finally realised the risk of rising gas levels, but regardless, their angles were wrong. They were shooting at shadows while Harper worked. He was fine with that as he armed the third charge.

One more to go.

Across the cavernous space and undetected while Aegis played "hunt the SRR operative", Harper saw Maggie's group reaching the maintenance tunnel entrance, almost clear now. He just had to place the last charge and get out before everything came down—

He rolled as Delaney dropped from a catwalk above. The older man's boot missed his head by inches. No gun, no blade – Delaney had come for a fight, up close and in Harper's face.

'Nothing personal,' Delaney said, moving with practised skill. 'But I'm afraid we've got too much invested here for you to screw it up. Especially on your dead daddy's request.'

He struck fast, using a military based hand-to-hand – possibly Force Recon or something similar. Harper recognised the style but couldn't quite place it, and frankly didn't care – The Special Services Regiment had taught him a lethal combination of Krav Maga, Aikido, Judo, boxing, and knife fighting, specifically designed to counter whatever they came up against. Harper blocked Delaney's first combination and countered with a spinning elbow strike that whistled just shy of Delaney's head. They moved into the confined space between machinery, sizing each other up and looking for weaknesses.

'Do you know what your father really wanted to make right?' Delaney asked, circling. He pulled off his hard hat and tossed it at Harper, a cheap distraction. Harper didn't fall for it, stepping back as it clattered to the ground.

'I'm sure you'll tell me, whatever I say.'

Delaney shrugged.

'The fact that he helped build all this, knew what it would cost. Your father wasn't worried about the town, Harper. He was worried about money – about whether we'd overextended ourselves.'

Harper didn't reply. He had the last charge in his hand and could see the final support column twenty feet away. But Delaney wasn't stupid. He knew Harper's plan, and kept him moving in the wrong direction, towards the waiting Aegis guards.

Who weren't shooting now.

'I'm guessing you realised not to keep firing guns at metal,' Harper smiled.

'We don't need guns to end you, now we see you,' Delaney continued. 'All that skill, all that training ... you really are your father's son. But like him at the end, you're bleeding out – trying to save people who'll never even remember your name.'

Delaney moved again, fast for his age, but Harper caught a tell in his stance. The punch came high while the actual attack went low, aiming to sweep Harper's legs. It was a classic combination, but one Harper had seen before. His Aikido training came into play - He let Delaney's momentum carry him past, then drove his knee into the man's kidney. Delaney spun, trapping Harper's leg and using the younger man's movement against him.

They crashed into a bank of gauges, metal edges digging into Harper's injured shoulder. Warning lights flashed as something cracked under their combined weight.

Harper broke free, but Delaney stayed close, denying him space to recover. Each impact jarred Harper's shoulder, sending fresh blood soaking into his shirt.

'You've got heart,' Delaney said, closing in again. 'But how long before the blood loss—'

Harper didn't let him finish. He swung the C4 block like a brick, a desperation move that forced Delaney to block reflexively.

The opening was enough. Harper's elbow caught Delaney's throat, followed by a knee to the solar plexus that doubled the older man over. Delaney recovered, and his counterstrike, while weak, hit Harper's shoulder again, sending him stumbling back into a tangle of pipes. Steam vented overhead, gauges spinning into red zones.

'Sorry to cost you all your yearly bonuses,' Harper gasped, his breathing ragged now.

'Do you think this is about money?' Delaney croaked back, his voice rough from the elbow strike. 'About government contracts? This is national security, Harper. Making sure we're not dependent on Chinese supplies.'

'Everything you're doing here is killing people,' Harper shot back, stepping in close to deny Delaney room to strike effectively. They grappled, each man searching for an advantage of the other, and as they did so, Harper could see the facility was now tearing itself apart. The warning sirens were deafening, and many Aegis personnel were fleeing, giving up on watching the two men punch the crap out of each other and abandoning Delaney to his fate.

Delaney was stronger than he looked, but Harper still had youth and reach on his side, even if his shoulder injury evened them out. Harper spotted his opening –as Delaney overextended, then tried to stabilise himself. Harper struck hard and fast, the movement pure instinct and training. A roundhouse spin kick connected with Delaney's temple, snapping the older man's head back. Harper followed up with a mule kick to the chest that sent Delaney sprawling into a heap against a processing unit.

For a moment, Harper thought it was over. Delaney didn't move. But there was no time to check; the last charge still needed placing, and the countdown on his watch told him he had barely two minutes left. He forced himself forward, his legs unsteady and his shoulder screaming in pain, the room already trembling as the facility shuddered.

He slapped the last charge onto the column and armed it. Blood now ran steadily down his arm, dripping from his fingertips as he leaned against the iron support, trying to catch his breath. His shoulder felt wrong – more than just torn muscle, something deep and vital had been damaged ... but he didn't have time to think about it. He'd set the charges in sequence. The first would go in just under three minutes, and the rest would follow, one by one, until the entire facility was buried under tons of rock.

Movement caught his attention – Delaney was gone. Harper scanned the area, his vision blurring from blood loss and exhaustion, but saw that two Aegis guards fleeing the scene were dragging Delaney's limp body towards a far corridor. They were retreating, finally recognising the inevitability of what was about to happen.

Good.

With the doors about to start their pressure cycles in a minute or two, locking anyone else in permanently, and leaving them to the fury of the explosive charges, Harper turned and staggered towards the maintenance tunnel entrance, every step sending fresh agony through his battered body. There was a borrowed key card still in his pocket from earlier, and he was hoping it would still work, but as he approached, he saw the door slide down, the pressure cycle beginning. It was too far to get to before it closed, Aegis guards already throwing aside rifles as they ran for it.

'All units converge on section three. Target is wounded, moving east,' the speakers blared; standard military tactics, ordering teams coordinating to limit his options, force him into a corner. Normally, in tight spaces like this, it would work.

But their teams were running for their lives, and Harper wasn't planning to take the obvious route.

He moved between processing vessels, staying in the shadows. The facility's layout worked in his favour for this, decades of additions bringing blind spots in their coverage. A lone Aegis guard appeared around the corner, assault rifle at low ready, but Harper was on him before he could react, using the man's own weapon to pull him off balance. The follow-up strike was sloppy but efficient – not enough force to kill, just enough to disarm and knock him back onto the floor as Harper continued to run through.

Two minutes now.

Somewhere above, hydraulics whined as more pressure doors engaged, sealing sections automatically. Through gaps in the machinery, he could see the last teams moving on parallel tracks, checking their watches, deciding on whether to coordinate their advance or make their way out as well.

It was professional work; *his father would have appreciated their efficiency.*

Gaining a second wind, he sprinted deeper into the facility, towards the primary processing vessels. He needed to be at least two levels up before the first charge went off, however, and the catwalk access ladder posed a problem. Harper's arm was pretty much useless now, the shoulder wound making climbing almost impossible, but he needed height. He tucked his arm close and started climbing one-handed, wincing with every step. Twenty feet up, as metal groaned under additional weight, two Aegis guards, obviously ones who hadn't gained the memo about getting out before it was too late, appeared on the far end of the catwalk moving fast. Harper pulled himself over the railing just as they opened fire, bullets sparking off metal where he'd been seconds before.

He rolled behind a ventilation unit, buying time to think.

One minute forty seconds.

'You've got a minute and a half before this blows,' he screamed out. 'You can chase me or you can save your lives.'

They chose the latter, thankfully, turning and running off at the news. As Harper continued through the environmental control centre, he saw to no surprise that it was now empty, with banks of computers monitoring the air quality, temperature, pressure systems all discarded, the scientists already clever enough to know to leave.

Harper found what he needed beside the door: industrial breathing gear.

It wasn't combat equipment, but it would help him.

Less than a minute left.

Harper climber higher on the ladder heading up the old ventilation shaft, pulling on the breathing gear, forcing himself to ignore the pain as he did so, the wet heat of fresh blood soaking his shirt.

Forty-five seconds.

Harper reached the shaft entrance just as flashbangs detonated below – Aegis guards still in the building, still believing they could save the day.

You bloody fools. I gave you all the time I could.

The noise in the confined spaces was disorientating, but he was already moving. The shaft was narrow, barely wide enough to climb through, and his shoulders screamed as he pulled himself up, using his legs to brace against the sides.

The first charge detonated right on schedule. The explosion hit like a physical wave, reverberating through iron and stone. As it passed him, Harper returned to quickly climbing one-handed, as the secondary and third charges blew in sequence, each detonation seemingly triggering the next. The shaft swayed with each blast, century-old engineering protesting at the force of the explosions.

The industrial breathing gear was awkward, designed for maintenance work rather than combat, but he could taste metal in the air now, feel something crystalline catching in his throat from before he pulled it on. Whatever they'd been processing down there had been released as the containment systems failed. He felt sorry for the operatives who had stayed, but then he remembered Moses Mathers and the others who had died.

You take the money, you take the risks.

Forty feet up now, the shaft narrowed even more, decades of dust and debris making progress harder. His shoulder had gone beyond pain into a kind of numbed detachment. Blood made his grip slippery on the iron handholds—

Another explosion, closer this time. The fourth charge taking out the primary support column. Metal screamed as the facility began collapsing on itself.

Thirty feet to go.

The shaft's cover was visible above, a grating that had probably not been opened since William Bickford's time. Harper's vision was blurring as he forced himself higher—

Shit.

The breathing gear had caught on something, nearly pulling him off the wall. He shrugged out of it, letting it fall.

Better to risk the air than get trapped here.

Twenty feet.

The entire mountain seemed to shake, the charges doing more than just destroying the facility. They were triggering the collapses in the old mine workings – a century and a half of half-structured tunnels finally hiding their secrets forever.

The grating, however, wouldn't move.

Harper braced himself against the shaft walls and pushed with his good arm. Nothing. Decades of rust had fused it shut. Below, he could hear the facility tearing itself apart; he couldn't see anything, but he knew the ventilation shaft wouldn't survive much longer, and soon he'd be falling. He tried again, placing his back against the wall and using his legs for leverage. The pain in his shoulder peaked and faded, replaced by a cold certainty that he was going to die in William Bickford's mine.

No. Not like this.

The grating finally gave with a shriek of tortured metal, and Harper pulled himself onto the rocky ground just as the shaft collapsed beneath him. He scrambled forwards, as the hill he had fallen out onto turned into effectively a crater, rolling away until he was on more stable ground, and the movement had stopped.

He lay there on his back for a moment, still feeling the mountains shudder beneath him, the sun directly ahead.

It was just past noon in Prosperity.

After a moment, his legs felt strong enough to move again, and he clambered slowly to his feet.

It was time to find out what damage Cortez had done at the town meeting.

29

AFTERMATH

THE GROUND WAS STILL SHAKING AS HARPER MADE HIS WAY down the hills from the ventilation shaft's exit.

His shoulder was now useless, hanging down at his side, and the blood darkened his shirt. Through the dust and debris clouding the air, he stared down at the main mine entrance as he walked along the ridge above, and glimpsed Delaney heading for vehicles – or some other escape route Harper hadn't known about – as several SUVs finally managed to drive out before the tunnels that led into the mine collapsed in on themselves.

Let him go. The charges had done their job. Whatever evidence the Feds found down the line would be enough.

The walk back to Prosperity felt longer than it should have; Harper had to stop twice, waiting for his vision to clear and his breath to ease, even vomiting up bile at one point. The sun was still almost directly overhead, turning the Nevada landscape into harsh contrasts of light and shadow, and his lucky stone, possibly one of the few things he had managed to bring out with him, was a familiar weight in his pocket as he moved, grounding him against blood loss and a growing weakness in his legs.

As he moved onto Main Street, finally stepping down from the hills, he heard Prosperity before he saw it. Not panic or chaos, but the sound of people organising, helping each other. There was no hysteria he could see, and no mass exodus; these people had faced crises before.

Main Street looked different somehow; there were the same buildings, the same weathered storefronts he had seen the previous day, but the atmosphere had changed, as he walked past O'Malley's, its windows dark but its door propped open. Inside, he could see people gathering, talking in low voices – but it didn't feel conspiratorial; it felt more like people planning what to do next.

A person in the room looked up, and seeing Harper standing there – nothing more than a silhouette, likely looking like Aegis – they stood and started towards him angrily, but before they could say or do anything, one of them, a young man with dark hair paused him.

'Harper,' he whispered, as if scared of the name as he recognised the battered figure in the doorway. 'Did you do this?'

Harper looked back at the mountain and shrugged.

'Kind of, I suppose. If you mean the mountain. I don't know what happened here.'

'Did you find Cassie?'

'She's out,' Harper smiled. 'They were going to escape near the Goldstrike; Maggie's leading them out. There's about five or six that Aegis had brought in with her.'

There was an excited muttering among the crowd, but Harper had already started moving on. He could see down a side street *The Prospector*'s office was still a blackened shell, but someone had already hung up a sign promising "back soon".

A Ford SSV turned onto the street, and Harper almost paused to hide, but stopped as it continued on. Carson was behind the wheel, and Bickford looked to be handcuffed in the back. The mayor's face was a mix of fury and disbelief as he saw Harper as they passed, screaming at Carson from the back, and Harper almost wondered if Carson was about to stop and try to arrest him as well, but the Ford just continued on. Harper also noted how people had stopped to watch, but there was no cheering or celebration, just quiet satisfaction as justice finally caught up ... or shock that things had changed so rapidly.

The town hall steps were crowded with familiar faces and some new ones. An older man stood with deputies and younger officers, and it sounded like decades of experience was being shared. Doctor Chen sat with the recently rescued Katie Martinez, checking her breathing, while others gathered around to hear her and the other rescuees explain what had really been happening in those mines.

Through the doorway, Harper could see Cortez in conversation with a group of town officials. It looked like she was already taking charge.

'You look like hell,' Maggie materialised behind him, a medical kit in hand.

'You made it out then,' Harper smiled.

'We've been waiting for you for ages,' she grinned. 'It was you being a diva, wanting to take all the glory that made it take longer.'

Harper checked his watch, wincing as his shoulder twinged.

'I missed my noon deadline to leave by a good couple of hours,' he said. 'Who exactly do I turn myself in to?'

'I think you're okay for a few more days,' Maggie nodded at the shoulder. 'How is it?'

'Not great,' he admitted.

'No shit,' she was already helping him towards a bench, professional efficiency in every movement. 'We got everyone clear through the maintenance tunnels. They'll need proper medical attention but they'll live.'

She started cutting away his shirt and examining the wound. There was definitely more blood than there should have been, but this was still just muscle damage and blood loss.

'Town hall?' he asked, wincing as Maggie probed the wound.

'Cortez handled it. Bickford tried to talk his way out but ...' Maggie's smile was fierce as she now re-cleaned the wound. 'Let's just say people aren't buying his stories anymore. Coble even gave away that he fired the rifle that killed her dad, while his phone turned out to be the one that sent the message to kill *my* dad. From what I can work out, it was quite a screw-up.'

She paused as Doctor Chen walked over, glaring at Harper.

'Why are you letting her clean you up?' she asked.

Maggie's eyebrows raised as she turned to face her.

'Doctor Chen—'

'I'm the town locum,' Doctor Chen smiled, taking the cleaning wipe from Maggie. 'You've got a father to take care of. This is my domain.'

Maggie smiled in return, nodding, and allowed Doctor

Chen to continue the tender ministrations of Liam Harper as she headed off to find Eddie.

'Mason Carrick?' he asked, as Doctor Chen started working on the wound.

'He's gone. The guy with the glasses, too. Probably off calling whoever they need to call,' Doctor Chen began applying a proper dressing, her movements precise. 'Coble didn't get that luxury, though. He's in holding along with Bickford. Reynolds is running the department until things settle.'

'Who's Reynolds?'

Doctor Chen paused, staring at Harper.

'You know, the fact you've only been here a couple of days is completely lost when I think about how much you've done for the town,' she said. 'Or *to* it, even. Reynolds was Robbie Cortez's old partner. Quit after he was killed. Let's just say he's found a new faith in law enforcement.'

Through the town hall doors, Harper could see Maggie walking over to Eddie, who was spreading papers on a table, townspeople gathering to hear the true story of their home. The Winchester rifle was secured in an evidence bag, no longer a symbol of Bickford authority, but proof of decades of corruption.

'You know they'll come back,' Harper said. 'Federal agencies, military contracts, people with badges and suits will appear, and they'll try to bury all of this.'

He looked up at the mountain.

'You know ... more than we've already done.'

'Let them try,' Doctor Chen finished taping the bandage. 'I've already sent copies of my data to news outlets and universities, and Eddie's got documents going back to 1870. They might have tried to destroy the library to remove them, but we had copies way before they started. Bickford's need to have his own museum, in a way, caused his own fall. And now that people are talking ...'

She was right. All around them, conversations were happening; neighbours comparing stories, sharing memories of accidents that never made sense, of families who disappeared after asking questions. The weight of one hundred and fifty years of secrets seemed to lift as truth finally found air. But Harper couldn't help wondering how many of these revelations were actually nothing more than simply "a family left because they were tired of the place", now placed into the urban legend without their permission.

'Hold still,' Doctor Chen muttered, starting a couple of smaller cuts. 'They got you good.'

'It was Delaney. He's better than he looks.'

As Doctor Chen checked him over, Harper watched Tucker moving through the crowd, no longer playing the conspiracy theorist drunk. 'They all were.'

'Yeah? Well, they didn't know Prosperity, did they?' Doctor Chen's voice carried pride now. 'Didn't understand what they were really facing.'

Cortez emerged from the town hall, people making way for her as she passed. Harper noted she seemed embarrassed about this, but was carrying herself with a new authority. She wasn't just a suspended deputy anymore. She looked like a leader who had earned her place the hard way.

'The state police are on their way,' she said as she reached them, giving nothing more than a simple nod to Harper, 'along with the FBI and God knows who else. Doctor Chen here has already been talking about studies and testings.'

'We need them,' Doctor Chen said. 'This could take years to sort out.'

'They'll try to classify everything,' Harper warned. 'National security, military contracts—'

'Maybe,' Cortez smiled. 'But they can't classify an entire town, and they can't hide what's already in the open.'

'The first priority is containment,' Doctor Chen said. 'We'll need monitoring stations around the perimeter, check the groundwater, test soil samples—'

'Samples? Already started,' Cortez interrupted. 'Tucker's been tracking spread patterns for ages now.'

'Of course he has,' Doctor Chen's smile was tired but genuine. 'Do you think he was ever really mad and drunk?'

'Only on Tuesdays, apparently.'

The man named Reynolds emerged from the sheriff's office, a badge on his shirt, and the old cop moved younger than his age belied, years seeming to drop away as he took command.

'State police just passed Casey's Junction,' Reynolds called out to Cortez. 'Ten, twenty minutes out, FBI's maybe an hour behind them.'

Cortez nodded, already moving to organise people – not giving orders, exactly, but helping coordinate what needed to be done.

Natural leadership, Harper thought.

'They'll want statements,' she said, 'from everyone. About the mine, about Bickford, all of that. We shouldn't hide anything.'

'Even the parts that make us look bad?' someone asked. 'The times we looked the other way?'

'Especially those parts,' Cortez's voice carried no judgement. 'We'll have no more secrets in Prosperity.'

'You're going to need a hospital.' Her ministrations

finished, Doctor Chen packed away Maggie's medical kit as if it was her own.

'Later.' Harper saw Maisie Brown directing people towards the diner, most likely organising food for those who'd been held at the mine. The town was already rebuilding itself and finding its new shape. Through gaps in the crowd, Harper caught glimpses of the mine in the distance. Smoke still rose from multiple points, but the collapse seemed to have contained whatever Aegis and Bickford had been processing up there, buried under tons of rock ... for now at least.

'They'll try to dig it out,' he repeated quietly. 'Too valuable to leave buried.'

'Let them try,' Maggie had walked up again beside him, and her voice carried the steel of a US Marine who had found something worth protecting. 'This time, we'll be ready. Hoo-rah.'

The first State Police cruisers appeared at the end of Main Street, lights flashing, but sirens silent. It was a professional courtesy, Harper assumed, or maybe they already understood this wasn't the kind of situation that needed sirens. As it was, Harper didn't want to be around when the police turned up, and so he slowly rose, turned to Maggie ...

And then passed out.

THREE DAYS HAD PASSED SINCE THE CHAOS IN PROSPERITY, before Harper finally left the hospital, his arm stitched up properly, and his body scrubbed of all traces of the mine.

The doctors had been thorough, more thorough than

Harper had expected, for a rural hospital. After tidying Doctor Chen's work on the gunshot wound and setting Harper up with a fresh line of antibiotics, they had also insisted on running additional tests, explaining to him that the heavy earth metals exposure he'd had wasn't something they took lightly, so they'd drawn blood and sent it to the lab, wherever it was, looking for traces of substances like dysprosium and terbium in his system.

Harper wasn't a scientist, but they had explained it plainly enough. The metals didn't belong in the human body, and when they found their way in through dust or fumes, they'd cling to bone, settle in soft tissue, or linger in the bloodstream like unwanted guests.

None of it sounded good.

They took a spectrometry analysis, breaking his blood into lines of numbers to detect what didn't belong; they'd even scanned his lungs using high-res imaging to spot any particles that might have lodged deep in his tissue. Harper had no problem with this at all, though; he still remembered how Moses Mathers looked when they found him, and the last thing he wanted was anything like that. He knew also that he'd walked through the mines without a breathing apparatus on, gasped in deep breaths of the air when he fought Delaney, and when the explosions had started, he'd had to cast his quickly borrowed one aside, to escape.

Surprisingly, the results had come back cleaner than expected; maybe his short time in the mine had saved him from worse. Still, they warned him to monitor his breathing, and to come back if he started feeling worse from that.

Now, three days after being admitted, having passed out because of exhaustion and lack of oxygen, he sat on Maggie's porch, watching federal vehicles drive through Prosperity's streets like black beetles in the morning sun.

The town had handled the invasion of authority better than he'd expected. State Police had arrived first, followed, as expected, by the FBI, then a parade of agencies with increasingly obscure acronyms had arrived, men and women in suits and tactical gear, all trying to contain a truth that had already broken free. Doctor Chen's data, apparently, had already spread through academic circles, while Eddie's historical documents had been copied, verified, and archived. Even Tucker's detailed notebooks had become evidence – although Harper found that amusing, and wondered what people would think when they found the notes that were very much more the tinfoil conspiracy side of Tucker.

Would they be classed as fact as well?

Cortez had handled them all with the same quiet authority she'd shown in the town hall. There was no grandstanding and no drama, just the facts, laid out with a patience her father would have been proud of.

Yes, the Bickfords had been processing rare earth elements without permits.

Yes, people had died.

Yes, a few remaining bars of 1875 gold were found in the Bickford safe – whether these were the ones once stolen was yet to be decided. But, what they'd also found, in Bickford's precious home museum, was a letter from William Bickford, claiming the mine was passed to Prosperity as a community enterprise, and therefore he couldn't be forced to pay exorbitant debts—a letter that, if proven to be true would not only show the Bickfords had gained everything illegally and would have to pay it back, but that Prosperity was about to become more than just a word in this town.

Of course the fact it appeared shortly after Eddie had explained such a letter would save the town made Harper wonder just how legit it truly was... but that was for someone else to sort out.

Yes, Aegis security had operated as a private military force on American soil.

The suits didn't seem to like those facts, but they couldn't hide them anymore. Bickford was still in custody, along with ex-Sheriff Coble and the Aegis "deputies" who had helped cover things up, but that was it. Mason had disappeared into whatever shadow world handled such things, but in a way his absence felt like its own kind of victory. Many of the remaining soldiers, including Blaine and Lucas, had been arrested while others, like Gomez, the Hispanic man with the dodgy beard had simply vanished. Either way, their hold on the town was broken, and people were talking of it almost in the same way they had about the Los Alamos biker gang when it had been run out of town.

The mine itself remained sealed; Harper's charges had done their job, and federal teams were talking about containment protocols and proper procedures for handling what laid buried up there, but everybody agreed that this would take time, authorisation and paperwork. For now, secured and unable to be entered, the mountain kept his secrets.

Maggie emerged from the guest house with coffee, handing him a mug. While Harper had been in the hospital, she'd been busy; the guest house had become a halfway house for many of the incoming authorities. Harper hadn't been happy about finding the other rooms filled with FBI and NSA agents, and they seemed *very* interested in the British tourist who had appeared. Maggie, however, had kept his role quiet; he was just a tourist who'd got caught up in all this at the wrong time. For the moment, they played along and let him be ... although his black redacted file had been commented on more than once.

'You're thinking too loud,' she said. 'I can hear the cogs working from inside.'

'Just trying to decide what happens next.'

'Above our pay grade,' Maggie said as she settled into the chair beside him. 'Although I do hear they're looking for a new mayor.'

Harper smiled at that. He'd seen Cortez that morning, watching her coordinate with federal agencies, while simultaneously helping organise clean-up efforts around town. The deputy badge she wore wasn't just for show; the state police had already returned her to deputy status, and people had considered making her sheriff – although she had agreed that the recently returned Reynolds should take that position.

That said, Harper knew there were other conversations happening, other possibilities being discussed, and that if they were right, then the Cortez name might finally move away from law enforcement and more towards public service and politics in a different town role.

Movement caught his eye; a familiar figure in round Lennon glasses walking down the other side of the street.

Ashfield.

The man's corporate manner was still perfect, but something had changed. For a start, he hadn't been arrested, so had either come in undercover, under an assumed identity, or something else had happened outside of the town which, as Maggie had said a moment ago, was "beyond their pay grade".

He caught Harper watching and gave a slight nod. As Maggie raised an eyebrow in a "you can't seriously be considering this" manner, Harper wearily rose and walked down to him, noticing that an SUV had been parked a short way behind him.

'Not arrested, then?'

'I had nothing to do with any of this,' Ashfield replied. 'I was working for Delaney. Delaney is the one they're looking for. I never went down past the main entrance, never went into the mine, and I've got proof that shows that.'

'Even when we went down there?'

'Nah, I don't remember that, Harper. I don't remember going down there, or even leading you to where we found Moses Mathers.'

Harper wasn't stupid, he understood what Ashfield was saying. *Ashfield had deliberately led them to the body. Had he even placed explosives nearby to reveal it on time?*

The message given, Ashfield paused, looked around and then shrugged.

'It doesn't matter, I think Aegis is pretty much done here, anyway. There are other sites, other towns, other operations that might need attention, though.'

'Is that an offer or a warning?'

'Consider it professional courtesy,' Ashfield moved towards the SUV parked behind him, and then stopped. 'Your father would have been proud, you know. Not just of what you did, but how you did it.'

'What about you?' Harper asked.

'There's always work for someone like me,' Ashfield shrugged. 'Not in military ... but you always guessed I wasn't military.'

He gave an almost mocking bow.

'I hope we catch up again, Harper,' he said. 'Maybe next time we'll be on the same side.'

'I felt that sometimes we were, while we were here.'

Ashfield grinned, and then he was gone before Harper could respond, the SUV pulling away quietly before anybody noticed.

Harper stood for a moment, watching it disappear around the corner.

Professional courtesy.

Of course, Ashfield still hadn't confirmed that he was the one who'd sent the video message to Harper from his father in the first place.

The morning sun was climbing higher when he returned to the porch, his coffee still steaming where he'd left it. The town was healing itself, finding its new shape around him. But Ashfield's words nagged at him. He knew that Aegis still had other sites in other towns and other secrets waiting to be exposed, but he didn't know if this was the job for him. There were other places he needed to go, things that his father had asked him to look into.

He still had a mission to focus on.

Maggie, sitting in the chair still, watched him approach.

'You've got that look,' she said.

'What look?'

'The one that says you're about to do something stupid,' she smiled. 'You want some company?'

Harper pulled his lucky stone from his pocket, feeling its familiar smoothness. The stone that had seen him through training, through combat, through this past week in Prosperity, even. He'd earned its luck, just like he'd earned every scar.

'You've got something more important going on here,' he said, looking at her directly. 'This town is finally breaking free. Not just from Bickford, but from its own past.'

'You're including me on that?' There was an edge to her question.

'Maggie, you loved Robbie,' Harper whispered. 'Maybe still do, in a way. But you've spent years trying to protect his memory by staying exactly who you were when he was around. Running this place, keeping to years-old routines, being what everyone expected.'

Maggie's expression hardened, but he continued.

'I saw you this week. Fighting. Leading. Being who you really are; the US Marine who could organise an evacuation, or the one taking down Aegis operations, the woman who kept medical supplies ready because she knew someday they'd be needed. This isn't about a bum leg, or Robbie's memory. This is about who you've always been.'

Maggie was silent for a long moment, staring out at the town she'd lived in most of her life.

'And what about you?' she asked, finally. 'Off to find more wrongs to right? The "Littlest Hobo" on a Triumph?'

'Something like that,' Harper grinned. 'Seems there are other towns out there, other secrets that need finding.'

'Alone?'

'Better that way,' he stood, shoulder protesting the movement. 'Besides, Prosperity needs you more than I do.'

'And Cortez?'

'You'll always have the love you lost,' he said. 'I don't think I reached that far, but I will miss her.'

'Well, you can say goodbye to her properly.' Maggie rose, finishing her coffee. 'Maisie's doing lunch for everyone at the diner. You coming?'

'Sure,' Harper stood, stretching his shoulder carefully. 'I just need to grab some painkillers from my room before I turn up, but I'll meet you there.'

'Damn right you'd better,' Maggie grinned, turning and walking off down the steps.

Harper watched her walk towards the diner, and then, when he felt it was safe enough, he turned towards his Triumph Bonneville. The bike was already packed; it had been since dawn, his helmet hanging from the handlebar, waiting.

Time to move on.

THE ENGINE'S PURR ECHOED OFF PROSPERITY'S BUILDINGS AS HE pulled away; in his mirrors, he caught a last glimpse of Main Street, of people rebuilding their town, and of Maggie Hawkins, standing near the diner, watching him go.

Some goodbyes were better left unsaid.

Besides, Harper was pretty sure this wasn't the last time he'd pass through Prosperity, Nevada.

Want the next Liam Harper Thriller? CLICK HERE on digital, or turn the page...

Liam Harper will return in his next thriller

BLOOD RIDGE

ACKNOWLEDGEMENTS

When you write books, you find that there are a ton of people out there who help you, and so I wanted to say thanks.

There are people I need to thank, and they know who they are, including my brother Chris Lee, Jacqueline Beard MBE, who has copyedited all my books since the very beginning, editor Sian Phillips and weapon specialist Eben Atwater, all of whom have made my books way better than they have every right to be.

Also, I couldn't have done this without my growing army of ARC and beta readers, who not only show me where I falter, but also raise awareness of me in the social media world, ensuring that other people learn of my books.

But mainly, I tip my hat and thank you. *The reader.* Who once took a chance on an unknown author in a pile of Kindle books, and thought you'd give them a go, and who has carried on this far with them, as well as the spin off books I now release.

I write these books for you. And with luck, I'll keep on writing them for a very long time.

Jack Gatland / Tony Lee,
London, May 2025

ABOUT THE AUTHOR

Jack Gatland is the pen name of *#1 New York Times Bestselling Author* Tony Lee, who has been writing in all media for thirty-five years, including comics, graphic novels, middle grade books, audio drama, TV and film for *DC Comics, Marvel, BBC, ITV, Random House, Penguin USA, Hachette* and a ton of other publishers and broadcasters.

These have included licenses such as ***Doctor Who, Spider Man, X-Men, Star Trek, Battlestar Galactica, MacGyver,*** BBC's ***Doctors, Wallace and Gromit*** and ***Shrek***, as well as work created with musicians such as ***Iron Maiden, Bruce Dickinson, Ozzy Osbourne, Joe Satriani*** and ***Megadeth.***

His recent novels include the urban fantasy comedy ***Twelve Tasks,*** and the *Playing Card War* series.

As Tony, he's toured the world talking to reluctant readers with his 'Change The Channel' school tours, and lectures on screenwriting and comic scripting for *Raindance* in London.

As Jack, he's written several book series now - a police procedural featuring *DI Declan Walsh and the officers of the Temple Inn Crime Unit*, a spinoff featuring "cop for criminals" *Ellie Reckless and her team,* a third espionage spinoff series featuring burnt MI5 agent *Tom Marlowe*, an action adventure series featuring conman-turned-treasure hunter *Damian Lucas*, a series of thriller books following ex-UKSP operative *Liam Harper* and a standalone novel set in a New York boardroom.

An introvert West Londoner by heart, he lives with his wife Tracy and dog Fosco, just outside London.

Feel free to follow Jack on all his social media by clicking on the links below. Over time these can be places where we can engage, discuss Declan, Ellie, Liam, Tom and others, and put the world to rights.

www.jackgatland.com
www.hoodemanmedia.com

Visit Jack's Reader's Group Page
(Mainly for fans to discuss his books):
https://www.facebook.com/groups/jackgatland

Subscribe to Jack's Readers List:
https://bit.ly/jackgatlandVIP

www.facebook.com/jackgatlandbooks
www.twitter.com/jackgatlandbook
ww.instagram.com/jackgatland

Want more books by Jack Gatland? Turn the page...

Hooded Man
MEDIA

Printed in Dunstable, United Kingdom

71457387R00224